What they're sayin … *g, Angus.*

"Play Me Something, Angus is a pleasure to read. You don't have to be a music lover to devour this book. You just have to love wonderful story-telling. Although this is his first novel, Charlie Rath writes like a seasoned pro."

Robert L. Shook, New York Times best selling author.

"Everyone who has an emotional feeling for what they have done and their accomplishments needs to read Charlie Rath's book. It will make you appreciate all you have done and the message you are sending to those close to you."

Robert L. Dilenschneider, Chairman, The Dilenschneider Group

"Charles Rath has captured the flavor of an era with his first novel. Drawing from his own life experience, he shares with the reader the flavor of his own "coming of age", a struggle with which many readers will identify. Charles motivates us to relive our own triumphs and disappointments, a worthy exercise."

Robert E. Byrnes, musician, psychologist, restaurateur.

"There's a depth and tenderness in this novel I look for in everything I read. The humor in Rath's voice belies the sadness and the loneliness of his characters. What at first might appear as a lighthearted romp is in fact a masterful exploration of estrangement, small-town isolation and human nature."

Katherine Taylor, author of RULES FOR SAYING GOODBYE

"In Play Me Something, Angus, Charlie Rath writes about family, friendship and dreams — both realized and shattered — with a wit, grace, and humanity rare in today's fiction. Readers will recognize in Rath's characters their own family, friends, nemeses, and neighbors, and be glad to go on this journey with them."

Eric Rickstad - author of REAP and *THE SILENT GIRLS,*

Play Me Something, Angus

A Novel by Charles W. Rath

To Linda
Great family friends for years. Much love and fond memories
Best Wishes
Charlie Rath
6/6/15

Significance Press
200 Park Avenue
New York, N.Y. 10166

ISBN: 978-0-9907574-3-6

DEDICATION

To my wife, Susie;
Annie & Tom; Katie & Bill; Charlie & Michele;
And to our nine real-life grand-characters: Zach, Evelyn, Henry, Gigi, Will, Charlie, Amelia, Ian and Madeline.

ACKNOWLEDGMENTS

My special thanks to friends who helped me get this story out of my head and onto paper (well, into my computer): Gotham Writers' Workshop, in particular, Katherine Taylor, novelist and faculty member. Eric Rickstad – *Idea2book.* Eric is not only a successful novelist, but also a skilled professional editor and story critic under whose guidance, *Play Me Something, Angus*, pushed well past my original notions of character depth, voice and plot. Additionally, Russell Kessler, who, along with Jim Bachmann, provided valuable advice regarding the legal and business portions of the story. And my sincere thanks to Joe Tessitore and Jim Zebora, *Significance Press,* who deftly guided me through the editorial and publication process. Many others along the way chipped in with various plot thoughts and suggestions. Collectively, I refer them as my fellow *Cascaders* in that we would enjoy an occasional round of golf at The Homestead Cascades, followed by beverages and food at Woodland Cottage Sporting Club and veranda discussions about odd topics including what I was trying to accomplish with my writing. Thanks to all sixteen of them.

I'm indebted to my long-time friend and voracious reader, Robert E. Byrnes. Bob has always been supportive of my writing efforts and helpful with his viewpoints about plot and character, his significant knowledge of culinary skills and his insights as an accomplished jazz pianist. Friends – both past and present – in particular, professionals in the field of music, medicine and culinary arts who have contributed so valuably to this story. They include my personal mentor and longtime friend, Donald J. Vincent, M.D. (deceased); pediatrician, Dr. Bruce Meyer; professional pianists/teachers Mark Flugge and Shelly Berg; guitarist, Gene Bertoncini; classical bassist, Dr. Mark Morton and jazz bassist, Dr. Lou Fischer; jazz educator, performer and historian, Ray Eubanks; culinary professionals, Chef Bryan Loveless; restaurateur, Kenny Yee; and Robert Burns, former Executive Chef, The Columbus Country Club; Joe Karpowicz, attorney.

Finally, a word about personal experience: From age 14, I've played piano, vibes and bass in local jazz/blues clubs, bistros, bars and ensemble workshops. I worked summers in a commercial kitchen at a resort and as a short order cook at different family restaurants where I benefitted from the counsel and guidance of those whose success and reputation were rooted in their dedication to good food, good service and good value. I acquired my experience in marketing and advertising under the tutelage of Joe Mack, Dancer Fitzgerald Sample (NYC); public relations under Bob Dilenschneider, The Dilenschneider Group (NYC); as well as the day-to-day rigors of my fifteen years as Chief Marketing Officer for Wendy's International. Thanks to my close personal association with its founder, R. David Thomas, I grew to appreciate the role that dedication to quality and customer satisfaction plays in business and the food service industry in particular. My late friend, Dominic Militello, gave me a joyful appreciation for *things Italian,* particularly food, and his secrets of making a great dish: *Linguine w/white clam sauce.*

PLAY ME SOMETHING, ANGUS

1985

When Aummie first took her grandson, Angus, into her country sitting room, he felt as if his heart would burst as he stood transfixed by the piano before him. His eyes gleamed as he studied its ornate lettering: Mason & Hamlin. Sunlight angling through the window danced on the burnished mahogany cabinetry.

Aummie nudged Angus. "Touch it, it won't bite," she said, her voice a squeak.

As Angus rubbed his fingers over the piano's lustrous surface, Aummie cracked her gum, ignored a long ash dangling perilously from the end of her burning Raleigh. Leaning to open the piano keyboard's dust cover, the ash fell. She blew it aside.

Angus gasped at the long row of beaming white keys facing him. He'd seen a piano in music class at St. Pat's grade school – a piano he'd been forbidden to touch – but it was nothing like this piano, Aummie's piano. Unlike the keys on St. Pat's piano – yellowed and cracked with age – Aummie's were polished pearls. The ivory keys – wider than the black keys – stood like attentive acolytes waiting to serve benediction.

Aummie doused her Raleigh in an old coffee can, lifted her wire-rimmed glasses high on her forehead and turned to Angus. "Sit down on the bench there and we'll have some fun."

Angus slipped sideways onto the bench. Aummie took his hand, held it just over the surface of the keyboard and touched his index finger to an ivory key.

"Push down," she said.

Angus pushed down. The piano's sound rang out as if a church bell, so unexpectedly resonant he arched his back then burst out giggling. He turned to Aummie who giggled with him.

"How… does it do that?" he asked, his eyes wide with mystery.

"A little hammer strikes a string inside the piano."

"A string?"

"A wire…" she said.

Aummie opened the piano's rectangular wood panel above the keyboard to reveal uncountable long metal wires wound tightly around square-headed black pins grouped in tight rows. Below the pins sat little oval wooden hammers stretching left to right and covered with hard white padding.

"Hit that white key again," Aummie said.

Angus hit the key and one of the white padded hammers jumped up and bounced off one of the strings. Again, the room filled with the sound of the ringing round tone, but the tone was different now from the one he'd first heard.

"That sounded different," he said.

Aummie cracked her gum, lowered her glasses and peered over them.

"That's because you didn't hit the same white key you hit the first time."

Puzzled, Angus hit the key again and again. Each time, the sound heightened his elation, a warm feeling swelled inside him.

"Can you play a song?" he asked.

He didn't realize it then, but "Now Is The Hour" would be the song that remained with him forever.

"If you put your mind to it," Aummie said when she finished playing, "You can learn to play the piano and enjoy it your whole life."

~~~~~~

Spring – Aummie continued to work the jewelry counter at Dee's Department store in Fountain Point and Angus visited her as often as he could after school. She gave him something one day that surprised him: a gold Claddagh ring.

"I've kept this Irish Claddagh for you," she said. "Someday you'll meet a nice young lady to give it to."

As Angus studied the Claddagh, Aummie said, "The heart means love, the clasping hands mean friendship. The crown means loyalty... it should always point to her fingertip."

Aummie took Angus' hand, kissed it as she tucked the Claddagh into it. He leaned toward her, kissed her cheek and hugged her gently as she held his hand tightly. She seemed frail... like a rusting old farm implement having borne the brunt of a thousand storms.

A month later, Angus' mother told him the crushing news of Aummie's passing.

After Aummie's wake, Angus's mother gave him an envelope. Inside was the sheet music for "Now Is The Hour" with a picture of Bing Crosby on the front. Below it, Aummie had scrawled a note: Angus... if
~~~~~~

you practice, you can learn to play the piano. You can do it! Love Aummie.

Angus trembled as his mother said, "Aummie left her piano to you."

~~~~~
~~~~~

Book I

1. ST. PAT'S – 1988

It was Friday night of the All Saint's Day mixer in the Parish Hall when Angus first fell in love – with both of them: Rosemary Gracewood and Bernice Walker. Riveted in place, he scanned them head to foot, first Bernie, then Rosemary. They glanced at him then turned back to each other.

Angus' mind raced at the thought of dancing with them during the mixer. Pushing past his friend, Buddy Hunt – who wore slouchy jeans and a shabby khaki vest over his white t-shirt – Angus shuffled toward the girls. Bernie stood in silhouette, elbows jutting out like a coat hanger, her tight-fitting white sweater clinging to her curvy bust. Though pudgy with bucked teeth, she oozed a sexiness that set her apart and stirred jealousy among the other girls.

As Angus approached, Rosemary stepped aside to make room for him. Uncertain what to say, Angus raked his fingers through his unruly black hair and felt his palms moisten. Though Rose was lanky, taller and less developed than Bernie, she had a quiet mystique that attracted Angus. Rose's curly black hair framed her oval face, short bangs at the top of her deep-set black eyes tickled her rounded black eyebrows. Wearing beige jeans, flat-heeled shoes and a knitted sweater over a dark brown short-sleeved blouse, Rose was the most dressed up of anyone attending the mixer.

"Let's go in," Rose said.

Inside the hall, Buddy huddled with Bernie and tried to kiss her, Angus sat next to Rose and leaned close to her as the DJ played the right song to set the mood: "You're The Only Woman," by Ambrosia.

"That's a good song for dancing," Angus said.

"It's too mushy," Rose said "I'm not very good at dancing, anyway."

Between songs, Angus groped for something to say until Rose gave him an opening.

"I took my first piano lesson from Mr. Chapman last week," she said.

How did you like it?" Angus said.

Rose shook her head.

"I can't even hum a tune, let alone play one."

"Maybe I could help," Angus said.

"I'm going to stick with basketball," Rose said.

When the DJ started playing, "The One You Love," Angus turned to Rose. "Let's dance… just this one time."

Moving slowly toward the dance floor, Rose said, "Remember…I'm not very good, OK?"

Embracing Rose gently, Angus took her right hand in his left. Making only the slightest moves, Angus guided Rose's tentative steps in unison with his. When the song came to Angus' favorite part: *When you remember those nights in his arms, you know you gotta make up your mind…* he pulled Rose to him. When they returned to their table, Rose smiled as Angus held the chair for her.

"Maybe next time I'll know how to dance a little better," she said.

"Sister Pauline said I could play the piano. Do you have a favorite song?"

"Not really," Rose said.

"Will you come up and sit with me while I play?"

Rose looked at her thin silver wristwatch.

"My dad is picking me up pretty soon," she said.

"I'll play "Now Is The Hour," Angus said.

Rose shrugged. "I've never heard it."

2. MOSS

In the McCrory neighborhood, Moss Brown made his rounds for Fountain Point's weekly trash pick-up on Friday afternoons. Under his bright yellow-striped work-vest, Moss was a slight-built, wiry black man. Angus' mother – who loved working in the yard – would talk with Moss as he rolled his large portable trash caddy up their driveway and around the side of the house to the collection area behind their garage. Moss always stopped to smile and tipped his hat to her.

One Friday, while Angus practiced piano in the basement, he heard Moss' voice through the open basement window.

"Afternoon, Mrs. McCrory. Them mums spreadin' a world of glory."

"Aren't they?" she said.

"Do I hear someone playing the piano?" Moss asked.

"That's Angus… he loves playing that old piano his grandmother gave him."

"Would you mind if I peeked in and listened to him play?"

She led Moss to the back door and called down the stairwell, "Ange! You have a visitor… say hello to Mr. Brown. He wants to hear you play the piano."

"Play me something, Angus," Moss said, as he entered the basement.

"I don't really know much… unless you like church songs or "Now Is the Hour."

Angus held out Aummie's sheet music for Moss to examine. He studied it for a moment, handed back to Angus and removed his ball cap revealing a slightly receding, V-patterned hairline. Moss' eyes were large, whites the color of straw and watery…his teeth were straight and white… his large hands weathered, fingers knobby and nicked up.

As Angus took the sheet music, Moss said, "I know them church songs. Best blues comes outta' church songs… gospel, too."

"Blues?" Angus said.

"Yeah, man… *blues*! Real soul music… New Orleans."

"You from all the way down there?" Angus asked.

"Can't you tell by lookin', man? I'm *Creole*."

Angus studied Moss' eyes. They were bluer than a robin's egg. Angus had never heard of a *Creole,* but his mom had some Dixieland tapes she played in the kitchen; a trumpet player named Al Hirt and a clarinetist, Pete Fountain.

"I thought the only music from New Orleans was Dixieland."

Moss chuckled, sat down at the piano. "Let me show you a couple of things."

As Moss spread his hands over the keyboard, Angus watched his fingers slide from one piano key to another using all five fingers on both hands… up and down together, then in opposite directions. Moss played a funky tune and hummed along as he said, "*C-seven, F-seven, G-seven.*"

Hypnotized, hearing sounds coming out of Aummie's piano he never knew were there, Angus listened as Moss played four notes at the same time. They sounded odd, as if there were something missing. Not waiting for Moss to explain, Angus said, "How do you make that sound?"

"It's all in the chord structure, man. You gotta listen," Moss said as he fingered a four-note formation. "This here's a *B-flat* chord. That top note I'm playin' is the flatted seventh tone on the B-flat scale."

Moss played the chord again, pulled his hands off the keyboard and stretched his fingers while looking at Angus.

"You hear the color in that chord?"

"I think so." Angus answered.

"Ain't no thinkin' to it, man, it's your ears!"

Moving away from the piano Moss said, "See you next Friday."

3. MR. PORK PIE

Sister Pauline had always permitted St. Pat's first after-Christmas mixer to coincide with the weekend around the Epiphany and had given Angus permission for his newly formed combo, The Five Saints, to play. When school resumed on the Monday after New Year's, Buddy Hunt – Angus' best friend and *Saints'* guitarist – stopped Angus after school.

"Bernice wants to sing with us at the mixer," he said.

"Bernie can sing?"

Buddy shrugged. "Who cares as long as she wears one of her tight sweaters?"

"I'll ask Sr. Pauline if we can practice on Friday after school," Angus said.

"She already knows 'Pennies From Heaven.'"

~~~~~

Performance time, Angus grabbed a funky Amish straw hat from the closet and headed for the Parish Hall where The Five Saints gathered around the bandstand. Angus plopped his music onto the piano and scanned the room. Seeing Rose traipse in with her friends, he adjusted his tie and sidled toward her. Rose wore a green-and-blue plaid jumper
~~~~~

over a pleated-front blouse and white knee socks. She grinned at Angus as he approached.

"You look like the scarecrow from the Wizard of Oz," she said as she pointed to Angus' straw hat.

Angus forced a weak grin as he ambled onto the stage with his best friend and guitarist, Buddy Hunt; bassist, Harry 'Lighthorse' Roberts; drummer, Georgie 'Sticks' Weaver; and clarinetist, Albert 'Ratface' Martin.

The Five Saints opened with two blues tunes then Angus took the microphone.

"We have a guest vocalist tonight," he said. "Here's Bernie Walker to sing 'Pennies From Heaven.' As Angus put the microphone back on its stand, he saw Rose gather with her friends and move to the front of the bandstand. Beaming broadly at Rose, Angus nodded to her then beckoned Bernie to the stage.

Bouncing up the steps, Bernie strolled downstage. Her pudgy legs appeared to be unshaven, stubbly hair visible down to the tops of her dilapidated sneakers. When she stood at the microphone and tugged her sweater down over an exposed slice of her chubby midriff, a hole appeared under her left armpit, hair peeking out. She doffed her thick glasses. Surprisingly, Angus thought, she looked a lot more attractive without them; her pretty amber eyes were clear and shining. She turned to Angus and smiled coyly as if to say, '*This is for you!*'

Bernie held the microphone close to her mouth and picked up the cue. Angus was shocked that her voice over the microphone sounded remarkably clear with a husky resonance. After her perfect performance, everyone broke into raucous applause. As Bernie edged toward the stage steps, Angus motioned her over. "Would you like to sing again at our next mixer?"

Bernie nuzzled close to Angus. "I'd love to but I don't know any other songs."

"I'll teach you," Angus said quietly. "We can practice at my house."

As Bernie stepped off the stage, Rose glowered at Angus. Deciding to take a quick break, he bounded off the stage and rushed to Rose's side.

"Can I play something for you?" he said.

"My friends and I are going to get something to drink," she said and turned on her heel.

~~~~~

The week following the mixer, Rose and Angus barely spoke. But despite having blown his chance to impress Rose, his spirits were lifted as he studied his sparse library of songs and picked out the ones he thought were good for Bernie. Having invited her to his home Sunday after mass and breakfast, Angus met her at the door and escorted her to the basement.

Her sweet scent trailed behind her as he followed Bernie down the stairs. At the bottom, Bernie turned and faced Angus. Her blond tresses, combed into a tight bundle lay close to her head, secured by a metal barrette. When she slipped out of her coat and tossed it onto a chair, Angus noticed she was wearing baggy blue fleece warm up pants torn at the knee. But, instead of her usual tight sweater, she wore a long-sleeve red-checked flannel shirt open to the second button. As Angus glanced at the hint of Bernie's cleavage, she turned to the piano.

"I don't know much about pianos, but yours looks very cool," she said.

"My grandma gave it to me when she passed away," Angus explained.

As Bernie moved toward the piano, she brushed lightly against Angus, as if sending him a friendly 'thank you' for inviting her into his private domain. Though timid at first, Angus pulled out the bench for Bernie and said, "You ready to practice?"

"Play something first," Bernie said, nestled close to Angus and put her hand on his arm.
~~~~~

Feeling Bernie's warmth, Angus glanced at her hand to see her skin was dry, chapped, her nails cracked, cuticle torn. With Bernie beside him, he played "Now Is The Hour."

When he finished, Bernie put her hand on Angus' shoulder. She smiled softly. "That was beautiful, what was it?"

"Now Is The Hour," Angus said. "It was Aummie's… my grandma's favorite song… she taught me how to play the piano."

Bernie dropped her eyes. "I wish I had a grandma... and real parents."

"Real parents?" Angus asked, confused.

"I live with foster parents," Bernie said flatly.

The basement fell silent. Sensing that Bernie wanted to say something, he waited and looked her in the eyes. But instead of speaking, she leaned over and kissed Angus on his cheek. Pulling back slowly, Bernie wagged her finger in front of Angus' face as she said, "I thought you were going to teach me some new songs."

"Let's try some blues," he said.

He sang and played "St. Louis Blues."

"I don't know if I can sing that," Bernie said.

"Listen to me sing it again, then we'll try it together."

After three tries, he was surprised at how well Bernie caught on. More surprising was Bernie's resonant sexiness. Her voice pure, her intonation nearly perfect, Angus marveled at the thought that despite no training, Bernie was imbued with natural talent and musical intuition.

"Let's try something else," Angus said. "Have you ever heard, 'S'Wonderful' by Ella Fitzgerald?"

"I've never heard of her," Bernie said.

"You can borrow a CD or some tapes at the library and listen to her," Angus said.

Bernie let her eyes drop.

"I… we don't have anything to play them on," she said. "My foster father gets pissed if I even ask him to let me listen to the radio."

"I'll lend you my CD player," Angus said. "You could listen when he's at work."

"He doesn't work," Bernie said. "He sits around all day and watches TV."

Taken aback, Angus forced a wry smile as he said, "It isn't really any of my business, but how does he… make a living?"

Her eyes misty, Bernie spoke softly.

"You can't ever say anything, Ange… promise me that you'll never ever tell anyone about this." She fixed her eyes on Angus. "Promise?"

Angus took Bernie's hand as she spoke in confidence.

"He and my foster mom live on welfare and the money they make from foster care for taking me in." Her face reddening, she continued. "I get seven dollars a week for doing the housework and the laundry."

"What about… your mom?" Angus asked.

"She…goes out a lot… with other men... " Bernie's voice trailed off.

Stunned, Angus realized that Bernie's life was nothing remotely similar to his. How did Bernie cope? "Is there anything… I can do to help you?" he asked.

"Sr. Pauline helps me a lot. She gives me clothes she finds at the church rummage sales." Bernie grinned. "I hide the sweaters she gives me under our trailer until I can smuggle them inside."

"That's… doesn't anyone from foster care check on that stuff?"

"I don't say anything," Bernie said. "My foster dad would kill me."

Angry, Angus ripped through the songs The Five Saints had rehearsed until his mother called from the head of the stairs.

"Are you two having fun?" she asked.

"We're almost finished," Angus replied and handed Bernie a few other songs from The Five Saints repertoire.

"You can take these home and check them out for the next time we rehearse," Angus said.

Bernie walked up the stairs ahead of Angus and into the kitchen.

"My mom will take you home if you want," he said.

"I'll walk," Bernie said. "It isn't that far."

"I'm having a Valentine's Day party," Angus said as Bernie stepped outside.

Bernie bundled her coat around her. "Cool," she said.

4. POETRY IN MOTION

At the stroke of 7:00, Anna Belle West, Mary Wiggins, Bernie Walker and Rosemary Gracewood arrived at Angus' house with everyone in his band plus Sammy (Fox) Silvers from Academy Middle School.

The boys hung their coats in the entryway closet and as Angus collected the girls' coats, he saw they were all decked out. Rose wore dark blue slacks and patent leather flat-heeled shoes and a bright red silk blouse with a knitted pink tunic. Bernie doffed her coat, a quilted khaki army surplus jacket. As she handed it to Angus, he fixed his eyes on her tight-fitting orange sweater and thought about what she had told him about having to smuggle her sweaters into her trailer. As they edged into Angus' living room, Buddy pulled Angus aside. "Hey man, I brought my ax… we could get the chicks in the basement and groove a little music… you know?"

Though he hadn't thought about playing the piano that night, Angus grinned at the prospect of impressing Rose after blowing his chances with her at the *Epiphany* mixer.

Gathered in the living room, they drank fruit punch served from a cavernous bowl filled with fruit frozen inside a floating ice ring. Earlier at school, Buddy told Angus that he'd gotten everyone together to work on the party entertainment with what Buddy called: Mother Goose-me rhymes.

At Angus' urging, the group got started with the poetry session while his mother went to the kitchen. To break the ice, Buddy read his poem imitating Alvin the Chipmunk.

"There was an old woman who lived in a shoe… she had so many children she had to work nights at Mickey-D's."

Mimicking Buddy ensued with spontaneous off-color innovations on Buddy's theme of what the old woman had to do to support her children. As the banter continued, Angus thought about what Bernie had told him about her foster mother and felt like a hypocrite laughing with the others. He glanced at Bernie to see her looking at him, embarrassed. She forced a wan smile as Buddy said, "Bern… you're next."

When she finished, Buddy signaled her to move over to where he sat cross-legged on the floor. She plopped down beside him. As she slipped out of her tattered sneakers and pulled her knees up, her skirt around her pudgy hair-stubbled legs was frayed at the hem; he tried not to notice that her sweater had hiked up revealing a naked band of her flabby midriff.

With Anna Belle and Lighthorse abstaining, all the poems had been delivered except Rose's. As the others slouched on the floor shoes off, Rosemary stood:

"'IF I WERE'… by Joanna Fuchs," she began.

"If I were a key, I would lock you;

If lightning, then I would shock you;

If I were a pier I would dock you;

If I had a band I would rock you.

If I were a spoon, I would feed you;

If I were a house, I would deed you;

On Valentine's Day, I must plead you,

Valentine, I really need you!"

When she read the line: *If I had a band I would rock you,* she smiled at Angus. Finished, Rose sat next to Angus on the pillow-back divan. Her perfume radiated a sweet fragrance that Angus could taste. Scooching over as close to Rose as possible, Angus stretched his arm over the top of the divan behind Rose's head. Her thick black hair brushed against his arm. His heart thumped.

"That was… where did you find that poem?" he asked.

"My mom has a zillion poetry books."

Angus said, "Have you ever tried to write any?"

"I have a little notebook I use," Rose said.

"May I see it some time?" Angus said.

Rose blushed.

"Do you write poetry?" she asked.

Never having tried to write a poem, Angus groped for an answer.

"No, I… I love song lyrics."

Out of the corner of his eye, Angus saw Buddy trying to kiss Bernie. Angus stood and helped Rose off the divan.

"OK, Bud-man… it's time to eat," he said, as he pulled both Buddy and Bernie into the dining room with the others.

Angus put his food plate on the floor and inched his chair closer to Rose to ask the question burning in his mind.

"Do you have a boyfriend?"

Rose shook her head.

"My mom won't let me," she said.

"Would she let you… let us go to a movie together?"

Rose frowned as Angus held his breath.

"My dad doesn't want me to go out with boys."

"Will you ask?" Angus pressed.

Before Rose could answer, Buddy piped up: "Me and Ange got a jam session planned... let's hit the basement."

Hoping it was a good opportunity to impress Rose, Angus led the group down the stairs into the basement. As Buddy plopped his guitar down on the piano bench, Rose pointed to the piano. "That's a lot nicer piano than the one at St. Pat's."

"Aummie... my grandma gave it to me when she passed away," Angus said. "Do you have a piano?"

"We have a big white one," Rose said.

Angus nudged Rose toward the piano. "Sit next to me," he said.

As they edged past the others, Angus' mother called from the kitchen.

"There's a car honking in the driveway," she said.

"That's my dad," Rose said. "Thanks for the party."

Dejected at again missing an opportunity to impress Rose, Angus got her coat from the hallway closet and helped her into it. His hands trembled as he decided to ask her again about the movie.

"Will you ask your parents about it?"

"About... ?"

"The *movie*," Angus said.

"I don't think they'll let me."

Frustrated at Rose's untimely departure, Angus waved as her father backed out of the driveway. In the kitchen, his mother pulled him aside.

"Mr. Brown called," she said. "He asked me to let you go with him to his club Saturday night and play piano. I'll drive you... he'll bring you home."

5. 151 CLUB

The 151 Club was more crowded than anywhere Angus had ever been. The air foggy with cigarette smoke made his eyes water. Amped-up jazz blared over the club's speakers. Men and women flirted, drank, danced close – a world of roiling, swirling motion bristling with pent-up energy.

A mirrored-back bar ran down the left wall to the restrooms in back. Tucked against the right wall, six booths stood opposite five tables centered between the booths and the bar. Toward the back of the seating area, an elevated bandstand overlooked the scuffed up linoleum dance pad. On the right side of the bandstand, a rickety upright piano sat tightly against the wall; a large wooden stand-up bass leaned against it. A set of drums sat cramped against the back wall; a floor-stand microphone stood at the front edge of the bandstand.

Angus ambled into a small room behind the bandstand and saw Moss smoking with four other men; the wafting aroma sweet, pungent. Moss' eyes looked rheumy. The four men glanced at Angus as he entered. Moss introduced them starting with a lanky black man standing beside him.

"This is my brother, Otis… bass man," Moss said.

Moss took a long drag on the cigarette, sucked in the smoke and held his breath. He stubbed out the butt with his fingers on the edge of a tin ashtray, pocketed the remainder and continued. "This here's J.J. on sax," he said then gestured to the third man. "James Jackson's my drummer."

As the musicians climbed onto the bandstand, Angus felt sweat coursing down his back, his armpits dripping. As Moss introduced the first tune, Angus tried to relax but couldn't. Images of jamming with

Moss at home flickered through his mind as he studied the piano keyboard. It was different from Aummie's piano; chipped yellowing keys, splintered and nicked wood… not at all like the pristine gem she had willed him. The piano bench sat higher than Aummie's, forcing Angus to slump to get comfortable. As Otis plunked random notes on his bass, J.J. squeaked a couple of tune-up tones. James Jackson checked the tension on his snare drum. Angus dried his hands on his pants and silently fingered the B-flat-7th chord to begin the first blues tune; Moss at the microphone, the crowd buzzed in readiness. Sweat dripped from Angus' brow onto the piano keyboard. A sudden chill seized him as Moss spoke to the noisy crowd.

"Gonna' kick off with a tune called, *Freddy The Freeloader,"* Moss announced. "Wanna' introduce my new piano player, Angus McCrory. Stand up, Ange, and take a bow."

To a smattering of applause, Angus felt his cheeks flush as he stood and nodded. A heightened sense of exhilaration surged through him as Moss quietly spoke to Angus and the other musicians.

"I'll play an eight-count solo intro," Moss said. "Ange, you come in when James hits his first drum lick... be cool, man."

Moss' compliment helped Angus relax as Moss counted off the swinging tempo for "Freddy The Freeloader" Angus had practiced a hundred times.

Moss played the solo intro… James hit his drum lick and Angus fingered the first chord. Otis picked up the groove. At first, Angus struggled to keep up, but settled in. After three choruses, Moss stopped playing as J. J. took over to play his improvisational chorus. Moss leaned over to Angus and said, "Good start, Ange. After J. J. finishes, James and me gonna' *trade fours."*

Angus panicked. Trying not to lose track of the beat, he turned to Moss. Moss grinned at Angus' stricken face.

"What are *fours?"* Angus whispered.

Moss chuckled, held his horn to the side.

"James and I alternate playing four bars, trading solos back and forth a couple of times through the tune," Moss said. "Then it's your turn to solo. After that, we start over at the top of the tune and play it through one last time."

"I…"

"Be cool, man... I'll cue you."

When J. J. finished his solo, Moss and James *traded fours,* Moss turned quickly to Angus. "Wail, Ange."

Holding his breath, Angus played the blues chords in tight rhythm with James's flitting fills and Otis' driving bass line. On the second pass through, Angus strained to play simple improvisational passages. At the end of the form, Moss yelled at him. "Keep wailin' man."

As the crowd applauded, Moss took the microphone.

"That was my piano man's first solo. Let's give him a hand," Moss bellowed.

Blushing under the heat of the overhead lights and Moss' praise, Angus stood and bowed. A sexy looking woman in a halter-top he'd seen dancing, reached up for Angus' hand, tickled it with her finger.

"You're cute," she said, as she held onto his hand. "Can I buy you a drink?"

"Got another blues number, so get down," Moss announced. "Here's "Blues in Hoss' Flat."

Lost in the reverie of the woman's touch, the hot lights, smoky air, the thrill of having lived up to Moss' expectations, Angus sat back down at the piano.

As if disappointed by the interruption, the woman turned away and mingled with the crowd.

"Better stay away from *that* stuff," Otis laughed, as he introduced Angus to a reddish-colored drink. "Try this," Otis said and handed

Angus two frosted glasses with a red cherries floating on top of their foamy contents. "S*loe gin fizz...* get ya' in the groove, man."

After the first tune of their second set, Angus chugged down one of the two pink drinks Otis had given him. Moss stopped bantering with a couple standing at the foot of the bandstand, turned and called the next tune, "C-Jam Blues." Time for his solo, Angus felt a heady buzz. Though slightly dizzy, he played with inspiration... his best solo ever.

"Nice, man... very cool," Moss said, nodding approval. An hour later – after finishing their third set – Moss pulled Angus into the back room, patted him on the back and said, "Let's have a joint."

6. FOUNTAIN POINT HIGH SCHOOL

Angus, Rose, Bernie and their little colony of St. Pat's graduates, clustered at the auditorium entrance for their first day at Fountain Point High School. A hulking kid – the biggest kid Angus had ever seen – stood with three others boys inside the auditorium by a bank of seats. The boy looked like a redheaded tree stump with stovepipe arms. He held up a hand-lettered sign with an arrow pointing to an empty section of the nearby seats: *MACKRIL SNAPPERS SECTION — WELCOME CATLICKERS.*

"I guess they don't teach spelling here," Rosemary said.

FPHS boasted a student body of more than 400. There were nearly 125 students in Angus' freshman class alone...more than the entire kindergarten through eighth grades at St. Pat's. When Angus looked around the packed auditorium, the only person he recognized other than his St. Pat's friends was his brother, Robby. cutting up with his baseball cronies in the upper balcony. Angus felt as if he were a nameless drone in the middle of a beehive.

Following the assembly and huddled around their hallway lockers, Angus reviewed his class schedule with Rosemary and Bernie. Rosemary had changed since they had danced at St. Pat's last mixer. Her dark curly hair was fixed in a French braid, her black eyes were now shaded with a faint tint of lavender, her eyebrows thinner, her lashes longer and more pronounced. She wore dark pink lipstick, her fingernails a matching tone. Angus had thought of her all summer and hoped he would have another chance to impress her with his piano playing.

Bernie too had changed over the summer… her fingernails once cracked and nubby were neatly filed into smooth oval shapes; her legs were cleanly shaven, more developed and shapely. Her bulky eyeglasses replaced with contact lenses made her amber eyes appear to be deeper and better aligned, eyelashes longer, her smile broader, her complexion, richer… creamier. Her longer flowing blond hair was pulled back into a ponytail and fixed with a ribbon. Though still pudgy but leaving all the boys drooling over her legendary boobs, she wore a tight brown sweater that looked too small, washed-out gray cotton footies and worn sneakers.

After school, the St. Pat's group met at Percy's Confectionary, the high school hangout, soda fountain, candy store and bakery owned by Tommy Percy. The Art-Deco interior featured brushed aluminum and stainless steel fixtures, black lacquered Bakelite appointments, stepped-form mirrors with etched figures of top hats along the bottom and geometric swirls curling around them. Painted pastel pink with dark green moldings, the walls were covered with pictures and graphics from high school athletic functions.

Except for Bernie, everyone ordered a milkshake. As the waitress served them, Angus whispered to Bernie, "Aren't you having anything?"

"I'm trying to lose some weight," Bernie said.

Angus nodded and sipped his milkshake.

"You'll never guess who I met," Bernie said. "Leon Muncy. The call him *Beef*."

"Who?" Anna Belle asked.

"We saw him at the assembly," Bernie said.

"Holding up *that* sign," Wiggs said.

"Looked like the *Hunchback of Notre Dame*," Angus quipped.

"Beef's our freshman football star," Bernie said. "He's *so* big!"

Nodding cynically, Angus turned to Rose.

"You meet any *big guys* yet?"

"I'm trying out for cheerleading," Rose said.

"Cheerleading? You?" Angus said, surprised as he was curious.

7. THE CHIEFTAINS

Angus and Rose stood at their hallway lockers. Rose wore knee stockings, pink tennis shoes, a dark blue kilt-like skirt and beige crew-neck sweater. A red satin hairband stretched over the top of her head, pushing her black curls just behind her ears. She wore a small gold pendant and matching earrings.

"Will you go to the football game with me Friday night?" Angus asked. "And the Victory Dance Saturday night?"

"I have some great news," Rose bubbled. "I was voted onto the freshman cheerleading squad. They only elect four freshman girls and I was one of them. Isn't that unbelievable?"

"I… congratulations."

"I can't go with you to the game," Rose said. "I'll be cheerleading and Saturday night I was invited to help lead cheers at the Victory Dance… isn't that just super?"

Angus rummaged through his locker. When he turned to look at Rose, she was leafing through several papers clipped together.

"Look at all these cheers I have to learn," Rose said. "Let's see…" she muttered as she went through the papers, "… there's twenty different routines I have to learn."

Angus stepped back to his locker, closed it, twirled the combination lock and ambled down the hallway for class.

~~~~~
~~~~~

It was a cool fall evening, the air light but damp and filled with the smell of smoke from the pre-game bonfire. With Fox on the reserve football squad, Ratface and Sticks in the band and Lighthorse, the team water boy, Angus looked for a seat in the mobbed grandstand. Wriggling into the first row, he sat by himself. Behind him, Bernie yelled, "Come and sit with me and my friends."

Stumbling over the other fans, Angus squeezed into a small space next to Bernie. She was decked out with a bright red sweater, a yellow mum perched just above her bulging chest.

"Do you like my corsage?" Bernie asked.

Angus glanced at her floral adornment.

"Beefy gave it to me for good luck," Bernie gushed.

Peering toward the sidelines, Angus couldn't help but notice Rosemary and one of the male cheerleaders hugging each other. His teeth gleaming like a television toothpaste model, he wore FP's school colors... black tights, a red sweater with a huge red chenille letter '*C*' on the front. As with the other girl cheerleaders, Rose wore a short red skirt and black sweater with the same red chenille letter. Whoever was hugging Rose, Angus couldn't help wishing he would drop dead.

Within minutes of the game beginning, Beef Muncy scored. With the crowd going berserk, Bernie pounded on Angus' back. "Ange! Did you see that? Beef just bulled over everyone. He's so big!"

The announcer's voice thundered:

> *"Where's the Beef? There's the*
> *Beef! Freshman Beef Muncy scores*
> *his first high school touchdown!*

At halftime – the Fountain Point Chieftains winning 24 – 3 over archrival, the Urbana Hill Climbers – Angus made his way to the sideline. Seeing Rose kiss her toothpaste hero, he skulked home and practiced for hours in preparation for The Saints first gig at the second Victory Dance, Saturday, the following weekend.

~~~~~

Monday morning, Rose bounced down the hall toward Angus and her locker.

"How did you like the game? Wasn't it just super?" Rose beamed.

Angus hesitated. It wasn't super... not even close.

"I tried to wave to you on the sidelines," he said.

"Did you see that cheerleader standing next to me? He's our captain," Rose said.

While checking her makeup in a small mirror fixed inside her locker door, she said, "Friday night, he's going to throw me up in the air and catch me."

Rose finished primping, closed her locker and turned to Angus.

"He's a junior… his name is Thurman Marks but everyone calls him *Thurmy.*"

8. VICTORY DANCE

A drenching downpour nearly washing out The Chieftains' second Friday night home game, Angus stayed home to practice for the Saints first gig at the Victory Dance where he hoped Rose would like the new song he'd polished just for her: "All I Do Is Dream of You."

The rain continuing all day Saturday, Angus raced into The Inn at Mary's Gate, hung his slicker in the coatroom, moseyed into the ballroom and was struck by its cavernous size. Larger than the auditorium at FPHS, Angus guessed that it could easily accommodate as many as five hundred people. The pristine ballroom was painted a neutral off-white tone. The center section was cleared for dancing, a stage serving both for meetings and a bandstand. Around the perimeter of the room stood twelve round tables with ten chairs tucked neatly under them. On each table was a floral centerpiece with a lit candle and ribbons featuring the Fountain Point High School colors… black and
~~~~~

red. A large, antique wooden Indian – the Chieftains mascot – stood sentry near the entryway.

After checking out the Inn's piano, Angus looked up to see Rose enter. Not seeing her toothpaste hero, he ambled to the coatroom where Rose was hanging up her raincoat.

"I've practiced a new song I think you'll like," Angus said. "Will you sit with me on the bandstand between cheering?"

As Rose chirped, "Thurmy is parking his car," Angus noticed a school ring on her finger.

"How did you get a class ring?" he said.

"Ange! It's Thurmy's ring. Were going steady... Isn't that just super?"

Hearing a commotion behind them, Rose turned and squealed, "Here's Thurmy now!" Angus turned to see Thurman entering the ballroom, Bernie and a cadre of other giddy girls following. Bernie rushed over to Angus, her sopping wet thin canvas sneakers squishing with every step. She wore tight black slacks and the red sweater she had worn at the first football game.

Still breathless, Bernie turned to Angus. "Beef should be here in a few minutes," she said, "We can say hi to him."

"I have to start playing," Angus said, skipped to the bandstand, counted off a brisk tempo for "Bye Bye Blackbird" until interrupted by the arrival of Beef and his cronies. With hands clasped over his head like a prize fighting champion, Beef preened for his boisterous devotees. While the rest of the football team mimicked Beef, Rose clutched onto her toothpaste hero, jumping up-and-down with him at the victorious team's raucous entrance.

All during the party, Angus tried not to watch Rose and Thurman on the dance floor. As Angus and his group got ready to take a break, he looked over at Bernie and Beef standing alone together in one of the forbidden alcoves reserved for chaperones. Angus jumped off the bandstand to ask Bernie if she wanted to sing with his group during the last set. As Angus approached, Bernie took a step away from Beef.

"C'mon up and sing a couple of tunes," Angus said.

"She's busy," Beef snarled, pulling her beneath his massive arm.

As Angus turned to leave, Beef flipped him the bird.

Gazing out over the dance floor during the last set, Angus wondered where Rose and her new steady had gone. Near the end of the set, he looked toward the exit to see Beef and Bernie leaving the ballroom; just behind them were Rose and Thurman.

~~~~~

While playing the 151 Club over the Thanksgiving break, Moss introduced Angus to a friend Moss had invited to sit in. The lanky, forty-something musician hopped onto the bandstand and extended his hand to Angus.

"This is Milt Davis," Moss said. "I told Milt it would be good with you if he played a couple of tunes with us. Cool?"

"Cool," Angus agreed.

"Moss tells me you're very good," Milt said, as he and Angus shook hands.

"Milt just moved here from Lima to teach in the public school system," Moss said.

As Milt hopped on the bandstand, Moss took Angus aside.

"Listen to Milt's solos… you'll hear some very cool improvisation," he said.

Moss bobbed his trumpet, snapped his fingers to count off a ripping version of "Blues For Pepper," by Oscar Peterson. Transfixed, Angus stood at the side of the bandstand. When it was Milt's turn to solo, Angus' eyes riveted on his deft hands, awestruck by his swinging improvisations. Finishing a laid-back version of Count Basie's "Blues in
~~~~~

Hoss' Flat," Moss beckoned to the group to take a break. In the back room, Moss lit a joint and turned to Angus.

"Milt said he'd teach you about improvising," Moss said.

"Thursdays after school," Milt said. "My office over at Academy Middle School."

~~~~~

Milt's office was a small, sparsely furnished space. A creaky relic of an air conditioner whined in the window behind his desk. As Milt extended his hand in greeting, Angus eyed an aging, beaten up piano against the wall.

"Welcome to my palatial dump," Milt said.

Angus scanned the cramped room to see volumes of music folders scattered over Milt's desk. In the corner, a conga drum served as a pedestal for a dusty fake fern.

Milt pulled out the piano bench and gestured to the relic of years gone by.

"This junky thing has a great tone. Go ahead and play something."

Angus ripped off a short version of "C-Jam Blues."

"Now, play it again and let me hear something besides the melody."

Angus played through the tune and turned to Milt.

"I can hear ideas, but they don't translate to the keyboard," he said.

"Hearing them is a good sign," Milt said. "If you know the chord structures, you can hear how the melody of any tune fits into them… then invent variations around it."

Hesitating, Angus squinted at Milt.

"I can hear it… it just isn't … working," he stammered.

"The pros use all kinds of different licks and phrases," Milt said. "Listen to what they do… you're good enough to borrow their ideas and embellish them with your own."

~~~~~

The first weekend of the New Year, Angus sauntered into the 151 Club. Moss met him and Milt at the bandstand.

"Milt says you're getting a lot better," Moss said. "You sit in on the first set and let's hear some of your new stuff."

A nervous chill ran through Angus as his Milt, his new mentor sat near the bandstand waiting for Angus to perform. Moss turned to Angus… "Gonna start with an old Muddy Waters tune, 'Got My MoJo Workin.'"

Angus quickly turned to Moss.

"I… I never heard it," Angus whispered.

"Use your ears, man," Moss said. It's a twenty-four bar blues. You'll feel it."

Moss counted off a groovy tempo. One by one, Angus' fingers started to function. Intuitively, he caught the feeling he thought had abandoned him. Reaching inside himself to the mysterious place where creativity resides, Angus could hear himself play things he had no idea he was capable of playing.

9. HANGIN'

Rose, having barely acknowledged Angus all spring since her announcement about going steady with her toothpaste hero. His heart raced at the sound of her voice over the phone.

"Hi Ange. I'm having a cookout on Saturday night over the Fourth of July," Rose said. "I hope you aren't busy playing piano somewhere."

"Who all's coming?" Angus quickly responded.

"Everyone. See you about four, OK?"

Angus muddled through the days before Rose's party as if he were waiting for a prison parole. The week of Rose's party, Bernie called.

"Guess what?" she said. "Rose invited me to her party. Can I ride with you?"

~~~~~

As he pulled his mom's car into Greenway Acres Trailer Par*k,* Angus gasped at the sight of the rundown cluttered property. Dumpsters crammed full of trash spilled out into the spaces between trailers. Torn garbage bags lay strewn over the ground where green-bottle flies and scrawny dogs fought each other for scraps of food spilling out of the bags. Laundry hanging out to dry looked grimy and gray; dirty, half-dressed children peered at Angus as he parked the car. Bernie stood outside a squatty, rusted-out trailer next to a beaten up propane tank. She waved to Angus, sauntered to his car and jumped into the front seat. She wore ragged-edge white denim short-shorts, a tight sleeveless red-white-and-blue sweater and tan chamois moccasins. Her hair was pulled back in a ponytail with a red ribbon.

"Glad you got here before my old man comes home," Bernie said. "Let's split before he shows up and makes me stay home."

~~~~~

Rose's home on Orchard Island sat directly on a northerly point looking west over the lake toward Paradise Island. A hand-lettered sign – *Gracewood Cottage* – stood at the edge of the driveway. Angus drove toward the two-story house built with Nantucket brick and cinnamon-stained cypress. Vaulted windows rose in elegant greeting. A canopy of leaves from four towering cottonwood trees shaded the house from the July sun. A three-car garage behind and to the left of the house stretched to a copse of tightly sculpted trees.

"You've got to be kidding," Bernie gasped. "This is a freaking mansion. You're sure this is where Rose lives?"

Angus took a deep breath and soaked up the scene.

"Her dad owns a bunch of Wendy's restaurants," he said.

As Angus parked his car and jumped out, Rose emerged from the house. She wore white capri pants, a hot-pink sleeveless blouse with matching wide-brimmed mesh sun hat and strappy pink sandals. She greeted Angus with a quick hug.

"You're early," Rose said. "Thurmy's the only one here so far."

Angus heart sank into his gut as Thurman slinked out of the house and sauntered toward them in white sateen pants, a yellow-and-blue, bold-striped collared soccer top and white loafers with no socks, a baby-blue silk scarf wrapped around his neck as if he were nursing a sore throat.

"*Bonjour, mes amis,*" Thurman intoned.

As Bernie stepped into the sunshine, Rose pulled back and scanned her skimpy attire. "Glad Ange could bring you," she said as she took Thurman's arm and pulled him toward Fox's car entering the driveway.

"C'mon Thurmy, let's say hello to the others."

Wiggs and Anna Belle jumped out of Fox's car and squealed greetings to everyone.

Rose rushed to greet them, gestured to Thurman.

"You all know Thurmy," Rose said. "This is his bon-voyage party."

Angus turned to Bernie and whispered, "Did I hear that right?"

"Wiggs said he's going to some swishy dance school in the East," Bernie said.

As more guests arrived, Rose gathered them together and said, "Let's go watch the sunset."

~~~~~

The lake rippled under a gentle breeze as Rose and Thurman swirled among the gathering. As Rose stopped to talk with Anna Belle and Wiggs, Thurman spotted Angus, Ratface, Fox and Bernie standing at the refreshment table. His usual sappy grin beaming, he minced over to them.

"Agnes! I love that name, *Agnes*. It sounds so… so explicit," Thurman said.

"Nice seeing you again," Angus said.
~~~~~

Thurman moved close to Angus, reached over, stroked Angus' arm.

"I love your shirt," Thurman said, as he withdrew his hand. "You're that musical person or something, no?"

Angus shrugged, stepped back.

"I hear you're going to dance school."

Thurman's drippy smile spread over his face like syrup on pancakes. "Hochstein School in Rochester. New York, you know?"

"I'll bet Rosemary is sorry to see you leave," Angus said.

"She's a darling little twit. But... as they say... the show must go on."

~~~~~

As the sky darkened, Rosemary herded everyone inside where the crowd clustered together in the largest living room Angus had ever seen. He remembered Rose telling him at his Valentine's Day party the her mother loved her big white piano, but he drew in his breath at the sight of the nine-foot, white Steinway Concert Grand. Pulling out the piano bench, he sat down and ran his fingers over the keyboard, then, played a trial note. The sound rang through the room like an *Angelus* summoning worshipers to *Vespers.* As Bernie sat next to Angus on the piano bench, Rose gave Angus a cool glance and motioned for him to start playing.

"Let's start with everyone's favorite, 'Kumbaya,'" Rose said.

The piano's silky soft keyboard action invited Angus' fingers to ignore the moronic song and feel the joy of just playing the pristine instrument. After the final chorus, Bernie turned to Angus.

"I saw you and Thurman," Bernie said. "Looked like you two were sucking up to each other."

"That's the last…" Angus started to say until Rose rasped, "*Shush,* you two."

Fox and Ratface smirked as Thurman launched into his triumphant tale.
~~~~~

"Well boys and girls, this spring," he began… "I auditioned for The Hockstein School in Rochester."

Bernie poked Angus in the ribs.

"Is he queer or what?"

Trying not to irritate Rose again, Angus listened as Thurman finished.

"… and… well… I hope someday you'll all come and see me on Broadway."

~~~~~

Finishing the main meal, two service people circulated through the guest tables pouring ice water from silver pitchers and serving a fudgy dessert cake with ice cream and chocolate sauce.

After Bernie finished her brownie and ice cream, she looked at her wristwatch and turned to Angus.

"I have to go. My foster-dad will be pissed if I'm not home by ten," she said.

As Bernie thanked Rose for the party, Angus extended his hand to Thurman.

"Good luck in Rochester," Angus said.

"Au revoir," Thurman cheeped.

As Angus turned to Rose to thank her for inviting him, Rose patted Thurman on the arm and grinned at Angus.

"Thurmy and I are going to get together in Rochester," she said.

"Good for you," Angus muttered as he and Bernie left.

10. HOMECOMING

The ballroom at the Inn at Mary's Gate for Saturday night's Homecoming Dance was festooned with banners streaming off a special
~~~~~

dais beside the bandstand for Queen Bernie Walker and her court. The five court chairs were draped with regal red velvet. The Queen's throne sat slightly elevated above the other chairs. A special stairway with flowered hoops arching overhead and green floor carpeting led up to the dais. As Angus organized his band's music charts, Rose approached the bandstand. Fishing a mirror out of her purse, Rose paused and studied her image. Finished dabbing, she looked over the top of her mirror at Angus.

"Is Bernie… singing with your band tonight?" Rose asked.

"I didn't ask her… she'll be tied up with the whole crowning thing."

"Maybe we can… dance or something, OK?" Rose said.

Puzzled at Rose's unexpected invitation, Angus picked up the sheaf of music charts for the night. As he leafed through them, he remembered the last thing Rose had said at her party: *I'm going to get together with Thurmy in Rochester.*

Ratface – having smuggled in a pint of sloe gin – hung out with Fox and Angus in the restroom sharing the contraband booze when Beef Muncy burst through the restroom door as if it were tissue paper.

"Gimme a swig of that shit," Beef demanded.

Fox handed the bottle to Beef who promptly drained it.

"Don't be a hog," Ratface protested.

"Fuck you, Ratface. You didn't score no touchdowns, did'ya?"

Beef pushed through the three of them and headed for the urinal.

"You fuckwads got any pussy lined up tonight?" he said, as he relieved himself.

"Yeah, Beef. We're all set," Angus said.

"I know you McCrory… you'd love to fuck Bernie. I better not see you looking at her or I'll smash your ugly face. Just go play your fucking piano like a good boy and quit asking her to sing with your stupid band."

Angus lunged toward Beef. "You're a moron," Angus shouted.

Beef backed up.

"You want a piece of me, asshole? Take your best shot."

Just as Angus drew back to swing at Beef, chaperone Mr. Walters, entered the restroom. "You boys break it up and get out of here right now!" he yelled.

Beef slammed Angus aside and stormed toward the restroom exit.

"Anytime, McCrory. You know where to find me," Beef grunted.

~~~~~

As Angus jumped onto the stage, Mr. Walters took over the microphone.

The students gathered at the foot of the bandstand, the chaperones ushered Queen Bernie Walker and her court down the grass carpet, under the flowered hoops and onto the dais. On her way to the dais, Bernie whispered to Angus. "I can't sing tonight. After the crowning, we're going for a ride in Beefy's *Corvette*!"

Suddenly, Beef jumped onto the bandstand and grabbed Angus. Pushing Angus against the piano, he spluttered in Angus' face.

"I thought I told you to fuck off McCrory!"

Before Angus could push back, Beef punched him in the face.

Reeling from Beef's powerful blow, Angus pinched his brow to staunch the blood trickling down his cheek. The room fell silent as Beef's voice rang out: "Stay away from Bernie or I'll cripple your ass for good."

His head throbbing with pain, Angus swiped the blood from his flowing brow and lunged at Beef just as Mr. Walters grabbed Beef by the collar.

"That's all for you tonight, Mr. Muncy!"

As Mr. Walters and two other chaperones escorted Beef to the exit, Rose sidled up to Angus.

"Ii feel sorry for Bernie," Rose said.
~~~~~

"I don't," Angus said.

As Angus turned to leave, Rose put her hand on his arm.

"I heard from Thurman…"

"I suppose he's some super star?" Angus said.

"He has a new friend."

"You're going to Rochester to meet his new friend?" Angus said.

"His name is… well, I guess his name doesn't matter," Rose said.

As Angus looked directly into Rose's eyes, she leaned close to him.

"Just so you know," she whispered. "I mailed Thurman's class ring back to him."

11. COME ON HOME

In the music room, Mr. Hamilton sat at a table filled with catalogs and flyers from an array of music schools. Angus took a chair opposite him.

"Here's several options," Mr. Hamilton said. "I've earmarked a few I think would be good for you."

Angus examined the pile of catalogs: *New England Conservatory of Music, The New School; Juilliard; University of Miami; Cincinnati Conservatory; University of Rochester; Berklee College of Music; Capital University.*

"Here's my recommendations," Hamilton said. "Capital, Rochester, Cincinnati and Berklee."

Angus gathered the catalogs and thanked Mr. Hamilton. "I'll talk with Milt and see what he thinks.

~~~~~

Angus trudged to Milt's office and handed a bundle of music school catalogs to him.
~~~~~

"Mr. Hamilton said I should ask you to look these over."

Milt sat the catalogs on his desk, plopped down in his rickety tilt-back swivel chair and said, "Cool, but let's talk about improvising, first."

Angus perched on the piano bench as Milt continued.

"I've been thinking about you since our last lesson," Milt said. "What have you been practicing?"

"The usual – scales, exercises… some new tunes…"

Milt pointed to the piano.

"Play 'All The Things You Are' and improvise two choruses for me," Milt said.

Angus sat at the keyboard and started playing. In the middle of his second improvisational pass through the tune, Milt stopped him.

"What do you think about while you improvise?" Milt said.

Angus paused, considered.

"I try to play things I hear in my head," Angus said.

"Who are you listening to?" Milt said.

"Oscar Peterson… Bill Evans… Chick Corea…"

"That's the third time I've heard you play 'All The Things You Are,'" Milt said. "You're using the same improvisational licks over and over."

Milt smiled and stood up.

"What do you suppose those players you're listening to think about when they improvise?"

"I have… no idea," Angus said.

"Good improvisers don't fear making mistakes," Milt said. "They know the song form, the chord structure and have a set of priorities when they practice."

"They practice?" Angus said.

"The best players put in four or five hours a day," Milt said. "They experiment. That's how they learn better creative choices and avoid regurgitating trite phrases when they improvise. If you listen closely, each one has a unique improvisational voice."

"What's *voice*?"

"Styling," Milt said. "Their personal musical palette. Their styling creates their *voice* signature. Like… everyone speaks differently."

"I'm not following… exactly," Angus said.

"Good artists don't paint the same picture fifty times," Milt said.

Angus rubbed his chin.

"How can I change what I hear in my head?" Angus said.

"Listen harder to the pros and *feel* their phrasing." Milt said. "And practice more!"

Milt handed Angus a sheet of paper filled with handwritten notes.

"I've written out twenty-five chords to practice," Milt said.

Angus scanned the chord notations.

"I know all these chords," he said.

"Take the chords one at a time and play each chord with your left hand while you play the major, minor, melodic and harmonic scales, arpeggios and triads with your right hand."

"Every one?" Angus said.

"That's your assignment for this fall," Milt said.

Angus folded the assignment sheet and stepped to the door.

"What about the music school catalogs?"

Milt sorted through the file of catalogs and nodded.

"Pretty impressive selection," he said. "I'll look them over and we'll talk."

~~~~~
~~~~~

Deciding to give Rose the *Claddagh* Aummie had given him, Angus carefully wrapped it and headed for the Saturday night Victory Dance at the Inn.

The crowd gabbed about the Chieftains' win. Beef's cluster of hero worshippers gathered for the usual round of adulation and boasting about having scored four touchdowns. His *coup de gras* was to hit the floor and do pushups to the number of points his touchdowns totaled. As Beef's group of admirers chanted *seventeen... eighteen... nineteen...* Angus and Rose pushed past them toward the tables near the bandstand. Rose whispered to Angus as Beef's sideshow ended.

"It's too hot in here. Let's go to Percy's."

~~~~~

Angus' favorite waitress, Percy's daughter, Beth, was tall and slender with straight brown hair and an engaging smile. When she put the menu in front of Angus and Rose, her silver charm bracelet clanked on the table.

"How was the dance?' Beth said.

"Big crowd," Angus said. "Hot in the ballroom."

"We'll share a chocolate sundae," Rose said. "OK, Ange?"

Beth nodded, picked up the menus and disappeared behind the soda fountain.

Angus reached into his pocket and pulled out the small package wrapped in green tissue paper, pushed it across the table to Rose.

"What's that?" she said, pointing to the package.

"A surprise."

Rose picked up the package, turned it over several times then teased the outer wrapper off. Studying the inner wrapper, Rose said, "OK, Ange... this is a trick... right?"

Angus scooped a bite of ice cream and said, "Why else would I wrap it up?"
~~~~~

Rose finished unwrapping the gift. Sitting in the middle of the green tissue paper, a small gold ring gleamed. Rose squinted at the figures embossed on it.

"What is this?" she said.

Angus' heart raced as he leaned across the table to Rose.

"It's a *Claddagh,* he said.

Rose studied the two hands clasping a heart with a crown sitting atop the heart.

"For me?"

Angus' palms moistened; his fingers trembled. He took the ring and slipped it onto Rose's ring finger of her right hand, the crown pointing to her fingertip.

Rose studied the ring again. "Are you serious?"

Angus stirred his melting ice cream.

"The heart means *love,* the clasping hands mean *friendship* and the crown means *loyalty,"* Angus said.

"It's beautiful," she said. "Is there a special way..."

Angus put his hand on hers. "The crown always points to your fingertip."

Rose turned her head and coughed sharply.

"You're coughing a lot," Angus said.

Turning her head again, Rose expelled another harsh cough.

Angus pushed a glass of water across the table.

"Have a sip," Angus said.

Rose sipped the water and looked at Angus.

"I hate to say it, but if I don't get home soon, my dad will think I've wrecked his precious BMW."

At her car in Percy's parking lot, Rose pulled Angus toward her and said softly, "Don't make a girl ask for a goodnight kiss… it's very rude."

~~~~~

Late Sunday afternoon, Angus couldn't wait to find out how Rose felt about going steady. He dialed her home and waited. When Rose answered, his hands shook.

"I just called to say hello," Angus said.

As if nothing had happened between them the night before, Rose sounded annoyingly blasé.

"Oh… hi Ange," she said.

"Hope you had a good time last night," Angus said, and waited for Rose to say something encouraging.

"My mom doesn't like me going steady," she said.

Brutally disappointed, Angus twirled the phone cord around his fingers.

"She wants me to give the *Claddagh* back," Rose said flatly.

Infuriated, Angus couldn't resist speaking his mind.

"What about when Thurman gave you his class ring? What about *that?"* Angus fumed. "You told me you were going *steady* with *him!* Did your mother tell you to give *his* ring back to *him*?"

His temper boiling, Angus waited.

"I can't talk anymore," Rose said. "My mom wants to use the phone."

Disheartened, Angus slumped at the kitchen table and shook his head. Trying to clam down, he called Milt to arrange to meet with him the next week after school to discuss his potential choices for music school.

~~~~~

Milt was on the phone when Angus entered his office. As Milt gestured for Angus to take a seat, Angus saw the catalogs on Milt's desk. Milt hung up and smiled at Angus, picked up the Berklee catalog and turned to him.

"Berklee's the best choice for you," Milt said. "They have the strongest jazz performance program."

Milt handed the catalog to Angus and pointed to a paper-clipped page near the back.

"Don't be shocked, Berklee's expensive," Milt said.

Angus turned to the clipped page. When he read the tuition information, he froze.

"Man… I don't have anywhere near that kind of bread," he said. "It's a hundred bucks just to apply."

Angus pushed the catalog back to Milt.

"If you can't find a hundred dollars, I'll loan it to you," Milt said.

Angus retracted the folder and opened it again, scanned the requirements.

"What about the audition?" Angus said.

"Cleveland, next February," Milt said.

"That's only a few months away."

"It's stuff you already know," Milt said.

Milt took the folder from Angus and pointed to the page, *Audition Requirements,* handed the catalog back to Angus and tapped on the paragraph.

"It says: *blues, standard song forms and vamps,"* Milt said. "You sure as hell know blues and a ton of standards. I can teach you the vamps in two weeks."

"What are *vamps*?" Angus said.

"R & B, rock, funk and fusion rhythms repeated in the same musical voice where each note always has the same weight," Milt said.

As if Milt were speaking Greek, Angus sat mute.

Grinning, Milt said, "The repeating rhythm pattern may be part of a tune or a complete melody."

Angus shook his head. "Is there any way you can boil that down?"

"Just think of vamps as improvising over repetitive chords and rhythms."

Angus studied the audition guidelines further.

"It says there's sight reading, too."

"We'll work on that," Milt said.

Angus nodded, rubbed his chin.

"Do they offer scholarships?" Angus said.

"Not the first year," Milt said. "Take the catalog home and talk with your folks."

~~~~~

At dinner, Angus pushed his beef and noodles around on the plate while his mother and father bantered about the fall weather and the leaves piling up in the yard.

"You're awfully quiet, tonight," she said. "Will you help me rake up the leaves after dinner?"

Angus put his fork down. "I talked with Milt today," he said.

"Did you have a lesson?" Angus' father said.

"Sort of," Angus said. "We talked about music school."

Angus' father finished eating and pushed his chair away from the table.

"What about it?" he said.
~~~~~

Angus stepped to the counter under the phone to retrieve the Berklee catalog he'd left handy, handed it to his father, took a deep breath and slowly exhaled.

"Berklee's in Boston," Angus said. "They have the jazz study programs I need."

Angus' father put the open catalog on the kitchen table and pointed to the fee schedule.

"Pretty expensive," he said.

Silence hung over the three of them as Angus rubbed his forehead.

"I'll get a job… something," Angus finally said. "I'll help pay for it."

Angus' father pushed the catalog across the table to Angus' mother.

"When do you have to apply?" his father said.

"Mr. Hamilton said if I apply now, I can audition in February."

Angus drew in a deeper breath and paused for a moment as his mother flipped through the catalog.

"Does Berklee offer scholarships?" she said.

"Milt told me there isn't much chance for the first year," Angus said.

Angus' father stood and patted Angus on the back.

"Go ahead and apply," he said. "If you get in… we'll work things out. Your mom can squeeze money out of a turnip."

As Angus' mother finished writing the check to Berklee, the phone rang.

"McCrory's," she said.

Angus picked up the empty decorations boxes and started toward the basement stairs but stopped when his mother said, "Phone call, Ange. I don't recognize her voice."

"Hello," Angus said.

"This is Mrs. Gracewood. Rose asked me to call."

Angus clutched the phone and stepped into the pantry for privacy.

When he returned to the dining room with a dour look on his face, his mother turned to him. "What is it?"

Angus eased his slumping body onto a kitchen chair.

Rose has… *mono*," he muttered. "She won't be back in school until after Christmas."

~~~~~

The week before Christmas vacation, Milt stopped in the middle of their hour-long lesson and tapped on the keyboard.

"You're just playin' notes, man," Milt said. "You're not *feeling* anything."

Angus moved away from the piano and looked out the window at the dingy snowdrifts covered with icy gray slush.

"I feel like I'm getting stale," he said.

Milt moseyed to his desk drawer, pulled out two CDs and handed them to Angus.

"Freshen up listening to these two over the holidays," Milt said.

Angus fingered the CDs of two pianists he'd never heard of: Red Garland and Hank Jones. Milt pointed to Red Garland's album, *Blues in the Night.*

"It's an old album, but listen to Red's block chords," Milt said.

Angus looked at the artist's picture on the CD cover. Red Garland appeared to be a slight-built black man with an easy smile covered by a splotchy black beard.

"Red plays three notes in his right hand and four notes in his left," Milt said. "You'll hear his right hand playing an octave above. Different sound."

Angus studied the tune list on the album.
~~~~~

"Any particular tune?"

"All of 'em. But start with 'Ahmad's Blues,'" Milt said

Angus nodded as Milt tapped his finger on the Hank Jones album, *Bluesette/London.*

"Take a minute and read that first paragraph of the notes," Milt said.

Angus squinted at the small type –

'... admired by his fellow musicians for his

imagination, Jones' versatility and distinctive

style blend urbanity and rhythmic drive of

Harlem stride pianists, the dexterity of

Art Tatum and the daring of bebop.'

Angus reread the album notes and shook his head.

"I wish I knew what all that means," he said.

"You have to do more than listen to these cats play," Milt said. "You have to *feel* how they play."

Milt opened the door for Angus to leave.

"Go to the library and get a couple of other CDs by Tommy Flanagan... Willie Smith, too. Listen to Willie's stride style," Milt said.

Angus turned to leave, then paused and looked back at Milt.

"What's stride?"

Milt sat at the piano and motioned for Angus to stand behind him and watch him demonstrate *stride* technique.

"Stride is your left hand playing a four-beat pulse with a single bass note, octave, seventh or tenth interval on the first and third beats and a chord on the second and fourth beats," Milt said.

"All that with my left hand?" Angus said.

Milt stepped away from the piano to his desk, opened a drawer filled with vintage cassette tapes, rummaged around and handed one of the tapes to Angus.

"They probably don't have this recording at the library, so I'll lend you mine. Willie's 'Pork and Beans' is a classic."

Angus opened the plastic container and read the insert.

"They called Willie Smith… *The Lion?"* Angus said.

"One of the top stride piano players *ever*," Milt said. "Fats Waller, James Johnson, Monk, Art Tatum... some others."

Angus slipped the cassette into his pocket while Milt opened the door for him to leave. "Try adding some stride to your improvisation," Milt said, "You'll dig it."

~~~~~

As Angus headed to the basement to practice, he glanced out the front window and saw the *UPS* truck pull into their driveway. Rushing to the door as the deliveryman knocked, Angus signed for the unexpected package addressed to him from: *Gracewood Cottage, #1 Orchard Island, Russells Point, OH. 43348.* He fumbled getting the package open. The outer wrapper fell to the floor as Angus studied the inner wrapper of Christmas paper sealed with holly stickers.

"I think it's from Rose," he said, to his mother

Angus' mother turned to go into the kitchen.

"You should call Rose and see how she's feeling," she said.

As his mother disappeared into the kitchen, Angus continued unwrapping the mysterious package. Underneath the first layer of paper with the holly stickers, a small tightly tied red bow was wrapped around an interior layer of sparkling Santa Claus paper. Angus hefted the package, untied the red ribbon and let the wrapping paper fall to the floor. Inside, was a delicate, ivory white porcelain plate glistening between more folds of red tissue paper. Gently, Angus removed the last fold of the paper and exposed the gift. On the surface facing him, he saw
~~~~~

the word, *Balleek,* imprinted below a brown ink illustration. Slowly, he flipped the plate over to the front side and read the hand-lettered inscription in the middle of the plate.

AN IRISH BLESSING ~

May the road rise to meet you,

May the wind be always at your back.

May the sun shine warm upon your face,

The rains fall soft upon your fields.

And until we meet again,

May God hold you in the palm of his hand.

Angus went to the kitchen and dialed Rose's number.

Rose's mother answered: "Gracewood Cottage."

"Merry Christmas. Is Rose there?"

Angus heard Rose's mother talking away from the phone, *"It's Angus… do you feel like talking?"*

Quickly, Rose came on the line.

"Merry Christmas, Ange. I miss you."

"Feeling better?"

"The doctor said I can't come back to school until January."

"January?"

"I'm wearing my *Claddagh,"* Rose said.

"I got your gift," Angus said cheerfully. "I'll call you on New Years"

Rose moaned softly.

"I won't be here. We're going to my mom and dad's condo in Florida."

"The whole time?" Angus said.

"I'll write to you," Rose said.

As Angus hung up, he was startled when the phone rang again. Maybe it was Rose calling back, he hoped, but a man's voice said, "Angus, please."

"Speaking," Angus said.

"This is Charles Sewell at the Inn at Mary's Gate."

"How are you?" Angus said, wondering why Mr. Sewell had called.

"How would you like to play a few weekends over the Christmas holidays?" Mr. Sewell said.

"I'd love it," Angus said.

"I'll book you for the Friday and Saturday nights the weekend before Christmas, only Saturday after Christmas and on New Year's Eve. Ten an hour plus your tips."

In his bedroom, Angus put Rose's *Irish Blessing* gift on his dresser.

12. BLUESETTE

Shuffling down the hallway at school in January, Anna Belle pulled Angus aside.

"I just saw Bernie cleaning out her locker," she said. "She was crying and didn't want to talk."

Angus stashed his parka in his locker, grabbed his notebook and rushed to find Bernie. Minutes before the bell rang for first period, he saw her rummaging through her locker and sidled up to her. "You and the Beef-man running off together?"

Her eyes red and swollen, Bernie said, "Meet me at Percy's after school?"

~~~~~

Bernie and Angus took a booth in the back of Percy's. She tossed her battered backpack down, slung her rumpled parka onto the booth bench and sat down. She wore a plain brown sweater with a wrinkled blouse; her hair was dull, raked to the side, clipped with two hairpins. Sitting silently, Bernie rummaged through her purse, extracted a small cosmetic mirror, blew on it and rubbed it against her sweater sleeve. She looked at Angus. Her eyes were more red and puffy than they were when Angus saw her at school that morning. Her cheeks blotchy, the corners of her nose inflamed, it was the first time Angus could remember seeing her so disheveled and unkempt. When she finally spoke, she drew out her words as if she wasn't sure what she wanted to say.

"Ange... I need your help," she said.

"I hope it isn't math," Angus said.

Unclipping her hairpins, she teased a length of her long blond hair.

"Not that kind of help," she said.

Her fingernails, usually well manicured, had been chewed down to nubs.

"The Beef-man dump you again?" Angus said.

Bernie looked away. Angus sensed that she knew what she wanted to say, but couldn't. Finally, she blurted, "I'm pregnant."

Angus reared back, put his hands over his eyes. He drew his hands slowly from his forehead to his chin, dropped his arms onto his lap and leaned across the table.

"Are… are you sure?" he whispered. "Couldn't there be a…"

"Sister Pauline took me to a doctor. I'm four months gone."

"What are you going to do? What about Beef… where's he?"

"He kicked me out of his car and told me to go get an abortion. Besides, even if I wanted to get an abortion– which I don't – four months is too late."
~~~~~

Angus couldn't recall ever seeing Bernie cry, but tears gushed down her cheeks as she took a napkin and dabbed at them.

Percy's daughter, Beth, put menus on their table.

"Happy New Year," Beth said. "Last semester for you two?"

Hoping Beth wouldn't linger, Angus quickly ordered, "Cokes and fries."

Beth turned toward the fountain as Bernie rubbed the tears from her eyes and looked at Angus.

"I'm leaving tonight, "Bernie said. "I need fifty dollars. I can't tell you why right now but I will later."

"Tonight? Where are you going?"

Bernie rooted through her purse and handed Angus a crumpled paper.

"Miss Ogletree informed me about the school rules," Bernie cried.

Angus unfolded the paper and read the terse note:

> *A pregnant, unmarried student must complete her classes by tutorial arrangements only. No personal class attendance is permitted. Signed – Josh Freeman, Principal.*

Before Angus could comment, Beth brought their order and Angus quickly thanked her. Hoping to calm Bernie, Angus pushed the Coke in front of her, but she ignored it.

Angus reread the note, passed it back to Bernie and studied her sullen countenance. She looked so different from the person Angus had known since grade school. There was no hint of a smile… her flirty grin and giggle, gone. Sitting there dumbfounded, Angus took her hand. When Bernie turned her head slightly into the light, her face was filled with angry bruises which her makeup had masked before her flooding tears washed it away.

"That son-of-a-bitch... he hurt you, didn't he?"

Bernie sobbed.

"My stepfather..." her voice trailed off.

"We should report him to the police. You can't let him get away with that!"

Bernie tried to choke back her tears.

"It's too late. He'll never see me again and that's exactly what he wants, so screw him and his bitchy wife. They only wanted me around for the money they got from foster care."

After sitting silent for a moment, Bernie stood up, wriggled into her parka.

"I have to go," she said.

Outside Percy's, Angus paused, searching for something to say, then finally, "Where are you going?"

Bernie hugged Angus.

"I'll write to you in a few days. Do you have the fifty dollars with you?"

Angus handed her two folded-up twenty-dollar bills he'd kept hidden in his wallet and the extra ten dollars from his pocket.

"Where are you going?"

"Walk me to the bus station, will you?"

~~~~~

When they arrived at the Greyhound station, Angus' held the door for Bernie. Inside the terminal, he watched the crowd of travelers line up at the ticket counter. Pangs of regret over Bernie's disaster clogged his throat as he put his arm around her slumping shoulders.

"Tell me where you're going," he said.

"My things are over there," Bernie said, gesturing to a bank of storage lockers on the wall next to the ticket counter.
~~~~~

As he watched Bernie open the locker and pull out a stuffed duffle bag, he felt his throat tighten again. Bernie handed the duffle bag to Angus and hiked her backpack over her shoulder.

"Thanks for helping me," she said.

"What about your bus ticket?" Angus said,

"I bought it when I dropped my stuff off earlier," Bernie said.

"You haven't told me where you're going," Angus persisted.

"Please, Ange. I need to work through this by myself. I'll write to you."

"You can't just leave. I'll help you..."

"You've always helped me," she said. "I can't tell you any more right now... just that... you know how I feel about you..."

As Bernie turned to board the bus, she held her hand out in goodbye.

~~~~~

Raging winter winds rattled the panes in Angus' bedroom window. Bleary-eyed and foggy from practicing late on Friday night, Angus slept in. When he bumbled into the kitchen at noon, his mother beamed at him.

"Something came for you in today's mail," she said, pointing to the kitchen counter. "It's right there by the phone."

Angus jumped to the counter and grabbed the ivory-colored business envelope with an engraved return address: *Berklee College of Music.* His hands shaking, he scanned the neatly printed corner card again, ripped the envelope open, paused with angst and read the neatly typed brief paragraph.

January 4, 1992 – cc. Mr. Milt Davis

Dear Mr. McCrory:
~~~~~

After reviewing your application and pending your audition with our Faculty Jury, you are tentatively accepted for admission to Berklee. You will be contacted for scheduling your audition.

Cordially,

The Berklee Office of Admissions

Angus whooped and kissed his mother.

13. PROM DATE

The first Monday of the New Year – like a pack of ravenous wolves on the scent of fresh meat – the high school gossip hounds began sniffing out the story about Bernie and Beef. Little cadres of rumormongers huddled in the hallways; girls yowling; boys howling.

The freezing winter weather virtually locked everyone into the school for lunch. In the cafeteria line at noon, Angus had the bad luck to stand in front of Beef as Rose waited ahead in line gabbing with one of her cheerleader friends. Angus was astonished when Rose suddenly turned around, pushed past him and confronted Beef.

"You should be ashamed of yourself, Leon," Rose said.

Beef tapped his finger on Rose's shoulder. "I don't take crap from no snob-puss like you, Gracewood," he growled. "Mind you own fucking business."

Angus grabbed Beef, pushed him out of the lunch line.

"Mind *your own* fucking business you moron!" Angus bellowed.

Beef grabbed Angus by the shirt and they both fell into a cafeteria table. Chairs flew, food scattered over the floor.

"I been waitin' to get a piece of you, McCrory!" Beef roared.

Angus swung wildly at Beef's head. His left fist connected with Beef's right ear and a cracking noise like firewood being split resounded through the cafeteria. Before Angus could duck, Beef's roundhouse punch smashed Angus on the bridge of his nose. Angus sprawled on the floor, blood spurting from his nose. Tears gushing from his eyes, Angus staggered to his feet. Seeing Beef taunt him with clenched fists, Angus lunged at him until Mr. Freeman yanked them apart.

"You two go straight to my office," Mr. Freeman ordered.

~~~~~

Inside Mr. Freeman's office, Angus and Beef sat next to each other, Mr. Freeman opposite them behind his desk. Angus touched his feverish swollen hand. Wincing with pain, he sulked over how fighting – especially with someone as stupid as Beef Muncy – would affect his audition for Berklee. Beef sat leering at Angus as Mr. Freeman pulled out a file from his desk drawer and scanned it.

"With your dismal record, Mr. Muncy, I have no choice but to expel you from school for a month," he said.

Beef stood towering over Mr. Freeman.

"Who gives a rat's ass," Beef bellowed and stomped out of Mr. Freeman's office.

As Angus held a bloody handkerchief over his nose, Mr. Freeman said, "You better go home and take care of that nose. Meanwhile, I'm putting you on probation."

~~~~~

Dr. Vincent examined Angus' broken nose and turned to Helga as the surly x-ray technician moseyed into the examination room. From somewhere under her camouflage moo-moo, Helga produced a large brown envelope and winked at the doctor.

"FYI, Doc, the film's still wet," she said, and plopped the envelope onto the x-ray reading console and pranced out.

Dr. Vincent removed a large, dark celluloid object from the envelope and stuck it onto a backlit fixture mounted on the wall. Angus saw the white areas illuminated by the backlight. As in a spooky

Halloween image, Angus saw the outline of his skeletal hand. Dr. Vincent studied the image and turned to Angus.

"So, you've been in a fight?"

"Not really… I…" Angus said.

Angus' mother moved closer to the examination table.

"Is it bad?" she said.

Dr. Vincent flicked off the x-ray reading panel light and wrote on a pad of paper. When he finished, he snatched the x-ray film from the reading light and stuffed it back into the envelope.

"You have what's called a *Boxer's Fracture,*" Dr. Vincent said. "Cracked your fourth metacarpal but you're lucky it isn't worse. Take a couple of aspirin twice a day for the pain and keep your hand iced."

"How soon can I start playing piano again?"

"Three weeks," Dr. Vincent said. "You can take the cast off."

Icing his hand in his room before bed, Angus tried not to sulk and Rose's *Irish Blessing.* Tossing down two aspirin, he gulped a glass of water and stewed most of the night over his Berklee audition.

~~~~~

Senior class vice president, Angus was appointed head of the Prom Decorations Committee by class president, Rosemary Gracewood. Worried about his audition, Angus struggled to be upbeat. But the prospect of taking Rose to the prom helped him ignore his ailing hand and he arrived early for the first planning meeting the second week of January. After Angus called the meeting to order, Rose said, "Do any of you remember the *Twelve Gods of Olympus*? *Aphrodite, Zeus, Poseidon, Athena?"*

"I want to be…*"* Wiggs paused with indecision.

Ratface shot Fox a sly smile and winked at Wiggs.

"Why don't you be *Pandora.* You can open your…"
~~~~~

"Shut up, you nitwit," Wiggs said.

"Will you please pay attention," Rose said.

Everyone sat erect as Rose continued.

"Angus will make up ballots and get them distributed for our class to vote on whom they want for the twelve gods and goddesses. OK, Ange?"

~~~~~

At home on Saturday morning, crystals of ice on his bedroom window broke up the rays of sunshine and formed fractured shadows on the wall, reminding Angus of his broken hand x-ray. He rubbed his sore hand, flipped the switch on his CD player and listened to Oscar Peterson. Caught up in Peterson's groovy rendition of "Joy Spring," Angus tried to ignore the pain in his hand.

Just before noon, he dressed in heavy sweats with a hooded top and ambled into the kitchen where his mother worked at the kitchen sink.

"Any mail today?" Angus said.

"I haven't checked yet," she said.

Angus hurried to the front door. Reaching into the mail slot, he extracted the few loose pieces. An envelope – larger than the usual bills – hung up in the mail chute. Yanking it out, Angus fingered the business size envelope and gasped: *Berklee School of Music.* Rushing back into the kitchen, he brandished the letter.

"It came! Berklee!" he yelled.

Angus ripped open the letter and devoured the news.

January 14, 1992   cc. Mr. Milt Davis

Dear Mr. McCrory:

In follow up to our letter of January 4, I'm writing to inform you that you have a choice of audition dates and location for final admission to Berklee.
~~~~~

Please choose between February 23, in Boston, or February 27 in Cleveland at the Tri-C Community College, Metro Campus, 2900 Community College Ave.

Please advise.

Cordially,

The Berklee Jury

"I'm going to see Milt!" Angus shouted.

~~~~~

A week later, the Prom Committee assembled in the cafeteria, Angus called the meeting to order and passed out a recap of the balloting for the twelve gods and goddesses. When everyone finished *oohing* and *aahing*, Rose took charge.

"Since Ace Cooper – our best track team's javelin thrower has been named Zeus – we'll have him start the prom by throwing a thunderbolt into the middle of the gym floor," Rose said. "After the thunderbolt, all the other gods and goddesses will follow Zeus and me into the Greek setting inside the gym," Rose continued. "We'll take up positions in front of the bandstand and welcome everyone with one brief memory of our senior year's experiences. I'll be the Master-of-Ceremonies."

Rose reached into a large plastic bag and produced a five-foot-long, handcrafted javelin-like object and held it up for all to see.

"This is the thunderbolt," Rose said.

Spanning the shaft, a gold painted bolt of lightning was surrounded by black and red, the FPHS colors. The tip of the thunderbolt resembled a badminton shuttlecock with a large Indian feather attached to the shaft just behind the tip. Staring in admiration of Rose's creation, the committee applauded. Nodding her appreciation, Rose tapped the end of the thunderbolt with authority.

"The tip of the thunderbolt holds a percussion cap which will explode on contact with the gym floor, signaling the beginning of the evening's fun," she said.
~~~~~

Angus took the floor.

"I've seen pictures of the *Parthenon,*" he said. "I think – with Mr. Noble and the shop guys – we can build a great one. I'll ask my dad to get us some of the large cardboard cores from the flooring company to use for columns… we can paint them white, and… "

"That's brilliant," Rose said. "And don't forget, lots of white draping."

Rose handed her homemade thunderbolt to Angus.

"See if you can tighten the tip," she said.

Angus inspected the tip of Rose's thunderbolt.

"Easy," he said.

Rose handed Angus a sheaf of papers.

"Here are some costume ideas for you to give to the gods and goddesses," she said.

As Rose stood with the others to leave the planning meeting, she tapped her finger on her thunderbolt and said to Angus, "Be sure to keep the tip dry, OK?"

~~~~~

In Milt's office, Angus studied Milt's wall calendar, Thursday, February 27, circled in red ink. He scanned Milt's practice schedule:

Jan. 18 - Week 1: Sight reading; scales and arpeggios.

Jan. 25 - Week 2: Improvisation on 'All The Things You Are.'

Feb. 1 - Week 3: Blues (five keys). Straight, No Chaser (Monk)

Feb. 8 - Week 4: Vamps - R&B, Rock, Funk & Fusion; ear training.

Feb. 15 - Week 5: Review and practice all the above.

Feb. 22 – Final Run through;

Thursday, Feb. 27: Audition at 11:00 a.m., Cleveland!
~~~~~

Angus' smile masked his anxiety.

"I don't think there's a lot to be gained by forcing the issue with your hand." Milt paused. "We can still cancel your audition."

"I'm not going to let this crap beat me," Angus said. "Let's go!"

Milt handed Angus an unfamiliar lead sheet for "Dearly Beloved."

"Alright," Milt said. "It's an upbeat tempo. Play it with your right hand only."

Angus blew through the tune it in thirty seconds. Before Milt could comment, Angus started over playing it again with both hands. When Angus finished, Milt cleared his throat, snatched the chart off the piano and slapped a different lead sheet, *Cottontail,* on the music desk. With his right hand playing the melody line, Angus comped with Red Garland-style chords and ripped through the tune.

Milt raised his eyebrows and stepped back.

"Ange... you're in the water, man. Let's hope to hell you can swim!"

BOOK II

1. I FEEL FINE

Entering the main auditorium at Tri-C Community College, Milt and Angus approached the reception desk to register. The handsome wood paneled room was constructed for perfect acoustics. Clanking noise from a workman moving a ladder to adjust an overhead stage light echoed through the hall. A heavy beige backdrop showcased a nine-foot ebony Steinway Concert Grand. On the stage floor next to the piano, a drum set gleamed in the lights. Next to the drum kit, an electric bass was hooked up to a large amp stack. A surge of anxiety seized him.

The receptionist was dressed in a wool suit with a gold treble-clef pin attached to her lapel, her cropped hair just over gold earrings complemented her matching gold necklace. Just below the clef pin, she wore a name badge reading "Jane Newton." She smiled as Angus introduced himself.

"I'm Angus McCrory… here for my audition."

"I'm Miss Newton. Welcome to our audition, Mr. McCrory," she said and handed Angus his audition credentials.

"You won't be permitted to sit in the auditorium while the others are auditioning," Miss Newton said, then leaned toward Angus and whispered, "But you may be able to overhear a bit from the back stage waiting room."

Miss Newton beckoned to a young woman standing behind her holding a clipboard. Looking as if she were waiting for a bus, the young woman – in her mid 20s, Angus guessed – wore a lavender satin vest over a dark blue turtleneck, camel hair brown slacks and ankle high short-heeled tan leather boots.

"This is Miss Crawford," Miss Newton said. "She'll escort you backstage to the waiting room."

Hefting his packet of audition credentials, Angus said, "How will I know when it's my turn?"

"Miss Crawford will get you," Miss Newton said.

~~~~~

At 10:55, Miss Crawford entered the room and tapped on her clipboard.

"You're up Mr. McCrory. I'll escort you to the stage."

Angus' muscles tensed tighter with every step he took following Miss Crawford.

At the stage wings, she pulled back the entrance curtain and said, "Good luck!"

He eased onto the stage and peered into the auditorium's dimly lit void. Squinting through the stage lights, he saw four people – three men and a woman – sitting at a long table on the floor of the auditorium in front of the first row of seats. Angus wasn't sure which of the three men were speaking, but he had a clipped British accent.

"Welcome to Berklee auditions, Mr. McCrory," the British voice said. "Please be seated at the piano, you have ten minutes to warm up."
~~~~~

Angus massaged his left hand, uttered a silent prayer, extended his fingers and furrowed his brow. Rambling through random scales and arpeggios, he began to perspire. Sweat dripped from his chin onto the keyboard. The ten minutes allotted for warming up passed in a blur.

"If you're ready, Mr. McCrory, let's begin with a simple blues form," the British voice said.

Angus launched into the first blues tune Moss had taught him: "C-Jam Blues." Nervous, he struggled at first with improvising over a harmonic vamp, but nailed the last pass. Without waiting for more instruction, Angus transitioned into Thelonious Monk's, "Straight, No Chaser." Six bars before the end, Angus felt a sharp pain in his left hand. Finishing quickly, he sat back, massaged his hand until the British voice echoed another instruction.

"We'll pause for a moment while Miss Crawford gives you a sight reading selection. You may look at it briefly and play through it when you're ready," the voice said. "Our bassist and drummer will accompany you."

Angus studied the single sheet of music entitled: "No Time Blues." Noting it was in the key of F, Angus visualized the chords in his head while the bassist and drummer took their positions. Confident from his gigs with Moss at the 151 Club, Angus nodded his readiness to play. The drummer clicked his drumsticks in metronome rhythm and counted off a groovy tempo. Angus muffed the timing of the eighth-note pickup on his entrance to the first bar, but quickly settled in. Improvising on the second pass, Angus felt a knife-like twinge in his left hand. Favoring his right hand, he comped sparsely with his left hand using simpler three-note chords. Pain shot up his left arm as the group finished playing and the drummer and bassist exited the stage. Angus sat back, pulled out a handkerchief, mopped his brow.

"Thank you, Mr. McCrory," the British voice said. "Please continue with any two of a fusion, rock or funk vamps of your choice, then you may finish with your chosen standard... 'All The Things You Are.'"

Wondering if Milt could hear him offstage, Angus struggled with the exact feeling Milt had coached him on for the fusion and funk vamps and completed his audition with an up-tempo version of "All The Things You Are." Feeling his improvisational choruses had redeemed him from his screw up on the vamps, he drew in a deep, relaxing breath and squinted when the house lights illuminated the cavernous auditorium. As he looked toward the stage wings, Miss Crawford motioned for him to take a seat at the judges' table. Satisfied that he had done his best, Angus rose from the piano bench. Ignoring the embarrassing sound of his sweat-dampened pants peeling off the piano bench's shiny surface, he stepped off the stage and sat down at the judges' table. With the pain pulsing in his left hand, he waited while the three middle-aged men in business suits and the slender woman – short auburn hair and dressed in a dark brown pants suit – studied their sheaves of papers. The woman handed Angus a bottle of water, sat back and crossed her legs. His pulse racing, he twisted off the bottle cap and felt a prickly sting penetrate his left hand from his fingertips to his elbow.

"You're very talented," the woman judge said.

Sweat pouring off his head onto his shirt collar, Angus nodded.

The man sitting on the left end of the table with white bushy eyebrows and piercing black eyes, looked over the top of his half-lens reading glasses perched on the end of his nose and cleared his throat.

"Mr. McCrory," he paused... "How long have you been studying piano?"

Connecting the man's voice to the British accent, Angus brushed his chin with his hand, "Since... I was about eleven."

As the questioner made notes on his paper, the heavy-set balding man sitting next to the man with the British accent leaned toward Angus.

"Mr. McCrory... what are your goals?" he said.

Angus paused, took a sip of water.

"Professional jazz pianist," Angus said. "... composer, too."

The third man – a wiry looking black man with a graying beard – addressed Angus.

"Which jazz composers are you most interested in?" he said.

Angus could feel the perspiration dripping from his armpits down his side and into his underwear waistband.

"I like Ellington. Cole Porter… Jerome Kern… Johnny Mercer… Oscar Levant…"

"Oscar Levant? Can you name one of his compositions?"

Angus reached back to the one time he'd seen Oscar Levant perform on television.

"Blame It On My Youth?" Angus said.

"Is that a question," the wiry man said.

Angus scratched his head.

"Sorry… the song…"

Sitting erect and uncrossing her legs, the woman jurist said: "I'm impressed. Not many young pianists have studied quite the range of composers you've mentioned. What is your practice routine?"

"I try to get two hours after school and four hours on weekend days."

The woman smiled and cleared her throat.

"I meant… *what* do you practice?"

Angus could feel the tension in his neck start to ease.

"Scales, arpeggios, chord voicing… standard songs, blues… some pop tunes."

"What are the qualities of a successful musician?" The hefty man said.

Thinking back to the time Milt blew up about Angus' lax practice habits, Angus paused, put his hand to his cheek and made a circular motion with his index finger.

"I think… being dedicated. Sacrifice."

The balding man made a notation on the paper in front of him.

"What are your musical strengths?" The wiry man said.

"Feeling. I feel the music," Angus said.

The judges nodded to each other.

"What is your favorite part of being a musician?" Bushy eyebrows with English accent said.

"Improvising… playing solos."

"Who has inspired you to pursue a career in music?" the wiry black man said.

Angus throat went dry.

"My grandmother... and a trumpeter friend…" Angus paused. "… my teacher, Milt Davis…and my mother."

" *What* motivates you?" the hefty balding man said.

Angus smiled at his questioner and said, "I just… love the music. My friends and I played together almost every week… my lessons with Moss and Milt."

Angus sat back as all four judges made notes. The balding man nodded ambiguously.

"What has been the biggest challenge in your musical learning and growth? How have you overcome it?" the woman asked.

Angus looked into her penetrating eyes. "My mom… especially since I broke my hand… she's…"

"You broke your hand?" the wiry black man interrupted.

"A few weeks ago," Angus said. "It's fine now."

The British man in the half-glasses fingered through the papers in front of him, nodded to the other panel members, arched his bushy eyebrows, peered at Angus over his half-glasses.

"Thank you for auditioning," he said. "For the moment, let's just say that we're interested in the possibility of you enrolling at Berklee."

The four judges stood and smiled as the man in the half-glasses extended his hand.

"You'll be hearing from us," he said, with clipped British certainty.

Angus shook his hand and the other three judges' hands and wondered if they felt him trembling. Miss Crawford appeared beside Angus as the judges kibitzed among themselves.

"Thank you, Mr. McCrory, I'll take your credentials and escort you and your friend to the exit."

Driving home in the still blustery blizzard conditions, Angus felt uncertain if he had said the right things to the judges.

"I couldn't hear everything, but what I did hear sounded great," Milt said.

"I screwed up a little on the sight reading."

"Everyone screws up," Milt said. "I blew a whole fucking tune when I auditioned for music school. Got lost in the middle of 'Basin Street Blues' for Christ's sake!"

Though comforted by Milt's remark, Angus still stewed over his audition.

"Do you want some lunch?" Milt said.

"Do you mind if I just flake out?" Angus said, leaning his head back on the car seat.

~~~~~

Saturday afternoon Angus joined Rose at their favorite booth at Percy's, the aisles cluttered with shopping bags and packages. A *Dee's Department Store* bag hung on a booth hook next to Angus. He felt a
~~~~~

pang of nostalgia as an image of Aummie working at Dee's jewelry counter flashed through his mind.

Angus sat across from Rose and eyed the menu.

"I ordered a grilled cheese and Cokes of us," Rose said. "OK?"

Angus tabled the menu and gestured at the plastic bag hanging next to Rose.

"What's in there?"

"You'll see at the prom," Rose said. "So? How did your Berklee audition go?"

"Sweaty... lots of questions."

"What were some of the questions they asked?"

As Angus rubbed his hand, he glanced at Rose's hand to see she *wasn't* wearing the *Claddagh!*

"Composers I like… you're not wearing the *Claddagh*," Angus said.

Rose blushed and touched her empty finger.

"I forgot and left it on my dresser," Rose said.

Hurt, Angus put his sandwich down.

"How could you forget? Does your mother check on you every time…"

Rose's tone left no doubt that she didn't appreciate Angus' remark. She arched her eyebrows as she said, "Ange… I just *forgot* it! OK?"

"I… just wondering."

"When will you find out?" Rose said.

"Find out?" Angus said.

"About your audition… getting accepted by Berklee?" Rose said.

Angus sipped his Coke and a glanced again at Rose's hand.

"Couple of weeks… I hope…"

"Oh, you'll get in," she said.

"What about you?" he said, "... after graduation."

"My dad wants to send me to hospitality management school," she said.

"What do you learn about there?"

"Managing hotels… and restaurants… or resorts," Rose said.

"Where do you have to go for that kind of a degree?"

"Farleigh Dickenson," Rose said. "New Jersey."

Angus felt his gut tighten at his sudden recognition of their being separated. He stopped chewing, put his sandwich down and reached for her arm.

"Isn't New Jersey a long way from here?" As soon as he said it, the thought dawned on him that so was Boston. "I mean… how will we talk… and everything?" he stammered.

Rose looked past Angus then back at him.

"Honestly, I'm looking forward to going away," she said. "Besides… you'll be in music school in Boston."

Angus' mind raced back to his audition. He hadn't given much thought to Berklee being based in Boston, but the tone of Rose's voice struck Angus as though the two of them being apart after high school wasn't a big deal. *Was Rose losing interest in him? Was that why she wasn't wearing the Claddagh? Was it her mother?*

"What does your mother think?" he said.

"She just hopes I meet someone to marry," she said.

The twinge in Angus' heart triggered a spasm in his hand. Angered at the thought of Rose being married, even dating someone other than him, he wished that he hadn't asked Rose about what her mother thought.

"What… about us?" he asked, his voice thick.

Rose pulled her arm away as she said, "Ange… we'll always be best friends."

2. THE LETTER

Easter Saturday, Angus' mother handed him a business size envelope that had just arrived. Embossed in the upper left hand corner of the envelope, his eyes widened as they riveted on the logo:

BERKLEE

College of

Music

Angus drew in a long breath, ripped open the letter and read the neatly typed content.

March 18, 1992

Dear Mr. McCrory:

After reviewing your application and your recent audition, our Faculty and Jury Panel believe that, all things considered, you proved to our judges how serious you are about becoming a professional jazz musician. Accordingly, it is the judges' belief that you would be a welcome addition to the Berklee School of Music and an asset to your fellow musicians. Please note however, that given the fact that your left hand is healing and in order to achieve competence, we strongly recommend that you spend your time the next few months working on your left hand skills.

Under separate cover, you will receive the matriculation details for entrance to Berklee for the fall semester beginning October 1. Our admissions officer, Ms. Jane Newton, will be in touch regarding financial affairs.

Congratulations! We look forward to your future success at Berklee!

Cordially,

The Berklee Faculty & Jury

Angus hugged his mother.

"I made it!"

"You deserve it, Ange… you worked hard for it!"

~~~~~

Seated at the kitchen table for dinner, Angus' father read the Berklee letter, nodded approval and turned to Angus.

"I guess there's only one catch in the ointment," he said. "Money."

"I'll get a job… I can save a lot between now and September," Angus said.

Angus' mother placed a giant portion of beef and noodles in front of Angus.

"Your father and I said we'd help you if you got into Berklee," she said, and turned a gentle smile to Angus' father.

"We'll burn that road when we come to it," Angus' father said. "I got a big flooring job coming up the week after Memorial Day at the Roma. You and Robby can help me."

3. APHRODITE

On prom evening, Angus toweled off, studied his stubbly beard in the bathroom mirror and reached for his razor. To quell his anxiety, he hummed the most popular show tune from *South Pacific:* "Some Enchanted Evening." Borrowing his dad's badger-hair shaving brush and old coffee cup with shaving soap, he whipped it into a thick rich lather and slathered it over his sparse facial growth. Not adept at angling the razor around the corners of his nose, he nicked the flesh and watched the mirror reflect the bright red blood trickling down past the corner of his
~~~~~

mouth into the sink. He tore off a corner of toilet paper and patched it over the oozing cut.

While waiting for the nick to dry up, he reached into the bathroom medicine cabinet for the nail clippers and fingernail file. After ten minutes of clipping and filing, Angus was satisfied with his self-administered manicure. He splashed *Canoe Cologne* over his face after gently teasing the crimson paper off the razor nick and winced at the astringent sting. Stepping back from the sink, he spritzed his unruly dark locks with hair spray and pushed around at the uncooperative mangle with a stiff brush. Satisfied, he flipped his bath towel into the clothes hamper and skipped into his bedroom and turned up the volume on Gene Harris' CD, *Listen Here!*

Donning his off-white, double-breasted tuxedo, Angus stepped back and checked his image in his dresser mirror. Ready to roll, he slipped into his black patent leather dress shoes, sat on the edge of his bed and tried to think of what else he had to do before driving up to the lake to pick up Rose: *Rose's thunderbolt! ... and her corsage!*

Angus grabbed the Gene Harris CD for the car. In the kitchen, he extracted a rectangular yellow florist's box from the refrigerator. Seeing Rose's corsage safely inside, he grabbed the car keys and ambled out the back door. Suddenly, he remembered: *Rose's thunderbolt!* Bolting down the basement stairs, he spotted the thunderbolt leaning up against his piano, grabbed it, bounded up the stairs two at a time to his father's new Pontiac Bonneville parked in the driveway.

Very carefully, Angus placed Rose's thunderbolt on the back seat, closed the door jumped behind the wheel, shoved the Gene Harris CD into the slot and dialed up the volume on Harris' rendition of "Sweet and Lovely." Arriving at Rose's a few minutes early, Angus was met at the door by Mrs. Gracewood. She escorted him into their living room. "I think Rose is almost ready," she said, "I'll tell her you're here."

Quelling the fleeting thought of what Mrs. Gracewood had said about Rose finding someone to marry at hospitality school, Angus waited for what seemed like an eternity.

When Rose appeared, his jaw dropped. Casting herself as Aphrodite, Rose wore a costume that was nothing Angus could have imagined if he'd seen Aphrodite in person. A thick, gold-braided rope cinched her waist, holding up a white draped toga-style robe over one shoulder, her other shoulder bare. The toga's irregular lower-calf hemline brushed the tops of the gold strapping of her Roman style sandals. Three gold armbands accented the gold tiara restraining her free-flowing, long, crinkly raven hair. Her sweet scent teased him as she kissed him.

Angus picked up the boxed flower, removed the corsage and reached for Rose's shoulder. Putting his hand under the toga strap, Angus felt her warm skin beneath his trembling fingers. Rose blushed as Angus pinned the cluster of white, miniature *Cymbidium* orchids to the toga strap.

"You look cool in your tux," she said.

~~~~~

As the gods and goddesses assembled for the gym doors to swing open, Rose tugged on Angus' arm.

"Where's the thunderbolt?"

Angus blanched. He'd left it on the back seat of his car!

"I'll be right back," he said and rushed out of the gym.

As he burst through the exit to the parking lot, a gust of wind accompanying a cloudburst nearly knocked him off his feet. He looked up at the ominous black sky and pulled his tux coat over his head. Sprinting for his car, Angus felt his stomach knot. The car windows! He'd left them open!

As he scrambled to wrest open the back door to see Rose's thunderbolt sitting drenched on the back seat, he jumped into the car, pulled out his handkerchief and tried to sop up the water from the soaking wet missile. Pursing his lips, he blew on the tip to dry it off. Satisfied that the tip of the thunderbolt and the percussion cap appeared to be dry and intact, he backed out of the car into the rain, carefully lifted
~~~~~

the thunderbolt out of the backseat, covered it with his tux coat and dashed back into the gym. Rose met him at the door.

“You’re sopping wet,” she said.

Disheveled, Angus brandished the thunderbolt. “I got it.”

“Let’s go!” Rose said. “Give the thunderbolt to Ace.”

As the crowd surged through the gym doors, the twelve gods and goddesses gathered around Rose as she yelled at Ace: “Throw it!”

Ace reared back and gave a mighty heave. Transfixed, everyone watched the thunderbolt arc through the air and strike the gym floor with a resounding crack. The percussion cap sparked as if to explode, but instead, belched a billow of toxic black smoke. Riveted in place, all eyes of the prom-goers followed the curling cloud as it rose to the rafters and set off the fire alarm’s piercing klaxon. Rose’s fierce stare at Angus made him feel as though he were guilty of a mortal sin. Mr. Walters yelled to the shocked onlookers: “Evacuate the gym! Right now!” As everyone scrambled to vacate the gym, he yelled again, “Everyone go down to the cafeteria and wait until I get there.”

Angus grabbed Rose’s arm and pushed toward the cafeteria. Her face red with fury, Rose wrenched her arm away. “What happened to my thunderbolt?” she screamed.

Angus heart sank to the bottom of his stomach as he explained.

“I… I left the car windows open. It was raining. It got wet… and…”

Rose scowled at Angus.

“How could you be so careless? You’ve ruined the prom!”

Embarrassed and angered by Rose’s tirade in front of his friends, Angus bristled, took Rose’s arm and tugged at her to follow him into the cafeteria. Rose jerked away.

“You don’t have to *drag* me,” she said. “I can walk on my own.”

While they waited for Mr. Walters, everyone but Rose and Angus sat around laughing about the botched start to the prom. A half hour later, Mr. Walters entered the cafeteria.

"Everything's fine," he said. "The smoke's cleared and you all can go back to the gym and enjoy the prom."

Rose stalked onto the stage and took the microphone. Everyone gathered around as she addressed the crowd.

"Thanks for your patience," she said, shooting Angus a withering frown.

"Look behind you," Rose yelled to the crowd. "Zeus!"

To a building drum roll, everyone turned and applauded as Zeus mounted the Parthenon steps, sat on the throne and waved to signal the official start of the prom.

Rose slinked off the stage and pushed past Angus.

"At least Zeus didn't screw up," she muttered.

~~~~~

The music of Karl Beach's big band cloaked Angus like a dense fog. Sullen and distant, Rose sat sulking at the prom committee's special table, Angus across from her. What he had dreamed would be a perfect night with Rose had turned into a nightmare.

"I'll get you something to drink," Angus said.

"Go ahead and get something for yourself," Rose said.

The night's special entertainment temporarily relieved Angus' frustration as Mr. Hamilton took the stage to play a trumpet solo. Squinting through the dim light, he spotted Angus and took the microphone.

"Come on up, Angus," he said. "I need some professional accompaniment."

To a chorus of applause, Angus stood up and glanced at Rose.
~~~~~

“I hope you don’t mind,” he said to her quietly

Rose shrugged her shoulders. “Why would I mind?”

Trudging back to the table after accompanying Mr. Hamilton’s performance of “Our Love Is Here to Stay,” Angus saw Rose walking toward the restroom with Wiggs and Anna Belle. As Angus sat down, Fox shot him a knowing smirk and said, “If I were you, man, I wouldn’t plan on getting in Rose’s pants tonight.”

The last dance signaling time to leave for the after-prom party at the Inn at Mary’s Gate, Angus whispered to Rose, “Sorry about the thunderbolt.”

Rose pulled back. “I think all that smoke made me sick,” she said. “Will you take me home?”

Rain lashing the windshield, Angus and Rose rode silently, Rose plastered against the door. As they listened to the Gene Harris CD, Angus tried to forget about the prom fiasco and tapped his hand on the steering wheel trying his best to be nonchalant. Lowering the volume, he turned to Rose. “I’m really sorry… I screwed up.”

Staring at the rainy roadway in front of her, Rose said, “Stop apologizing… it’s over.”

At Gracewood Cottage, Rose opened the car door. Jumping out of his side of the car, Angus rushed to help Rose get out on her side. He shielded her from the rain with his rumpled tux coat as they scrambled to her front door. Waiting in awkward silence for Rose to make some sort of gesture… anything… he watched her quickly step into the foyer. After a terse, “Thanks,” Rose closed the door behind her.

Driving home, Angus couldn’t get Rose’s words out of his mind: *You’ve ruined the prom!* Her accusation of him being careless was undeniable; he felt guilty but resented Rose’s making a scene about it in front of their friends. More galling was that she had virtually ignored him the entire evening. He thought about all the times he and Rose had been together, talked at their school lockers; Percy’s; the *Claddagh;* the times they’d confided in each other, supported each other, complimented each other making him feel special. "Screw the thunderbolt," he muttered as he cranked up the volume on Gene Harris' version of "The Song Is Ended."

4. A FINE ROMANCE

Friday of Memorial Day weekend, classes over, graduation looming and still irked by Rose's indifference toward him, Angus sat in the kitchen as the warm sun streamed through the kitchen window and splashed across the table where he studied his *Czerny* exercise assignment for the day. His mother came in from working in the yard, slipped out of her gardening shoes and went to the sink to wash her hands.

"You love working in the yard, don't you?" Angus said.

"I'd go crazy if I didn't have that," she said.

As Angus returned to his exercise book, his mother sat down next to him.

"You seem down in the dumps," she said.

"Thinking about graduation and paying for Berklee," he said.

His mother filled a glass with tap water and turned to him.

"I was at the bank yesterday," she said. "I met someone who knows you."

"Me?" Angus said, looking up.

"Claire Sewell. She said to say hello."

"I barely know Claire," Angus said. "She graduated with Robby."

"She's very attractive," Angus' mother said. "You should call her."

"I still like Rose," Angus said. "We're just…"

"I'm not saying you should forget about Rose... I'm just saying Claire is a nice person."

Angus looked past his mother to a plump redbird perched on the feeder outside the kitchen window.

"I have the money you've saved in my account," his mother said. "I'll call her and tell her I want to transfer the money to your account."

"I don't have an account," Angus said.

Angus' mother put her hand on his arm.

"All you'll have to do is go in and see Claire and sign some papers."

~~~~~

Angus parked in the Logan County Citizens Bank visitors lot and sauntered into the bank lobby. Seated at the reception desk, he was surprised to see Anna Belle West. "You work here?" Angus said.

"Part time," Anna Belle said.

Angus glanced around the lobby and fixed his gaze on an enormous portrait of a portly man on the wall behind Anna Belle's desk.

"Who is *that*?" Angus said, pointing to the portrait.

"Mr. Carter Duffy," she said. "He owns the bank."

"Doesn't having him looking over your shoulder all day make you nervous?"

"Is he expecting you?" Anna Belle said.

"I doubt it," Angus said. "I'm here to open a savings account. Where would I find Claire Sewell?"

"Take a seat and I'll ring her," Anna Belle said.

As Angus sat surveying the bank's lavishly appointed interior, Claire emerged from a small office to the left of a row of teller cages. She wore a tastefully tailored dark blue business suit over a white pleated-front blouse and medium height black pumps.

"Welcome," Claire said. "We can go to my office."
~~~~~

Claire led the way, took a seat behind a round conference table next to her desk and gestured for Angus to sit next to her.

"Your mother called about transferring some money to your account."

"A little I've saved from my gigs," Angus said.

"Gigs?" Claire said.

"Playing the piano."

"It's a nice amount of money. Are you saving for something special?"

"I got accepted to music school... Berklee in Boston," Angus said.

Claire studied a single sheet of paper on the conference table.

"You have almost two thousand dollars."

Clair passed the document to Angus. At the bottom of the paper, the sum of $1,995.77 caught his attention.

"Really?"

"All you need to do is sign the New Savings Account form, and you can come visit your money anytime," Claire said. "Before I forget, Dad wants you to play on weekends at the Pub this summer and especially for you and Robby to come to Mom and Dad's big Fourth-of-July cookout."

"Love to," Angus said as he signed the form and slid the papers across the conference table to Claire.

5. VINCENZO

Angus' first day of working for his father was to lay the new floor at Roma Ristorante. Vincenzo Seccareccio – owner of the Roma – was a forty-something burly Italian restaurateur with thinning black hair. He greeted them with his arms spread wide and a baritone welcome: "*Buongiorno*!"

"Brought the big muscle with me," Angus' father said, gesturing to his sons.

"Tough getting help these days," Vincenzo said. "You boys looking for work?"

Angus' father pointed to Robby.

"This guy's in college," he said. "Angus there," he nodded to Angus… "… is a musician. Going to music school."

Angus crunched on a *pizzelle,* sat upright and addressed Vincenzo. "I'm working for Dad to help pay for school," he said.

"You ever work in a restaurant?" Vincenzo said.

Angus glanced from his father to Vincenzo.

"No… I…"

"Good! That means you don't have bad habits," Vincenzo said.

"Robby here," Angus' father said, "… worked at a fast food joint for a while."

Vincenzo wrinkled his nose. "I make everything to order so it's always fresh… no heat lamps and crap like that."

Vincenzo sipped his coffee and peered over the rim at Angus. "You ever been around a grill?"

"Just cook outs," Angus said.

"The boys' mother is a great cook," Angus' father said. "Wouldn't be surprised if some of her talents rubbed off on them."

Angus father stood, thanked Vincenzo for giving him the flooring job and gestured through the window toward his 1977 white Dodge Sportsman Van sitting in the parking lot. Emblazoned on the door side in red block letters was the company name and slogan:

McCrory floors – Underfoot since 1971!

"Time to get our brains circulating," Angus' father said. "Good flooring job starts with prepping the substrate."

Angus and Robby nodded ambiguously.

"I'll scrape and you two can haul out the old crap," Angus' father said. "Or the other way around… we can switch off."

~~~~~

The installation finished, Vincenzo inspected it. Nodding in appreciation of the McCrory Company's craftsmanship, he squeezed into a booth next to Angus and held his hand out to his father.

"*Buono*!" he said. "*Buon lavoro! Grazie mille*!"

Uncertain if he should bring up the subject pressing on his mind, Angus sat forward, tentative, and said, "Do you have a job opening… on the grill?"

"When is school over?" Vincenzo asked.

"We're out… graduation the weekend after next," Angus said.

Vincenzo squinted at Angus.

You come in on Friday and I'll train you. You work out… I'll pay you fifteen dollars an hour… breakfast through closing, *capice*?"

Vincenzo clapped Angus on the back. "You'll need to be here at six-thirty... I show you how to light the grill."

6. OVER EASY

Angus' first day at the Roma – a blur of machine-gun instructions from Vincenzo, memory-boggling lists of cupboard contents, cooler inventory, freezer products, dry goods, utensil usage, knife sharpening procedures, work surface sanitizing, sweeping and mopping – crammed his brain. He practiced prepping produce – Vincenzo swearing, "*Spazzatura!*" as he hurled heads of offending lettuce – frying bacon, cracking eggs without breaking the yolks, mixing, whisking, ladling pancake batter onto a cooler section of the grill and learning when to flip them by the bubbles on top, dredging bread in egg batter for French toast and worst of all, making an omelet with five ingredients.
~~~~~

At the end of the day, Vincenzo pulled Angus aside.

"You come-a in the next three days and practice," he said. "Friday... friends of mine are coming in for a free breakfast."

~~~~~

Friday morning, Vincenzo and seven of his friends filed into the Roma and sat at two different booths. The Roma's best waitress, Theda, winked at Angus and ambled over to Angus' test customers. Angus counted the cooked bacon, checked the prepared vegetables and sat the basket of eggs in easy reach on the prep table. Minutes later, Theda approached with her order pad poised: "Here are two batches of four orders," she said. "Good luck."

Feeling confident, Angus finished the first orders and sat the egg platters on the pick-up table. Theda took all four platters at once and hustled into the dining area to serve the first foursome. Just as Angus was finishing the second group of orders, Vincenzo stormed into the kitchen holding two of the egg platters… one in each hand… and slammed them on the worktable.

"*Amico…* this stuff looks-a like crap! The bacon burned, the eggs a stones... toast is limp!"

Angus stepped back and wiped his hands on a clean towel as Vincenzo sputtered.

"Do over and get it right! *Capice*?"

Struggling to recover from Vincenzo's rebuke, Angus cringed and turned away as his boss stomped out of the kitchen. Sweating over the hot grill, Angus mopped his brow and followed orders. Minutes after Theda served the newly prepared platters, she bounced into the kitchen and whispered to Angus.

"Vincenzo looked happy."

Glancing at the clock over the cash register… only an hour had passed since the test customers had arrived. Angus wiped off the prep
~~~~~

table and scraped the grill until Vincenzo sidled up to him and patted him on the back.

"*Buono, amico,*" he said.

Feeling the tension drain from his shoulders, he glanced over Vincenzo's shoulder to see Theda grinning.

~~~~~

At home, Angus labored playing the Czerny, Brahms and Hanon exercises Milt had given him until his left hand gave out from fatigue. Sitting back, his mind drifted to his Roma job. He added up the weekly hours he guessed he could log in with Vincenzo… fifty total. At the $15.00 an hour Vincenzo had promised, that was $750.00 per week. Angus pulled the little plastic calendar out of his wallet and counted the weeks until he would leave for Berklee in late September – fifteen – then did the calculation: $11,250! After taxes, he estimated he could save over $8,000… enough to get started at Berklee… with a little help from his Mom and Dad.

7. GRADUATION

Rivulets of water sloshed across the high school parking lot as the worst downpour of the summer let loose a half-hour before the graduation ceremony. Inside the auditorium, the air was humid enough to grow orchids.

Parents, siblings, friends, Robby and Angus' parents fanned themselves with everything from funeral home paddles to floppy graduation programs and flapping hands. As the jammed auditorium settled in to test their endurance for discomfort, FPHS Principal, Josh Freeman, School Superintendent, Hermione Detman, guest vocalist Gracious Maxy, from Bountiful AME Church and guest speaker, Edwina "Bunny" Carpenter, president of the School Board and Fountain Point mayor, sweltered under the stage lights.
~~~~~

As Mayor Bunny waxed on about citizenship and academic achievement by the graduating class, Angus glanced at Rose but she looked away.

Finally, as Mr. Hamilton raised his baton for the orchestra to play the traditional "Pomp and Circumstance," the graduates queued up for the diploma presentation. When it was Angus' turn to receive his diploma, sophomore pianist, Richie Turner, sat in. Stepping away from the piano and squeezing into line at the stairs leading up to the stage, Angus felt the invisible presence of his past four years at FPHS. Ratface, seven paces ahead of Angus in the alphabetical queue – pointed to Mayor Carpenter's gradually spreading perspiration rings spreading under her arms. Barely keeping a straight face, Angus shuffled in snail time toward Mr. Freeman and thought of the times he had been on stage, played in the school orchestra for theatrical presentations and recitals... of Aummie teaching him to play piano... of giving Rose the *Claddagh.*

Angus leaned out of line to watch Rose accept her diploma. While not audible to Angus, it was clear that Mr. Freeman had said something complimentary to Rose, because she curtsied and shook his hand in the most pretentious manner he could imagine. Angus' eyes followed Rose offstage and back to her seat to wait for her valedictory address.

Waiting to be awarded his diploma and feeling perspiration beading on his upper lip, Angus edged closer to Mr. Freeman. By the time it was Angus' turn to receive his diploma, his sentiments about graduation and moving on to music school were swallowed up by the realization that being with his friends the last time… together at that moment... he felt a wave of melancholy.

Hearing his name over the auditorium speaker as Mr. Freeman congratulated him, handed Angus his diploma and shook his hand, Angus was jolted by the applause from his family and relatives sitting in the front section of the auditorium. Angus nodded in appreciation and glanced at Rose to see her clapping and he wondered how he would make up with her in the coming weeks. When the diploma ceremony came to an end, Mr. Freeman welcomed Rose to the podium for her valedictory speech.

Stressing the idea that "*No matter what anyone thinks, be yourself,*" Rose exuded self-confidence. Angus stood and held his hand out to Rose as she returned to her seat near where he waited to perform with Ratface. Rose touched Angus' outstretched hand and took her seat.

Basking in the honor of being invited to perform Gershwin's "Rhapsody in Blue," Angus opened the thick score, spread it out on the piano's music desk, sat erect and signaled Ratface who stepped downstage, nodded to the audience applause and extended his right hand toward Angus.

Angus stood, bowed quickly, turned back to the piano and sounded an A for Ratface to tune his clarinet. Exchanging eye contact with Angus, Ratface began the composition's rapturous opening… a clarinet trill followed by a legato 17-note rising diatonic glissando. Feeling the pace, hearing the blue notes and jazz rhythms of the Gershwin work, Angus reveled in their duet. Brisk, prolonged applause rang through the auditorium. As Ratface stepped offstage, Angus regretted that it would be his last performance as high school student.

The ceremony concluded, Angus' family waved to him; Robby silently mouthed congratulations and meandered with the family toward the auditorium exit with the company of heat-weary guests. Angus gathered up his music folio, edged his way through the other orchestra members and shook Mr. Hamilton's hand.

"Thanks for all of your help," Angus said.

"Nice job," Mr. Hamilton said. "Don't forget to turn in your music."

Backstage, Ratface and Angus tossed their music into a cardboard box and hugged each other.

Suddenly appearing backstage, Rose interrupted their celebration. Speechless, Angus blanked at seeing her, but rallied quickly and said, "Great speech." As Rose extended her hand in return, he saw that she wasn't wearing the *Claddagh.*

"I'm glad you're still here," she said. "I wanted to say goodbye."

"Goodbye?" Angus said, puzzled.

"I'm leaving this week for the Farleigh-Dickinson School of Hospitality Management."

Angus' cheeks flushed.

"This week? I thought you weren't leaving until September. You won't be here for the summer... at all?"

"I get my choice of dorm rooms by going early," Rose said.

Angus arched his shoulders.

"When will you be home again?"

"Maybe... on breaks," Rose said. "Toodles 'til then."

"*Toodles?*" he muttered as Rose sauntered off. "Fucking *toodles?*"

8. BERNIE'S TUNE

A week after graduation, Angus' mother handed him a letter with no return address on it, but Angus' name and address were in Bernie's handwriting.

"I'm sorry, Ange. This letter came last week but with all the graduation commotion, I forgot it."

Angus tore open the letter and scanned the one-page content.

June 7, 1992
Hi Ange...
I hope graduation was a blast! Sorry I missed it. My baby is due in a few days. Hope your piano playing is still fun. Have a good summer and thanks again for your help.
As always... Bernie.
P.S. I'm at the Florence Crittenden Home in Columbus.
Say 'hi' to Rosemary. BW

Angus showed Bernie's note to his mother.

"You think I could drive over to Columbus to see her?"

"I don't see why not," his mother said. "I'll call and make arrangements."

After calling information, she dialed the number in Columbus as Angus listened in on the phone extension in the living room.

"Crittenden Home," a woman said.

"This is Mrs. McCrory. My son would like to come visit a Bernie Walker. He's her friend and..."

"I'm sorry. Miss Walker left the Crittenden Home yesterday. She left no forwarding address."

"She left? On her own?" Angus shouted.

"I'm sorry... all of our mothers are free to leave at any time."

"You're telling us that she just had a baby and walked out and you have no idea where she went?" Angus' mother said.

The woman's voice turned icy.

"We don't require any forwarding information. She was free to go on her own. I can only tell you that she said she was going to live with a friend."

Angus fury resounded over the line. "That's *crazy*!"

"I resent your tone," the woman said. "I can't tell you anything more."

The line disconnect still ringing in his ears, Angus stomped into the kitchen, slammed his fist on the table and winced at the pain from his still sensitive injury.

"Angus... I'm so sorry I didn't give you the letter sooner," his mother said. "I'm sure Bernie will be in touch. Have faith."

Angus scowled. "You're *sorry?* Have *faith?* I'll have faith when I find out where she went. I can't believe she wouldn't let me know where she was going."

Angus sat motionless, stared out the window, slammed his hand on the kitchen table and winced at the smarting pain.

9. FIREWORKS

The morning of Claire's Fourth-of-July cookout, Angus practiced *Hanon - The Virtuoso Pianist,* for an hour, committed the first two *Czerny* exercises to memory then turned to the *Brahms' 51 Exercises.* At 9:30, he bounced into his bedroom to see Robby balled up in fetal position, a pillow muffling his comatose snoring.

"Hit the deck," Angus yelled, as he threw open the window curtains.

Robby rolled to the edge of his bed and mumbled, "Jeez-us, little bro'. It's still the middle of the night."

"Mom's got our seats set up to watch the parade," Angus said.

Robby uncovered his head and squinted at Angus.

"What time's the parade?"

Angus glanced at Robby's sallow, puffy eyes. "Man, your eyes look like two piss holes in the snow."

Robby launched into a coughing fit and rolled over to his other side.

"Go back to sleep. I'll tell Claire you're hung over," Angus said.

"Pick me up after lunch," Robby mumbled and slumped down into the bed with the pillow over his head. "I'll be ready," he mumbled.

~~~~~

As Angus drove, Robby nursed his hangover in the front seat. Angus slowed down at the eastern edge of Russells Point.

"I want to stop by the Gracewoods and see how Rose is doing in school," Angus said.

Robby turned to Angus and peered between his fingers covering his bleary eyes.
~~~~~

"I thought Lady Rose dumped you," he said.

"She didn't dump me. She's just… away at school."

Parking in Rose's driveway, Angus thoughts drifted to prom night… how beautiful Rose was as *Aphrodite*. As Angus jumped out of the car, Robby moaned, "Don't slam the friggin' door!"

Angus slammed the car door as hard as he could. Robby reared up, glared through the back window and gave Angus the finger.

Angus knocked on Rose's front door. Mrs. Gracewood answered; she opened the door and gestured for him to step inside.

"We haven't seen *you* for a while," she said. "Rose will be happy to see you."

Stepping into the foyer, Angus' shock couldn't have been more jolting.

"Rose… is here?"

"She got home yesterday," Mrs. Gracewood said. "She's … out in the lanai… with a friend."

Though sensing he was intruding, Angus stepped further into the house.

"I just stopped by to say hello and see how Rose was doing… at school."

"I'll tell her you're here."

Seated, Angus took in the Gracewood's lush living room and eyed the Steinway Concert Grand glistening in the sun at the far end of the room. While Angus smiled to himself at the thought of Thurman's cookout, Rose entered from the lanai. She wore a blue terry cloth swimsuit cover-up and white sandals. Angus stood to greet her.

"I just… I didn't know you were home," he said.

"School is on break over the Fourth," she said.

"Your mother said you have a guest."

"Come out to the lanai, I'll introduce you," Rose said.

Rose turned toward the lanai, Angus following. As he entered, Angus paused at the sight of a well-built twenty-something man with black hair seated in a lounge chair near the shallow end of the pool and wearing a black Speedo swimsuit. As the man stood and turned to Angus, Rose gestured to him.

"Angus… I'd like you to meet my friend, Patrick O'Meara. Patrick is a year ahead of me at Farleigh Dickenson. He's my advisor."

Patrick stepped toward to Angus and extended his hand.

"Always glad to meet another *Mick,"* Patrick said.

Angus wanted to scream *FUCK YOU!* – but he quickly smirked at Rose's guest and said, "Me, too."

"Do you want something to drink," Rose said.

"Robby's in the car," Angus said. "We're going over to Claire Sewell's for a cookout."

Rose clutched at her cover up and leaned against the swimming pool handrail and said, "Tell Claire hello."

Angus looked from Rose to Patrick then stepped back and gave Patrick a wan smile. "Good luck at school," Angus lied and turned to leave.

Rose led Angus back to the living room. Halfway to the door, Rose stopped. "Can you wait here for a minute, Ange?"

Rose left Angus standing at the door. Returning quickly, she handed him a small package.

"I thought you might want this back," she said.

Angus teased the outer wrapper off and stared at the *Claddagh.*

"You're giving it back?" Angus said, gulping for air.

"Patrick... it wouldn't be fair of me to keep it."

"He's your... boyfriend? Already?" Angus sputtered.

"You make it sound so dramatic," Rose said. "Patrick and I are just friends."

Angus scowled as he tucked the *Claddagh* into his pocket, opened the front door and glared at Rose. "We're late for Claire's cookout," he said, and slammed the door behind him.

Charging toward the car, Angus turned and looked back at Rose's house and to the beach beyond. Squinting through the sun at the sandy expanse, he regretted the times he'd done everything possible to show Rose his feelings for her… even through the stupid thunderbolt fiasco. "Fucking *toodles* to you, too," Angus muttered as he slumped behind the wheel of the car. Robby – still nursing his hangover – groaned, "Where you been, little bro'? Did you give Rose a little Fourth of July bang for old times?"

Wheeling the car around, Angus said, "We're going home, swill face."

At home in the kitchen, Angus went to the refrigerator, poured a glass of milk and sat sulking at the kitchen table. Taking the *Claddagh* out of his pocket, he lumbered up to his bedroom and tucked it into his dresser drawer – out of sight – along with Rose's *Irish Blessing* plate.

10. DOG DAYS

Playing his last weekend gig at the Inn, Angus was surprised when Claire came into the Pub and sat at the piano bar.

"We missed you and Robby at our cookout," Claire said. "Did you hear the news about Rosemary Gracewood?"

Angus stopped playing, stared at Claire.

"Her mother and father were here at the Inn for a party last night and told my dad that Rose is getting married," Claire said. "Isn't that great?"

Angus fingered the piano keys and dropped his eyes as Claire continued.

"Some guy she met at school named Patrick O'Meara," Claire said.

Angus forced his face to stay pleasant.

"I have to run," Claire said. "Hope we can stay in touch."

~~~~~

As if serving a jail sentence, Angus counted off the days before his departure for Berklee. After scrubbing the grill one afternoon, he returned the prep items to the refrigerator and watched Vincenzo stuff cash into a canvas bank bag for the day's deposit. Zipping up the bag, Vincenzo called for Angus to come into his tiny office just off the kitchen. Finished sanitizing the prep table, Angus washed his hands and stepped into Vincenzo's office.

"What's up?" Angus said.

"Big church group coming for lunch tomorrow."

"Great," Angus said. "No problem."

Vincenzo tapped on his desk as he said, "*Un momento, amico,...* They want chicken cacciatore for sixteen. Need a triple batch."

"Triple?"

"You'll have to work tonight," Vincenzo said. "Here's the key to the door. I'll come back in around eight and help you finish."

Angus took the door key, folded his arms and smiled at his boss and said, "I'll be here at seven sharp to prep."

"Put the recipe together on the stove, come back in every hour starting at nine and add two ounces of my special Chianti Reserva," Vincenzo said as he reached under his desk and handed Angus a bottle of Villa Antinori, Chianti Classico, Reserva, 1989. As Vincenzo tapped on the label, Angus noticed an image of what looked like a black chicken.

"What's the chicken?" he said.

Vincenzo spoke reverently.
~~~~~

"It's no 'chicken,' *amico,*" Vincenzo corrected. "*Gallo nero…* the black rooster crows *authentico!*"

Angus nodded in respect as Vincenzo continued.

"Solomente…oncia due!" Vincenzo said and held up his middle and index fingers together for Angus to acknowledge. "Stir good and turn off the range at midnight to let it cure, *capice?*"

"*Capice!*" Angus said.

~~~~~

Angus arrived at the Roma with his CD player, unlocked the side door, assembled the cacciatore ingredients on the prep table and grabbed three plump chickens from the cooler. Slipping a Chick Corea CD into the player, Angus turned up the volume on, "Sophisticated Lady," his favorite cut. He selected one of Vincenzo's razor-sharp butcher knives from the wooden cutlery block and studied the owner's ornately hand-scripted recipe.

Mentally, he tripled the ingredients as he chopped the vegetables. Grabbing the first chicken, Angus slapped the glistening carcass onto the cutting board. Testing the knife blade with his thumb to be sure it was honed to do its job, Angus murmured to the chicken: *Your little butt is history.*

He inserted the knife blade into the big joint at the underside of the breast quickly separating the leg and wing from the carcass. Pushing it aside, he spun the chicken around and severed the other big joint. Finishing the second bird, Angus stepped back for a minute before attacking the third chicken and listened to the beginning of Chick Corea's rendition of "Autumn Leaves."

Glancing at the clock, he turned to the third plump victim waiting to join his friends in the cacciatore pot. When the blade balked at severing the fowl's joint, he bore down, forcing the blade as hard as he could. Angus wrenched back in shock as the blade slipped. Staring at his hand in disbelief to see raw bone peeking out from where the errant knife had nearly severed his right thumb from the palm of his hand, he reeled
~~~~~

in pain as the knife clattered to the floor. The rush of nausea at the sight of his dangling appendage and the bloody tissue surrounding the wound brought heaves of vomit to his throat. With blood streaming onto the floor, he rushed to the sink and grabbed a bundle of kitchen towels to staunch the flow. His vision blurred, vomit pouring from his mouth and nose, Angus slumped to the floor.

BOOK III

1. DARK CANTICLE

Darkness… a coffin! Piercing shards of light sneak into dark corners where nothing lives. A piano with no bass clef. Mingling voices… a bulldog. Voice-faces empty… gray shadows for eyes. Feet spattered with blood, he walked to a corner of the wall. Gone. An abyss. Gore. Fans whirling in waltz time. A barking black rooster pecks at the eyes of a trespasser. A graveyard. A burly man frying bacon in his hat. Staccato pinging... B-flat... echoes of his mind. Trampling feet. Voices chant… leave your love behind…the bulldog calls out…faintly…

Sugna? Sugna!

The door opened. A rush of air stirred the window curtain. Gray light peeked into his hospital room. Partially covered with a sheet, Angus roused, turned toward the door. Blinked. His right hand throbbing, the gauzy picture in Angus' mind sharpened. The image of Berklee's acceptance letter danced before him, as if mocking him, teasing him with the hellish truth. He moaned, turned toward the window shaking his head in agonizing regret for having been so stupidly clumsy. He moved his bandaged hand and felt a rush of piercing pain as the vague image of his father leaned toward him. “Ange... quit worryin’…you’ll come outta’ this lookin’ like a rose.”

Murky memories cloaked Angus’ morbid ennui.

“Rose? Where’s Rose?”

Seized with despair, he wrenched violently and vomited.

… and Morpheus said to Angus: ‘Take the A-Train, man.’

~~~~~

Angus felt a tug on his arm and squinted into the overhead light.

“Dr. Vincent is coming to see you with Dr. Devoe,” his mother said. “Can you sit up?”

“I don’t want to see any freaking doctor!”

His mother stepped to the window and threw open the curtains.

“It’s two-thirty. They’ll be here in fifteen minutes,” she said and turned back to Angus. “If you want the use of your hand again, you’ll have to cooperate.”

Angus reared up. “What’s the point? I’m fucked!”

“You can save that language for someone else,” she said. “Meanwhile, if you want to feel sorry for yourself, do it when I’m not around”

Nurse Sonja cranked up Angus’ bed and turned toward the door as two doctors entered the room. Dr. Vincent touched Angus’ injured hand. “Angus, this is Dr. Devoe. He operated on your hand last night.”

Dr. Devoe stood smiling under his green pillbox surgical cap; a matching surgical mask rested on his chest. Angus scanned the tall sturdy frame of the man peering at him through heavy tortoise shell glasses. His bulbous nose spread widely beneath his glasses overpowered his sparse mouth jutting out above a closely trimmed, V-shaped mottled goatee.
~~~~~

"Dr. Vincent told me that you've had some bad accidents with your hands," Dr. Devoe said. "Looks like this one is a doozy... let's have a look."

Unwrapping the last layer of surgical dressing, Dr. Devoe examined Angus' hand and turned to Dr. Vincent.

"First-class wound," Devoe said. "Good thing the knife was sharp. Fishtail wound about six centimeters through most of the flesh… trapped blood… severed vessels… nerve damage no doubt. Underlying bone probably scored by the knife."

Angus pulled his throbbing hand away and said, "Jee-Zus! I just cut myself a little."

Dr. Vincent glanced at Angus' mother, then back to Angus.

"You did more than just cut yourself, Angus," he said. "You have a serious wound that needs more surgery."

"I'll get the radiologist to look at the X-rays again this evening," Dr. Devoe said. "Meantime, I'll book a surgical suite for seven tomorrow morning."

Angus' mother wrung her hands and timidly interrupted.

"Do you think Angus will be… will he be able to…"

"I'm concerned about the nerve damage," Dr. Devoe said and winked at Angus. "Use the morphine pump and try to get some rest."

Nurse Sonja put a new surgical dressing on Angus' hand, cranked his bed down, refreshed the bedside water carafe and turned to Angus' mother.

"Angus can't have anything to eat. Only ice chips until after surgery."

Angus squinted at his mother and pushed the morphine pump five times.

"I'll be here before you go to surgery," his mother said as she stepped to the door. "Just trust in Jesus and Mother Mary... I'll light a candle for you at church."

Angus heard the door shut, laid back and closed his eyes to the pain radiating up his arm.

"Gonna' take more than a freaking candle to fix this shit," he muttered.

~~~~~

Splinters of sound... a voice speaking... words plying his ears ... who? Angus felt himself being elevated... his head aching... dizzy... squinting... irritated.

"Where... where am I...?" he murmured.

"Calm down, Ange, please," his mother said. "Dr. Devoe is coming in to see you in a few minutes."

Angus raised his left hand and pinched his brow.

"What... time is it?"

"Five o'clock," a man's voice said. Angus looked at the man standing next to his mother.

"Dad?"

Angus seized his bandaged right hand.

"What'd they do to my hand?" he gasped. "I can't feel anything!"

"You're all doped up," his father said. "Doc said you wouldn't know whether to wind your watch or bark at the moon."

"Dr. Devoe is at the nursing station checking your chart," nurse Sonja said. "He'll be in to see you in a minute."

"I don't want to see any more doctors."

As Angus slumped into the bed sheets, he heard someone enter the room.

"Well... how's the piano player?" a man's voice said.

Angus rolled back to see Dr. Devoe's hulking frame.
~~~~~

"Piano player, my ass," Angus muttered. "What happened to my hand?"

"You had a tough operation," Dr. Devoe said.

Angus glanced at his mother, then to his father and back to Dr. Devoe.

"I hate to use this old expression, but I have some good news and some bad news," Dr. Devoe said.

Angus sat up, shook the cobwebs from his head and glared at the doctor.

"You're lucky you still have your thumb," Dr. Devoe said.

"That's the freaking *good* news?" Angus rasped.

Dr. Devoe put his hand on the bulging surgical dressing on Angus' hand and said, "It won't be as functional as it was." Pausing to give Angus a moment to grasp the bad news, Dr. Devoe studied Angus' reaction. "You won't have as much feeling as before… and that'll be a problem sensing heat and cold. With all the nerve and tendon damage, your thumb's lateral movement is going to be restricted."

Angus dropped his eyes.

"I know you play the piano and your injury will affect that," Devoe said. "I'm not sure how much, but we'll know more in a few weeks."

Groaning in despair, Angus rolled toward the window, away from Dr. Devoe.

"I've written orders for you to use the morphine pump," Devoe said. "I'll be looking in on you for the next few days."

"When can I go home?" Angus said to the window.

"Friday... maybe," Dr. Devoe said. "We'll have to see how things go."

Angus punched the narcotic button five times... *blues… Moss… Willie 'The Lion' Smith … the Berklee letter buzzing... taunting…*

2. I GOT PLENTY O'NOTHIN'

Dozing on the couch Sunday afternoon, Angus answered the doorbell to see Moss and Milt; Milt had a brightly wrapped package under his arm.

Angus escorted them into the kitchen and sat down at the table with them. Before anyone said anything, Angus hoisted his injured hand onto the table and said, "Looks like all that stuff you taught me is in the dumper."

Angus' jazz mentors shuffled uneasily in their chairs, each waiting for the other to speak until Milt pushed the package he'd brought with him across the table to Angus.

"We brought you a welcome home gift," Milt said, folded his hands and waited for Angus to open the package.

"Is this a bunch of exercises for a sawed off right thumb?" Angus said.

Moss grinned. "The book's about butchering chickens. Cats want you to be their poster boy."

Angus grabbed the book with his left hand and feigned throwing it at Moss. Moss ducked reflexively as Angus dropped it on the kitchen table.

"Some days you screw the chicken... some days the chicken screws you," Angus quipped.

"Before you get too philosophical," Milt said, "You might want to open the package."

Angus hefted the package again and tore open the wrapper revealing a softbound book slightly larger than his hand and little more than a half-inch thick. On its cover was a striking picture of a dark-complected man with a cigarette dangling from his mustachioed lips, his head tilted down, eyes focused on his left hand holding a guitar. It wasn't completely clear from what Angus could see, but the man's left hand appeared to be quite deformed. Above his head in distinct red type, the word *DJANGO* spanned the margin of the cover and rested atop the word *Reinhardt.* Below that was a smaller name in white type: *Charles Delaunay.*

Angus brushed his hand over the cover … up and down three times. Pausing… groping… Angus raised his bandaged hand. "I'm… thanks," he managed to say and looked at Milt, then Moss, then back to Milt. "I never heard of... who's Django Reinhardt?"

Moss crossed his legs, bounced his foot up and down.

"You never heard of Django Reinhardt?"

Angus shook his head, wished Moss would stop trying to cheer him up but Moss kept bouncing his foot up and down.

"No... I" Angus said.

Moss leaned toward Angus and touched his wounded hand.

"Gypsy cat… hell of a jazz guitarist, man. "Django got burned bad in a fire. Lost the use of most of his left hand and two fingers. Composed more songs than you can count and formed a swinging quintet he named The Hot Club of France and hunkered down in Paris.

Angus pushed his chair back. "So?"

"So… shit happens," Moss said. "But the man had the balls to get past it."

Angus studied the picture of Reinhardt, winced at the image of his deformed left hand and looked up at Moss.

"What's that got to do with me?"

"Hey man," Moss said, "I ain't telling you no fairy tale. Cat didn't quit... worked out a system of reaching the frets on his guitar and played his ass off the rest of his life."

Angus nodded at Moss with a flat smile. "Maybe I should take up guitar."

Moss and Milt stood up to leave and reached for their coats.

"Whatever you do, man, keep playing," Milt said. "You've got more talent with a bad thumb than most players have in their whole body. Don't *ever* give up!"

His spirits lifted by Moss and Milt's visit, Angus led them to the front door.

"Thanks for the book," Angus said. "I'm going in for a check up next week."

~~~~~

A thick folder tucked under his arm, Dr. Devoe burst through the door into the examination room where Angus waited after being x-rayed.

"Angus... your X-rays look pretty good... but I'm going to test your nerve responses," he said and unfurled a device with wires and needle-like attachments.

"What's that thing?" Angus said pointing at the device.

"An EMG... *electromyogram...* tests the nerve and muscle responses," Dr. Devoe said. "Lay back and relax... test takes about an hour."

~~~~~

As Angus sat up, Dr. Devoe stashed the EMG apparatus in a cabinet behind him and turned back to Angus. "Your nerve response wasn't as bad as I thought... but it's not as good as it needs to be," he said.

Angus furrowed his brow and hopped off the examining table.

"So... what's the bad news? Angus said.

"Quit thinking about bad news, Angus. If you do what I tell you, we might not have to do another surgery and I'm confident you'll have good functionality with that hand."

"Functionality?"

Dr. Devoe folded his arms over his chest. "I'm telling you that you'll be able to play the piano again." Dr. Devoe paused, then added, "Maybe not perfectly, but pretty good. There's no guarantees... but with physical therapy, I think you'll have a very positive outcome."

"What if I can't... what if...?"

"You're very lucky Angus. Get your head in the right place and you might surprise yourself."

3. DO NOTHIN' TIL YOU HEAR FROM ME

By the time another three weeks of physical therapy droned by, Angus had virtually memorized the key points of Django's life and career.

Waking up to warm sunbeams splashing through his bedroom window, Angus slid out of bed, dressed in cargo shorts and a light sweatshirt. Champing at the bit to get back to playing, he tapped his encasted hand with alacrity. "Gonna lose your ass this afternoon," he muttered and ambled down the stairs to the kitchen to see his father slathering a piece of toast with *Nutella.* As Angus finished his cereal and started to reload with another helping, his mother ambled into the kitchen, handed him the morning Examiner and pointed to a notice in the Fountain Point Community Life column. As Angus scanned the column, his heart sank.

Mr. and Mrs. James A. Gracewood, Russells Point,
Ohio, announce the marriage of their daughter,
Rosemary Anne, to Mr. Patrick J. O'Meara...

Angus stopped reading, turned away from his mother and muttered: "At least someone got fucked besides me."

Rummaging through the refrigerator, his mother turned to Angus and said, "Did you say something?"

"I was just... congratulating the newlyweds."

~~~~~
~~~~~

Dr. Devoe flexed Angus' bare hand and gently rotated his thumb in a semicircle.

"How's it feel?" he asked Angus.

Expecting to feel more pain, Angus was relieved when he felt only slight discomfort.

"Pretty good," Angus said. "But my thumb feels numb and tingles like needles pricking it."

Dr. Devoe unraveled the EMG wires and swathed Angus' hand with antibacterial solution.

An hour later, Angus sat up, searched Dr. Devoe's face for some clue about the test results.

"Well?" he said, anxiously.

"The tingling in your thumb doesn't surprise me," Dr. Devoe said. "It's very common for your type of injury to cause *paresthesia*."

Angus' eyes narrowed as he said, "Paris-*what?*"

Dr. Devoe pushed his glasses up on his forehead and leaned against the examining table.

"It's a condition resulting in damaged nerves that makes your hand tingle like it's falling asleep."

"Ice your hand and take the naproxen I prescribed... but don't overdo the medicine."

"How long will it take to get over it? Angus asked, his tone anxious.

Dr. Devoe folded his arms and shifted his stance.

"Angus… here's the bottom line," he began. "There's no doubt that your thumb *will* have restricted motion… and the paresthesia will very likely become chronic." The doctor paused, watching Angus' grim reaction then said, "That means you'll have to live with it… maybe forever."

Angus drew in a deep breath and looked past the doctor.

"What about... playing the piano?" he said shifting his eyes back to the doctor.

"Here's my advice. Start practicing... easy at first. You'll find out very quickly how much stress your thumb can handle."

"How... will I know when...?" Angus said plaintively.

"Trust me, when you've reached your limit, your hand will spasm like it's in a vise. Stop playing and massage it. Eventually... you'll adjust."

"For crissakes..."

"You're young, Angus. Just take it slow and don't get into any fist fights."

4. MOOD INDIGO

Alone at home – Angus sidled down the basement stairs and sat at Aummie's piano. He rubbed his healing hand as he studied the keyboard. Fearful to even touch the keys, his eyes welled at the thought that he might never be able to play the way he once could. As if frozen in space, his right thumb hovered over Middle C, then pressed down. The mellow sound of Aummie's piano resounded in his ears, reminding him of what she had told him years ago: *You can do it... practice and you'll have something to enjoy your whole life.* But he *had* practiced; practiced for hours – days and weeks, months and years on end. But now, he realized the disheartening truth that he *couldn't* do it – not in the way he had dreamed.

In his room that night, Angus delved into the Reinhardt book again.

Sentence upon sentence, page after page, Angus relished the vivid, bittersweet story of the legendary Django Reinhardt, a quirky, unforgettable portrait of a bizarre figure who threw his fortunes to the wind and lived the spectrum of opulence to poverty. Quick tempered but forgiving and generous to a fault, he never learned to read or write and let friends forge his autograph, lived in a fairytale world fueled by his own imagination, ignored schedules and was known to gamble away a week's income in a night.

The more Angus read the more he empathized with the man who lived in a gypsy caravan. A resolute musician who triumphed over the agonizing pain inflicted by the disastrous fire he survived only to endure a grueling recovery from the horrendous burns to his right leg and left hand and taught himself to walk again with a cane. Angus smiled at how Django charmed his way out of jail by serenading the police officer with his guitar. And yet... despite the hellish torture he suffered, he willed himself to go on... doggedly holding on somehow to his passion for playing jazz guitar like nobody before or since... and never quit living his dream! Angus was struck by a sense of vicarious loss when he read that Django died of a stroke at the age of forty-three.

Angus closed the book and thought about the many times Milt and Moss had encouraged him... spurred him on. With jazz still his passion, he couldn't give up, wouldn't give up...ever. His fervor reignited, he closed his eyes and visualized Django Reinhart's life-altering injury and vowed again that he would do his best to live up to Aummie's challenge: *You can do it!*

~~~~~

Every night, Angus tested his thumb's endurance as he practiced with increasing intensity. By the weekend, he'd been able to play for nearly an hour before the spasms in his hand radiated up his arm in grim reminder of his limitations. Giving in, Angus lumbered up to the kitchen and downed a dose of the naproxen. As he massaged his hand, he glanced at a pile of mail sitting on the kitchen counter. Though rarely finding anything addressed to him, he leafed through mostly catalogs and other junk mail, stopped abruptly when he discovered a letter for him from *Berklee School of Music.* His hands shaking, he ripped open the envelope.
~~~~~

BERKLEE

College of

Music

September 20, 1992

Dear Mr. McCrory:

I'm writing in regard to your pending enrollment at Berklee for the fall term beginning October 1. At the present time, we have not received your final application, accommodation preferences or first term fees.

Since the deadline for matriculation is September 28, I would encourage you to contact me at your earliest convenience to confirm your enrollment. Due to the fact that our curriculum is very demanding, we will not be able to extend our enrollment deadline beyond September 28.

I look forward to hearing from you soon.

Cordially,

(Ms.) Jane Newton

Director of Admissions

His eyes misting, he reread the letter, tucked it into his jeans and lumbered up to his bedroom. Disheartened, he doused his reading light, closed his eyes.

Awakened in the middle of the night by an excruciating seizure in his right hand, Angus bolted upright. Tears welling in his eyes, he buried his head in his pillow and screamed in agony. He gripped his thumb hoping to sooth the fierce throbbing and began massaging it gently, but in the darkness of his bedroom, his thumb felt different, swollen, fevered and totally numb. He reached for his overhead reading light, switched it on. Squinting in disbelief, he saw that his entire right hand was nearly twice its normal size, the skin turgid and red, finger nails splotchy white. He glanced at the clock – 4:23 – wobbled to his feet and lurched down the stairs to the kitchen where he filled a mixing bowl with ice from the freezer and added water to the half-full point. Seated at the table, he plunged his hand into the freezing slurry and recoiled at the icy assault. Though still numb, he could feel the familiar needle-like prickles raging through his thumb until, suddenly, another spasm. Wrenching back, Angus felt a wave of nausea. Seconds later, he pulled his hand from the ice bath and vomited into the bowl. Angus slumped to the floor, his head pounding, heart racing and ears ringing.

His mother's voice: "Ange… Angus?"

Dazed and disoriented, Angus peered at his mother kneeling beside him.

"I heard all the crashing around down here… what happened?" she said.

Hunching up on his elbows, Angus blinked, turned away as the smell of vomit repelled him.

"I was icing my hand and I felt like I was…"

Before Angus could finish the thought, his mother's eyes caught sight of his hand. Her voice quaked as she said, "Ange. Your hand!"

Angus staggered to his feet. "I… guess I over did it practicing."

His mother put her hand on Angus' arm.

"I can't tell you how worried I am about you… but this is getting to the point where you have to start thinking more about your future."

"I have thought about it… I think about it every day…" Angus words trailed off.

"I can't stand the thought of finding you passed out on the floor again. It's beyond me why you won't just quit playing until your hand completely recovers."

Angus closed his eyes, rocked his head back.

"I'm afraid… if I stop I won't ever get back to where I used to be."

"You have to have a little faith in God… He knows you need help."

Angus reached into his jeans pocket and produced a folded over paper and handed it to his mother.

"If God knows what I need, maybe he'll tell me how to answer this letter."

While waiting for his mother to read the letter from Berklee, Angus' mind churned at the thought that his dream of becoming a professional jazz pianist had turned into a haunting nightmare.

Slowly, his mother handed the letter back to him.

"Angus," she began, "I'm sorry… but for now, you just have to try and understand that some things don't always work out the way…"

"Don't always work out? My whole goddamned life isn't working out!"

Angus' mother slapped her hands on her hips and scowled at him.

"That's the most ridiculous… *selfish* remark I could ever imagine."

Angus slammed his right fist on the table and winced with pain.

"It's the truth! Everything I've lived for is fucked."

For the first time in Angus' memory, his mother's temper erupted.

"I'll tell you something… my self-pitying little boy… it might come as news to you that not only has everyone sympathized with you, we've all supported you every step of the way. Stop moping around like you're the first person to ever have had a setback."

5. WHEN THE SUN COMES OUT

The morning of his first day back at the Roma, Angus ran on autopilot until he looked up to see Claire and her parents stroll in and take a booth. The crowd sparse, Angus ambled out of the kitchen to greet them.

"I saw Mr. Seccareccio at the Inn last week," Charlie Sewell said. "He told me you were coming back to work for him."

"I love cooking," Angus said.

"Maybe it's a calling," Marianne Sewell said. "We're always worried what we'd do if our chef ever left the Inn."

"Marianne's right," Charlie said. "Running a kitchen is hard work and long hours but my guess is, it's very rewarding. Have you ever thought about becoming a professional chef?"

Angus shook his head and pointed to his right hand. "Vincenzo's chicken cacciatore killed that idea." Immediately, Angus felt guilty about blaming his thumb injury– at least, indirectly – on Vincenzo; but that's the way it sounded and it took a few beats of silence before anyone spoke.

"Didn't Rosemary Gracewood go to culinary school?" Marianne said.

"Hospitality management," Charlie said.

"Maybe she would have a suggestion," Marianne said.

Angus' first thought was that maybe Rose could stuff her suggestions where they belonged... along with Patrick Whosit.

"I heard she's expecting a baby," Claire said.

Trying not to gag, Angus bit his lip.

"Claire," Marianne said. "You never tell me anything. When?"

"Sometime in the spring. April... I think."

"Almost every chef I've hired at the Inn got their training at the hands of a master chef. It's called *staging,*" Charlie said. "You ever heard of it?"

"Can't say as I have," Angus said.

"The best way to explain it is that you find a chef who would be willing to teach you all the basic kitchen skills," Sewell said. "They don't pay you, but you get all the training you need to be a good chef without spending a lot of money on culinary school."

~~~~~

Sitting in the living room with his parents and Robby watching *Murder She Wrote,* Angus mulled over the lunchtime conversation with Charlie Sewell. As *Angela Lansbury's* came on the screen, Angus' father stretched back in his La-Z-Boy recliner and balanced a cup of coffee on his stomach.

"I like that Fletcher woman," he said. "She's got spunk. I just can't figure out why anybody would want to live in a place like Cabot Cove."

"Why not?" Angus' mother said. "It looks very pretty."

"Looks to me like someone gets murdered there every week," Angus' father said.

Angus' mother got up from the sofa, Angus following into the kitchen.

"At lunch today… Mr. Sewell told me about a way I could learn to be a chef without going to an expensive culinary school," Angus said.

"He knows a lot about food," she said. "The Inn's coffee shop is the best restaurant for miles."

"He said maybe I should try… working for a master chef to learn how to do things."

"The good Lord will lead you," his mother said. "I'll light a candle."

Angus broke into a smile at her persistent habit of lighting a candle on the altar at St. Pat's every Sunday after mass.

"You always say that," he said. "Do you really think that helps?"

"It's gotten me through a lot of problems… like your father's drinking. God answered my prayers. Your dad's been sober for five years now."

Angus leaned over and kissed his mother.
~~~~~

"I'll work something out with my piano… but for now, I'll going to talk with Vincenzo about becoming a chef."

As Angus and his mother finished talking, Robby and his father ambled into the kitchen.

"That Fletcher woman is a pretty damn good detective," his father said and turned to Robby. "You get that job at the Cincy PD, you might want to push for being a detective. You could learn a lot watching *Murder She Wrote.*

Angus grinned at Robby as they burst into laughter.

MERIBAH

In his bedroom, Angus opened the Reinhardt book. Reading the passages he had underlined, he thought about what Moss had said about Django: *Cat didn't quit... worked out a system... played his ass off for the rest of his life."*

Sitting in silence, Angus knew he had learned a hard lesson about perseverance in face of trial. And faith. Faith in his family, faith in his friends and faith in himself to stay true to the thing he loved most… jazz piano. It would always be part of who he was and would be forever.

BOOK IV

1. AS TIME GOES BY

Angus' mother finished placing the vibrant autumn colors of her Halloween and Thanksgiving table decorations. Startled to see Angus meander into the room, she looked up.

"You're home early," she said. "Things slow at the Roma?"

Angus kicked off his boots and gave her a kiss.

"Vincenzo is a saint," he said. "He's fixing me up to meet his cousin in Columbus... Dominic Militello. He has an Italian food specialty business."

His mother turned back to the table decorations and moved one of the skaters.

"I thought you wanted... to go to work for a chef?" she said.

Angus sensed there was more to her question and stepped to her side.

"Vincenzo said his cousin knows every chef in Columbus," he said. "He'll help me make some contacts."

"Will you have to move... to Columbus?" she asked.

Angus put his arm around her shoulders and hugged her.

"If I get the job," he said.

"But..." her tone querulous, "... where will you live?"

"Vincenzo said that Dominic will work it out."

His mother turned away as she said, "You had a phone call... Mr. Sewell."

Curious as to why Charles Sewell had called, Angus showered and thought about how Mr. Sewell had pointed him toward learning chef skills without the expense of culinary school. Excited to tell him about Vincenzo's arrangements for him to meet with Vincenzo's cousin Dominic, Angus dialed the Inn.

"Thanks for returning my call," Charlie Sewell said. "I'm hoping you can help me out over the holidays in the Pub."

"I took your advice," Angus said. "I'm moving to Columbus... Vincenzo at the Roma is helping me relocate so I can look for a job working for a chef."

"When are you leaving?"

"Right after the New Year," Angus said.

"Can you play piano for me over the holidays? We're booked up and our Pub needs your smooth touch."

2. NAGHTEN STREET

Amid snow squalls and blustering winds, Angus arrived in Columbus at the Militello Macaroni Company housed in a three-story building that had seen better days. Angus stepped through the doorway into a noisy sales room bustling with customers. Three phones jangled incessantly. A cigarette sat burning on the edge of the counter near the phones. A tall man with a broad flat nose and receding salt-and-pepper hair, wearing dark slacks, dressy loafers and a beige cardigan sweater over a tan dress shirt open at the collar, shouted orders over his shoulder to someone unseen.

"Pinky! Two cases of Genoa for Rocco's!"

Angus eased into the work area and stood to the side. The aroma of Italian spices, cheeses and meat products piqued his senses. Several men – dressed neatly – sat on spaghetti cases drinking coffee. After two women settled their bill at the counter, the cardigan-sweater man took a quick drag on the burning cigarette and stubbed it out with his foot on the rotting and creaky wooden floor. One of the three men standing closest to him called out, "Domenico… cut me a wedge of provolone… the good stuff," he said. Mesmerized, Angus edged away to make room for the chaos and watched the man called Domenico grab a two-foot-long, two-handled knife blade and hack through a loaf-shaped three-foot-long round of creamy white cheese protected by a wax shell dotted with red-ink markings. Finished hacking off a slab of the provolone, Domenico turned to Angus.

"You waitin' for an order?" he said.

Angus short-stepped toward him.

"I'm Angus," he said. "Vincenzo… sent me."

Dominic squinted at Angus. "Vincenzo who?"

Before Angus could answer, Dominic yelled toward the back of the warehouse.

"Pinky, goddammit! Where's the Genoa?"

The man Angus assumed to be Pinky emerged from a back room toting two cases. Angus was surprised to see that Pinky – not tall and muscular as Angus expected of a stock person– was short and rotund with pink eyes, pinkish skin and reddish-blond kinky hair. His mouth was collapsed from lack of teeth but his thin pink lips bore a wry smile as if to say: "I got one speed and it ain't hurry up!" He wore thick amber eyeglasses, a weight lifter's belt around his bulky gut and a ratty white cotton headband with the word *"Stugotz"* penned on it in bold black marker.

"Two Genoa!" Pinky yelled and slammed the cases on the counter top.

Dominic snatched a deli apron from a wall hook and tossed it to Angus.

"Put this on and help Pinky," he said. "We'll talk later."

~~~~~

At noon, Dominic lit a Pall Mall and leaned against the service counter.

"Vinnie says you want to be a chef," he said. "You got the coglioni for it?"

"Vincenzo… taught me a lot," said Angus.

"He told me you played the piano before you screwed up your hand."

Angus folded his arms and tried to relax.

"You work here for a couple of months and we'll see," Dominic said. "You got a place to stay?"

"Vincenzo said you might be able to set something up."

"Vinnie says a lot of things. Where's your stuff?"

"In my car," Angus said.

Dominic lit another Pall Mall and pointed to a closed door on the west wall.

"You need to see Etta. She's my office manager."

Dominic led Angus though the west door into a cramped room stacked with file folders and relics of old office equipment. Seated at a metal desk littered with paperwork, a slight built woman, about Angus' age, hovered over a computer screen. When she looked up, Angus was surprised to see that she wore her hair a lot like Rosemary's… bangs teasing her black eyebrows, long black curls trailing over her shoulders and wide-set black eyes. She smiled and said, "Can I help you, Uncle Dom?"

Dominic raised his eyebrows and tilted his head toward Angus.
~~~~~

"This is Angus…" he turned to Angus, "… what's your last name?"

"McCrory," Angus said.

"Be nice to Etta, she does the payroll," Dominic said.

Etta picked up a sheaf of papers from her desk, turned to Angus and said, "My real name is Concetta… but everyone calls me Etta."

Dominic stubbed out his cigarette on the floor and turned to her.

"Angus is hourly… ten bucks," he said. "Is the upstairs room open?"

Etta leaned back and stretched.

"I haven't been up there in months," she said.

"Get your stuff, " Dominic said to Angus.

~~~~~

Following behind Dominic, Angus hauled his suitcase and a box of personal belongings up the narrow stairway and into the room on the third floor. Dominic flipped on the overhead light and motioned for Angus to put his things down.

"This was my father's sleeping room when he first started the business," he said. "That's him in the picture over the table. His name was Gaspar."

Angus squinted at the picture of Gaspar to see the portrait of a benign-looking, elderly gentleman.

"My brother Louie used this room for his private little love nest… until he had a heart attack while he was humping some floozie," Dominic said.

"I'll try not to let that happen to me," Angus quipped.

"I don't care what you do with your private time, but don't fool around with Etta. She's spoken for, *capice*?"

Angus smiled. "Capice."
~~~~~

Out of the corner of his eye, a partially draped object caught Angus' attention.

"You being a piano man, you can use this anytime," Dominic said as he pulled off the drape to reveal a piano. "Might need to be tuned," he said. "Louie used to think he could woo the ladies by acting like he was a musician. He couldn't play "Mary Had a Little Lamb" but he'd sit there and plunk on the keys hoping some broad would start breathing heavy."

Angus stepped over to the piano. "I'll work on it," he said

"Friday's and Saturday's are big days, so tomorrow morning, you be down in the retail room by six," Dominic said. "Pinky needs help."

Dominic paused at the head of the stairs and turned back to Angus.

"Pinky's an albino… has a hard time reading. You can be his eyes while you're learning the stock."

~~~~~

Saturday afternoon, Dominic clapped Angus on the back and lit a Pall Mall.

"We don't usually run this late on Saturdays," he said. "You getting your bearings?"

"Pinky got me checked out," Angus said.

"Monday, I'll show you how we run the regular weekly orders. Our supplier trucks come in here at six. We get our own delivery truck loaded up and on the way by nine. If we're short on anything, you hand deliver the late items in the afternoon."

Dominic handed Angus a piece of paper with a phone number on it.

"You need me… call. See you at seven Monday morning. Ciao!
~~~~~

3. STUFFED A FEATHER IN HIS HAT

Sharp winds rattled the windows in Angus' sleeping room as he showered, jumped into his work jeans and sneakers and headed down to the Militello retail room. As Angus entered, Dominic handed him a clipboard full of papers.

"Pinky's under the weather so I want you to personally deliver the order to the Columbus Country Club. Chef Byrnes is my best customer. Etta will tell you how to get there. Make the delivery by no later than ten-thirty, capice?"

~~~~~

When Angus rambled into her office at nine-thirty, Etta looked up from leafing through a stack of files.

"Uncle Dom will be here by the time you get back from the CCC."

"CCC?" Angus asked.

"Columbus Country Club," Etta said and handed Angus a sheet of paper with the driving directions.

"Chef Byrnes wants his order no later than ten-thirty," Etta said. "When you get back, stop and see me… I'll have your paycheck."

~~~~~

Angus turned the delivery truck into the winding driveway entrance to the Columbus Country Club. Backing the truck into the loading dock, he jumped out, scrambled up the stairway to the kitchen entrance where a lanky black man greeted him.

"I'm Glenn," he said, "Can I help you?"

Angus handed him the delivery receipt, "Militello delivery."

Glenn pointed to the kitchen area. "You'll find Chef Byrnes in there," he said.

The aromas of food preparation greeted Angus as he meandered into the kitchen buzzing with workers. Before he could ask for Chef

Byrnes, a man in a chef's toque peered at him from the doorway of a cubbyhole space adjacent to the kitchen.

"Whadya' got, lad?" he said.

Angus stepped toward the man and proffered the delivery receipt.

"Militello delivery," Angus said.

The man squinted at Angus and waved him into his office.

"I'm Chef Byrnes," he said as he sat down at a cluttered desk. "You new?"

Angus eased inside the office.

"Few weeks… working for Dominic…"

"Good man… knows his stuff," Chef Byrnes said. "Where're ya' from?"

Angus relaxed, took a short step toward an empty chair.

"Fountain Point," he said. "I worked as a chef… well… cook… for the Roma over there."

"Have a seat," the chef said.

Angus slid onto the chair and waited.

"How'd you get hooked up with the Militello boys?" the chef said as he dropped the delivery receipt into a desk drawer.

"Dominic's cousin, Vincenzo… he owns the Roma… he set it up."

The chef sat back and clasped his hands behind his head.

"You moved here to be a delivery boy?"

"No," Angus paused, "I… was a musician, Dominic's helping me find a job."

"What's he know about the music business?"

Angus scooched back in his chair and furrowed his brow.

"No… I'm hoping to become a chef," Angus said.

"Good luck with that," the chef said. "Cordell will help you unload the truck. See you around." As the chef picked up the phone to make a call, he motioned for Angus to leave.

~~~~~

Just past noon, Angus parked the delivery truck and hustled into the retail room.

Dominic stubbed out his cigarette on the floor.

"Go get your check… but remember what I said about not fooling around with Etta… she's a hot little fox but she's getting married in a couple of months, capice?"

Slowly easing into Etta's office, Angus tried not to look interested but couldn't resist checking out her appearance as she stood to greet him. She had removed her green jacket. Unable to avert his eyes, Angus' gaze drifted to Etta's flowered blouse gaping at her bust line. Etta blinked her long black eyelashes at him and handed him an envelope.

"I heard you're a musician," she said.

"Was," Angus said.

Etta stepped toward Angus and put her hands on her hips. A teasing pout formed on her lips as she said, "I'd love to hear you play sometime."

"Maybe… sometime."

Etta stepped back to her desk and spoke over her shoulder.

"Don't disappoint me," she said. "I don't bite."

~~~~~

The following week, Angus swept up as Dominic hung up the phone and turned to him.

"That was Chef Byrnes at the CCC," he said. "The chef said you two had a little chat last Monday."

Angus stopped wiping the counter.

"We did…"

"Chef said you handled yourself well."

Dominic lit the last cigarette from the Pall Mall pack, squashed the empty package and tossed it into the trash barrel.

"Chef said he could use some extra help over Valentine's weekend at the Club. No pay… you interested?"

Angus felt his adrenalin surge.

"You call him tomorrow morning at ten," Dominic said and handed Angus a folded up note. "Here's his direct line."

~~~~~

Reveling in Chef Byrnes' invitation to work at the CCC over Valentine's Day, Angus sat at the piano in his sleeping room after work and played until he looked up to see Etta in the doorway. Her gait slow, slinky, she eased toward him.

"You promised to play something for me," she said. "I'm off work for the night."

Angus' hands moistened at the sight of Etta's loose fitting coral silk blouse opened to the second button; her skin-tight green skirt clung to the tops of her knees. Her hair swirled over her shoulders, cascading down her back.

"I better go sweep up," Angus said.

"Don't you have time to play one song?" she said.

Reluctantly, Angus turned back to the piano.

"Here's the first song I learned," he said and played a lazy version of "Now Is The Hour." Finishing quickly, Angus stood and turned around. Before he could move away, Etta stepped in front of him and opened the third button on her blouse.

"We have time… everyone's gone for the day," she said as she pushed close to Angus.
~~~~~

Angus moved to the side. "I thought you were getting married."

"Not until May," she said. "I'm still a free woman."

Angus pushed back. "I'm…"

Etta puckered her face into a sour frown.

"You're not one of those… *fanuks*, are you?" she said.

"A what?" Angus said.

"Gay… homo…"

Angus rolled his eyes.

"Hardly," he said.

A broad grin spread over Etta's face as she finished unbuttoning her blouse, slipped out of it and tossed it on the floor.

"I told you I don't bite," she whispered, reached behind her back and released her lacy black bra.

"You're staring… are you waiting for an invitation?" she murmured.

As Angus caressed her, the thought of Dominic's warning flitted through his mind, but quickly dissolved into oblivion.

Angus pulled Etta close, opened his mouth and touched her parted lips with his tongue. He felt her tongue respond as she smothered his mouth with hers. She stepped back and unzipped her skirt, letting it fall to the floor. Unbuckling Angus' jeans, she pushed them off his legs and gently tugged him toward the bed. Legs entwining, they clung to each other.

~~~~~

Awakened by a distant siren, Angus sat up on the edge of his bed and squinted at the clock on his nightstand: 2:43. He didn't know how long Etta had been gone; it couldn't have been long… her sweet feminine scent lingered in the dim light. Scrubbing his face with his palms, he pulled the blanket around him, stepped to the window overlooking the sidewalk below. The snow had drifted around the base of
~~~~~

the street lamp blocking the entryway to the retail room. Peering through the ambient light emanating from the street lamp, he thought about Etta. His virginity joyfully subsumed in their passion, how soon would they be together again? Tomorrow? He glanced at the clock again; it was already tomorrow! Dominic! What if Dominic found out about them? Shivering at the thought, he scrambled back into bed, covered his head with the pillow. He would compose a song to Etta, romantic lyrics and a hint of humor. In the still of the night, his mind spinning, he dozed off.

~~~~~

Bolting upright in bed, Angus glanced at the clock: 7:49. Lost in his night of bliss, he had forgotten to set his alarm. Dominic, he thought. DOMINIC! Saturday! The busiest day of the week in the retail room! Angus leapt from his bed into the bathroom and flipped on the shower to a torrent of body-numbing streams of icy water. He shuddered. Toweling off, Angus checked his image in the vanity mirror, grinned at the giant hickey on his neck and scrambled to dress.

~~~~~

Dominic's cold scowl bespoke his ire.

"You're late! I got enough problems without babysitting for you!" he barked as he pointed to a stack of pick up orders for the morning. "Pinky's car won't start so I'm going to get him while you get busy on those orders."

Hoping to mollify his boss, Angus said, "I'll shovel the walk..."

"I shoveled it an hour ago," Dominic said. "Start ganging the orders for me to check when I get back... customers start coming in at nine so get your ass in gear!"

~~~~~

Noon. Angus and Pinky stood exhausted as Dominic locked the front door and handed Angus a slip of paper.
~~~~~

"Etta called for you," he said. "She's working on the payroll at home and needs your hours. That's her number... you can call her from the office."

Knowing that he had left his work hours on Etta's desk earlier Friday, Angus sat at her desk in the office and anxiously dialed her number. His heart raced as he waited for her to answer. When she did, Angus' hands moistened.

"This is Etta..."

"Sorry I missed your call," he whispered. "Can we get together tonight?"

As he waited for her to reply, Angus heard a man's muffled voice in the background: "Get off the phone and let's go," he said.

"I can't," Etta said softly, apologetically.

"Can we just..." Angus started to say, but Etta interrupted and spoke as if she were on a business call.

"Yes... thanks for letting me know," she said. "I'll get the information to you next week."

Angus hung up the phone. Was that Etta's fiancé? Was that the end of Angus' romance with Etta? That quick?

~~~~~

All the following week, Angus made excuses to go into the office at the warehouse and talk with Etta, but curiously, Etta was never there. Finally, on Thursday, Angus caught up with Etta in the doorway as she left her office for the day.

"Can't we get together... for drinks... or something?" he asked peevishly.

Etta furrowed her brow.

"I can't... my fiancé is waiting for me," she said nodding toward the front door. She patted him on the arm. "I'm sorry."
~~~~~

As Etta squeezed past Angus and took three steps toward the door leading to the street, Angus bounced to her side. "You're fiancé is waiting? That's it? What about me… us?"

Etta pulled back.

"This is not a good time for me," she said. "I have to go."

Angus shook his head. How could he and Etta have made passionate love only days ago and now, she treated him like he was an outdated warehouse item?

4. STAGING

Anxious to meet Chef Byrnes, Angus sat in the club foyer until a thirty-something statuesque woman appeared and extended her hand.

"Mr. McCrory? I'm Alyssa Porter, our dining room manager. Chef Byrnes asked me to have you wait a few minutes for him in the Shock Room."

Grinning as he mused over the room name as though it might be a special torture cell for interrogating prospective employees, Angus rose quickly from his chair, extended his hand in greeting and said, "Shock room?"

"It's a small dining room named after our golf pro, Don Shock. The chef said you were going to help out in the kitchen for our Valentine's Day parties," Alyssa said and led Angus around the corner into the cozy, nicely appointed Shock Room.

"Take a seat," she said, "Chef will be here in a few minutes. Would you care for coffee or a soft drink?"

"I'm fine," Angus said and sat down in a royal blue, plush upholstered chair.

Within minutes, Chef Byrnes appeared with two cups of a steaming beverage and sat them on the table.

"Tomato bisque," Chef Byrnes said. "You'll be making a lot of it this weekend."

Angus sampled the creamy concoction, nodded and said, "Tastes great."

"Less filling, too," the chef quipped.

Chef Robert Byrnes, a tall, slightly graying, trim and well sculpted man – Angus guessed to be in his mid-fifties – turned suddenly serious and handed Angus a pad of paper, a sharpened pencil.

"I need to know exactly what experience you've had in a commercial kitchen," he said. "Write down everything you think I should know."

As Angus took the pencil and pad, the chef stood and – as if struck by an afterthought – amplified on his request.

"If I know what you're capable of, I won't let you get in over your head with our kitchen staff. They can be brutal if they think you're a dullard."

Finished detailing his work experience, Angus leafed over to the third page of his hand written resume, re-read it and added a footnote:

> *As a jazz musician, I appreciate the art of improvisation. Like musical notes, ingredients in food can be assembled to make a harmonically pleasing and satisfying composition. – Angus McCrory*

He waited until the chef bustled into the room with a bulky bundle under his arm and handed it to Angus.

"Here's a kitchen smock and a pair of work pants," Chef said. "If these don't fit, talk to Ruby Tanner… Rube's my sous chef… she runs the kitchen, makes out the work schedules and assigns the prep chores. You best make friends with her… she can make it easy on you or she can bust your balls. Any questions?"

Angus unbundled the kitchen garb and held up the pair of black-and-white checked work pants to gauge the fit. The pants looked as if two people could fit into them; the smock was closer to his size.

"Get dressed in the locker room and come see me. I'll introduce you around."

~~~~~

Decked out in his kitchen garb, Angus strolled into the kitchen to see a woman talking with Chef Byrnes. Chef beckoned him to join them.

"Angus, meet my sous chef, Ruby Tanner," Chef said.

Willowy, erect in bearing and tall, Ruby wore a red gabardine rodeo shirt with pearl snaps and white piping… around her neck, a metal tipped bolo tie, its fastener a hand carved turquoise and coral bucking bronco. Skinny denim jeans pushed down her long legs into white leggings resting on top of her black Converse All Star sneakers. Her fiery red hair, straight cut just above the eyebrows framed her heart-shaped face and accented her nose and chin – both pointy and sincere. Ruby wore a smoky peach shade of lipstick and matching but sparse eye shadow. Sous Chef Ruby Tanner, took one look at Angus and burst out laughing.

"Get you a grind-organ and a monkey with a tin cup, you could be our weekend entertainment," said Ruby. "Get some new duds... we got enough problems without your pants falling down."

~~~~~

Chef nodded to the assembled kitchen staff, gestured to Angus and said, "This is Angus McCrory. Joey's assistant, Jewell… is off to a family wedding this weekend so…" Chef looked at Angus, "…Angus is filling in for her."

Angus exchanged nods with the other kitchen staff as Chef gestured to a man and woman standing in front of a bank of Viking gas ranges.

"Franky and Selma are our main line cooks. We get extra busy, Ruby helps out." Chef nodded to a short, stocky, heavily muscled black man standing at the back of the group. "That's Cordell," Chef said. "He helped you unload the truck. He's our dishwasher, floor-mopper, part-time philosopher and music critic." As Cordell took a bow, Chef pointed to a heavyset man standing next to him. "Larry's our pastry chef... he'll let you sample his pecan rolls if you're nice to him." Chef shuffled a few steps toward the prep area and nodded to a slump-shouldered, slouchy man, his head wrapped with a blue paisley bandana. "This is Joey Black, our go-to prep man." Chef paused. "Prep gets screwed up, the whole operation gets out of sync."

Chef placed his hands palm down on Joey's workstation and arched his eyebrows toward Angus.

"Joey will tell you what to do… any disputes, Rube kicks somebody's ass."

Angus smiled at the kitchen staff's sigh of agreement, but out of the corner of his eye, he saw Joey sneering at him.

Chef handed Angus a copy of the weekend menu. "Look this over and get familiar with it. A good chef knows the ingredients for every menu offering by heart. Any questions… see Rube."

As Chef swooshed his hand overhead and stepped into his office, the group disbanded. Joey motioned for Angus to move to his prep table.

"OK, pal… I'm showin' you how to dice an onion," Joey muttered.

"I know how to chop an onion," Angus said.

Joey assumed the military stance of a drill sergeant, rolled his eyes and handed Angus a fresh Spanish onion.

"OK, prep man… let's see what ya' got," Joey mumbled.

As Angus took the onion, he thought he detected a hint of alcohol on Joey's breath. While Joey slouched against the prep table and yawned, Angus chopped six onions and filled the prep wells for the cooking stations. Joey nodded ambiguously and pointed to a pile of carrots, mushrooms, celery and peppers stacked up on the worktable.

"You ought to be able to chop the rest of that crap on your own," Joey said and pointed to a pan of boiling water on the range top. "Blanch the tomatoes in that hot water for about ten seconds and slip the skins off before you slice them."

"I can handle it," Angus said.

"Keep potatoes peeled and under cold water. Don't slice an apple until you hear an order requiring it. If the apple's brown, the salad bitch will raise hell." Joey smirked at Angus. "I got my own work settin' up the Stag Grill…so don't bug me unless you go brain dead."

~~~~~

After the lunch period – torn between appeasing Joey, pleasing Ruby and impressing Chef Byrnes – Angus wiped his brow, checked his Timex: 2:12 – sat down for the first time since he'd arrived that morning and sipped a cup of fresh-brewed coffee. Savoring the third sip, a voice behind him startled him.

"You takin' a fucking vacation, or what?" Joey rasped.

Angus stood and sat his coffee cup on the counter.

"Just… a quick break," he said. "I'm…"

"Go home and take a freaking nap," Joey said. "You ain't cut out for this kind of work."

Flushed and angry, Angus jabbed his finger in Joey's face and said, "Lay off… you didn't hire me."

Joey retreated two steps and scowled at Angus.

"Maybe not… but I can fire your sorry ass. Ask the sous-bitch."

Searching the kitchen to see Ruby seated in the chef's office on the phone pounding the desk, Angus stepped to the doorway and peered in as Ruby slammed the receiver down. When she looked up and saw Angus, her anger abated under a wan smile.

"You need something?" she asked, sharply.

"Joey told me to go home… I guess he's pissed I'm here."

Before Angus could jump aside, Ruby bolted past him out of the chef's office and grabbed Joey by the arm. Angus didn't have to strain to overhear her fury.
~~~~~

"You're not running this goddamned kitchen," she yelled. "Don't let the door hit you in the ass on the way out!"

Angus watched Joey stalk to the back door. Before exiting, Joey turned and gave Angus the finger. "Kiss my ass!" he shouted.

Ruby stormed back to the chef's office and turned to Angus.

"Forget about Joey's crap and be here at six in the morning."

~~~~~

At 5:45 Sunday morning, Angus motored into the staff locker room, donned his kitchen garb and marched into the kitchen to be greeted by the mouth-watering scent of roasting meat. The lemony scent of the chef's court bouillon for poaching fish – with notes of onion, thyme and bay leaf – teased Angus' senses. As he approached the prep station, Ruby burst out of her office.

"Chop-chop, McCrory," she said. "We got four hours to have that dining room buffet humming. Button your coat and see me in Chef's office."

Angus nodded to Larry and drafted behind Ruby into the chef's office.

"Joey showed up drunk a few minutes ago and hassled Chef in the parking lot," Ruby said. "Chef told him to get lost."

Angus pressed his fingers against his temples and sat back.

"Should I say something to Chef?"

"Don't say a damn thing… just bust your butt and keep quiet." She handed Angus a list of prep items for the brunch. "Yell if you need help."

~~~~~

After the brunch guests had departed, Chef invited Angus into his office.

"Take a seat," Chef said.

Angus eased into the chair opposite the chef and waited. After a slow minute, Chef raised his eyes, studied Angus' as if Angus were on trial. "I read that note you wrote on your resume," Chef said, paused, drummed his fingers on the desk and continued. "You made a good point. Great dining is on a par with great music. Great meals have a rhythm and a harmony all their own... flavors, aromas, textures and visual surprises."

Uncertain if the chef wanted him to respond, Angus said nothing.

"You did a good job today," chef said, "I'm impressed."

Angus' hands moistened as Chef continued.

"You want to be my *stagiaire*?"

Angus froze.

"Joey's in rehab. Jewell is back in tomorrow. You can start working for her... unless you like driving a truck for Dominic."

Angus jumped to his feet, banged his knee on the chef's desk.

"When?" he blustered.

"Wednesday morning. You got a place to live?"

Angus plopped down on the chair, rubbed his chin.

"A little room at Dominic's... just temporary."

The chef put his arms on the desk and leaned toward Angus.

"See Alyssa when you come in. We have an old vacant apartment upstairs our club manager, Bowman, used to let members live in if they got kicked out of their house for an unscheduled vacation."

The chef stood, shook hands with Angus, "One more thing... I don't believe in slave labor. You paid your dues working gratis over the weekend." Chef paused, stepped back and said, "Pays ten bucks an hour."

Angus raised his eyebrows and nodded in appreciation as Chef motioned for Angus to leave. As Angus was halfway out the door, he turned back when Chef said, "Plan on seventy hours a week."

~~~~~

Exhausted, Angus trudged up the stairs to his sleeping room at the Militello warehouse and stopped halfway. The tune, "The Shadow of Your Smile" from Gene Bertoncini's album, *Body & Soul*, drifted down the stairwell from his room. He didn't remember leaving his CD player on. Stepping into the dimly lit room, he was surprised to see Etta sitting in his bed wearing a bright red satin teddy. Completely baffled by her tantalizing appearance, he felt confused. Etta had blown him off just days ago. As he approached, Etta reached for a bottle of Prosecco on the nightstand and said, "Happy Valentine's Day… I hope you're not too tired to celebrate."

~~~~~

Bursting into the retail room at the warehouse Monday morning, Angus greeted Dominic with a hug and said, "Chef Byrnes hired me... I start tomorrow..."

"Good for you," Dominic said in an angry tone. "It's a good thing you're leaving because I had two very pissed off visitors last night."

Angus arched his eyebrows, but as he started to speak, Dominic put his hand up.

"I warned you about Etta being engaged," he said. "I should have told you it was my godfather's son, Nello. Nello and his father showed up at my house demanding that I fire you."

"For what?" Angus blurted.

"Etta broke her engagement with Nello. She told him all about you!"

"She blamed me?" Angus yelled, bristling. "I didn't start it… Etta..."

"Don't blame it on her," Dominic growled. "You dishonored me!"

Angus felt the blood drain from his face. "I didn't… it was…"

Dominic stubbed out his cigarette and stepped in front of Angus' face.

"Pack your things and have a good time at the country club."

~~~~~

Packed and ready to leave, Angus snuck into the warehouse office to talk with Etta. She was seated at her desk, her wardrobe – black and somber – reminded Angus of a wake. Her eyes were red and teary; she wore no makeup.

"I'm sorry about what happened," he said. "Your uncle is pretty pissed at me."

Etta looked past Angus and frowned.

"He'll calm down when he finds out that his *goombah's* son has been cheating on me with some *putana* he's been keeping on the side."

"A what?" Angus asked.

"A whore!" Etta yelled.

"How did you find out about that?" Angus said.

"Right after you started working here, I took his coat to the dry cleaner and found a note with a phone number on it when I went through the pockets. I called the number and some woman said 'Hi Nello baby… see you tonight?'"

For an instant, Angus wondered if Etta's reason for making love with him was revenge.

"What about... what about us?"

Etta's tone turned somber.

"We can't get together until some bullshit gets worked out between the families."

"What has to get worked out?" Angus said. "Can't you just call it off?"

"Our engagement was a formal Catholic ceremony… in the church. A priest consecrated it. It's the same as making a vow."

"Sounds archaic to me," Angus said.
~~~~~

"I can't push it," Etta said. "I have to honor my parents wishes."

"How long?" Angus asked.

"We're supposed to see a priest over at St. John's. I'll call you as soon as we get this crap over with."

5. DÉJÀ VU AGAIN

Angus bounded down the staircase from the once-secret apartment on the club's second floor to the foyer, doffed his Amish straw hat and saluted the portrait hanging on the west wall in tribute to Columbus Country Club Founder, Orlando A. Miller.

As he rambled down the hallway past the Shock Room and into the kitchen, Alyssa intercepted him.

"Ange, you have a phone call."

"Can you…"

"You better take it… pretty sexy voice on the line."

Angus hustled into the kitchen, stepped into Chef Byrnes' office and punched the blinking phone button.

"This is Angus…"

"Ange! I finally caught up with you."

Glancing toward the ceiling in wonderment, Angus arched his eyebrows and clutched the phone.

"Bernie?"

"You're a hard person to track down," Bernie said.

"Where the hell have you been?"

"Right here… in Columbus."

"Why didn't you get in touch?"

"A lot's happened... I heard about your thumb accident…."

Angus glanced at his old wound and thought of the times he had taught Bernie to sing in his basement.

"How'd you find me?"

"Your mom. Can we meet sometime soon?"

"You name it..."

"I dance at The Golden Gentleman... on the East side of Columbus. I'm the part-time manager, too."

"You're a dancer? In a strip club for crissakes?" Angus said.

"Can you meet me Saturday night... around eleven?" Bernie said.

~~~~~

As Angus entered The Golden Gentleman, a scantily clad hostess met him and escorted him to a small stage-side table.

"I'm looking for Bernie Walker," Angus said.

"I'm Misty. Bernie told me all about you," she said. "I'll tell her you're here."

The scent of cheap perfume, stale cigarette smoke and sweat reeked in the dim light. Two bare-breasted brass pole artists shucked and jived to the stage lights' throbbing in rhythm to Pat Benatar's, "Hit Me With Your Best Shot." A crowd of young men celebrating a bachelor party tucked dollar bills into the dancers' garters. Through the haze, Angus could see Misty disappear backstage. A minute later, she emerged with a woman... unmistakably, Bernie. Misty pointed to Angus and as he stood to greet Bernie wending her way toward him, her skimpy costume revealed her still voluptuous figure.

"Ange... I've been dying to see you."

"You had your baby... everything's cool?"

Bernie scooched her chair next to Angus and said, "Except for this dump!"

"Is there anywhere we can talk?" Angus asked.
~~~~~

Bernie nodded toward the back of the room.

"The owner lets me use his office. I'm his bookkeeper," she said.

The owner's backstage office was dim and dank and reeked of mildew and stale air. As they sat on folding chairs next to a clunky metal desk, Angus said, "What are you doing in this place?"

Bernie grimaced.

"Ange... I'm in trouble... again," she said.

Massaging his forehead, Angus said, "You're... pregnant?"

"No way, thank God!" she said and shuddered.

"Then what's the deal?"

"I owe the guy who owns this place a lot of money," she said.

"How much, Bern?"

"After I had my baby, I worked as a waitress in a bar where I met what I thought was a very nice guy. His name is Mort Toney. He offered me a job here and I took it."

Bernie paused, looked past Angus and continued.

"Mort loaned me money to take accounting classes at Columbus State," she said. She glanced over her shoulder toward the office door, then back to Angus. "I got certified as a bookkeeper and payroll manager. After that, I went to work for Ames Payroll Service here in Columbus," Bernie said. "Misty helped me get the job, she was dating the owner."

Angus put his elbows on his knees, clasped his hands and leaned forward.

"How much do you owe?"

"After six months, I got promoted to account supervisor." Bernie cleared her throat and took a sip of her drink. "A woman who worked for me got caught embezzling money from one of our clients." She paused. "My boss had her arrested. At her hearing, she accused me of helping her cover it up. I hadn't done a damn thing and even when she couldn't prove I did, my boss fired me anyway."

"How did she do the embezzling?" Angus asked.

"She never took people off the payroll who had left the client's employment. She put their payroll checks into a phony bank account and stole nearly twenty-thousand dollars."

Bernie stood and shuffled toward the door. She peered through the slatted window blind then turned back to Angus.

"I've paid off my Columbus State fees, but still owe that Toney jerk for the rest of it… about three thousand dollars. That's the problem, Ange… "

Angus stood, stretched out the kinks and leaned back against the metal desk.

"Three thousand... for crissakes? " he said.

Bernie slumped down in her chair.

"Mort started hitting on me right after I came back. He told me to put out or get out. He's taking money out of my dancing check… and I have to give him the tips I get from the slime balls out there by the stage. I don't have any way of fighting him."

They sat in silence as Angus mentally traced through the déjà vu saga of what seemed to be Bernie's ongoing disasters.

"Let me see what I can do. Where are you living?"

"I rent a condo in German Village. I'm barely holding things together but if you can help me get out of here, I know I can find a job as an accountant."

She wrote her phone number and address on a notepaper and handed it to Angus.

"I have to get ready to dance," Bernie said. "Call me… soon?"

~~~~~
~~~~~

Monday, after Bernie dumped the bad news on him at The Golden Gentleman, Claire answered Angus' call. "This is Claire... may I help you?"

"Hi Claire... this is Angus."

"Angus McCrory... the famous pianist turned chef?"

"Nice of you to remember. How's the food over at the Roma these days?"

"Vincenzo needs you back. Wait... I forgot; you're my dad's protégé now. How's your chef career going?"

"I'm working at the Columbus Country Club"

"A country club's pretty fancy, Angus. When are you coming back to the Inn? My dad would love to get you back here. What can I do for you?"

"You know the money I was saving for music school? Can you tell me how much I have in my savings account?"

"Sure. Let me check." Seconds later, Claire said, "As of this morning, you have a little over forty-three hundred dollars."

"Could you deposit three thousand into my checking account?"

"It'll be there by tomorrow morning. Have you talked to your brother lately?"

"Last week," Angus said. "He told me he was thinking about moving back to Fountain Point to be a detective for the Police Department."

There were a few beats of silence before Claire spoke again.

"You should call him."

His curiosity piqued by Claire's vague reference to Robby, Angus dialed the number Robby had given him in Cincinnati where he worked as an assistant detective .

"City Hall... may I help you?" a woman's voice said.

"Detective McCrory, please," Angus said.

"Is this an emergency?" she barked.

"Yes… I'm trying to help a lunatic in trouble," Angus quipped.

Her tone quickly changed from passive to hostile.

"I'm sorry… we're very busy… is this some sort of practical joke?"

"Yes… I'm his brother. Will you connect me… please?"

Angus waited long enough to wonder what would've happened if it really were an emergency.

"Ange! I tried to call a couple of times."

"Yes, Detective McCrory… a likely story. Where were you on the night of the alleged crime?"

"Lemme' see… I was in the arms of my betrothed. You can check with her. How are you?"

"Worrying about you. You had any petty murders to solve lately?"

"We're still working on who killed Cock Robin. Do you have any tips?"

"Not since I quit working circumcision parties," Angus said.

"That's the kind of stuff you should be saving for my wedding reception." He paused… "Will you be my best man?"

As if struck by lightning, Angus yelled, "You're… getting married? Who?"

"Who do you think, little bro'? … Claire!"

Angus sucked in a shocked breath.

"Claire… you're … getting married…?" Angus sputtered.

"FYI little bro'," Robby said. "I got a job with the Fountain Point PD. Claire and I are going to live there after we tie the knot."

"I… I'll be honored… to be your best man," Angus said.

~~~~~

When Angus called Bernie the next morning, her voice sounded nothing like her at all; it was hoarse and raspy as if raw and inflamed.

"Ange… I've been praying you'd call."

"You sound terrible," Angus said.

"It's worse than what I told you Saturday night."

"Bernie?"

"Last night… Mort… Mort tried to rape me!"

"Bernie… listen to me! You've got to get out of there!"

"He's threatening to hurt me if I don't pay him."

"I have the money. You can get the hell out of there today."

"Ange… don't kid around."

"I'll get it to you today… this afternoon… we can meet at Wendy's on the corner of Hamilton Road and East Main Street."

~~~~~

When Angus hustled into the restaurant expecting to see Bernie, he was surprised to see Misty sitting at a corner table.

"Where's Bern?" Angus said.

"She's a mess… she's hiding." Misty said.

"Where's she hiding?" Angus said.

"My apartment… 210 Thurman, just south of downtown," Misty said.

Angus plopped down and frowned.

"What the hell is she going to do after this fiasco?"

"I'll help her," Misty said. "My folks have a condo in Florida. I'm going to take her there for a few days to get back on her feet."

"I have the money for that Toney jerk," Angus said.

Misty shook her head and said, "She couldn't bear seeing him again. Can you deliver it for her?"

Angus nodded slowly as Misty said, "Toney's a bad actor, Ange… I'd take someone with you."

"I'm working tomorrow, but I'll stop by and see you after lunch," Angus said.

Misty put her hand on Angus' arm. "Bernie loves you… she's just horribly upset and confused right now."

~~~~~

Knute (Butch) Ohlsen was a hulking Scandinavian man who did the maintenance and heavy work at the Columbus Country Club. At 8:30 that night – to the blaring sound of Van Halen's "Hot For Teacher" – Angus and Butch Ohlsen stepped into The Golden Gentleman and powered their way through the tables backstage to Mort Toney's lair where Bernie and Angus had met. The door was locked. Angus knocked sharply.

"Delivery for Mr. Toney," Angus yelled.

"I'm busy!" a man's voice barked.

Angus turned to his friend. "Mr. Butcher… would you please open the door?"

One massive lunge from Butch's left shoulder pounded the door wide open… slamming it against the interior wall. Inside, Mort Toney was entertaining his favorite lap dancer.

"Who the fuck are you two?" he yelled, as the naked woman ducked behind him.

"We won't stay long," Angus said. "Just making a delivery."

"Get the fuck out of here. I didn't order nothin'," Mort yelled.

"Relax bud," Butch said, as he moved to the front of Mort's desk.

"I don't take orders from no scumbag like you," Mort said.
~~~~~

Before Angus could say anything, Butch pushed Mort's desk backward, pinning him to the wall behind it. The nude lady disappeared out the door as Mort gasped for air.

"What the fuck do you want?"

"Just sign this receipt I have here for this check," Angus said and waved the check in front of Mort's nose. "It says: All debts paid-in-full… Bernice Walker. You remember her, asshole?"

"You're telling me that little cunt's finally paying up?"

"If you want to keep your face nice, bud, watch your mouth and do what the man asked," Butch said.

"Sign right here," Angus said, as Butch pulled the desk back just enough to give Mort Toney room to write.

Angus tucked the receipt into his pocket, threw the check on Mort's desk and at 8:53, Butch and Angus sauntered past two nude dancers teasing five businessmen to Ted Nugent's "Cat Scratch Fever." The taller of the two dancers winked at Butch as he and Angus exited The Golden Gentleman. Jumping into his car, Angus turned to his helper and said, "Jeez, Butcher… I didn't realize what a gentleman you are."

~~~~~

Angus drove to Thurman Street on his afternoon break at the CCC. Bending his head against the driving snow, he waded through the icy drifts and checked the mailboxes. Bounding up the stairwell to apartment 3-C, he reached for the buzzer, but there was a note covering it, addressed to him.

Dear Ange… we're on our way to Florida.

We'll be in touch. Misty.

6. WEARING O'THE GREEN

Saturday morning a week later – as if Bernie had sensed Angus was thinking about her – Alyssa handed Angus an envelope addressed to him
~~~~~

at the Columbus Country Club. Angus tore open the envelope and scanned the hand scrawled note:

Dear Ange –

Nope… haven't died as you might have wondered. I don't have a phone so that's why I'm sending this to you at work. We're still in Florida but Misty and I are coming back to Columbus this weekend. Can we meet on St. Paddy's Day for dinner or lunch… or, maybe breakfast? (But I don't get up very early!) You're a doll Ange… plan on staying at my place overnight.

My address is 185 S. Third St., Columbus, Ohio 43206

I'll have a phone by then: 555-3434 XOXO - Bernie

~~~~~

On a dismal, ugly, blustery day, Angus arrived at Bernie's place. She was waiting for him with a green beer and a giant St. Paddy's Day card with their high school pictures pasted on the cover. Her condo was small but inviting. Inside the German village cottage, a cozy sitting room with a fireplace greeted Angus as he entered. The ornately carved wooden mantle held a grouping of pictures from their days at St. Pat's and FPHS. Angus studied a picture of Rosemary standing with him and Bernie with Buddy in the middle of the dance floor at the Parish Hall. To the right was a sparsely furnished kitchenette and eating area. Stepping to the open bedroom down a narrow hallway, Angus peered in to see Bernie's bedroom, several stuffed animals propped on the bed.

"Welcome to Bernie's Bed & Breakfast," she said. "I have a shamrock for that funky straw hat you're wearing… it'll look cool."

As she pinned the green cloverleaf onto his Amish straw hat, she moved her body so close he could smell the fragrance of her perfume.

"What's that sex potion you're wearing?" Angus said.

"Satin Blush… let's go over to Murph's for lunch."

Within an hour, they had moved from the bar to a table at the back of the pub. They sat close all afternoon… played shuffleboard, listened to
~~~~~

Irish music, danced and talked about Fountain Point. Angus was shocked when a gigantic cake with flaming candles was placed on the table in front of him.

"I told Murph it was your birthday," Bernie said and led the bar staff singing "Happy Birthday." Murph handed Angus a shooter of Powers Irish Whiskey to be tossed back after blowing out the candles. Two hours later – more Powers chased down with more Harp Lager – Angus felt the effects of their celebration as Bernie leaned over and whispered in his ear, "Let's go home."

~~~~~

Inside her condo, Angus shivered from the cold walk, sat down on the sofa and watched Bernie light the fireplace. She turned toward her bedroom and said, "I'll be right back... need to change out of these jeans."

She returned wearing a loose fitting terry robe... her long blond hair spilled over her shoulders. She went to a portable Bose Stereo unit and turned it on to an older album Angus had heard: Chet Baker Sings. She adjusted the volume on the song, "That Old Feeling," and sat next to Angus on the sofa. He inhaled the scent of her Satin Blush as she leaned her head on his shoulder. She scrunched close to him... her robe opening slightly.

"Touch me," she whispered as she moved his hand inside her robe. She moaned softly and pulled Angus to his feet, led him to her bedroom. It was dimly lit. Fragrant.

~~~~~

As Bernie lay sleeping, Angus felt edgy, uneasy, as if he had cheated on Etta. But Angus wasn't married to Etta or engaged or even living with her. His thoughts drifted to how Etta would survive her confrontation with the priest at St. Johns. Maybe Etta wasn't the free woman she had claimed to be. At the same time, Angus felt as though Bernie's feelings for him were honest. He felt good about having helped her by giving her the money she so desperately needed. He thought about what Misty had said: "Bernie loves you… she's just horribly upset and confused right now." Despite what Misty had told him, did Bernie really feel that way about him? Or was he the confused one? Making love with Bernie had been spontaneous, as if they both secretly knew it would eventually happen. Fighting his jumbled thoughts, Angus slept in fits and starts.

~~~~~

Dressed to leave, Angus sat on the bed and put his hand on Bernie's arm.

"My guess is that you don't want a big plate of corned beef and cabbage," he said.

Bernie flopped back of the bed.

"I feel like I need a casket," she said then leaned up again, noting Angus was dressed. "You're… leaving? Ange! Don't go…"

"I'll call you," Angus said as he lifted her arm and kissed her hand.

Trying to get her bearings, Bernie sat on the edge the bed, spoke haltingly, "I… there's an envelope for you… on the mantle by the front door… let me get it…"

Struggling to get up, Bernie coughed violently and slumped back on the bed.

"I'll find it," Angus said. "Go back to la-la land."

As he sat in his car, Angus opened Bernie's envelope. There was a small note card… just two words neatly penned on it: Thanks, Ange. Clipped to the note were five, ten-dollar bills. Despite thinking about Etta as he drove back to the club, it was as if the devil were roosting on his shoulder. He couldn't get the sweet aroma of Bernie's Satin Blush out of his mind.

~~~~~

As Angus dressed to check in with Ruby in the kitchen for the Saturday night menu, he thought about Bernie. But he still felt conflicted about Etta and her uncertain situation with her family over her engagement. Who knew how that would turn out, he mused. Having promised Bernie that he would call, Angus put aside his thoughts about Etta and dialed Bernie's number. He got a recorded intercept:

"This line has been temporarily disconnected."

"I just saw her two freaking days ago!" Angus yelled at the recording as he slammed the receiver.

~~~~~

Late Saturday night – on a hunch – Angus visited The Golden Gentleman to see Misty, but learned that she had quit the day before and had left for Florida with her friend Bernie-something... no forwarding information. Stepping out into the blustery March wind, Angus shook his head and pondered the paradox of Bernie Walker: Once again… she had bowed out of his life.

~~~~~

Sunday the week following, Angus sat alone in his room and thought about Misty telling him: "Bernie loves you… she's just horribly upset and confused right now." Though torn between his feelings for Bernie and Etta, Angus struggled to understand why Bernie had left for Florida without bothering to contact him.

His emotions a muddle, Angus stretched out on his bed and tried to sort out what was going on in his life: His job obligations, Robby's announcement of his engagement to Claire, Rose having dumped him, gotten married, his dreams of music school dashed, Etta and the crazy situation with her family about her engagement to a lothario. His thoughts churning, he closed his eyes. Moments later, the tolling bells from a nearby cathedral sounded vespers. Etta's meeting with the priest was scheduled for that afternoon. Angus put aside his swirling anxieties and dialed her number. Her voice sounded as if she were in the throes of despair.

"Thanks for calling. I need a shoulder to cry on," Etta said.

Hearing Etta's somber tone, Angus' heart dropped.

"I take it you had your meeting?"

"Oh yes! This afternoon… Father Mario Panelli."

"You don't sound… happy."

"Actually… I am… for the most part." Etta said. "I want to see you… but for the time being my father has forbidden me," Etta cried.

"Forbidden… why?"

"Don't ask, Ange… It's all part of being Italian."

"How long?" Angus said.

"My dad made me promise I would go with him and my mother to visit his family in Sicily. He won't get over all this crap until I make a retreat at a convent near where they live in Messina… get absolution and do penance."

"How long will you be gone?"

"About a month," Etta said.

"Sounds like a helluva long penance," said Angus.

7. ROSEMARY REDUX

Rosemary approached the Inn at Mary's Gate and strolled from the original carriage step-block up a gently inclining slope to the Inn's wrap-around veranda. Massive terra-cotta planters filled with poinsettia dotted the planked floors.

As she sat on the veranda waiting for her ten o'clock meeting with Charles Sewell, a black woman in a maid's uniform lumbered past her toward the entrance.

"Honey… my name's Gracious," the woman said. "Can I get you something… a glass of tea?"

"No thank you, Mr. Sewell is meeting me," Rose said.

As Gracious nodded and walked toward the Inn's entrance and went inside, a man emerged from the Inn dressed in a sport coat with a lapel flower. Carrying a notepad and a tray with two cups of coffee, Charles Sewell strolled over to Rose and placed the tray on a glass-top table between a pair of rattan rocking chairs. In one fluid motion, he pulled the rocker away from the table, sat down and crossed his legs.

"Help yourself to the coffee," he said, leaning back and brushing a random thatch of unruly dark hair from his brow. An easy smile warming his eyes, he sipped from his cup and silently studied Rose as if reading her thoughts.

For the past year, Rose had tried to forget about her disastrous marriage to Patrick O'Meara, but memories of the aftermath still clung… her messy divorce, her fifteen-month-old son... making a new life…

"Your father filled me in on your situation," Sewell said.

Rose returned her cup to the service tray and said, "I worked at the Fox Hollow Inn for a year right after getting married." Dabbing her lips on a napkin, she continued, "I've been working for my father for a few months…" she paused, "…but it's time for me to branch out and Dad thought…you might have something for me."

"Your timing is perfect," Charlie said. "We just finished a major refurbishing project. Marianne and I would be proud to have you here at our Inn."

Charlie brushed away the obstinate lock of hair.

"For starters, you'll be my Assistant Operations Manager," he said. "You'll be involved in every phase of our business and I'll want to introduce you to Mr. Carter Duffy at the Logan County Citizens Bank. Mr. Duffy and his bank gave us a generous line of credit to do our remodeling."

A surge of excitement radiated from Rosemary's face as she said, "I'm planning to move into my own place here in town."

"Is next Monday convenient to start?" he said.

Rose stood, extended her hand in appreciation.

"I'll be here early," she said.

As they shook hands, Charlie Sewell turned to leave, then paused.

"In the meantime, browse around the Inn and stop by the Pub," he said. "You remember Nikko our Pub manager? He'd love to see you."

The Pub's décor featured traditional Arts & Crafts furnishings, stylish art and antiques. Over the bar, Roycroft mica lamps hung from the ceiling, eight barstools were carved wooden replicas of Stickley design. A blue-toned neon light – secreted behind a decorative chase – circled the ceiling.

As Rose surveyed the Pub, from behind her came a man's familiar voice. Rose turned to see that Nicolo Marsala looked exactly as she remembered him from her earlier visits to the Pub.

"I hear you're talking to the boss about working here," Nikko said.

"Starting next Monday," Rose said.

"Your friend, Angus, used to tickle the ivories over there," Nikko said, gesturing to the piano. "Here's a picture of him performing one night."

He reached for the picture from the back bar, handed it to Rose, then filled two tumblers with soda and offered her one.

"Cheers," he toasted.

"Cheers," Rose said and studied the photograph.

Reminding her of their senior prom, the smirking Angus at the piano flooded her with pangs of wistful affection. She had been upset and cruel to Angus over the thunderbolt fiasco. Standing there looking at his picture, Rose wished she had kissed him when he'd taken her home early, missing the after-prom party.

"I knew he wanted to be a musician, but I heard he had an accident," Rose said.

"I guess after that thumb injury, he gave up the music thing and hauled ass out of town," Nikko said. "He's a big time country club chef now."

8. SPRING IS HERE

Following the Mother's Day Buffet rush, Chef Byrnes strolled into the kitchen with a tray loaded with shots of whiskey. Chef hoisted a glass of Black Bush and saluted his crew. As the kitchen staff finished toasting, Alyssa entered the kitchen and whispered to Angus, "Ange… you have a phone call on line one. She wouldn't tell me her name. You can take it in the Shock Room."

"Probably my mother," Angus said. "I've been meaning to call her."

Angus nodded to his fellow kitchen staff, ambled into the Shock Room and punched the blinking phone button. The familiar voice said, "Angus! You'll never guess what!"

"Bernice? Jee-zus! I've been trying to get in touch… "

"Guess what!"

Angus rolled his eyes, cradled the phone on his shoulder.

"I talked to Sr. Pauline. She said Mr. Sewell has an accounting job for me at the Inn at Mary's Gate," Bernie bubbled. "I'm moving back to Fountain Point. Do you believe it?"

"What the hell happened to you after our St. Paddy's Day party?"

"Ange… you're a doll."

"Bernie…?"

"I never in the world could have told you about it, but at the time I saw you on St. Paddy's Day, I was involved with another guy Misty had fixed me up with at the Golden Gentlemen's Club. You know? "

"No… I don't know. How involved…?"

"I won't bore you with the details, Ange, but I made a bad mistake.

I thought he was Mister Right and we got married." After a deafening pause… "I just rushed into the whole damn thing."

Stupefied, Angus pinched his brow in amazement. He had always given Bernie credit for being smart, but now, had she become so self-deluded that she had lost every ounce of common sense? What had she been thinking sleeping with him over St. Patrick's Day? Was he just another tumble for her ego? Trying to stifle his frustration, he regretted how he, too, had behaved.

"Would you care to tell me what happened?" Angus asked, his tone resigned.

"I loved Florida when Misty and I were there and, well… that's where my new husband and I moved. He was a private investigator… of sorts."

"Was…?"

"I feel so stupid, Ange. He left me after six weeks for some floozy he was investigating for marital infidelity. Can you believe that?"

"So… you're divorced?"

"Very," she said, "And a nice settlement, too… no more money problems."

"I'm happy for you…"

"I have the three thousand I owe you with interest… plus a nice little nest egg left over for me," Bernie said. "Give me your address and I'll send you a check."

~~~~~

After the club's monthly twilight mixed partners golf outing with dinner following, Tim Bowman, handed Angus an envelope from the Huntington Bank in Columbus. Tearing it open, Angus extracted a bank check payable to him for $3,500.00. Scanning the check, Angus noted it was from the account of Bernie Walker.

Angus returned to his apartment on the second floor, shaved,
~~~~~

showered and flopped on his bed. Not noticing that his message light was blinking, he was surprised when the phone rang. When he answered, he was more surprised by Etta's testy greeting.

"Don't you ever check your messages?" she said.

"I'm… I apologize… I didn't know you were home."

Etta's reprimand stung: "I called two times," she said.

"I promise… I didn't know…" Angus stammered. "Can we get together?"

"Only if you bring something good to eat… I'm tired of Italian food," Etta said.

"I'll be there… half an hour."

~~~~~

Seated with Angus on her sofa grazing their impromptu meal, Etta finished detailing her trip to Sicily with her parents and said, "Would you like to see a few of the million pictures my dad took of Noninna and Nonno's wedding anniversary? They're in my bedroom… be back in a sec."

A moment later, she appeared with a folder of pictures, spread them out on the coffee table and cuddled close to Angus. Flipping through the bundle of pictures, Angus picked up one of the photographs, examined it closely and pointed to the image of a young man standing next to Etta.

"Who's the Adonis standing next to you?"

Etta grinned at Angus' petulance. "My cousin, Lorenzo. Actually, he's my second cousin."

"Any rules about cousins getting together in Italy?" Angus said.

"Don't be jealous, Ange… I lived a chaste life while I was in Sicily."

"Me too," Angus said, grinning.

Etta took Angus' hand and stood up. "Help me carry these photographs back to my bedroom."
~~~~~

9. GOLDEN JUBILEE

While Rose busied herself hosting the Labor Day celebration of the Inn's Golden Jubilee, Bernie surveyed the crowd mingling in the lobby of the Inn and spotted the handsome face of JoJo Gardini. Working with his Lima-based partner, Johnny Mocha, JoJo managed Mouse's Pool Emporium and Recreation Parlor – an obscure and secretive gaming operation where nightly high-stakes poker games supplanted JoJo's income, which was principally derived from Johnny's kickback schemes he'd set up with Lima Linen Supply and State Wholesale Food Services for restaurant operators.

He gestured to her and squeezed through the crowd.

"I'm JoJo… "

"I remember. We talked in my office about your business."

"Being old friends, let's have a drink," JoJo said.

JoJo moved closer. The exotic scent of his cologne flooded the narrow space between them. Bernie's skin tingled; her eyes betrayed her thoughts. JoJo...handsome... his scent… his curly black hair, classic Italian features with slow gray eyes, a broad smile and perfect white teeth… his mouth, sensual and inviting. Their bodies nearly touching, a heady tension flowed through her as JoJo pushed ahead of her through the crowded lobby toward the Pub's entrance.

Inside the Pub, Bernie chose to sit at the bar.

"I like sitting at the bar… makes me feel very adult," she said.

"I love adult fun," JoJo whispered in her ear as he rubbed Bernie's back.

The bar was dim, not in direct sight of the lobby area but the exit was close by. Sitting high on her barstool – her feet adorned with Stuart Weitzman Laceswoon black pumps – Bernie crossed her shapely legs at the generous slit-opening in her jet black Halston Heritage one-shoulder ruched cocktail dress she'd recently acquired from Stylings by Monique in Columbus. Seeing JoJo eye her fleshy calf, her pulse raced; a prickly shiver coursed down her spine as she turned to the Pub's veteran bartender, Nicolo Marsala, and said, "Cosmo please, Nikko." She straightened her back and swung around to face JoJo. "Grey Goose… rocks… stuffed olives," JoJo ordered.

His knees resting against hers, JoJo said, "How in the world did a good-looking woman like you end up here in Fountain Point?"

"To work for Charles Sewell, I'm his business manager here at the Inn," she said, hoisted the Cosmo to her lips and teased them on the glass rim.

"I can save you a lot of money on linens and food products," JoJo said as he placed his hand on Bernie's exposed knee. Let's drive to the Lake tomorrow and talk."

A thin bead of perspiration glistened on his forehead as Bernie patted his hand and turned her knees slightly out of reach as she felt a tap on her shoulder.

"Oh… there you are," Rose said. "Let's go, OK?"

As Bernie slid off her barstool she whispered to JoJo, "Pick me up at noon."

10. INDIAN LAKE

Bernie stood before the full-length mirror in her bedroom. In her head, she pictured herself dazzling JoJo, glanced at her reflection and whispered: "I like you!"

She donned her $1,200.00 ensemble from Stylings By Monique… a delectable French-lace bra with matching satin thong and a stylish Herve Leger bright magenta, strapless dress. The final touch…a pair of new Prada, strappy backless wine-toned pumps. Scanning her reflection one last time, she turned left, then right, to check the seams on her sexy new black silk stockings. She spritzed a mist of Satin Blush onto her neck and cleavage and sauntered out the front door of her apartment as JoJo pulled up in his shiny new Mercedes SL500 convertible.

"You're looking sweet," he said, as he opened the passenger door for her.

~~~~~

The Cottonwood's dining room featured ceiling-to-floor windows overlooking the western expanse of Indian Lake. Shafts of the late summer sunset speckled the cranberry and lavender toned walls... the hostess seated them at the most preferred table... reserved by JoJo.

"Grey Goose," JoJo ordered.

"Margarita for me," Bernie said.

JoJo's eyes lingered on the waitress' legs as she strutted to the bar and disappeared. Turning back to Bernie, he drummed his fingers on the tabletop.

"Let's talk business," he said. "I can make you a lot of money."

Pursing her ruby-glossed lips, Bernie shifted her gaze toward the glassy smooth lake surface. Swallows flitted, swooped around the eaves of the roof; wisps of sun-tinged clouds drifted capriciously above the warm glowing horizon.

Bernie turned back to JoJo.

"We shouldn't waste such a beautiful evening talking about business," she said.

JoJo reached over, touched Bernie's hand.

"No big deal," he said. "Just a couple of thoughts."

As JoJo stroked Bernie's hand, the waitress returned and sat their drinks in front of them and said, "I'm Babs... you guys having dinner?"

"Couple of drinks, first," JoJo said. "Any chef's specials tonight?"

"Several. Let me know when you're ready," Babs said.

Bernie hoisted her margarita and toasted JoJo, "Cheers!"

JoJo shifted positions on his chair and leaned forward.
~~~~~

"The Inn buys a lot of food… right? Linens too?"

Bernie acknowledged JoJo's question with a coy nod.

"My business partners and I have very sweet deals," JoJo said. "Lima Linen and State Wholesale… we pay commission on all your purchases."

"We do our own linens," Bernie said. "I order food based on the chef's menu."

"Don't you ever have an emergency… short on linens?"

"Sometimes," Bernie said.

"It's simple," JoJo said. "Restaurants put us on standby… pay a small monthly retainer fee and bam… you need something, you got it… cheap and quick."

Bernie folded her hands under her chin. "I see how that helps the Inn, but…" her voice trailed off as she took another sip of her margarita.

JoJo spread his arms on the table.

"We pay our clients a consulting fee to be our contact in emergencies… not a ton, but good dough," he said.

Bernie eased back into the chair.

"How's the food supplier thing work?"

Before JoJo could answer, Babs appeared at their table and said, "You want to hear the chef's specials?"

JoJo furrowed his brow and answered, "Few more minutes, sweetheart."

As Babs slinked away at his rebuke, JoJo turned back to Bernie.

"State Wholesale has an arrangement called price buffering," he said. "It's like insurance… protects your annual purchases against unexpected price increases." JoJo paused. "Same deal… you get a nice monthly spiff."

Bernie tongued the salt from the rim of her margarita glass and said, "I'm just curious… how much are we talking?"

JoJo finished his Grey Goose and signaled Babs for a refill.

"For an operation the size of Mary's Gate... I'd say – all together – about a thousand bucks a month… easy."

Babs handed the menus to JoJo and Bernie.

"Chef's special," she intoned… "Pan-roasted duck breast and slowly cooked leg confit… baby turnips, baby carrots, and spinach leaves with natural duck jus."

"What's that confit thing?" Bernie asked.

As if she were a peacock ready to peck out Bernie's eyes, Babs smirked, "You'll love it."

There was a moment of awkward silence then Bernie said, "I'll have a steak and French fries." She turned to JoJo. "What are you having?"

"I'll try the special," JoJo said. "And bring me another drink."

This time, Babs stalked toward the kitchen bristling at JoJo's curt orders. JoJo grinned at Bernie.

"After she brings my drink, I have one more thing to discuss."

"I'm going to the powder room," said Bernie.

By the time Bernie returned, JoJo had finished his third vodka and ordered the fourth. Bernie gathered her skirt, sat down and focused on JoJo's chiseled features.

"What's the other thing you mentioned?" she said.

JoJo scanned Bernie's teasing ripe lips, inviting eyes.

"Advertising," JoJo said. "My friends and I own a big piece of Fountain Point's radio station… WOFP."

Bernie took a deep breath, relaxed.

"We use a lot of radio advertising… I buy it," she said.

"I've seen the Inn's broadcast affidavits," JoJo said. "Good numbers."

"About seventy-five thousand dollars a year," Bernie said.

"You should be getting a fifteen percent commission," JoJo said. "That's how the advertising agencies make money."

"The Inn could use that," Bernie said.

"The Inn doesn't get a discount," JoJo said. "Only an agency gets the discount."

Bernie studied JoJo's confident wide-eyed grin.

"What's the joke?" she said.

"No joke," he said. "All you have to do is set up a simple little agency… everyone does it… capture the commission for yourself.

"What about the Inn?" Bernie asked.

"Nothing changes… they pay the same amount as always… stations don't give their broadcast clients any commission… only to agencies… like one you could set up."

As the waitress plopped down their entrees, JoJo reached across the table and took Bernie's hand.

"Deal? I can help you set up your own agency in a heartbeat."

Bernie scanned the thick steak and mound of French fries.

"Let me think about it," she said.

As JoJo cut into his confit, he nodded to Bernie.

"I'll give you a break," he said. "I'll go back to July to start the advertising commissions."

After post-dinner vodkas for JoJo and two Crème de Cocoa Angel Tip's for Bernie, JoJo pushed back, stepped around the table and held Bernie's chair for them to leave.

"I have to go to Lima tomorrow," JoJo said. "But let's come back up for a swim on Monday."

"Love to," Bernie said and looked at her Movado Rondiro eBay bargain with its pretty black face. "But let's go to my place for a nightcap."

~~~~~

They sat in Bernie's living room, finished a bottle of Chardonnay she had kept stashed in her refrigerator for just the right occasion. Their well-lubricated conversation lasted only a short time before JoJo pulled Bernie to her feet and unhooked the clasps on the back of her dress. They flirted – fondled each other as they drifted down the hallway to her bedroom, where JoJo made Bernie's day. She smiled as his deft hands undid her strapless bra. The matching satin thong disappeared amid the bed sheets.

In her dreamy state after JoJo quietly departed, she rested her head on the silk pillowcases she'd recently purchased and promised herself that she'd visit St. Patrick's for confession sometime soon. Before dozing off, a fleeting thought tickled… JoJo had moaned his own name when they'd made love. She giggled… and slept soundly.

~~~~~

Late Sunday morning, invigorated by her Saturday night romp with JoJo, Bernie sat at her desk at the Inn and sipped a cup of stale coffee. A folder marked Private: Bernie Walker, peeked out from under the stack of accounting records spread out over her desk. She opened the folder and reviewed the Inn's payroll records. At the beginning of the year, Charlie laid-off three employees and payroll savings for the thirty-four weeks to date totaled $20,230… just under $31,000, annually, Bernie noted.

She turned to the idea JoJo had suggested about capturing the fifteen percent commission on the Inn's advertising purchases from WOFP.

Charlie had approved the year's advertising budget of $75,000. Knowing that her $50,000.00 divorce settlement account at the Huntington Bank had been depleted to less than $25,000 because of her wardrobe, a fifteen percent advertising commission – $11,250.00 over the year – was not to be sneezed at; enough to keep her credit cards paid up.

The other bit of frosting on JoJo's cake was the arrangement she would agree to for emergency service from Lima Table Linens and food items from State Wholesale Foods. Together – assuming her monthly commissions from JoJo would total $1,000, adding that to the advertising commission from the beginning of the year plus her salary of $45,240 – she smiled at her projected annual income… $63,000.

Later that evening, she dialed JoJo's number.

"Hey you… thanks for yesterday. We still on for tomorrow?"

~~~~~

Sunset, after a generous dose of sunshine, water frolics and changing out of their swimwear, JoJo and Bernie sat comfortably on the Cottonwood Inn's veranda and ordered drinks. Bernie held her margarita up in toast to JoJo and the day.

"I just wanted to talk with you about our agency commission deal," she said and touched the salted glass rim with her tongue. "The fifteen percent you promised."

"If you set things up like I suggested, it's a no-brainer," JoJo said and tossed off his first vodka on the rocks.

"Do you like the name, High Point Advertising?" she asked.

"Congratulations… I'll go back and pay you the commissions since July."

She leaned toward JoJo… "But you said I could go back to the first of this year," she huffed. "Isn't that our deal?"

JoJo stroked his chin as he said, "Let's talk about it back at your place."

~~~~~

Inside her apartment, Bernie turned to JoJo. "I want to change into something light, flip on the air conditioner, I'll be right back."

Dutifully, JoJo flipped the on switch to the air-conditioning unit then opened the refrigerator, found a bottle of Bernie's preferred Chardonnay and popped the cork. Minutes later – intent on making sure

JoJo would agree to their advertising commission arrangement from the first of the year – Bernie slinked into the kitchen and sidled up to him.

JoJo handed her a glass of chilled Rombauer. Watching JoJo's eyes scan the promise of her glorious body under her recently purchased silk kimono with kanji calligraphy, she tipped the wine to her lips and peered at him over the rim of the glass.

"You like this little thing?" she said as she fingered the lapel of her kimono and moved toward the living room. JoJo followed, fixated on her shapely form.

"Let's sit over here and talk," she said.

JoJo, next to Bernie on the sofa, studied his quarry.

"OK… let's talk," he said.

Leaning back, she wrinkled her brow and said, "I just want to be sure about our arrangement going back to January. It's my accountant's blood."

Against his preference for starting their commission arrangements in July, JoJo wavered momentarily. Paying her retroactive commissions from the first of the year would cost him an extra six thousand dollars.

"You're being too quiet," Bernie said. "Did I say something wrong?"

"Just thinking," JoJo said. "I…"

"You won't regret it, JoJo… I promise," she interrupted, "It's business as usual, right?"

He paused… took another sip of wine and said, "I suppose… I can work things out."

Springing from the sofa, Bernie took JoJo's head in her hands. As her kimono blossomed open, she kissed him passionately. Pulling back slowly, she reached for her glass from the end table, gathered her kimono around her and hoisted her wine in tribute to JoJo.

"Nice doing business with you, JoJo," she toasted.

Sitting down, JoJo reached for the white envelope Johnny Mocha had given him for running the very profitable poker game at Mouse's Pool Emporium and placed it on the coffee table in front of them. Bernie glanced at the envelope.

"What's that, JoJo? A love letter?"

"Just a little something… help us celebrate our deal," he said.

JoJo opened the envelope and sprinkled the cocaine onto the tabletop. With his business card, he prodded the coke into four narrow, parallel lines. She watched as he rolled up a new, crisp fifty-dollar bill into a straw-like tube.

"It's easy, Bernie," he said as he placed one end of the straw into his nose, bent over one of the lines and snorted it quickly.

"Just like inhaling flowers," JoJo said. "Your turn."

Tentatively, she took the rolled-up $50 and let him guide her hand to follow his action.

"I don't know about this, JoJo… "

"Just do like I did, Little Flower. You'll love it."

She sniffed a line of cocaine into her nose, sat back slowly to see JoJo beaming a devilish smile.

"I like that name Little Flower," he said. "Catholic Church has a saint named Little Flower… somewhere in France… St. Theresa of something or other."

Bernie smiled at JoJo's humor of associating her with a devout, saintly woman. She breathed deeply, feeling the drug's euphoric rush.

"I've heard about this, but wow…" she purred.

Minutes later, after they'd finished the coke, Bernie exhaled a giddy giggle, stood up, took JoJo's hand and pulled him down the narrow hallway leading to her bedroom.

Reprising Saturday night's ecstasy with JoJo, she closed her eyes and muttered a fervent aside: Thank God…I've finally found the right man!

11. ASSISTANT SOUS CHEF

Shades of Indian summer painted the CCC golf course landscape for the season's closing day. As Angus wrapped up the kitchen cleanup chores, Ruby summoned him to the chef's office. Uncertain if he had screwed up, Angus slid behind the chef's desk opposite Ruby and anxiously waited. Ruby pushed a printed letter-sized paper across the desk to Angus. Tentatively, he read the typed page:

ANGUS MCCRORY NAMED ASSISTANT SOUS CHEF

CCC Executive Chef Robert Byrnes announces the promotion of Angus McCrory, to the position of Assistant Sous Chef. Club Members and guests are invited to meet Angus at a complimentary reception in the club living room, on Wednesday, October 26, at 5:00 p.m. Please RSVP to our dining room manager, Alyssa Porter...ext. 545.

You are cordially invited to congratulate Angus and sample his culinary offerings.

Chef Robert E. Byrnes

Angus leaned back, rested his head on the wall behind him and reread the announcement of his promotion.

"What about Jewell?

Ruby folded her hands on the desktop and said, "Jewell couldn't care less... she's a home body... thrilled you're getting the promotion." Ruby rocked back in her chair. "If were you... I'd be very nice to her."

Angus nodded and squinted at Ruby: "Any other advice?"

~~~~~

As Ruby suggested – after cleaning up from dinner for more than two hundred sated golfers – Angus peeked into Chef's office.
~~~~~

Chef looked up and gestured for Angus to take a seat. From his desk drawer, Chef produced a bottle of Black Bush Reserve, poured a generous portion into a glass and handed it to Angus.

"*Sláinte*!" he said, and tipped his glass in salute.

"*Sláinte, agus Táinte*!" Angus replied and sipped a taste of Chef's private stock. "Ruby talked to me... thanks for the good news."

"You do a great job," Chef said and swigged his whiskey. "You won't go wrong working for Rube. The Board is keeping an eye on her."

"She's the best," Angus said,

"I've recommended that the Board consider her for my job," Chef said and downed his second whiskey.

Angus moved to the edge of his chair and sat his glass on the desk.

"Your job?"

"Dublin's my home," Chef said. "Gonna be the head chef at the Shelbourne. Leaving a few days after we close on New Year's."

12. HIGH SOCIETY

"My bachelor party is on Wednesday, October twenty-six," Robby crowed over the phone to Angus. "I'm going to import a couple of dancing girls from Lima. Maybe one of them will let you tickle her fancy."

"I was going to call you and Mom, Dad too," Angus said. "I got a great promotion this week. I'm the assistant sous chef!"

"You deserve it," Robby said. "Luck must be running our way, I'm full time now with the Fountain Point PD."

"Nice to have a family connection with the law," Angus said.

See you the twenty-sixth," Robby said. "I'll have a gross of condoms for you in case you get lucky."

"I hate to tell you, officer, but your bachelor party is the same night of my big debut here at the CCC."

"No way you can change it?"

"I can't… but I'm looking forward to being your best man."

~~~~~

Later the night of his introduction at the CCC as assistant sous chef, Etta put on Mozart's opera buffa, *The Marriage of Figaro* and cuddled next to Angus. Pulling his arm around her, she said, "This is one of my favorite operas… there's a great love scene near the end."

"Speaking of love scenes, my brother is getting married this Saturday. Will you come with me? I want to introduce you to my friends."

Etta paused, sipped her wine.

"That's a special time for you to be with your family," she said. "Do you mind if I don't go?"

Hoping to persuade her, Angus said, "I'd love for you to meet my family."

Etta leaned over and kissed Angus' cheek.

"I know… but you go. I'm planning a surprise so hurry back."

Before the conclusion to Act I, Angus fell sound asleep… but by 2:00 in the morning, he'd recovered sufficiently to enjoy Etta's bedroom version of the love scene between Figaro and Susanna.

13. A NUPTIAL GATHERING

Inside the Inn's ballroom, Angus knew instantly that his mother had had a hand in the wedding party decorations. Welcoming the celebrants at the entrance to the Inn's refurbished ballroom, was a male mannequin wearing a trench coat, crumpled fedora and stogie hanging between its lips… the uncanny replica of popular television detective Columbo sat mounted on a policeman's motorcycle. A female
~~~~~

companion mannequin – wearing a wedding veil styled into a witch's hat – sat in the motorcycle's sidecar. Fear contorted the mannequins' expressions as if they were about to plummet over a cliff into a deadly abyss.

Along the west wall of the room where the ballroom's ceiling–to-floor windows showcased the Inn's external courtyard garden surrounding its mini-Fountain of Trevi, hand-tied floral buntings of white and yellow mums hung from wall sconces.

Standing next to Robby and Claire, Angus and the wedding party greeted the arriving guests. A half-hour later, Robby leaned toward Angus and said, "Gotta cut out for pictures, little bro'… I'll catch up with you."

Angus moseyed around the ballroom and studied the room's elegant remodeling. Stopping in the middle of the dance floor, he felt a sense of something missing. As if rising out of the ashes of Angus' resentment toward Rose's spurning him, a hollowness crept over him as he remembered: Rose cheerleading at the Victory Dances, their dancing closely, him playing with The Saints… giving Rose the Claddagh… Rose's marriage…

"Hi Ange… would you care for a glass of champagne?"

Angus turned to see the smiling face of Susie Merriman.

"Don't mind if I do," Angus said and lifted a brimming crystal flute from her service tray.

"You'll be seated at the main table," Susie said and pointed to the linen draped table centered in front of the bandstand. "Okey-dokey?"

After the wedding guests took their seats, Msgr. Vinnie Sullivan invoked the formal blessing on the newlyweds and the sumptuous meal prepared by the Inn's head chef, Byron Lovelace. Charles Sewell welcomed everyone, hoisted a flute of 1984 Veuve Clicquot Brut, offered the first official marriage toast, then turned the microphone over to Robby's father.

"First, let me say... this is a special time on the McCrory family plate," he said. "I've always told my two sons: get in the boat or swim..." he paused, "...or get out. Personally, I think that message has finally sunk home with Robby... but I ain't sure about Ange." Angus' father turned to the head table where Robby and Claire were sitting. "Me and the missus welcome you, Claire, just the same as if you... like we'd raised you from a pup."

To a round of boisterous "hear-hears," Angus stepped to the microphone.

"Robby... Claire... it's an honor to be here with you today. Despite the fact that I'm the one who made this marriage possible by encouraging Robby to find someone besides his baseball buddies to hang out with, I can say that I'll miss him and his brotherly counsel. Just the other day, he told me that Claire thought of him as Mr. Right." Angus nodded to Claire and winked. "Claire...I hope you aren't too surprised when you find out his real first name is Always."

Angus stepped over to the Inn's gleaming new Kawai satin ebony-finished seven-foot grand piano and sat at the keyboard.

"At Robby's request – and as a tribute to Claire – I've chosen a Richard Rodgers song from South Pacific to play," Angus said and turned to the keyboard. Smiling at the irony only he could appreciate, he played a lyrical rendition of "This Nearly Was Mine."

After acknowledging his new wife – toasting and kissing at every clinking of glasses – Robby took the microphone, thanked his family, the Sewell family and turned to Angus.

"That was a stirring musical treat, little bro'," he said. 'I'm just thankful that you didn't play "Hanging By The Moment." I wouldn't want Claire to get nervous."

As the celebrants chatted and sat waiting for the wedding dinner, the ballroom's side stage door swung open and the figures of Moss, Milt, Otis, James and J. J. pushed an equipment cart through the ballroom door. Angus spotted Milt as they guided the cart to the bandstand, hailed him and stepped off the dais to greet them. Seeing Angus, Milt and Moss cruised toward him.

"Was going to give you a heads up," Milt said, "But we wanted to surprise you."

"I'm blown away," Angus grinned as he clapped them both on the shoulder.

"Your brother and his bride want you to play piano tonight... Milt brought his vibes," Moss said.

Angus looked over Milt's shoulder as the others began setting up.

"What's the book?" Angus asked.

"Mostly standards, some Broadway stuff... here're the cheat sheets," Milt said and handed Angus a folder of tunes.

"We'll play a little mood music while you have dinner, then we'll hit the dance stuff before the bride cuts the cake," Milt said.

Seated next to Angus for dinner, Robby said, "You living in Columbus, we don't talk much anymore little bro'. That fancy country club... must be loaded with rich chicks lookin' for love. You got any talent on tap?"

"I don't mess around where I work," Angus said.

Robby smirked at Angus. "Very noble of you, little bro'. What about off campus?"

"I'm seeing a very nice lady," Angus said.

"Don't be so freaking private," Robby said. "Does she have a name?"

"Her name is Etta," Angus said.

"Little bro', I can tell by that moony look on your face, you're in love!"

~~~~~

After dinner – as if it were old times jamming with Moss and Milt at the 151 Club – Angus played with passion; tunes he hadn't
~~~~~

played in more than a year: the first blues tunes Moss had taught him: "C-Jam Blues"; "Freddy the Freeloader"; "Blues in Hoss' Flat." Listening to his musician friends improvise, Angus mentally paged through the taunting memories of what might have been, but those thoughts evaporated when Moss called Cy Oliver's tune, "Easy Does It." Immediately, Angus remembered it from his first Oscar Peterson album, *Night Train*; Angus smiled as he recalled that "Easy Does It" was the sixth cut on *Night Train*'s ten-tune platter. As Angus traced his fingers over the keys in quick refresher of the melody notes, Milt leaned toward him: "The four of us play the lead in unison then we'll rotate solos… let's wail!"

Midway through his third solo chorus, Angus knew he was improvising as creatively as ever he could remember. When Milt called, "Here's That Rainy Day," Angus remembered the time he and Rose had danced close together to that same song right in the very ballroom where he now sat at the piano. As he played his solo on Michele Legrand's romantic ballad, Angus surveyed the dance floor filled with wedding guests and thought of the times The Five Saints had played the same tunes.

After Claire requested, "My One and Only Love," for her and Robby to dance their first official dance as husband and wife, Angus thoughts drifted to Rose. He grinned as they played 'St. Louis Blues," remembering how he taught Bernie to sing it.

The grooving ensemble – Otis' driving bass lines, J.J.'s lyrical passages, Moss' soulful solos, Milt's vibes resonating – gripped Angus' gut; he nodded to them in silent praise as he bore in and found the cool notes for his swinging phrases.

Angus sat back, wringing wet after wrapping up for the night. Having played for two hours, his thumb tingled with the prickly needles but his heart thudded with exhilaration. He swept the ballroom with a gaze that might have been wistful, but the challenge of overcoming his fears of ever playing as well as he once had, had transformed into sublime joy: You can do it! It was no longer a fearsome boogeyman. Having once believed that his dreams of being a professional pianist had been altered by the cruel hand of fate, he now realized that he had just proven to himself that he could play at a level that rejuvenated his passion for jazz. As Aummie had told him – he DID have something special for himself. For the first time, Angus felt a sense of closure about his knife accident having dashed his dreams of music school. As he basked in that contentment, he knew that he had made the right decision to move on to a new life, a life as a chef and a life with Etta. A life of renewed musical fulfillment. A good life!

~~~~~

Returning to Columbus Sunday afternoon, Angus showered, dressed, and drove to Etta's apartment. Etta's surprise jolted him as she met him at the door; she had guests. When she escorted Angus the short distance from the door to her living room, a man and woman – about Angus' parents' age – stood to greet him.

"This is my father, Angelo," Etta said then turned to the woman. "And this is my mother, Margherita."

"*Come stai?*" Angelo said.

"*Placere di conscerti*," Margherita said.

Thrown by Etta's ambush, Angus extended his hand and said to each of them, "*Buonasera... Buonasera.*"

Etta put her arm through Angus' arm, nudged him to take a seat and whispered, "Not bad for a Mick."

Feeling as though he were a plump salmon invited to dinner by a famished grizzly bear, Angus edged into a chair, sat tentatively and crossed his legs.

"Etta tells us that you are a chef," Angelo said. "*Si?*"

"Sous chef… at a country club," Angus said as he sat down.

"You worked for Margherita's brother Dominic, *si?*" Angelo said.

Angus connected Etta's referring to Dominic as her uncle and nodded.
~~~~~

"Dominic helped me get my job as a chef," Angus said.

Etta filled four glasses with ice and poured Campari over the cubes, topped it with a splash of soda water, squeezed a wedge of fresh lemon into each of the drinks and passed them around… handing the first one to her father.

"*Alla goccia*," Angelo said, nodded to Angus and drained his glass in one draught.

Trying to hide his smile at Etta's father consuming the drink so quickly, Angus tipped his glass and said, "*Saluté*."

Before Etta's mother acknowledged Angus' toast, she turned to him, and said: "If you wish to court our daughter, Concetta, you must assure me that you are single… and Catholic. Do you attend mass?"

Realizing that both he and Etta's mutual feelings were well past a purely physical stage, the thought about what meeting her parents implied was unnerving. Clearly, while he wanted Etta to be content and satisfied with their growing relationship, the prospect of marriage unnerved him. Hoping for relief, he glanced at Etta but she sat like a sphinx with a stone smile.

"I am… and I go to mass as often as I can," he said to Etta's mother.

"*Buono*," she said, tippled half of her Campari and turned to Etta.

"*Grazie... arrivaderci.* Saturday night of Thanksgiving... a dinner for you two in our home with family and friends." She nodded to Angelo and said, "*Andiamo*."

Alone with Angus after her parents left, Etta refreshed Angus' Campari cocktail and nestled next to him.

"I think you passed the test," she said.

"What about that dinner with your family?"

"Everyone will be impressed with your Irish charm," Etta said.

"Who is everyone?"

"My cousin... my best friend and their husbands. Uncle Dom… and a few other relatives."

"Should I wear my bulletproof vest?"

"You'll be fine. Just be sure to act like you love my father's homemade *grappa.*"

Etta leaned over and kissed Angus' cheek.

"Mom and I are going to Italy over Christmas," Etta said. "Can you go?"

"You're not serving another penance are you?"

"Nonno's having eye surgery and Noninna needs help until he recovers and gets back to his olive trees."

"How long will you be gone?"

"Most of January," Etta said.

"I'd love to, but with my new job and my boss on vacation all January, I need to work on a new menu and have it ready when the club reopens in February."

Angus tasted the last of his Campari cocktail and shivered.

"How does anyone like this stuff? It's tastes like medicine."

Etta kissed Angus' ear and whispered, "It's an aphrodisiac… it works best in bed."

14. WEDDING SOUP

Amid snow flurries and gusting winds, Angus jumped into his car at 6:00 on Saturday evening after Thanksgiving, and drove to the Bianco home on the corner of Hubbard and Kerr Streets. As he had envisioned from Etta's briefings, her parents met him at the door.

"*Buonasera*!" Angelo, said as he clapped Angus on the back.

Having prepared himself with the basics of Italian introductions, Angus said, "*Molto leito*!"

Angelo gripped Angus' hand like a vise as he said, "*Non c' é male*!" and whisked Angus into the living room to meet the other guests.

A burly man offered his hand and said, "I'm Angelo's cousin, Pasquale." Then pointing to a portly woman at his side, he said, "And this is *la sposa*, Gabriella." Angus nodded as another handsome couple stepped forward. "This is my husband, Umberto," the woman said. "And I'm Sophia, Etta's cousin." Angus shook their hands and caught Etta's wide grin as she pushed toward him with another beaming couple.

"Ange, this is my best friend Lucille Monaco and her husband Gaspar... my cousin... uncle Dominic's son."

"I've heard Etta carry on about you for months," Lucille said. "Gaspar and I are looking forward to seeing a lot of you."

Standing next to Lucille and Gaspar, Dominic grinned broadly and leaned close to Angus as he said, "I owe you an apology... I was wrong about Etta and Nello," Dominic pulled back, nodded to the woman standing behind Gaspar and said, "Meet my wife, Carmella."

Hoping to impress Carmella, Angus said, "*Que lastima*!"

When everyone roared with laughter, Angus turned to Etta. "Did I say something... wrong?"

Etta shook her head and smiled. "You said, 'What a pity!'"

Dominic winked at Angus as Etta approached with her mother. "*Buonasera*!" her mother said and hugged Angus.

Seated around the family dinner table, the number of dishes Etta's mother had prepared reminded Angus of his mother's special occasions. Following an elaborate antipasto of salami, prosciutto-wrapped caponeta, mortadella, gorgonzola and manchego cheese, Etta's mother served what Angus thought was the most superb veal parmigiana he had ever tasted.

Over dinner, the group talked about olive oils, balsamic vinegars, how to bake crusty bread and ricotta cheese pastries, wedding soup recipes, which of the women made the best meatballs and where to buy the best veal.

After the women cleared the table, Carmella brought a silver platter of her homemade cannoli and sat it in the middle of the table. As the cannoli quickly disappeared, Etta's father reached behind him to an elegant marble table where a cut glass bottle filled with clear liquid stood amid several square-footed crystal cordial glasses. Out of the corner of his eye, Angus saw Etta grinning as if reminding him of her warning: act like you love my father's homemade *grappa.*

Angelo filled the glasses and passed them around to each of the diners. "*Fatto in casa. Salute!*" he said as he hoisted his glass in toast. "*I migliori auguri, Concetta e Angusto!*"

Realizing that he and Etta were being toasted, Angus hoisted his glass, nodded to Etta's father and downed the *grappa.* When the taste of the caustic liquid seared his palate, Angus stifled a choke. His eyes watering, he shot Etta an agonized smile. She nodded and gestured to her father as he rounded the table and refilled Angus' glass. Angus grimaced as Angelo patted him on the shoulder and said, "*Ancora... amico mio.*"

His head throbbing as the after dinner conversation wound down, Angus nursed his fifth glass of grappa. Muddling through, Angus hoped dinner was over when Etta's mother suggested they retreat to the living room to listen to Gaspar play his guitar and sing "Ave Maria."

As Gaspar tuned up, Angus leaned close to Etta and whispered, "Where's the bathroom... I think I'm going to be sick."

~~~~~

When Angus awoke the next morning, he was curled up on the sofa and covered with a knitted afghan. His mouth dry, his head pounding, he tried to sit up. Falling back, he glanced up at the pictures hanging over the sofa. As if mocking him, his eyes fell on the image of The Madonna Dolorosa who looked pained and sorrowful. Trying to shrug off the after effects of the grappa, Angus vowed never to indulge again.
~~~~~

Suddenly, Etta was kneeling beside him. "Everyone's gone to mass," she said. "They said to say… arrivederci."

"I hope I didn't embarrass you," Angus muttered. "It was a… fun time."

"My father left a bottle of his *grappa* for you on the entryway table," she said. "He said he'd never met anyone who loved it as much as you do."

15. I'LL BE HOME FOR CHRISTMAS

Disappointed he wouldn't see Etta until late January, Angus went home to celebrate Christmas Eve dinner with the newlyweds. When Robby and Claire arrived, Angus jumped off the sofa to greet them as they stomped the snow from their feet and embraced Angus.

Angus' father carved the huge turkey and after serving generous portions on each of the five plates, he tucked a slab of turkey into his mouth and turned to his wife.

"Katherine… great meal. Hit me with a little more of that cranberry sauce…"

As his father ladled a dollop of the sauce on top of his turkey, Claire nudged Robby.

"Should we tell Ange who we saw at the Inn last week?"

Pointing to Angus with his fork, Robby said, "Yeah, little bro'. Couple of your old flames holding down the fort over there."

Angus looked at Claire for enlightenment.

"Dad hired Rosemary Gracewood to be his assistant manager and Bernie Walker as his business manager," Claire said.

"It's so nice to see young people come back to Fountain Point after they've been away," Angus' mother said.

As if clobbered by a truncheon, Angus slumped in his seat…his voice cracking as he said, "I heard about Bernie… but Rose… works at the Inn, too?"

"She started working for Dad last summer," Claire said.

Angus reached for his iced tea and drained it in one tortured draught.

Angus' mother tapped him on arm. "You look pale," she said. "You feeling OK?"

Wrinkling his brow, Angus muttered, "Something just went down the wrong way..."

~~~~~

Angus pushed the mound of whipped cream off his pie and tested Aummie's mincemeat recipe and its rich fruity texture of apples, raisins, tart cherries, shredded beef and red currants.

Claire nodded to him from across the table.

"After dinner, Dad and Mom want to meet us for a drink at the Inn," she said.

"We can go together," Robby said. "The Chief lets me use a cruiser... it'll be fun to roll up in front of the Inn and watch that old doorman, Milsey Meeks, piss his pants."

"Robby!" Claire said. "That's very crude."

"You three have fun," Angus' mother said. "Loved having you for dinner."

"I'm gonna catch the Browns-Seattle wrap up," Angus' father said as he ambled into the living room.

Angus pushed away from the table. "You guys go... I'm going to stay here and watch the game with Dad."

Robby reached for the last of his apple juice and downed it in one gulp.

"What's with you, little bro'?" Robby said. "You never gave a damn about football."

"C'mon, Ange," Claire said. "Dad would love to see you. He keeps
~~~~~

saying he hopes you'll come back home someday and work for him at the Inn."

Feeling trapped, Angus conceded. "I'll go… but I don't want to stay very long."

~~~~~

Reluctantly, Angus followed Robby and Claire as they dashed through the snow and stepped into the Inn. Stomping the slush off his boots, Angus doffed his parka and followed them into the Pub bar. Glancing quickly at the crowd – Charlie and Marianne Sewell seated at a nearby table – Charlie beckoned for Angus and the newlyweds to join them. Susie Merriman sauntered over as they sat down.

"Merry Christmas," she bubbled and slapped a bundle of cocktail napkins on the table. "Drinks?"

Charlie Sewell tapped his chest and turned to Susie.

"All on me, tonight," he said.

"Okey-dokey," Susie said.

As Susie wound her way through the tables back to the bar with their order, Charlie grimaced.

"I've been trying to get Susie to say something besides that corny okey-dokey, when she waits on people… "

"She's cute," Marianne interrupted. "She's just being herself."

"I hear you're a sous chef, now," Charlie said. "Keep us in mind when you get tired of country club work."

"Very happy at the moment," Angus said.

As Susie sat their drinks on the table, she turned to Angus and said, "Are you playing piano tonight?"

"Better not… haven't been practicing," Angus said.
~~~~~

Glancing at Charlie as he poured his Heineken and examined the frosty glass, it was as if Angus could intuit his thoughts when Charlie said, "Play something for us, Angus... get the holiday spirit pumped up."

"Play that 'chestnuts roasting' song," Claire said.

"Please Ange," Marianne Sewell said. "Play "Jolly Old St. Nicholas." It's one of my favorites."

Not to disappoint, Angus shrugged and stood up.

"Don't listen too close," he said.

Angus wended his way through the crowd, slid onto the piano bench and blindly tested the keyboard. Glancing toward the bar to see Nikko giving him a thumbs up, Angus played "The Christmas Song"… faked his way through "Jolly Old St. Nicholas," finished to an outburst of applause – led by Marianne Sewell – and played his favorite, "I'll Be Home For Christmas."

As he played, a woman squeezed into the last seat next to him at the piano bar.

Angus looked up. The sight of Rose tightened his every muscle. A rivulet of perspiration trickled into his eye; his heart quickened. Rose wore a bright green cashmere blazer with the Inn's logo on its breast pocket, a mint green pleated blouse, her jet-black hair neatly coiffed in a French braid. As if her dark eyes were uncertain, they didn't seem as bright as he remembered. But that didn't fit with the Rose he once knew; that Rose would never be uncertain about anything. Yet, when he saw tiny wrinkles gathered at the corners of her eyes, he was struck by the thought that Rose looked vulnerable.

"Surprised?" Rose said with a teasing grin.

"I… I had no idea," Angus stammered. "I just found out you're working here."

"You still have the touch," Rose said. "I heard about your injury… doesn't seem to bother you."

Angus looked away from Rose, surveyed the crowd to see the

Sewells preparing to leave, Robby and Claire behind them.

"I… can we go out into the Grand Parlor and talk?" Angus said.

"I want to say hello first to the Sewells," Rose said. "Claire and Robby, too."

~~~~~

The Grand Parlor hummed with guests drinking and chatting.

"There's a little nook in the coffee shop," Rose said. "It'll be quieter there."

Rose led the way, stopped at the waitress station, filled two glasses with water and handed one to Angus. "Water's the best I can do," she said.

As they sat at a cozy table overlooking the garden fountain, Rose put her hand on Angus' arm. "Ange…" she paused, "I could say I've missed you… but it would sound a little corny."

"You don't have to say anything… maybe it's better if we forgot all the history."

"I don't want to forget," Rose said. "I'd rather… get a few things off my mind."

Feeling as if it were his day for the deck to be stacked against him, Angus tensed with exasperation at having allowed himself to get talked into coming to the Inn in the first place.

"Go ahead," Angus said sharply. "I'll shut up."

Rose reached for her handbag, extracted a white linen handkerchief, dabbed the corner of her eye then dropped her hands onto her lap.

"Ange… what I want to tell you… is very hard for me."

As Rose sighed, Angus was stung with painful memories of Rose playing him a fool. Now, she had something hard to say?

"Go ahead," Angus said. "You've never had any trouble telling me anything."
~~~~~

Rose stood, paced to the window overlooking the snow-laden courtyard garden. The Christmas tree lights cast colorful shadows about the room. She peered out over the courtyard as if searching for a lost thought or a forgotten memory. Angus resisted saying anything and waited for her to break the silence. It was as if he were running out of heartbeats when finally Rose spoke to him with what seemed an overly dramatic tone.

"A lot of things are different for me now," she said and sat again at the table. "I just want to be sure I say this right."

As long as Angus had known Rose, she'd never worried about saying something right. His patience waning, Angus sat back.

"Do you remember the day I introduced you to Patrick O'Meara?"

Angus felt his gut tighten. "What I remember is you giving me back my Claddagh."

"That summer, Patrick got a job for me working at the Fox Hollow Inn in Teaneck. I'd never met anyone like Patrick," Rose paused. "I was so infatuated with him… we got married that fall."

"For crissakes... I couldn't care less about how you hooked up with that guy."

Rose broke into tears. "I'm sorry... it's just part of what's been in my heart… what I've hoped you would understand."

Angus sat mute.

"I was pregnant when we got married," Rose said and rested her arms on the table.

Angus rocked back in disbelief: Miss Puritanical? Pregnant out of wedlock?

As Angus groped for something to say, Rose stood. "I hate to leave, but it's Christmas Eve and my baby sitter needs to be home by eleven."

Reaching inside her purse, Rose extracted her business card and handed it to Angus. Then she reached for her coat, turned to Angus and said, "Maybe we can talk again… sometime."

At the Inn's entryway, Angus opened the door for Rose and stepped back. A blast of icy winter wind froze the tears on Rose's cheeks.

She smiled faintly as she wiped them away.

BOOK V

1. MOANIN'

In her office the first Friday of January, Rose reviewed the memo Mr. Sewell had sent to all employees at the Inn:

January 6, 1993

To all employees of the Inn at Mary's Gate –

It's my pleasure to announce that, effective immediately, Rosemary Gracewood has been promoted to Assistant General Manager and Director, Food and Beverage Operations. Please join me in congratulating her and wishing her well in her new position.

Cordially, Charles Sewell, CEO

Putting the memo aside, she worried about her meeting with Chef Lovelace. Over the time Rose had worked at the Inn, Lovelace had made it clear that he expected his loyalty and years of service to be rewarded with a promotion, more responsibility and more money. As recently as the Inn's employee Christmas party in mid-December, Byron had sidled up to Rose and – feeling no pain – clarified his wishes: "Now that Mr. Sewell has dumped a bundle on refurbishing this place – none of it in my kitchen, by the way – I want to be promoted to Director of Food and Beverage. Put a bug in his ear for me… will ya sweetheart?"

~~~~~

At Rose's year-end performance evaluation with Charlie the week after Christmas, Charlie had opened the door, letting Rose honor Byron's request.

"Now that you've been here several months," Charlie said, "Give me your assessment of our key people."

After pausing in thought, Rose commented to her best ability on the Inn's staff. When she paused to form her thoughts about Chef Byron, Charlie nudged her on.

"You haven't mentioned Chef Byron," Charlie said.

Rose glanced over at the flowers Gracious put on Charlie's worktable every morning and shifted her eyes back to him.

"We spoke… at our employee Christmas party," Rose said. "He'd like to be promoted to our Food and Beverage Manager… some more money, too."

Charlie leaned back in his executive chair and clasped his hands behind his head.

"I appreciate the fact that Byron's been loyal," he said. "But I think he's losing his grip."

Charlie glanced at the fresh snow falling on the Inn's courtyard garden.

"Byron's wife left him for another man," Charlie said. "Since then, he's been very testy. He was miffed that I deferred upgrading the kitchen when we refurbished the Inn last spring. I think he's been hitting the sauce but I'm willing to give him a five-percent raise after the first of the year."

"He does seem a little antsy," Rose said.

Charlie sat forward and put his arms on his desk.
~~~~~

"That's why I'm promoting you to Assistant General Manager and Director of Food and Beverage Operations," Charlie said as he handed Rose a stack of new business cards.

~~~~~

Rose examined her new business cards and ran her finger over the embossed type: *Rosemary Gracewood, Assistant General Manager and Director, Food and Beverage Operations, The Inn at Mary's Gate.* She resisted the impulse to be puffed-up about her new position, shuffled through a stack of vendor bills and reminded herself that after her meeting with Chef Lovelace, she'd talk about the bills with Bernie.

Rose finished her third cup of coffee, stood, stretched the tension out of her neck and braced herself for her first official meeting with an Inn employee as the Director of Food and Beverage Operations. Admittedly, she knew few specifics about the Inn's kitchen, but even as protective as Chef Byron was about his operation, she felt confident he'd help her. As she scribbled a note to talk with Bernie about the vendor bills, Susie Merriman appeared at her door.

"You left a message with Hattie in the Coffee Shop to have me stop by and see you," Susie said. "Is this a good time?"

"Perfect," Rose said. "I wanted to ask you if you would be willing to organize Fountain Point's May Day Parade."

Susie arched back, a look of surprise covering her face.

"Me? ... organize the parade... the whole thing?! I'd... I haven't done anything like that before, I..."

It wasn't the first time Rose had marveled at Susie's charming innocence. A talented watercolor artist, Charlie Sewell had allowed Susie to exhibit many of her paintings in the lobby foyer. She was just the right antidote for Fountain Point's City Council and its stuffy reputation for clinging to the predictable ho-hum annual regurgitation of the city's May Day Parade. When Mayor Bunny Carpenter had asked Rose if she had any suggestions as to who might be able to help out on the parade committee, Rose had immediately recommended Susie. Mayor Bunny
~~~~~

was quick to say, "We need some new blood. You think she'll work out, we'll give her a try."

"You'll do a great job and the Mayor wants someone new for a change," Rose said to Susie.

"When is it? I guess… I mean… May first?'

"I'll let the Mayor know you're available and we'll go meet her," Rose said. "I want you to work on designing the Inn's float, too."

"Okey-dokey… super!"

Gathering her thoughts for meeting with Byron, Rose stepped into the hallway to go to the kitchen and bumped into Bernie.

"I'm working on the payroll," Bernie said. "Any changes I need to know about?"

"Mr. Sewell approved giving Chef Byron a five percent raise. And there's one other hourly employee's raise," Rose said backpedaling down the hall. "He approved giving Gracious Maxy a twenty-cent per hour increase. I'll get the paper work to you later today."

Bernie hunched her shoulders in a huff. "What the hell has she done to deserve a raise? All I hear from her is a lot of bitching about being short on housekeeping help."

"Can't talk now, Bernie. Just do it please, I'll explain later."

~~~~~

Entering Chef Lovelace's office, Rose was struck by his surly manner. Not only did he look bored, but sullen – his greeting arrogant and unprofcssional.

"Guess you're the big mama, now," he said and slouched behind his desk without offering Rose a seat. "Hope this won't take long… coffee shop's jammed on Fridays."

As Byron draped his leg over an open desk drawer and folded his arms, Rose sat on the folding metal chair across from him.
~~~~~

"We need to set up a regular meeting to be sure we're on the same page," Rose said.

Byron shrugged. If there was one thing he hated, it was the thought of regular meetings with anyone. And that old *same-page* crap – a smoke screen for prying.

"I'll check my calendar," he said. He reached for his appointment book buried under the papers on his desk but stopped when Rose's pager interrupted with Bernie's voice.

"Just got a call from Hattie Tilton," Bernie said. "Morning sickness. She's having a tough pregnancy… can't come in today."

"No problem, I'll fill in for her. It'll be good for me to get some direct customer contact," Rose said and clicked off.

"Sorry, Byron… you heard it," she said.

As Rose stepped out of Byron's office, Clifford Williams, the Inn's best cook, poked his head in and said, "All set for lunch, Chief. Big pot of your chili simmering."

2. BLACK FRIDAY

As Chef Byron had predicted, the coffee shop bustled with the noon crowd. Taking Hattie's usual place, Rose stood at the hostess stand near the coffee shop entrance – menus in hand – and welcomed an approaching couple.

"Welcome to the Inn. May I help you?" Rose said.

"I'm Buster Thompson and this is my wife Blanche," he said. "My law office has had many meetings here at the Inn… lovely place. Would you have a table in the center of the room?"

In the months Rose had handled group meetings for the Inn, she had no recall of the Thompson law firm booking any meetings. Ignoring her curiosity, Rose accommodated the Thompson's request and watched intermittently as they ordered lunch and appeared to be enjoying the meal placed before them by Susie Merriman. That was, until Blanche Thompson jumped to her feet and shrieked: "There's a dead mouse in my chili!"

Buster Thompson rushed to administer to his wife's shock as she peeled over in a dead faint, crashing into a service tray, dishes flying… her red hat turned upside-down on the floor. Buster Thompson shed his bright yellow coat and fanned his wife as if he were a bullfighter.

"Call a doctor," he yelled. "My wife's been poisoned! Call the emergency squad!"

All eyes turned to the couple as Rosemary rushed over to get Rob McCrory who was having lunch at the counter with his assistant, Boris Detman.

"Rob! Did you see that?" Rosemary gasped, frantically pointing to where the Thompson's had been seated.

Rob pushed past Rosemary toward the people gathering in the center of the coffee shop.

"Everyone, calm down! I'll handle this," he ordered as he worked his way into the center of the room. Seeing his uniform and modest, but conspicuous side arm – people stepped aside as he hovered over the scene.

"Rose… call the paramedics," Rob instructed. "We need to attend to the victim."

Wishing that Rob had used another word other than *victim*, Rose dialed *911*. Waiting anxiously for the squad to arrive, Rose's mind reeled: *How could a mouse get in the chili? Was Chef Byron that lax? Or was this revenge?*

Within minutes, EMTs rolled in with a gurney and administered first aid to Blanche Thompson, lifted her onto the gurney and wheeled her out of the coffee shop through the lobby to the ambulance parked under the portico by the Inn's main entrance.

Chester (Scoop) Wilson, managing editor of the *Fountain Point Examiner*, entered the coffee shop just as the Thompsons were leaving amid the hubbub.

"What's going on?" Scoop asked Thompson.

Buster's face lit up. "You're with the newspaper, aren't you?"

"Chester Wilson," Scoop said. "Someone get hurt?"

Buster Thompson studied Scoop then blurted, "It's my wife. She was just poisoned!" Thompson threw his hands in the air as he said, "Mister, we need to get to the bottom of this, we need to inform the Health Department that my wife's been poisoned." Thompson's eyes narrowed. "There was a dead mouse in her chili. It's an open and shut case of food poisoning!"

Thompson rummaged through his coat pocket, extracted a card and said, "Here's my business card. I'll be available to talk after my wife gets out of the hospital."

Scoop scanned the business card.

> *Harrison (Buster) Thompson,* ESQ.
> *Thompson and Clarke, LLC*
> *5595 Lincoln Ave., Fountain Point, Ohio*
> *Office: 293-5555 - Home Tel: 293-2222 (after 5:00 p.m.)*

Pocketing the card, Scoop wended his way through the murmuring crowd to Rob McCrory, who was still surveying the scene of the incident.

"Whatcha' got, Rob?" Scoop said.

"Don't know for sure yet," Rob said as he rubbed his chin. "Something about a mouse in the lady's soup. Doesn't figure. Charles Sewell runs a good place here. Rosemary saw the whole thing… you can get the details from her." Robby turned abruptly toward the scene of the incident. "Excuse me… gotta collect the evidence."

Scoop retreated to where Rosemary stood wringing her hands.

"Rose, what's all this about?" he asked.

"Something tells me this is a bad joke," Rose said.

"Could be… but it *is* news," Scoop said. "Have to cover it."

"Do what you have to Scoop, but there's something fishy about this whole thing."

They both turned to watch Detective McCrory as he issued instructions to his assistant, Boris Detman. "Handle that mouse easy," Rob said. "Put it in an evidence bag and don't forget that chili bowl."

3. BUSINESS AS USUAL

Bernie tapped on Charlie's open office door and sauntered in. Since it was nearly noon, he had planned on a light lunch at the Inn's coffee shop and had invited Bernie to join him after reviewing the Inn's year-end financials.

"You look tired today," Charlie said, as she sidled up to his conference table and sat down.

"Didn't sleep good last night," Bernie said, thinking about her late night celebration when JoJo delivered her commission checks.

"I can sympathize," Charlie said. "But you need to finish next week's payroll today. We can't miss payday."

Charlie glanced at the skimpy dress Bernie wore. He admitted that moral standards had evolved to a hazy muddle along with all the craziness of digital this-and-that distracting people from getting their work donc. Grudgingly, he had resigned himself to the new order and given as much latitude as possible, especially when it came to Bernie. After all, she was talented and loyal… as well as an astute accountant.

"Got the final numbers for our year-end," Bernie said as she opened a folder of accounting papers. "Had a few extra expenses over the holidays. We'll need to tap our line of credit to keep current on the payables."

"Shouldn't be a problem," Charlie said. "I'll call Dab Merritt at the bank and have him transfer some funds to our checking account."

Before they got started reviewing Bernie's financial report, a screaming siren and the screeching tires outside the Inn startled them.

"We'd better go see what that's all about," Charlie said, as the two of them rose from their chairs and hurried out of the office to the Inn's lobby. A few steps down the hallway, Snuff Guffy, the Inn's gardener, security and maintenance manager, intercepted them and frantically gestured toward the lobby. "There's something happening in the coffee shop. Miss Gracewood called the paramedics. I heard it on my handset."

Charlie and Bernie rushed toward the coffee shop just as Chester Wilson entered. Seeing Charlie, Rose hurried to his side.

"What the devil happened?" Charlie asked.

"I wish I could explain it," Rose said.

Together, they watched as the emergency squad wheeled Blanche Thompson out of the coffee shop on a gurney and headed toward the Inn's main door. Both Bernie and Charlie saw the unfamiliar figure of a man dressed in a yellow sports coat. He stood less than a foot away from Scoop Wilson ranting about his wife finding a mouse in her chili.

"Oh my God," Charlie whispered as he overheard the man's entreaty with Scoop. "This is all we need!" Charlie turned to Rose. "Rosemary! Calm everyone down and come to my office as soon as you can!" Scowling, he turned back to Bernie. "We'll have to postpone our financial review until later," he said and stalked toward his office.

~~~~~

The Thompson incident hung foul in the air, as the few remaining ruffled patrons trickled out of Mary's Gate Coffee Shop. Rose's calming assurances to the contrary, something unmistakably disagreeable had rocked the coffee shop's noontime serenity. Amid the whispered notions of what had happened, Rose fought to find words to assuage the disruption. Blanche Thompson's accusation of finding a mouse in her chili was nauseating, but Rose's crisis management training
~~~~~

at The Fox Hollow Inn helped: *Don't admit to anything until you have the facts.*

"Everything is fine, we look forward to seeing you again, soon," Rose said as she booked all of the patron's meals to her *house account.* Amid the confusion, Rose thought about Scoop Wilson's comment: '*It's news… have to cover it.*' Deciding she would deal with whatever the *Examiner* reported later, she grabbed her notebook and hurried down the hall to Charlie's office.

Upset and frustrated that she had let Charlie Sewell down after he had promoted her, Rose stood at attention by his desk, clutched her notebook. Charlie greeted her with a frosty frown.

"Have a seat, Rosemary."

Sitting across from her mentor, she felt foolish, like an errant schoolgirl caught in the act of fibbing. Charlie had entrusted the Inn's food service to her and – through no fault of her own – she'd been blind-sided by the Thompson incident.

"Mr. Sewell… I just…"

"Tell me what happened in the coffee shop today," Charlie snapped.

Shifting nervously in her seat, Rose paused to collect her thoughts, then said, "I can't explain it, Mr. Sewell. I was filling in for our regular hostess, Hattie Tilton, who called in sick. I had just seated the Thompsons and was watching to be sure that our best waitress, Susie Merriman, was being attentive."

Charlie pursed his lips. "And?"

Rose hands trembled but her memory was as clear as she hoped it would be, there was no mistaking what happened next.

"I'd looked away to greet another guest, when I heard the commotion."

"Tell me exactly what you saw, Rosemary, and don't leave anything out!"

"I heard Mrs. Thompson scream and I looked at her as she stood yelling: '*There's a dead mouse in my chili!*' I thought it was a joke. After that, she collapsed on the floor and her husband went berserk."

Charlie's face flushed crimson as he glowered across the desk at Rosemary.

"This can devastate the Inn's reputation!" he said sharply. "Even if it proves to be untrue, it'll kill our business for months."

"Please, Mr. Sewell... I *will* get to the bottom of this. I have a meeting with Chef Lovelace right after we finish here." Rose stood, gathered up her notepad and said, "I'm sorry to say, but I'm sure the *Examiner* will have a story in tomorrow's paper."

"Probably so," Charlie said. "Unfortunately, if I find out that we've been lax about food safety, I won't have any choice – Byron will lose his job."

Feeling blood rush to her cheeks, Rose turned to her mentor.

"I don't know all the kitchen details, but I promise, I'll know about it by the end of the day."

"I don't want to be heavy handed and confront Byron myself right now, so let me know what he says as soon as you talk with him."

~~~~~

Rose tapped on Chef Lovelace's office door and stepped inside. He sat slouching in his chair, his eyes noticeably bleary.

"I just met with Mr. Sewell," Rose began. "He's quite upset about what happened in the Coffee Shop today. I don't have time to stand on ceremony, so tell me how a mouse got into your chili..."

"Don't take that tone with me, *Ms. Gracewood,"* Byron broke in. "I've forgotten more about running a kitchen than you'll ever know."

"I'm not taking any *tone*..."

"I don't run a second-rate kitchen!" Byron barked. "There wasn't any goddamned mouse in my chili!"
~~~~~

Rose leaned forward, her face crimson.

"You better talk with detective McCrory and ask him what *was* in the chili," Rosemary blurted. "It was a mouse… plain and simple."

Byron slammed his fist on the desk and bellowed, "That's ridiculous. If you can point to one thing I've done wrong, I'll get the hell out of here."

"You might think it's ridiculous, but Mr. Sewell would differ," Rose said. "I'm trying to get to the bottom of this thing and he's not in the mood for mystery." "Well, I suggest you start clearing up any mystery about me by accepting my resignation," Byron hissed.

Rose leaned toward the chef. "I'm not trying to insult you, but I would appreciate it if you would get off your high horse and help me."

"Now that you're in charge, Ms. Gracewood... have our lovely business manager cut my final check."

Byron stood up, ripped off his chef's coat, wadded it up and tossed it at Rose.

"You might want to have this laundered to get all that mouse shit off it," he said then hoisted a half-pint bottle of *Smirnoff* from his desk drawer, cocked one eye at Rose over the upended bottle and drained it.

"Happy trails, sweetheart," he rasped as he stomped out.

4. STAND BY ME

Back in her office, Rose steeled herself to the task of telling Charlie the bad news about Byron. Beyond that, she needed to prove to Charlie that she deserved her promotion to Director of Food and Beverage and doodled her ideas for not only covering the kitchen staff shortage but also dealing with the mouse fiasco:

- *Cliff Williams – knows the recipes – interim chef;*
- *Work with Rob McCrory – mouse investigation*
- *Handle PR – news – inquiries – written statements*

- *Bernie – business as usual…*
- *Housekeeping – no change*
- *Snuff Guffy – inspect kitchen for any possible vermin issues!*
- *Front Desk – business as usual*

After double-checking the list, Rose rummaged through her purse, extracted her cosmetic mirror and freshened her lipstick. Another thought struck her as she blotted her lips. Glancing at her desk clock, she didn't have time to write it on her doodle pad, she would easily remember to mention it to Charlie – depending on how their conversation unfolded regarding her other suggestions.

~~~~~

Rose stepped cautiously into Charlie's office. On the phone, he nodded for Rose to take a seat. His tie down, collar undone, shirtsleeves rolled up – his face and neck purple – Charlie's hand trembled as he hung up the receiver and slammed his fist on the desk.

"God---dammit!" he roared and reared back in his seat.

Startled by Charlie's outburst and hopeful that she wouldn't be late getting home to Aidan, Rose stood to leave.

"I can come back in the morning," she said. "Aidan can play in my office while we talk."

Charlie glanced as his wristwatch, glowered at Rosemary.

"I know you need to get home to Aidan, but we can cover this crap in plenty of time for you to get out of here. I'll be glad to get the hell out of here myself… go home and have a stiff drink."

Relieved that she would be home in time to feed Aidan, Rose sat down, slid her doodled notes across the desk to Charlie.

"Before you look at that, you should know that Chef Byron resigned and huffed out of the kitchen when I asked him about his chili," she said.

Charlie slammed his hand on the desk and picked up Rose's notes.
~~~~~

"So much for loyalty," he said. "I knew the clock was ticking with him."

Charlie read Rose's notes, arched his eyebrows and said, "Some good ideas here." His temper abating, he looked across his desk and with a much calmer demeanor, continued. "Cliff's a good choice for the kitchen, but based on that phone call I was on when you came in, our kitchen staff might be looking at a few weeks of vacation."

Rose's puzzled frown sparked Charlie's clarification.

"That was the Health Department," he said, tapping on his desk. "A written complaint was filed against us this afternoon – Mr. Harrison Thompson – on behalf of his wife, Blanche."

Rose shook her head.

"That was quick…"

"Monday morning at eight, we'll be hosting a visit from one of the Health Department's crack investigators," Charlie said. "Some joker named Dallas Humply. I met him once when he was here on a routine inspection. He has a weird twitch in his left eye… they call him *Wink*."

Rose's chuckle lightened Charlie's tension; he forced a wan smile and read Rose's other ideas.

"Good idea about Rob McCrory," Charlie said. "Someone is likely to say being my son-in-law, he has a conflict of interest but I want you, him, our attorney and anyone else you think would be helpful to get started on the investigation."

Charlie tossed Rose's note pad back across the desk to her.

"The rest of your thoughts are fine. We'll schedule an employee meeting for Monday afternoon to keep everyone in the loop. Anything else?"

"One more thing," Rose said as her last idea formed in her mind.

"Shoot," Charlie said.

"This might not work out," Rose said and paused. "Angus is a chef.

I'm sure he knows a lot about kitchens, food handling, cooking… and with Byron gone, Angus could be a big help to us – especially with the Health Department."

Charlie rocked back in his chair and inhaled a deep breath.

"Excellent idea. Do you know how to contact him?"

"Robby and Claire know. I'll call them tonight."

"Ask Angus if he would be willing to sit in on the investigation meetings. I'll be glad to pay him for his time."

~~~~~

The headline on Saturday morning's *Fountain Point Examiner* screamed the news:

LOCAL COUPLE CLAIMS FOOD POISONING
INN AT MARY'S GATE CITED

~~~~~

5. SLÁN… AGUS HALÓ

Club Manager Tim Bowman always left town every January for the month when the CCC was closed. This year, at Chef's request in acknowledgement of the many favors Chef had done for him, Bowman's quid-pro-quo was to allow Angus to live for the month of January in the Club's once secret bachelor's apartment on the second floor. Accordingly, late Saturday morning, standing in the kitchen just inside the door from the dining room, Angus stood patiently as Bowman recited his *'Miranda Act'* of do's-and-don'ts, cautions and caveats he expected Angus to follow in his absence. Out of the corner of his eye Angus saw Chef Byrnes wink at him as Bowman droned on…

> *"Keep the heat at no more than sixty-degrees, report any trespassers to the police, I'll bill you for your telephone charges and don't bring any women in here… I'll know!"*

After shaking hands with Bowman, Angus stepped over to Chef Byrnes. "I thought you left for Ireland."

"Your new boss is stopping by on her way to Texas for the month off," Chef said, "I wanted to give you a heads-up before I leave."

Chef motioned for Angus to lead the way into his office. As they sat in their customary seats, Chef handed Angus a bottle of his private stock, Black Bush, 12-Year-Old Distillery Reserve. Tapping on the ornate blue and gold label, he said, "You'll have to come visit me in Ireland to get any more."

Angus cracked open the bottle and pulled two glasses off the shelf next to Chef's desk. "I won't forget what you've done for me," Angus said.

After the two clinked glasses, quaffed the amber spirits, Angus said, "What's the heads up?"

"Ruby's got her own way of doing things," Chef said. "So don't be surprised if she throws you a couple of curveballs. She'll want to put her thumbprint on your new menu ideas so stay flexible."

In farewell to Angus, Chef smiled and said, "*Slán!*"

~~~~~

Angus stashed Chef's gift in his locker and meandered back into the kitchen to brew a fresh pot of coffee to share with Ruby. As if seized by an apparition, Angus gawked at Ruby when she strutted into the kitchen dressed like a cattle drover with her fringed buckskin suede vest, an aquamarine and black accented Western shirt and stone-washed jeans neatly tucked into the most dazzling pair of cowboy boots Angus had even seen. A blue Stetson hat cocked on the back of her head left just enough room for tufts of her fiery red hair to peek out. Angus folded his arms, chuckled and said, "Should I get a bucket of oats for your nag?"

Ruby doffed her Stetson, released her hair and raked her fingers through it.
~~~~~

"Where I come from, greenhorns get shot for insulting a horse," she said. "I smell coffee… or is that your deodorant?"

Coffee in hand and crossing her lavishly booted feet at the ankle, Ruby hoisted them onto the edge of Chef's old desk, leaned back in his creaking tilt-back wooden chair, and carefully placed her hat on the rarely uncluttered desktop.

"So, hombre… you had a pretty good year," she said "Other than a gun fight with Joey, a couple of cuts and burns and a batch of screwed up lobster bisque – not to mention letting that hot little Simplot saleswoman overload us – you managed not to piss me off too bad."

"She isn't that hot," Angus said and took a sip of coffee.

"I wouldn't kick her out of bed for eating jerky," Ruby said. "What are you going to do all month knocking around in this morgue by yourself?"

"Gonna do some experimenting with a few of my own recipes," he said.

"You used to work in an Italian restaurant, didn't you?" she said.

"The Roma… back in Fountain Point," Angus said and glanced at his scarred thumb.

"Something Italian might work – some *nouvelle* items too,' she said. "Any ideas?"

Angus pursed his lips and rubbed his chin.

"I think candied squirrel heads would be a big hit."

"Our gardener would kiss your tenderfoot butt if you could get rid of a few hundred of those critters," she said.

"I'll walk you out to your buckboard," Angus said.

Lingering in the driveway, Ruby gave Angus a hug and handed him a note.

"Here's my number," she said. "Call me if you get lonely while I'm gone."

Ruby stepped into her car and started the engine. She pointed a warning finger at Angus and said, "Remember this, hombre, don't ever eat blue food or fuck with a woman named Ruby."

Angus slapped his hand on her car roof and stepped back.

"Don't throw a shoe on your way to Texas," he said and waved to the departing new Head Chef of the Columbus Country Club.

A gust of crisp January wind prickling his skin, Angus returned to the Club's warmth, strolled through the foyer toward the living room and stopped to admire the Club's Knabe Louis XV Scalloped Grand, Burled Walnut piano. Often, he had heard it played by a lady whom Angus guessed was at least 80, but – other than on the one occasion at the Club's employee dinner at Thanksgiving – he had side-stepped the occasional, *'Play me something, Angus,'* requests from Alyssa. In the solemnity of the winter quiet and his mind on Etta, Angus sat at the piano, opened the keyboard, played Etta's favorite tune, *Al Di La,* and spent an hour losing himself in the jazz repertoire he had kept tucked in the back of his mind until the phone jangled the fifth time. He ignored Alyssa's syrupy recorded greeting…

> *"Happy New Year. The Club is closed until Wednesday, February first. You may call with reservations beginning on Tuesday, January thirty-first. If this is an emergency, you may leave a message for our resident manager."*

… until he heard a familiar voice leaving a message.

"This is Rosemary Gracewood calling for Angus McCrory. Would you please ask him to return my call? My number is…"

Angus stared at the phone, bounded for it.

"Rose… don't hang up… it's me," he huffed out of breath.

"I hope you're not too busy to talk for a minute," she said.

"No… yes, I… the club's closed until February," he stammered. "I'm coming home tomorrow for Robby's birthday dinner."

Rose paused then said, "I don't want to interfere with Robby's birthday dinner… but do you think we could get together and talk?"

"You sound uptight," Angus said.

"The coffee shop… we had an incident… our chef quit and the Health Department is coming over on Monday morning to inspect our kitchen." Angus could hear Rose's deep sigh. "I… hate to impose, but I need some advice," she said. "We could meet at my house."

"We don't have to meet," Angus said. "I'll call when I get home… we can talk on the phone."

"Ange… with Aidan, it would be a lot easier for me if we talked in person, OK?"

"Same old same old," Angus thought: Rose, pushing to have her way.

"All right, Rose… I guess I can spare a half hour."

~~~~~

Rose welcomed Angus into her home on East Chillicothe Avenue. Seeing that she lived amid fairly luxurious furnishings, Angus felt awkward standing in the foyer and thinking about his apartment in Columbus and its bare necessities. As Rose hugged him and led him into her living room, Angus thought about Etta and felt ill at ease about being alone with Rose. He doffed his straw hat and winter parka and spotted a miniature metal xylophone in the corner of the living room, next to it a mound of children's toys and stuffed animals.

"Looks like you have a busy little boy," he said.

"Not very cooperative about putting his toys away," Rose said and pointed to Angus' straw hat lying askew on the sofa. "You actually wear that thing in the middle of winter?"

"My good luck charm," Angus said as he sat on the edge of the sofa. "I read the mouse story in the *Examiner.*"
~~~~~

Rose looked down and studied the back of her hand, then back to Angus.

"Mr. Sewell is worried the Health Department will shut us down for a food safety violation," she said and looked past Angus at the toys piled in the corner. "He's concerned about the coffee shop being closed if we have to do any kitchen remodeling."

"I don't blame him," Angus said. "People are fickle."

"We'd have to close until spring," Rose said. "He's worried about our regular customers canceling their room reservations."

"Restaurants close all the time to remodel," Angus said. "I think people understand..."

"But this is different. Those people – that Thomson guy and his wife – are going to sue us!" Rose furrowed her brow. "Besides... I think it's a scam. Something like that just doesn't happen... not in a kitchen like ours."

"I think you're right... but it *has* happened. Restaurants have been blackmailed by people who plant things in food and try to bilk money out of the owner." Angus brushed his hand through his hair. "What's your chef say?"

"He thought I was accusing him about the mouse… he got pissed and resigned."

"Was it his fault?" Angus said.

"I have no clue. The *Examiner* called and talked with Mr. Sewell. His response was 'no comment' until we have time to review the facts. Can you help us get through this mess?"

Having been through two extensive Health Department certifications at the Club over the past year, Angus knew how to fend off food handling issues.

"You have to play their game," Angus said. "Just do what they say and they'll back off."

"Maybe you could… talk with the Health Department guy tomorrow? I know Mr. Sewell would appreciate it," Rose said.

"I'm sure Mr. Sewell knows all about that stuff," Angus said.

"It would be doing us both a huge favor if you would stay a few days and help," Rose said.

Angus lifted his hands, tented them over his nose, considered.

"Ange," Rose said. "Mr. Sewell said he would be glad to pay you for your time."

How ironic, Angus thought. Rose had always been so independent and self-sufficient, but now she was asking *him* to help *her*? Had her botched marriage completely deflated her ego to the point where she was *asking* now instead of *telling*? Angus felt a pang of loyalty to Charlie Sewell. It would be more than a concession to Rose, he decided, it would be a gesture of appreciation to Charlie for all the things he had done to help him.

"I won't take any money," Angus said. "Mr. Sewell has been very good to me."

Rose cocked her head toward the hallway leading off the living room.

"Aidan's fussing… he wants to get up," she said and headed down the hallway.

Returning with Aidan – sucking his thumb and bundled in her arms – Rose nestled the boy against her shoulder and patted his back as she said to Angus, "Would you like to hold him?"

"I don't have much experience with babies," he said.

Rose grinned as she passed Aidan to Angus.

"Sit down with him while I get us something to drink," she said.

Whether it was Aidan coming full awake or the change in position, he resisted being handed off from his mother's comforting arms and bellowed, "No!"

"He reminds me of you," Rose said. "He knows what he wants."

"Trust me," Angus said. "When he has a little brother or sister to pick on..."

Suddenly, Aidan lurched back and slipped out of Angus' arms, nearly falling to the floor. As Angus held him tighter, Aidan flailed his arms, striking Angus squarely on the nose. Tears welling and nearly dropping Aidan as he squirmed to get out of his grasp, Angus thrust him at Rose.

"Uh-h... you better take him," he said.

As Rose cuddled Aidan, Angus donned his parka and straw hat, waved goodbye and left.

6. A WINK AND A SMILE

Angus sauntered into the Inn Monday morning and hurried to the kitchen to see a solemn, thickset man holding court. Under the man's gray suit coat with a health department logo on the breast pocket and a badge pinned just above the logo, he wore a zippered black sweater over a black tie on a white shirt. Busy leafing through a dog-eared manual, the inspector didn't notice Angus enter the kitchen. Standing near the man, notepad in hand, Rosemary motioned for Angus to approach as the inspector proceeded with his officious commentary.

"I hate to write you up, Miss Gracewood," he said. "But this kitchen is pretty sad. You've got at least five violations."

Before Rose could introduce Angus, the inspector turned to him and said, "You got business here, bud?"

"I'm sorry, Mr. Humply. This is Chef Angus McCrory," Rose said and turned to Angus. "Angus, meet Mr. Humply with the city Health Department."

After the slightest of nods to Angus, the inspector made several hurried notations on his clipboard. When he looked up, his left eye twitched at the corner of his thin dour face.

"McCoy, huh? I hope you know something about running a kitchen."

"It's *McCrory*… Angus Mc…"

"McCrory? You kin to that detective over at City Hall?"
"Rob McCrory's my brother. He's…"

"Tell ya' what bud… I'm gonna let you off easy," Humply said and turned to Rose. "I'm giving you a warning for improper food handling, cooler temperatures too high and personal hygiene deficiency on one of your workers."

"You said five violations… that's only three," Angus said.

"Don't wise-off bud, I ain't finished."

Humply stepped over to the gas range and peered into the vent hood.

"This hood isn't working right. One of the fans is busted."

"I'll get right on it, Mr. Humply," Angus said.

"You need new floor mats and a new mop bucket, too. Don't see how anyone figures you can have a clean floor with a filthy damned mop bucket."

"We'll replace them today," Angus said.

Humply slammed his clipboard on the counter, smiled, his left eye twitching.

"The good news is, I don't see no signs of vermin… as of yet," Humply said.

"We've never seen that, Mr. Humply," Rose said.

"You get vermin in here and I'll give you a red sticker," Humply huffed.

Humply's eye twitched again as he donned his heavy winter parka.

"So Robby's your brother, huh? Don't make 'em any better than him."

"No sir, they sure don't," Angus said, wryly.

"OK… ya' got two weeks," Humply barked and stalked out of the kitchen.

As the inspector disappeared, a man dressed in kitchen garb emerged from Chef Byron's former office. Rose turned to Angus and said, "This is Cliff Williams. He's in charge of the kitchen since our chef quit."

Angus extended his hand to Cliff. "I guess you have your hands full."

"Plenty to do," Cliff said. "If you'll excuse me, gotta prep for lunch."

Angus nodded to Cliff and dropped his straw hat on the counter.

"Coffee... or whiskey?" Rose said.

"Yes," Angus said.

Rose added cream and sugar to her cup and took a sip.

"I hope your hat brings us good luck," she said. "I don't trust that inspector."

"What about all the citations?"

"I didn't know about them," Rose said.

"I can get it all fixed in a few days," Angus said.

"What about that personal hygiene problem in the kitchen?" Rose asked

"I spotted the guy when I walked through the door. Apron… shoes… full of grease. Do you know his name?"

"Clarence… Clarence Dickey," Rose said. "He works for Cliff."

"I'll send him home and tell him what I expect when he comes back tomorrow."

"We can't miss our *Winter Festival* event on Saturday," Rose said. "I've already sent out the flyers. We have an ad scheduled in the newspaper over the weekend... and..."

"I'll have things good to go," Angus said. "Stop worrying."

"What about the floor mats... and that hood vent?"

"Rose... relax and let me handle it."

"I'm worried about the food handling."

"I'll handle it, Rose. I know what to do."

"Will you let me know how much... ?"

"I'll have something for you by Wednesday," Angus assured.

"What about the cooler problem?"

"Rose... *stop.*"

"Alright... just... let me know if I can help, OK?"

~~~~~

Angus' eyes followed Rose as she pushed open the two-way kitchen door and disappeared into the coffee shop. Putting his hands on his hips, it struck him that Rose seemed very different – less sure or herself – tentative and anxious. He turned his attention back to the kitchen and surveyed its state of disrepair. Not only was it seriously outdated but also not nearly well enough equipped for cost-effective meal production. Engrossed in his assessment, Angus didn't notice that Mr. Sewell had entered the kitchen until he tapped Angus on the shoulder and said, "I hear you met the honorable Mr. Wink Humply."

"Oh yes... Rose told me all about the *Winkster.*"

"I can't thank you enough for pitching in to help us," Charlie said.

"Few days, I'll have everything in good shape. Might need a little money to make some fixes," Angus said.

"Work with Rosemary," Charlie said. "She'll get you what you need."
~~~~~

~~~~~

Rosemary's office was small and tidy. Two shelves of a glass étagère were jammed with photographs. On the center shelf sat a picture of a young boy dressed in a snowsuit. Recognizing it was Aidan, Angus picked up the picture for closer inspection as Rose walked through the door.

"I see you found my rogues gallery," she said. "If you look hard enough, you might find yourself in one of those pictures… and Bernie, too."

"Cute picture of Aidan," Angus said as he replaced the framed photograph on the shelf. "If I didn't know better, I'd swear he was your little brother."

"What do you think about the kitchen?" Rose said as she sat behind her desk and motioned for Angus to take a seat.

"Besides all the stuff on the citation, I found a tiny hole in a corner of the storage pantry window – it was out of sight at the bottom of the window. I fixed it… but can't say a mouse didn't get in there."

"For God's sake," Rose said.

"The only real bad news is that you need a new range," Angus said.

"A new range could cost more than ten thousand dollars. We'll have to wait on that until next year."

"I saw a ton of items in the food pantry," Angus said. "Who handles the ordering?"

"Bernie. She works with someone in Lima."

"I took the liberty of checking on your table linens," Angus said. "Based on the table count in the coffee shop, you're way overloaded."

"Chef Byron let Bernie handle it. It would be helpful if you talked to her," Rose said, stood and beckoned for Angus to follow her out the door and down the corridor.

"She's in her office, I'm sure she'd love to see you."
~~~~~

~~~~~

When Rose and Angus entered Bernie's office, she jumped up, embraced Angus and pressed against him. Rose frowned as Angus quickly pulled back. Though always attractive, Angus thought Bernie looked too dressy in her rich navy blue blazer with white pearl buttons. Her thick blond tresses cut in a blunt bob just under her jawline framed her round face.

"Rose told me you were going to be here," Bernie bubbled. "All that mouse business… the chef walking out… you're a godsend."

As Rose stepped back toward the office door, she said, "I asked Angus to let you fill him in on some of our operations. You mind talking with him while I meet with Mr. Sewell?" Rose turned to Angus. "We're preparing to meet with your brother tomorrow morning on that stupid mouse investigation."

As Rose left Bernie's office, Bernie plopped down in her chair and rolled her eyes; they were red and inflamed.

"I think your previous chef wasn't minding the store," Angus said. "Looks to me like you're overloaded with inventory… food and linens."

Bernie pushed back, tapped her pencil on the desk.

"The chef had a drinking problem," she said. "I set up annual food purchasing plans but he ignored them and bought whatever he wanted. Linens… we were always running out at the last minute and I had to scramble."

"Doesn't the Inn do its own laundry?" Angus asked.

"Our slouch housekeeper never kept up… I was always ordering emergency linen service."

"Who are you working with?"

"A Mr. Gardini," Bernie said. "He calls on us for our food and linens… he's been great."

Angus nodded, sat back in his chair.
~~~~~

"You surprised me when you told me you'd gotten married... and divorced," Angus said.

"I made out pretty good," Bernie said. "Did you get my check?"

"All tucked away, thanks."

Bernie stood, moved from behind her desk and sidled over to Angus. A whiff of her Satin Blush catching him off guard, Angus edged back as Bernie whispered, "I own my own place and I'd love to get with you while you're here."

Before Angus could reply, Bernie's phone rang. Seconds later, she hung up and smirked at Angus. "Miss Rose would like to speak with you before her big meeting tomorrow.

As Angus turned to leave, Bernie scribbled on a piece of paper and handed it to him.

Angus glanced at the note: *BW - 218 S. Park St. 509-7591.*

"I'm not busy tonight... or any night except Friday," she said.

His pulse rising, Angus nodded.

"I'd love for you to come over for dinner," Bernie said.

Angus stepped to Bernie's office door and stopped. "Maybe next week," he said.

Bernie winked. "Don't be a stranger."

~~~~~

After Angus disappeared through the door, Bernie locked it, returned to her desk, opened the secret zippered pocket on the inside of her new *Prada* black calfskin leather purse, extracted a plastic zip-pouch and arranged a long line of coke on her credenza. She rolled up a crispy ten-dollar bill into a straw, put one end in her nose, the other end at the tip of the line and snorted it in one long breath. The coke's glorious euphoria engulfed her. She'd need to impose on JoJo for more... and take care of him in bed. She closed her eyes and thought about getting together with Angus. On an impulse, she opened the most recent bank
~~~~~

statement for her account at Huntington Bank, and was shocked to see the balance at $9,895.99. How had it gotten so low? The last time she'd checked, the balance was nearly $13,000.00. There *had* to be an error! She would check with the Huntington and clear up the obvious mistake on their part.

~~~~~

Ambling down the hall, Angus pocketed Bernie's note, entered Rose's office and as he strolled over to her desk, he sensed Rose was irritated.

"I didn't appreciate that welcome you got from Bernie," Rose said.

Taken aback by Rose's edgy tone, Angus said, "Bernie's just being Bernie."

"Bernie can be *Bernie* when she's not in this office working," Rose said.

"Don't blame me," Angus said. "Talk to her."

"Was she helpful?" Rose asked, her tone gruff.

"My only concerns are with the food inventory and the linens," Angus said. "You might want to review those with her."

"I appreciate your advice, but until this mouse issue gets resolved, I have to let people do their jobs," Rose said. "

Gesturing toward the door, Rose said, "I don't mean to be rude, but I have to pull things together for tomorrow. Mr. Sewell wants to meet with our attorney and I have to get home to feed Aidan."

7. THE INQUEST

Tuesday morning, Rose welcomed the Inn's attorney, Lewis (Speed) Watkins, and his assistant, Nora Cronin, to Charlie Sewell's office to discuss the Inn's defense of the Thompson lawsuit.
~~~~~

"This is not going to be much fun," Charlie began, glancing from Rose to Lewis Watkins. "The *Examiner* is all over this and I was told off the record that the Thompsons submitted a statement to the newspaper it plans to run tomorrow morning."

"Can't they delay it for a day or two?" Rosemary asked.

"The paper doesn't have any choice," Speed explained. "The last thing it needs is a bias complaint from Thompson's attorney."

"What are we looking at?" Charlie asked.

"Well, for starters," Speed said, "We have to get your kitchen's detailed procedures for how your chef prepared his chili."

"I have the info," Angus said. "Looks like he was the final link in the preparation."

Angus spread the contents of the file out on the center of the conference table.

"The prep cooks sauté the ground beef, onion, peppers, and the usual spices," Angus said.

"That's it?" Rose asked.

"He probably added some secret ingredients he didn't want anyone to know about so he didn't make any note of it. That's typical of chefs."

"We'll need the exact written procedures for the meat and produce ordering and storage. We want to know how everything's handled," Speed said.

"Here it is," Angus said and tossed the manila folder across the table to Rosemary. "I have to give a lot of credit to your ex-chef… he did a good job of record keeping."

Rose opened the folder, scanned the record and passed it to Speed who passed it to Nora Cronin. "Better make a couple copies of this… and mark it as evidence," Speed said to Nora and continued. "Angus, if we end up in court... you might have to testify about the kitchen procedures. There's always a loophole the prosecutors look for."

"When was the last Health Department inspection of the kitchen?" Nora asked.

"Other than yesterday morning, the last one was before Christmas," Charlie Sewell said. "We got a clean bill of health." Pointing to a document, Charlie continued. "Here's the Health Department's report. The only mention was a missing light bulb in the food prep area. I was there when Byron replaced it."

"Yesterday… did the Health Department say anything about any evidence of rodents?" Speed asked.

"Mr. Humply said he didn't see any signs of vermin," Rose said as she and Angus exchanged knowing glances.

"I will say," Angus paused, "I fixed a small hole in the supply room window. But… I didn't see any trace of mouse droppings."

"What proof do the Thompson's have about finding that mouse in the chili?" Speed asked.

"The woman screamed like a maniac and pointed to it," Rose said. "Robby and his assistant confiscated the chili bowl on the spot."

"I've checked it out," Speed said. "There's a couple of documented previous incidents with some of the fast food chains. Only one case went to trial in Chicago and the judge threw it out. It'll be the Thompson's word against ours."

"I know Robby has a forensics friend in Cincinnati at TruTech Labs," Speed said. "I'll ask Robby to call him and set up a meeting for next week. Let's see what he says and go from there. That alright with you, Mr. Sewell?"

"Do we really need to call in Robby? Won't that be more fodder for the newspaper if we tip our hand that we think it's a criminal matter?" Charlie said.

"We need to load every gun we have, Charlie. That's the best way to let Thompson know we aren't going to roll over and let him try to blackmail us without a fight," Speed said.

"Don't waste any time," Charlie said. "We're already getting room cancellations."

Charlie turned to Angus and said, "Are you going to be available to help us for a while?"

"For a week or so," Angus said. "But I have to get back to the club and work on our new menu for our reopening in February."

"Let's break for now," Rose said. "Angus, would you meet me in my office?"

As the group filed out of Charlie Sewell's office, Charlie turned to Angus. His face colored with anxiety, he said, "You and Rose keep me posted."

~~~~~

Retreating to her office with Angus, Rose wrung her hands and turned to him. "I know I was rude to you yesterday about Bernie," she said. "But I'm worried about her. She comes in late and leaves early. She's moody... and not friendly, either."

"I think she's just stressed out about business," Angus said.

"I can appreciate that," Rose said. "This whole thing... I feel swamped."

As Rose sat heavily in her desk chair, her phone rang. She motioned for Angus to stay and pushed the speaker button.

"I hate to bother you at work, but are you coming home soon?" Marcy said.

"I'm in the middle of an important meeting right now, I…"

Before she could finish, Marcy broke in.

"Aidan threw up… all over the floor."

Rose jumped to her feet and glanced anxiously at Angus.

"And now he's wedged himself under the sofa and I can't get him to come out," Marcy said.
~~~~~

Rose pinched her eyebrows. "I'll be home in ten minutes," she said, rushed to get her coat, shooting Angus a wan grin as she bounded out the door.

"Aren't you glad you don't have a two-year-old?" she said.

~~~~~

Rose scrambled into the living room where Marcy stood sobbing. "I'm sorry I had to bother you at work," Marcy said, "But I didn't know what to do."

Hearing Aidan whimpering, Rose spotted his foot sticking out from under the edge of the sofa. She knelt down in the drying vomit on the carpeting and tugged gently on Aidan's foot.

"Aid… it's Mommy. Please come out from under there," Rose coaxed.

Aidan's crying turned into a muffled scream: "No!"

When Rose pulled harder on his leg, Aidan's violent kick struck her hand.

"Stop kicking me and come out from under there right now!" Rose ordered.

"No! No!"

"Please come out, Aid… Mommy will fix pancakes for dinner… they're your favorite…"

As Aidan kicked his feet again, Rose stood and turned to Marcy.

"Help me move the sofa," Rose said.

Together, Rose and Marcy struggled to lift the sofa and moved it to see Aidan curled up covering his head with his hands. As Rose lifted him into her arms, Marcy stepped back.

"I'm sorry I had to bother you at work, but…" Marcy's words trailed off as she dropped her eyes.
~~~~~

"You didn't *bother* me," Rose said. "You did the right thing. I couldn't get along without you."

~~~~~

Aidan slept soundly after Rose had taken his temperature and was relieved to see he didn't have a fever. She turned him over to Marcy the next morning, assuring her that Aidan was OK and drove to the Inn to meet Angus.

As predicted by Charlie, the *Fountain Point Examiner's* headline about the mouse-in-the-chili incident blazed on the front page:

LOCAL COUPLE FILES $10-MILLION LAWSUIT AGAINST THE INN AT MARY'S GATE

Blanche and Harrison Thompson
Claim Mouse Found in Inn's Chili

Rosemary folded up the newspaper, slammed it on the breakfast table and turned to Angus.

"This is a complete crock of crap!"

8. GOIN' DOWN SLOW

The morning after the *Examiner* story, the Inn's Reservations Manager, Theresa Loar, fielded what she hoped was the last of the morning's calls to cancel room reservations. As she poured her third cup of coffee, Charles Sewell strode into the lobby, cut the angle across to the registration desk and snatched the reservations list off the workspace next to Theresa's computer. Theresa could all but hear the gurgle of blood rushing to darken Charlie's face.

"You've got to be kidding!" Charlie snapped and recounted the cancellations. Slapping the list down on Theresa's workspace, he shook his head. "We have forty-four rooms to rent! Thirty-nine booked as of
~~~~~

last week... twenty-seven cancellations as of this morning!" Charlie scowled at Theresa. "Give me an hourly update."

~~~~~

Friday afternoon, Charlie Sewell popped a handful of antacid tablets into his mouth, fingered the recap of the Inn's reservations and glowered across his desk at Bernie, Rose and Angus.

"We're in trouble," he said. "We're down to only four bookings for the weekend. They've already checked in – fifteen guests *counting* kids."

"I personally delivered a basket of fresh fruit to each of their rooms, and left a complimentary breakfast coupon, " Rose said. "Should we comp their dinners, too?"

"I don't want to send a complete panic message," Charlie said. "They may hear something about the mouse lawsuit, but we'll have to see how it plays out."

They sat in silence as Charlie tapped his pencil on the desk.

"Angus... what about the kitchen?"

"Assuming the guests eat all their meals in the coffee shop, how many walk-ins do you think there'll be?" Angus asked.

"Just a guess, but I'd say maybe twenty-five in addition to the Inn guests," Charlie said. "Pub might get some action... Nikko does pretty good on weekends."

"I looked over the menu," Angus said. "There're too many entrées to deliver quality. I'd clip a sheet of specials – maybe five entrées – to the menu and make the price extra attractive."

Charlie stretched his neck to one side then the other and turned to Angus.

"When you have to be back to work in Columbus?" he said.

"Monday or Tuesday," Angus said.

"I don't want to be presumptuous, but is there any way you can work on them here?" Charlie asked, his tone plaintive.
~~~~~

Thinking about Etta, Angus looked past Charlie for a moment. Other than playing piano in the pub for which Charlie had paid him very generously, Charlie had never asked Angus for a favor. He considered Charlie's request then, "I'll stay for another couple of days."

Rose opened her notebook to several items she had written down and turned to Angus.

"I have a three column by five-inch ad space reserved for tomorrow morning's *Examiner*," she said to Angus. "I asked Cliff to pull together the kitchen inventory. I can make up the ad for your specials and drop it off by their five o'clock deadline."

~~~~~

Steeling himself to the tedious task of auditing food inventory, Angus trudged behind Rose to the kitchen to review the food items he could cobble together for the menu specials. Plunking down at Chef Byron's clunky desk in his kitchen office, Angus greeted Cliff Williams as he entered Byron's former office and handed Angus a bundle of loose papers.

Rose sat on the edge of her wobbly folding chair, hunched her elbows on the desk and watched Angus trace his fingers down the inventory sheets. Leafing through its seven pages, Angus shook his head and turned to Cliff.

"There's more stuff on here than I keep on hand at the country club," he said. "Half of it's crapola… eleven half-gallons of pure maple syrup?… nine gallons of olive oil?… seven gallons of vinegar?… two quarts of vanilla extract… ?"

Angus tossed the clipboard aside and turned to Cliff.

"What's in the cooler?" Angus said.

"Fourteen whole fresh chickens, ten dozen eggs, ham, country sausage, about eight pounds of bacon, five different frozen veggies..."

"Fresh produce and fruit?"
~~~~~

"Got a delivery this morning… potatoes, mushrooms, lettuce, peppers, tomatoes and onions…."

Angus reached for a note pad on the corner of the desk and drew up a menu featuring:

- *The Famous Inn 'Wedge' w/Blue Cheese & Bacon Bits*
- *Rosemary Roasted Half-chicken and Fettuccini In Cream Sauce with Fresh Vegetables*

He handed the pad to Rose.

"I didn't know we had a *Famous Wedge,"* Rose said.

"You do now," Angus said.

Bouncing to his feet, Cliff asked, "What about tonight?"

"Tonight, we'll handle whoever shows up by improvising," Angus said, glanced at his co-conspirators then held his gaze on Rose.

"You ready to rock-and-roll?"

"Will you come by and have a glass of wine with me… after the coffee shop closes?" Rose said.

Thinking about Etta, Angus first instinct was to say *no,* but after a long day, *what could it hurt?*

~~~~~

Before Angus could touch Rose's doorbell – the door flung open and Rose put her finger to her lips to shush Angus and wave him in.

"I just got Aidan quieted down," Rose whispered. "He's been upset since I got home."

Rose led Angus into her living room and motioned for him to be seated.

"What upset him?" Angus said.

"He didn't like the pasta I fixed him for dinner," Rose said. "By the time I made scrambled eggs, he was in such a bad mood, he wouldn't touch them."
~~~~~

"Finicky... like you," Angus said.

"I'm going to check on him," Rose said.

She whispered over her shoulder as she stepped toward the bedroom hallway, "I set out a bottle of red for us... do you mind opening it?"

Meandering into Rose's kitchen, Angus picked up the bottle of Robert Mondavi Cabernet '89, peeled off the foil cap and pulled the cork. He heard Aidan whining as he filled the two glasses Rose had set out. Returning to the living room to see Aidan slamming his hand on Rose's arm as Rose sat rocking him, she nodded toward the coffee table. "Might as well put mine down," she said as she nestled Aidan's head into her neck.

As if in a cloistered monastery, no words were exchanged while Aidan fussed until Rosemary nodded to the toy pile and whispered to Angus: "Will you hand me that stuffed monkey... he usually likes that."

Angus retrieved the monkey and handed it to Rose. Before Angus could return to the sofa, Aidan threw the monkey on the floor and burst into a raging fit... his fists slamming into Rose's shoulder. Hoping to help Rose calm Aidan down, Angus picked up the toy xylophone and wooden mallet and pinged out the tune to "Old MacDonald Had A Farm." As he played, Aidan gradually stopped wailing, wriggled out of his mother's arms and scampered over to Angus.

"Me!... Me!" he yelled.

Angus handed Aidan the mallet and held the xylophone while Aidan ping-ponged over the metal tone bars. Squealing with delight, Aidan ping-ponged until Rose intervened.

"Aidan... that's enough. It's time for bed," she said.

Rose stood as Aidan ran toward Angus and bellowed back at his mother: "*NO! NO!*" ... and hoisted the xylophone mallet in the air: *"ME! ME!"*

As Aidan banged away on the xylophone, Angus handed Rose her glass of wine and nodded at Aidan.

"Nothing like a man and his music," Angus said.

As they sipped their wine and watched Aidan's wonderment, Rose – in contrast to her ruffled angst in Charlie's office that afternoon – appeared relaxed. Twenty minutes later – when Aidan yawned and slumped on the floor – Rose picked him up and hurried with him to his bedroom. She returned moments later to the living room, her face radiating contentment.

"I hope you realize that you are now in charge of Aidan's tantrums," she said.

"As long as he doesn't want me to make a thunderbolt… I'm cool," Angus said.

Rose broke into a laugh but quickly stifled it so as not to waken Aidan.

"I knew that would come back to haunt me," she said, pulled Angus off of the sofa and cradled his face in her hands. When she kissed him, Angus could feel her body tremble as she pushed tighter against him.

Though immersed in their lingering kiss, he flushed and finally pulled back. His thoughts a muddle, Angus donned his coat and said, "I'll be in early tomorrow morning." Rose put her hand on his back as he eased toward the door and gently stroked it as she said, "I can't tell you how much I appreciate your helping me."

~~~~~

At home in his old bedroom, Angus stretched out on the bed and thought about what had happened in Rose's living room. Had he misread her intentions for inviting him to come by for a *glass of wine?* When he and Rose had talked on Christmas Eve, he'd made no secret of his bitter feelings toward her. He couldn't deny that as much as Rose's kiss had caught him off guard, it lingered with him even now and though he didn't feel guilty about it, he felt unsettled.

As Angus flipped off his reading light, his last thought before closing his eyes was that Etta would be back from Sicily soon; they would get back together and move on.
~~~~~

~~~~~

Saturday evening's crowd was nowhere near Charlie Sewell's hopes. By 8:30, the last couple from the Inn's guest roster had finished eating. As was his custom on Saturday nights – and in his most cordial manner – Charlie bid the pair goodnight and went directly to the kitchen.

"Goddammit," he roared. "I thought that newspaper ad would spark some business. What was the meal count?"

Angus flipped through the kitchen copies of the guest checks.

"Twenty-seven," he said and handed the copies to Charlie.

"At this rate, we might as well surrender to that goddamned mouse," Charlie muttered as he stalked out of the kitchen.

9. MOOD INDIGO

Following the dismal weekend weather and sparse crowd at the Inn – Charlie entered his office and glanced at the blueberry muffins in the warmer basket left on his worktable by the staff.

"Where are Rose and Bernie?" Charlie said to Angus.

Before the echo of his question died out, they entered.

"We're ready," Rose said as she took a seat next to Angus at Charlie's worktable, Bernie on the other side of Angus.

Angus was taken aback by Bernie's garb; a cropped leatherette jacket busy with zippers, and high-heeled leather biker boots to match. Bernie's complexion looked washed out, her makeup blotchy, her lipstick uneven. As she sat down next to Angus, she whispered, "I want to get together for a drink before you go back to Columbus. Wednesday after work?"

Glancing at Rose to see her frown, he felt a rush of angst.

Charlie sat down at his desk, shook six antacid tablets into his hand, downed them, opened a folder of papers and handed one page to each of the three sitting across from him.
~~~~~

"We had the worst weekend I've seen in over twenty years," he said.

Without waiting for them to digest the report, Charlie hunched up on his elbows and talked through the details.

"In case there's any doubt – not counting overhead or the cost of that newspaper ad –we would've been better off if we had closed the whole Inn all last week after that goddamned mouse fiasco." Turning to Angus, Charlie said, "What's your guess on the amount of food we wasted?"

"I don't know your costs, but based on what we buy at the Country Club, I'd say just food… at least three hundred dollars," Angus said.

"I can check our supplier invoices," Bernie said. "But I doubt it would be that much."

Charlie raised his eyebrows and turned to Bernie.

"While you're at it, you and Rose work on a list of payroll cuts. We can't keep going on willy-nilly."

Turning back to Angus, Charlie said, "Figure out a minimum menu for the next two weeks… just the basics… and give Bernie a list of what she needs to order… but keep it tight!"

As Angus turned to Bernie and said, "I'll have the list for you by tomorrow," she was blotting her upper lip with a tissue.

Charlie munched on more antacids and turned to Rose. "Tell Gracious she's got two maids to help her until we see where we're going. And cancel any advertising we have scheduled."

Her nose red and swollen, Bernie blotted her nose again and said, "I'll handle it… it's only some radio time."

"Just to remind you, Mr. Sewell," Rose said, "We have the meeting at ten tomorrow morning with Robby and his assistant, Boris Detman. Robby is bringing his forensic friend from Cincinnati, Zach Barton."

"We'll meet right here in my office," Charlie said and looked at Bernie.

"You don't need to be in that meeting," he said. "I want you to get busy on a new operating budget with the worst assumptions. Give me pro-forma occupancy rates as low as sixty percent and tell me what we need to cut to break even... and factor in the note payments to the Logan County Citizens Bank."

~~~~~

Seated alone in her locked office after the meeting, Bernie made notes about Charlie's directives. She opened her supplier file and scribbled a note to herself to call JoJo and cancel the advertising schedule on WOFP. She would also have to tell him to hold all pending food orders from State Wholesale until she got the new list of items from Angus for the menu changes. She sat back, pinched her eyebrows and pulled out JoJo's most recent supply of cocaine. She sniffed two lines and muttered, "Screw you, Rose and your whole bullshit act." She felt a tickle on her upper lip. Checking her image in her cosmetic mirror, she saw a trace of blood at the edges of her nose and swore under her breath at the nagging cold she'd been fighting.

10. MAMMALIA RODENTIA

Promptly at ten o'clock, Robby introduced Zach Barton to Lewis Watkins, Charlie, Angus and Rose. Robby's assistant detective, Boris Detman, placed a sheaf of papers marked *Evidence Report* on the conference table.

"Zach and I talked over the weekend," Robby said. "I told him as much as we know about the mouse incident and the lawsuit. He's agreed to help us."

Zach nodded as Robby continued, "As you know, we collected the specimens from the crime site... excuse me... the *alleged* crime scene."

Everyone exchanged nods, as Boris produced a document and held it up.
~~~~~

"We've confirmed the identity of the foreign object the claimant says she found in her soup. Technically speaking, it's the body of a *Mammalia-Rodentia…* specifically, *Muridae Pennslyvanicus.*"

"Could you give us a layman's description?" Rose asked.

"A Meadow Vole," Detman said.

"Common field mouse," Robby clarified.

"So… it really *was* a mouse?" Rose said. "It couldn't have come out of our kitchen! We've never seen any evidence of one... ever!"

"What else did you find out about the mouse?" Zach Barton asked.

"That's all we know," Detman said. "It looks like the mouse drowned in the soup. It was covered with a residue we've identified as chili. As best we can tell, the residue is very common with what most chefs use in their chili recipes."

"I assume the Thompsons have this information?" Speed asked.

"They've asked for our report," Robby said. "We'll have to give it to his attorney."

They exchanged glances around the table. "Do you still have all the evidence intact?" Zach asked.

"We got the critter on ice over at the morgue," Detman said.

"Are there any restrictions on further analysis?" Zach asked.

"As long as it's within the law and rules of evidence," Robby said.

Zach studied the back of his hand and leaned forward.

"The mouse could have been placed in the chili seconds before Mrs. Thompson discovered it," he said. "I'll take the mouse back to Cincinnati and run a few more definitive tests. I'm confident that the results will take all the guesswork out of things."

"What about that waitress… that Susie… what's her last name?" Detman said.

"Are you kidding? Rose retorted. "That girl is the sweetest, gentlest young lady you'll ever find. Other than the minute or so when I looked away, there was no one near the Thompsons after Susie put the chili on their table. She's said she didn't see anything. I asked her ten times: *'Did you see anything in the chili?'* She swears she didn't."

"What about the old chef?" Detman asked.

"Byron Lovelace? I don't think so," Charlie said.

"But he blew up and quit when I asked him about it," Rose said.

"Byron had his shortcomings," Charlie said. "But in the five years he was our chef, I never knew him to be anything but honest."

"So… where do we go from here?" Angus asked.

"I'd like to arrange for a transfer of the deceased mouse to my lab in Cincinnati," Zach said.

As the meeting adjourned, Charlie pulled Rose aside.

"I like the way you're handling this… stay on it."

~~~~~

As Rose pondered the meeting, her phone rang. Theresa at the front desk.

"I'm glad I caught you," she said, "Your babysitter called in a panic."

"What?..."

"Something about a gas leak... just get home right away."

Arriving home to see a fire truck parked in the drive, Rose burst into her living room. A fireman in uniform was playing with Aidan. Rose rushed to greet a tearful Marcy.

"What in God's name happened," Rose said as she pulled Aidan to her.

"After Aidan got up from his nap… he wanted to play with his xylophone. I went to the kitchen to get him a glass of juice… and…"
~~~~~

Marcy shuddered... "... and when I came back to give it to him, I smelled gas."

"From where?" Rose sputtered.

"Aidan was pointing to the fireplace... luckily, I knew instantly where the gas smell was coming from. I glanced over and saw that the knob was missing from the gas log starter valve." Marcy broke into tears. "Aidan had it in his hand and... I tried to get it away from him but he had a complete melt down and wouldn't give it to me... I... I just grabbed him and... grabbed the phone... and... ran outside and called 911."

As Rose recoiled, Marcy pointed to the uniformed man standing quietly listening to Marcy's anguished account of what had happened. "Mr. Marmon... thank God, he was here in five minutes."

Marmon stepped forward and said, "Everything's under control Miss Gracewood. I replaced the gas-valve knob and took your son and your sitter to the station while some of the boys checked out the house. Nothing to worry about," Red said. "Your boy sure had fun traipsing around on that old fire truck at the engine house."

Rose gathered Marcy and Aidan in her arms. A sense of guilt gripped Rose as she hugged them and said, "Thank God for you, Marcy."

~~~~~

Wednesday morning, Angus cruised into Rose's office and handed her his hand-written interim menu Charlie Sewell had requested.

"I thought you got good grades in penmanship," she said. "Sister Pauline would be disgraced."

"Maybe I should've been a doctor," Angus said. "Want me to translate?"

Rose looked up frowning.

"It would help... I have the worst headache."
~~~~~

Angus took the list from Rose's hand and sat down across from her.

Giving in to an impulse, Angus said, "I'll treat you to a drink in the Pub this evening… maybe that will help."

"If Aidan cooperates," Rose said quietly.

"Here's my simplified menu," Angus said. "Easiest thing to do is a winter buffet… light stuff. At dinner, I'd have a carving station for turkey breast and brisket… with some easy sauces like au jus and Dijon mustard."

Rose squeezed her temples, sat back and said, "What about the labor?"

"Cliff and Shirleen have been covering since Charlie laid-off one of Cliff's helpers... I don't know his full name. They call him '*Jack-rabbit.*'"

"That's Jack Clancy. He's on Bernie's payroll roster."

"I don't want to add to your headache, but..." Angus said.

"I don't know if I can handle many more *buts.*"

"I have to get back to Columbus."

Rose closed her eyes, sagged in her chair.

"Please… don't tell me that. Can't you get a few more emergency days off?"

"*Rose…* I have a *new* job! I have to have some new recipes when we fire up again at the club and I need to have them ready or my boss will be pissed."

An uncomfortable silence filled the room as Rose dropped her eyes.

"Selfish of me to ask… see you tonight in the Pub."

~~~~~

Disheartened by the reality that Angus would be leaving to return to Columbus, Rose read his menu ideas, pushed them aside and prepared to go home. As she reached for her coat, her phone jangled.
~~~~~

"This is Rose..."

"Bunny Carpenter here," the voice said. "I got your nomination for..." Rose heard a shuffle of papers as the mayor paused, "... that young lady... Sally...Merritt..." Rose heard more paper shuffling as the mayor paused again, "... Merriwell," Mayor Bunny said.

"Good morning Mrs. Mayor," Rose said. "Susie... *Merriman.*"

"You think she can handle our May Day Parade?"

"Definitely," Rose said. "Susie's very organized... and artistic."

"I'll get back to you with some meeting dates," Bunny interrupted. "We can jaw about it some more but far as I'm concerned, it's a done deal."

"She'll be thrilled."

"The Inn always has a big float for the parade," Bunny said. "We're counting on it again this year."

"We won't disappoint you Mrs. Mayor."

As Rose walked past the reception counter in the lobby to go home and fix Aidan's dinner, Theresa beckoned to her and handed her several telephone messages.

"Some messages there for Angus," Theresa said.

"I'll give them to him when I see him later," Rose said.

To be sure it wasn't urgent, Rose scanned the messages, frowned and tucked them into her purse.

~~~~~

Hoping Rose had been successful getting Aidan to bed, Angus arrived early to meet her at the Pub for a farewell drink.

Nikko leaned back against the bar and gestured to the piano.

"No one's played that piano since you were here at Christmas and Lady Rose collared you. She runs things like a pro... can't get away with giving out very many free drinks."
~~~~~

Angus sipped his Black Bush. "She's coming in to have a drink with me. Maybe she'll give you a special dispensation to comp her."

"I'll get my best people to chill up a New Zealand Marlborough. She likes Sauvignon Blanc," Nikko said.

Angus struck a quizzical pose and said, "Your *best people?*"

"That'd be me," Nikko said. "Play something before I die of boredom."

As Angus pitched the piano's protective cover to the side, he felt a pang of regret for having agreed to meet Rose for a drink. But one last drink with Rose would be a quickie. He'd get home, pack and leave early in the morning.

As Angus played a medley of blues tunes, he thought about Etta and played "Al Di La." Getting back with Etta was long overdue, he mused, until Rose entered the Pub. She looked refreshed and sharp, but with a hint of fatigue in her eyes. She'd pinned her hair up into a neat knot and wore short dangling earrings. Her pale yellow skirt flowed in rhythm with her stride; her radiance reminded Angus of a song he loved, "Summer Breeze."

"Glad you could make it," he said. Catching a flirtatious nod of her head, Angus played through a chorus of "Summer Breeze."

"Too bad it isn't summer… dead tonight," she said.

"You remember *Field of Dreams*, 'If you build it, they will come?'"

As Nikko approached – bearing a chill-fogged glass and a linen napkin-wrapped bottle of wine – Rose sat down at the piano bar. Nikko placed the glass on a cocktail napkin in front of her and poured a generous portion of her favorite vintage.

"*Saluté…*" Nikko said and nodded to Angus. "Marlborough, Sauvignon Blanc… Mr. Angus ordered it."

Rose lowered her eyes then looked up and spoke in a low tone. "Sorry I'm late. It took longer than usual to get Aidan settled down."

"How *is* the little music man?" Angus said.

Rose forced a smile. "I feel like I'm talking to a wall. He's so obsessed with that xylophone, he won't eat unless I promise to let him play it afterward."

"What's his doctor say?"

"He said he's a healthy little boy."

"Don't you think you should tell him about Aidan's behavior?"

"*Angus*...I told you what the doctor said. I'll handle it."

"That's just it, Rose... you can't be handling it if you keep on ignoring it. Why don't you face it and get him to a different doctor?"

"I appreciate your advice, but I'm doing the best I can!" Rose said, her tone sharp.

Turning to the keyboard, Angus fingered a lazy chord until Rose broke the tension.

"I love old Broadway musicals, especially *Man of La Mancha,*" she said. "'Impossible Dream' is my favorite song."

As Angus played her request and a medley of other love songs from Broadway hits, he thought about Etta Angus pushed away from the piano and pointed to a booth near the entrance by the foyer, he said, "Let's sit over there."

"You're a hopeless romantic," Rose said as she slid into the booth. "Where did you learn all of those love songs?"

Angus slipped into the booth next to Rose, keeping a generous space between them.

"Played a lot of weddings," he said. "How's your headache?"

"Gone, for now," Rose said. "But I spent the last two days wrangling with Bernie about the staff cuts... and all of that excess kitchen inventory."

"Was she friendly?" Angus asked.

"She's so irritable, I feel like I have to pry everything out of her." Rose swirled her glass around. "She wants to fire Gracious along with three of her maids and she blames the inventory mess on Byron."

"For crissakes… Bernie's good with numbers. Isn't she looking at them? How many maids does Gracious have?" Angus said.

"Eight… two part time. But only six on the payroll now."

As they sipped on their drinks, Rose said, "When Bernie showed me the kitchen payroll list, I saw Jack Clancy's name with an asterisk… the one Cliff calls *Jack-rabbit*. Bernie said he was laid off when Charlie put the two maids on leave before the remodeling last January."

"Did she say anything about Cliff?" Angus asked.

"I showed her the new menu and all she said was she'd order anything Cliff needed."

"Have you seen this year's operating budget?" Angus said.

"Charlie said he and Bernie are working on it and he'll review it with me when he revises things with our recommendations for the cuts."

"Charlie's so stressed out he looks like he's ready to keel over," Angus said.

"God forbid," Rose said and placed her hand on Angus' arm.

"Ange… I can't stay…Marcy is waiting to go home. We can go back to my house and have a drink."

Angus felt the tension rise from his back to his neck. He had told himself that the one quick drink with Rose was it. The thought of revisiting the scene of their kiss was more than he wanted to deal with.

"I better get home and pack," Angus said.

Rose squeezed Angus' arm. "I know… just one last goodbye drink… *please*? But I don't have any of that… what's that your drinking?"

Against his better judgment, Angus pledged to himself that he would have *one* goodbye drink and leave. He turned to Rose and said, "Black Bush… but I like beer, too."

Rose's house was lit up as though on exhibition. As Angus ambled onto Rose's porch, a tortured wail pierced the air. The door flew open. Harried and exasperated, her hair wild, eyes red and wet, Marcy flailed her arms in the direction of the living room where Rose was restraining Aidan and screaming: "Stop crying and give me that mallet right now!"

Angus pushed past Marcy into the house. Shards of shattered glass littered the coffee table. As he tried to intervene, Rose glowered at him.

"This is *not* your problem!" she shouted.

"I'm trying to help," Angus said and turned to Marcy. "What happened?"

"I tried to put Aidan to bed and he had a melt down," Marcy sobbed. "He took his xylophone mallet and smashed three of Rose's crystal candle sticks."

"I'll help you clean things up," Angus said as Rose wrested the mallet from Aidan's hand and threw it across the room.

"Do me a favor and hide this somewhere!" Rose bellowed.

"Rose… get a grip," Angus said.

"I don't have any grip *left*!" Rose cried.

"Let me take Aidan," Marcy said and lifted Aidan into her arms.

Squirming to free himself from Marcy's grasp, Aidan screamed, "No!" – clamped his mouth on Marcy's arm and bit into her flesh. Howling at the sight of blood blooming through her blouse sleeve, Marcy dropped the boy.

Rose jumped to Marcy's side and caught Aidan before he hit the floor. As she tried to control him, Aidan bit his own hand opening the skin. Seeing Aidan's bloody wound, Angus gasped, immobilized with panic.

"Angus!" Rose yelled. "Get a towel from the bathroom!"

Bounding into the bathroom, Angus slammed open the linen cupboard to find only bed sheets and pillow cases. He reached for the largest drawer, yanked on the metal pull and swore when it came off in his hand.

"Angus! Hurry up!" Rose shouted.

Prying the drawer open with his fingernails, Angus grabbed two large towels, rushed back into the living room, tossed one to Marcy and pressed the other one on Aidan's wound to stanch the bleeding. "Do you need a disinfectant...or something?" Angus panted.

"Get two gauze pads from the medicine cabinet and the antibiotic ointment," Rose ordered. "They're on the first shelf."

Angus bolted into the bathroom again, swung open the medicine cabinet, grabbed the pads and ointment and rushed back to Rose.

"Open one of those gauze pads and hold it so I can put some ointment on it," Rose said.

"*I'll* do it," Angus said.

Aidan wailed and writhed as Angus held the sterile gauze pad in the palm of his hand, took the tube of ointment, spread some of it on the gauze pad and applied it to Aidan's arm. At the touch of the gauze to his injury, Aidan pushed Angus' hand away and screamed, "No! No!"

"It's OK, Aid," Rose said. "We're fixing your boo-boo." Angus nodded to Marcy and handed the medicine to her. "Put this on your arm, too, Marce," he said and turned back to Rose as she said, "Bring in the box of Band-Aids from the bathroom... the ones with the little bunny rabbits."

After the half-hour it took for everyone to regain their composure, Angus stepped back to survey the scene and shook his head as Rose cradled Aidan in her arms and rocked him to sleep.

"Should I call a doctor?" he said.

"I can *handle* it," Rose said.

Angus glanced at Aidan and took a deep breath.

"I don't think Aidan is fine, I think there's something *really wrong.*"

Rose squinted at Angus.

"I'll try to remember that," she said sharply and turned to Marcy.

"Please go home, Marcy, we'll be fine," Rose said.

Suppressing her tears, Marcy donned her coat. At the door, she turned back to Rose. "I'm sorry… but I can't. I just can't do this anymore," she said blinking her tears away.

"Marcy… *wait*!" Rose pleaded.

"I'm sorry," Marcy repeated, shutting the door behind her with a soft click.

As Marcy left, Rose choked back tears, dropped her eyes and cradled Aidan.

"I apologize for getting so… angry…" her voice drifted off as she cuddled Aidan and wept silently.

Angus put his hand on Rose's shoulder.

"What about… Marcy?"

"I don't… know," Rose whispered. "I'll ask my mother to help until I find a new nanny."

Angus looked at Aidan and took a deep breath. "I think we should call it a night," he said.

Aidan sound asleep, Rose stopped rocking him. Her eyes watery, she narrowed them, knit her brow and said, "Before I left to come home from the Inn this evening, Theresa gave me a few messages for you," Rose said. "They're over there… in the side pocket of my purse."

Grabbing the pink message slips from Rose's purse, Angus sat on the sofa's edge and said, "I never think to check for messages."

"Maybe you should start checking," Rose said, her tone petulant. "You had three calls from someone named Etta."

"Etta?" Angus said.

Her eyes narrowing, Rose's mouth curled into a sour frown.

"I don't want to be nosy, but…" Rose said.

"Then don't be," Angus said, irritably.

Quietly rocking Aidan again, Rose glanced at her wristwatch. Looking up at Angus, her voice cracked. "It's nearly nine o'clock," she said. "If I don't get Aidan to bed, he'll be a mess in the morning."

11. WELCOME HOME

Etta met Angus at her door in a loose shorty nightshirt of bright green silk trimmed with satin. They kissed, embraced. As they parted, Etta put her finger on Angus' cheek and teased it in light circles.

"You look worn out," she said.

They moved in *pas de deux* to Etta's sofa, sat close and listened to the music Etta had chosen for their reunion… *Frank Sinatra's Greatest Love Songs.*

Etta filled two Picardie glasses with Santero Fragalino and handed one to Angus. Entwining their arms, they kissed and sipped the sparkling wine flavored with wild strawberries.

"Sweet," Angus said.

"Me or the strawberries?" Etta said.

"Both."

"I missed you," she said, "Tell me what you did while I was in Sicily."

"I got into a fight with a mouse."

Etta shot Angus a puzzled frown.

"My friends at home asked me to help out with a chili problem," Angus clarified. "Someone slipped a mouse into their chili recipe and all hell broke loose."

Etta sipped her Fragalino and said, "Your friends?"

"Where you called and left the messages," Angus said. "The Inn at Mary's Gate."

"Do your friends there involve any… *women*?"

Angus felt the blood rush to his face. Now, the guilt he hadn't felt at the time he kissed Rose pounded his conscience as though it had been waiting for the perfect moment to strike. But it was *over* with Rose, permanently. He was home now. Guarding against giving Etta any hint of his thoughts, he finished his drink and grinned at her.

"Did you make any new boyfriends in Sicily?"

As Etta played back the details of her trip, Angus felt an emptiness that made him wish he had never gone back to Fountain Point to help Rose; a feeling very different from what he'd anticipated when Etta returned from Sicily. Etta looked the same, acted the same, kissed the same – more passionately, in fact. It was *him. He* didn't *feel* the same. It frightened and confused him. Etta's jab in his ribs cleared his ennui as she said, "You look like your mind is a million miles away. Am I boring you?"

"Just thinking about a happy ending to your story," Angus said.

"I have a surprise for you," she said and handed Angus a sheaf of papers that were sitting on the sofa table behind them. "These are some of Noninna's secret recipes. I hand-copied them… I thought you might like to try them."

Angus paged through the recipes, his eyes riveted on them as if they were sacred relics from a saint's personal artifacts. "Um…" Angus murmured as several of the recipes caught his attention. "Help me out with these names."

Glancing over Angus' shoulder, Etta pointed to a few recipes and translated: "*Pollo Ripieno,* baked stuffed chicken; *Gnocchi con Spinacci*, potato dumplings with spinach; *Carciofi Ripieni*, stuffed artichokes; *Mallusco Bianco*, white clam sauce."

Angus grinned broadly as he said, "I think you just saved my life."

Etta reached past Angus to the lamp on the end table and switched it off. As she moved back past Angus, she lingered for a moment to let Angus' hands explore her. They kissed again. As Frank Sinatra sang, *All The Way,* they made love.

12. THE EYES OF TEXAS

Ruby kicked back, propped her cowboy boots on the desk and sipped her coffee.

"So… whadya' get done over the last three weeks? Any brainstorms?"

Angus opened his folder and handed Ruby a copy of Noninna's recipe for the clam sauce. Ruby eyed it for a moment then looked up at Angus.

"I like your clam sauce idea," Ruby said. "What else ya' got?"

Angus felt his gut tighten at the thought that overextending his time helping out at the Inn had jeopardized his credibility.

"I had to spend time at home… with… a friend," Angus said.

"You *do* have more than this, I hope," Ruby said. "A one pony rodeo won't cut it."

"Family problems took a lot longer to work out than I thought," Angus said.

"I respect family problems," Ruby said. "But for a whole damned month?"

Ruby scanned the recipe again and shoved a hand written paper across the desk to Angus. "Just read that and don't give me any more sob stories."

Feeling squeamish about having fudged the truth about what he had spent his time doing while Ruby was away, Angus squinted at Ruby's flowery handwriting:

To all employees:
Agnes McCrory named Head Sous Chef

Columbus Country Club Head Chef Ruby Tanner announces the promotion of Angus McCrory to the position of Head Sous Chef, effective February 1, 1995

Angus felt his jaw drop as he re-read Ruby's announcement.

"You're sittin' there like a pole-axed mule," Ruby said. "You want the job or do you want to peel potatoes for the rest of your life?"

Angus broke into a wide grin.

"What's so damned funny?" Ruby asked.

Angus picked up a pencil, circled his name at the top of Ruby's announcement, slipped it back across the desk to her and said, "I didn't have a sex-change operation over the vacation."

"I was hoping you would," Ruby said then noticed her misspelling of Angus' name: *Agnes.* "OK, *Agnes...*Bowman approved a salary of thirty-five thousand. Not too bad for a greenhorn."

Angus stood to leave, paused for a beat, then said, "What's on the docket for this week?"

"Bowman wants to see the Valentine's Day menu," Ruby said. "I'll work on my own ideas and we'll go over them in the morning."

13. MONEY CAN'T BUY YOU LOVE

Carter Duffy's administrative assistant Anna Belle West, arrived early to set up Duffy's private conference room for the special meeting of the Logan County Citizens Bank Board of Directors to review credit risks. Minutes before the 9:00 a.m. scheduled meeting, Duffy took his customary seat at the head of the executive conference table and greeted his colleagues. Seized with an urge to cough, he turned his head and expelled a rumbling hack over the shoulder of his dark blue Armani silk-suit coat. Scanning the solemn faces of the five attending Board members – not counting himself and the approved absence of ailing Board member, Tahlman Krumm – Duffy noted that Charlie Sewell, the bank's eighth Board member, was not present. As he was about to address the Board, Charlie rushed into Duffy's office. Before Charlie could greet the Board members, Duffy barked, "Charlie, we need to talk!"

The other Board members nodded perfunctorily but none stood to greet him as Charlie eased into his chair on the long side of Duffy's mahogany inlaid conference table.

"How's the banking business?" Charlie asked.

"Mortgage business stinks. Hate to turn down so many people, but…"

A monotone, "Un-huh... bad times..." rose in unison from the other Board members as Duffy turned toward the window behind him. He coughed harshly into his fat fist, brushed his hair with his left hand, reached for the Purell, glanced around the conference table, gestured to the pastries and silver coffee samovar on the sideboard.

"You boys have a sweet tooth, get some coffee and a roll… Charlie's baker is the best."

Seeing that no one made a move for the refreshments, Duffy focused on Charlie.

"Charlie… we have a problem," he grunted, sat back and twiddled his thumbs. Duffy's piercing eyes bore in on Charlie as Charlie sat upright and fidgeted.

"Not sure what you mean, Carter," Charlie said.

Duffy rocked back in his executive chair. Straining the spring mechanism with his bulk, an ominous creaking like a sinking yacht punctured the air. He picked up a letter opener, repeatedly tap-tapped the point of it on the conference table.

"This isn't any fun for our Board, Charlie, but looking at your line of credit, you have a big payment coming up."

As the other Board members shrugged and frowned in faux sympathy, Duffy riffled through a stack of papers on his desk, coughed into his shoulder, looked over his half-glasses at Charlie and said, "It says here you have a one-hundred twenty-five thousand dollar principal payment – plus interest – due March first."

"I've just gone over that with my business manager at the Inn… sounds about right," Charlie said. "Haven't missed a payment yet."

"Our Loan Committee…" Duffy paused to cough. "Lord love a mallard, Charlie… they're all sitting right here at the table… we're worried."

Charlie peered at the Board members as they nodded in concurrence but quickly shifted their gaze back to Duffy.

"All the publicity about that Thompson lawsuit… has us concerned," Duffy said. "On top of that, Dabney Merritt pulled the most recent appraisal on your Inn. It isn't a pretty picture." Duffy turned his head, coughed. "It says your Inn's value is down about four-hundred thousand. You took a big hit since we loaned you the money to do all that refurbishing."

Charlie was well aware of the note payment, but to have the rug pulled out from under him with Dabney's appraisal… that was a gut shot he didn't see coming.

"That can't be. Who did the appraisal?"

"U. S. Realty… they're the best."

"That's... the Inn's a gem," Charlie said peevishly.

"I hear you my friend, but we're facing a helluva situation," Duffy said and leaned forward. "Unfortunately, the bank can't ignore these things. It's the damned examiners. They see something like this and bam!" Duffy pounded his fat fist on the conference table. "They're on it like flies."

"But… I…"

"What's your room bookings with all the bad publicity?" Duffy said.

Charlie swallowed hard, tried to relax.

"Down at the moment," he said. "But it'll bounce back when that mouse business gets behind us."

Duffy rocked back, turned his head, coughed into his fist, slathered his hands with a squirt of Purell and said, "Trouble is... people soak up the first story but don't read the later reports. I know of situations where restaurants have to close up and re-open a few months later under a different name."

Bristling, Charlie said, "Be a little tricky for us to close the coffee shop and call it something else later. It's the centerpiece of the Inn."

"I appreciate your problems my friend, but we've already renewed your credit line a couple of times. The bank examiners aren't going to hold still for us giving anyone any special treatment."

"Not looking for special treatment... just a little consideration," Charlie said.

Duffy's eyes – as if they were heat-seeking missiles zeroing in on a doomed target – studied Charlie's grim frown. "I hate to say it my friend," Duffy coughed, "But with you're business in the tank and the Inn's appraisal down, our bank will have to rethink your credit status." Duffy made a roundhouse gesture to the dour-faced men seated around the conference table. "The other boys here and I have discussed it," Duffy said. "We know you understand we're not in the lodging business."

"Dammit Carter, the Inn's my life. Don't quit on me now."

"Not quitting on you, pal. Just have to keep everything kosher... my hands are tied."

Duffy's intercom buzzed. As prearranged with Anna Belle, the time limit Duffy had set for Charlie's meeting had expired. Dutifully punctual, at 9:20, Anna Belle had followed through.

"Yes, Anna Belle?" Duffy paused, "OK... thanks."

"Sorry Charlie… gotta run to another meeting. Let me know if there's anything else I can do for you and the Inn… marvelous place you got there."

As Charlie sat dumbfounded, the other Board members traipsed out of the conference room, stone-faced.

~~~~~

As Bernie completed the Inn's bi-monthly payroll, JoJo appeared at her office, tapped on the door and said, "Hey Little Flower… you open for business?"

"If you brought something good," Bernie said as she bounced over to JoJo, kissed him and locked the door behind him as he stepped into her office.

JoJo's eyes stopped at the hem of Bernie's red pencil skirt barely touching her knees. Shifting his gaze to her low cut blouse, JoJo put his index finger to his lips, blew on it, placed it on her chest just above her tempting cleavage. "Can we talk for a minute?"

"I'll finish up and we can sneak out to my place and relax," Bernie said.

"Got another appointment in a half hour… just a couple of things we need to discuss."

"You sound so damned official, "Bernie said. "Is something wrong?"

Watching Bernie slink around the desk and sit down, JoJo eased into a chair across from her. His tone icy, he said, "I haven't seen any orders for food and linens, lately."

"That goddamned mouse has everything on hold," Bernie said.

Reaching inside his jacket pocket, JoJo produced a baggie of cocaine and tossed it on Bernie's desk in front of him. Tapping on the pouch, he said, "This is the last of the freebies until we work out a new arrangement."

"New arrangement?"
~~~~~

"With our commission arrangement down the tubes," JoJo said, "My friends and I have another idea… big money."

Bernie sat quietly, her bleary eyes questioning.

"My friends in Lima don't like the commission deal, anyway… it's peanuts… even if the Inn gets out of the mess it's in."

Envisioning her wardrobe-depleted bank account, Bernie tried to fathom the meaning of JoJo's remark as she said, "It isn't freaking *peanuts* to me. I need the money!"

"My friends got a bigger idea," JoJo said.

"Don't jerk me around, JoJo… we've got a good thing going!" Bernie snapped.

"We *had* a good thing going," JoJo said.

"I have no fucking control over what's happened since that goddamned mouse screwed everything up," Bernie said. "It'll blow over for crissakes!"

"Goddammit, *listen* to me," JoJo said. "You'll make a helluva lot more money than on the commission deal."

Bernie looked past JoJo, her eyes fixed on nothing.

"I'm listening," she said.

"Here's the new deal," JoJo said. "You have access to all the Inn's financial records, right?"

Bernie nodded.

"How many people use credit cards to pay their bill?" JoJo asked.

Bernie spread her hands in a *so-what* gesture.

"Almost everyone…"

"You've got a record of their credit card numbers, right?"

"I keep them right there," she said pointing to a file cabinet.

"Get the list for me and we're in business," JoJo said.

"*Give* you the list…for what?"

"Get that beautiful blond head of yours in gear… I use the credit cards to buy merchandise and get cash advances. Everything happens in Chicago, so by the time anyone notices the charges, we've banked a pile of dough."

Bernie rolled her eyes, shot JoJo a frown.

"But… that's… ?"

"No one gets hurt. The credit card companies work it out with the banks. The card holders don't have to pay."

"I wouldn't want to hurt anyone, especially someone we know," Bernie said pensively.

"If you're worried about the locals, hold onto them and give me just the out-of-towners."

"I don't know..."

JoJo reached for the bag of coke, arranged two lines on the desktop, rolled up a new fifty-dollar bill and handed it to Bernie who quickly snorted a line and leaned back in her chair. Anticipating the coke's gratifying rush, she exhaled, closed her eyes and waited… but the high was mixed with worry that tightened her chest as if her heart were skipping a beat.

After snorting his line, JoJo looked at Bernie and winked. "The way you love those designer clothes, it's a sweet deal."

JoJo pushed more coke into a single fat line and gestured for Bernie to help herself as he said, "You give me the numbers and I do all the work," he said. "Have another hit."

Bernie snorted the line. Much faster than her first snort, the coke's effect gripped her with an intensity that left her breathless, lifting her into a sublime high. Closing her eyes, she muttered: "When do you want the credit cards?"

"Soon," JoJo said as he eased to the door and left Bernie to her bliss.

A smile spreading across her face, Bernie ignored the raw tingle inside her nose and the trickle of blood on her upper lip.

14. MR. CHARLES BLUES

Skipping his usual lunch at the coffee shop, Charlie mouthed another handful of antacids and lay back in his executive chair. Dozing fitfully, he was awakened by his ringing phone. His mind fogged, he barely understood Rose.

"Doctor Barton called to postpone our meeting today," Rose said. "TruTech won't be finished with its analysis on the mouse for another week or so."

Charlie took a deep breath, looked out the window and heard the freezing rain clacking against the courtyard's rhododendrons.

"I've been going over the budget," he said. "I'll leave a copy for you on my desk."

"Do you want to talk about it now?" Rose said.

"I'm going home... feel like I'm catching a bug," Charlie said.

~~~~~

Rose reviewed her notes about Speed's plans to confront the Thompsons, tucked them into her file folder, noted the time on her desk clock and glanced out her office window at the dismal winter gloom. She would get home a few minutes early, play with Aidan and his xylophone and fix his dinner. She pulled on her snow boots. As she lifted her coat off the hook from the back of her office door, her phone jangled. "*Now what?*" she whispered as she lifted the receiver. Claire's voice cracked. "Rose… it's Dad. Can you come to the hospital… right now? He's in the ICU."

~~~~~

After completing the angiography on Charles Sewell, Dr. Wesley Silvers found the family in the ICU lounge.

"Looks like we have some good news and some not so good news," he said. "The angiogram shows significant aortal and small vessel blockage. That's the bad news. The good news is, a coronary bypass will fix things… he'll be a new man in six weeks," Silvers said. "I've scheduled the OR for tomorrow morning at seven. We'll know where we are by noon."

"Can we see him?" Marianne asked.

"Yes... he's awake and stable. See you tomorrow morning."

~~~~~

Charlie's family and Rose gathered around his bed in the ICU. In a weakened voice, Charlie spoke over the sound of the beeping heart monitor.

"Now first… don't everyone get crazy, I'm going to be fine," he said.

"Yes sir, commander," Speed replied. "How can we help?"

"You have all of my personal information, Speed," Charlie said. "You and Rose handle the Thompson lawsuit. If necessary, be sure that Marianne understands the details."

"Thompson's lawyer is playing games," Speed said. "He claims he can't meet with us for a couple of weeks."

Charlie nodded and turned to Rose.

"I want you to take over as interim general manager," he said. "If necessary, you can call me with any questions."

"No phone calls, Dad!" Claire ordered. "Speed can work with Rose to wind up that mess with the Thompsons. " Claire turned to Rose. "Let me know if I can help. Now let's all go home and let Dad rest."

15. IT'S A BLUE WORLD

The orderly wheeled Charlie Sewell through the double doors into the icy cold Surgical Suite, 1-A.
~~~~~

"Yo, Sweet Georgia… got a customer for ya'," he said, as he handed the surgery orders to Head Surgical Nurse, Georgia Brown, who confirmed Charlie's ID taped to his wrist and handed the surgical orders to cardiac surgeon, Dr. Wesley Silvers.

As the orderly sauntered out of the surgical suite, Dr. Silvers nodded and gestured to anesthesiologist, Dr. Silvia Weeks, to proceed with injecting Charlie with the anesthetic.

~~~~~

Four hours later, with a healthy graft in place, Dr. Silvers worked to restart Charlie's dormant heart, kneading the vital organ for more than a minute. He held his head up for Georgia Brown to mop his sweating brow with a sterile pad then returned to kneading Charlie's flaccid heart. But the heart muscle did not respond. He kneaded it harder. Nothing.

"Syl! … Defib!" he ordered.

"Clear!" Sylvia shouted and shocked Charlie's exposed heart with the defibrillator.

Charlie's heart quivered but fell still.

"Again! Dr. Silvers yelled.

"Clear!" Dr. Weeks shouted, jolted Charlie's heart again, waited an instant then said: "Nothing!"

"Epinephrine!" Silvers barked. "Four milligrams in the drip, one cc into his heart – STAT!"

Immediately, the anesthesiologist injected the stimulant directly into Charlie's heart.

"Potassium?" Dr. Silvers asked.

"Elevated!"

"Pump up the oxygen to a hundred percent," Silvers barked.

"Got it!"

Laboring to restore Charlie's heartbeat, Dr. Silvers' strong hands
~~~~~

worked frantically.

~~~~~

Charlie's family sat in the surgical lounge waiting to hear the outcome of his bypass surgery. Dr. Silvers came through the lounge's waiting area door, his face sullen. The family stood quickly, joined hands.

"How is he?" Marianne asked.

Dr. Wes Silvers took Marianne's hand in his and pulled her gently to him.

"I'm sorry, Mrs. Sewell… terribly sorry."
~~~~~

BOOK VI

1. IN MY SOLITUDE

The pounding on his apartment door like a battering ram, Angus squinted at his Timex – 7:09 – "What the hell…" he muttered, lumbered out bed and stumbled to the door to see Chef Ruby. "Your father needs to talk with you... he's on your line," she said.

Lurching back to his nightstand, Angus picked up the phone and sat on the edge of his bed. "Dad? It's… you're up pretty early."

"Your mother went to mass," Angus' father said. "I told her I'd call you."

"What… what's happening?" Angus said as he rubbed the sleep from his eyes.

"Charlie Sewell died."

Staggering to his feet, Angus gasped.

"Mr. Sewell?"

"After heart surgery yesterday," his father said. "Visiting hours on Sunday afternoon and evening… funeral mass on Monday morning."

Angus hung up, rolled back on his bed. His throat dry, he called Etta.

2. REQUIESCAT IN PACE

Huddled together under umbrellas at Charlie's graveside, Angus, Etta, Rose, Claire, Robby and Marianne – along with more than a hundred mourners – bid a final farewell to their beloved Charlie, as Father Stenz intoned the final petition:

"Through the mercy of God, may his soul and the souls of all the faithfully departed rest in peace."

After sprinkling Charlie's casket with holy water, he stepped aside to allow Mayor Bunny Carpenter to present the Sewell family with the American flag and an engraved plaque that read: *For Outstanding Community Service.*

"Please accept this token of our appreciation," Mayor Bunny said to Marianne and Claire, then stepped away.

As the graveside mourners moved somberly to their waiting automobiles, the family, along with Angus, Etta and Rose, quietly entered the limousine and rode in silence to the Inn at Mary's Gate for the family's reception. Dodging the wet snowfall, the three dashed into the Inn, shook icy crystals from their coats and headed for the coatroom. As Robby entered the coatroom with Claire and Marianne's coats, he turned to Rose.

"Before everyone else arrives," he said, "Claire and her mother would like to speak with you in private."

At the entryway to the Ballroom, Rose spotted Claire and her mother and whispered to Angus and Etta, "I'll be right back."

Etta shook her head as she and Angus sat down. "I thought we were going back to Columbus right after the funeral mass."

"I don't want to be rude," Angus said. "We'll leave in a few minutes."

Glancing around the ballroom, Angus smiled at the memory of Fountain Point High School's Victory Dances. As he beckoned a waiter offering water and soft drinks, Rose approached.

"I'm going to the powder room," Etta said coolly.

Rose sat down, turned to Angus.

"I hope Etta doesn't mind us talking," she said.

"It's awkward for her not knowing anyone," Angus said.

"I'm sorry, but Claire and her mother were anxious to talk." Rose paused then looked directly into Angus' eyes. "They asked me to take over as general manager of the Inn until they decide what to do."

"That was fast."

"Claire and I talked about it on Saturday, but I wanted to assure Marianne," Rose said as she sat forward and put her arms on the table.

"Do you want a drink?" Angus said.

Rose shook her head.

"I know you and Etta are in a hurry," she said, "But I'd like to ask you to think about something."

Her eyes dark with anxiety, Rose reached for Angus' hand and gripped it firmly.

"Will you come back to Fountain Point and take over the food and beverage management at the Inn?"

Rose's question was so far beyond what Angus had anticipated, he groped for a way to respond without hurting her feelings, especially now. He felt a knot in his throat, pulled his hand back. "I'm flattered, but I have a great job and...Etta..."

"I'm just asking you to think about it," Rose said. "Please?"

"I can't just quit my job... and move back here."

"You make it sound like you'd be banished to Siberia," Rose said.

Angus rolled his head to scrunch the tension out of his neck and shoulders.

"I can't do it," he said. "I just got promoted to sous chef at the Club."

Angus looked past Rose as Etta sat down beside him.

"Will you think about it some more… before you decide for sure?" Rose said.

Etta glanced at Rose and back to Angus.

"I hope I'm not intruding," she said.

"We were just talking…" Angus said.

"I was asking Angus to consider coming back to Fountain Point and taking over the chef's job at the Inn," Rose said.

Her face somber, Etta stood and stepped back from the table. "I think we should leave… it's getting late."

"Etta… I'm sorry," Rose said. "It was very rude of me to hold you up."

Rose, if she knew anything, it was how to be cordial. In the past though, she'd have been sour about Angus turning her down; she'd make him feel as if she expected him to automatically agree with her. And though she seemed very gracious in the face of disappointment, it still felt that way. As they shook hands and he and Etta readied to leave for Columbus, Angus felt a pang of regret at turning Rose down, but knew he couldn't come back to Fountain Point.

~~~~~

Physically and emotionally drained, Angus climbed the stairs to his apartment and stretched out on the bed. Was the empty feeling in the pit of his stomach from grief or anxiety, he wondered?

Hours later, Angus awoke drenched in sweat. His mind reeling, he glanced at the clock – 4:19 a.m. Icy sleet cracked against his window. His eyes wide open, he stared up at the flaking plaster of his bedroom ceiling as if it held magic advice for curing his anxiety. He lay back and told himself he had made the right decision about declining Rose's request to
~~~~~

return to Fountain Point. Even so, an unsettled feeling lingered…

3. MY FUNNY VALENTINE

With bad weather, the Columbus Country Club's Valentine's Day dinner crowd was sparse. Toward the end of the main course, Angus peeked through the door leading to the dining room to see Gary Taylor, the Club's most experienced busboy, cleaning up the dirty dishes and carrying the loaded trays into the kitchen. A tap came on Angus' shoulder and he turned to see Alyssa. She winked at him, tugged him into the dining room and announced to the diners: "As a special treat tonight, Chef Angus will play the piano."

Before he could say anything, Alyssa nudged him toward the kitchen and said, "Hurry up… they're all waiting for you to play."

"I don't have anything to wear except my chef's coat," Angus protested.

The words having barely left his lips, Alyssa stepped to a hallway closet and extracted a men's jacket that had been left behind by someone.

"This should fit," she said.

Donning the musty brown blazer – its sleeves more than two inches too short – Angus crept into the dining room, eased onto the bench of the club's piano and played, "My Funny Valentine." Reaching to the back of his mind for an encore, he played "Now Is The Hour." Digging deeper into his repertoire, Angus played tunes that he, Milt and Moss played at Robby's wedding reception. As he finished playing "All The Things You Are," he glanced at the scar on his thumb and wondered how different his life might have been had he been able to enroll at Berklee. After playing "Al Di Là," it was as if by subliminal impulse, he played Rose's favorite song, "The Impossible Dream." The thought of Rose and her plea for him to move back to Fountain Point nagged him.

An hour and two more rounds of vodka-laced ice cream Hummers later – and to the surprisingly good and well-lubricated Irish tenor voice of Club member, Tait Roberts, Angus played the fourth and final run through of "Danny Boy." Angus retreated to his room to clean up and meet Etta as the few remaining dinner guests trudged out of the Club to their iced-over vehicles.

~~~~~

When Etta met Angus at her door, she was barefoot and wore a sexy red satin teddy. She kissed him as he entered her apartment and sat together on her sofa. Though having looked forward to relaxing with Etta after a long day at the club, Angus felt moody, tense, his thoughts disconnected. On the coffee table next to three sweet-scented burning candles stood a bottle of Lillet Blanc chilling in a marble wine crock. Etta filled two stemmed glasses with the golden-orange aperitif and handed one to Angus.

"Happy Valentine's Day. You look like you could use some relaxation," she said.

"Busy night," Angus said as they clinked glasses. "Can you put on some music?"

"Opera?"

"Maybe something lighter… something I can understand."

"I have an album by Michel Legrand," she said. "*Windmills of Your Mind.*"

"Perfect," Angus said.

They listened in silence to the first cut, "Summer of '42" and sipped the Lillet. As the second song began, Etta nestled close to Angus.

"'Where Love Begins' is one of my favorite songs," she said. "It reminds me of you."

"Me?

"How we met… at the warehouse with Uncle Dominic."

Angus chuckled.

"Dominic said I should watch out for you."
~~~~~

"*You*… watch out for me? I think you have that backwards," Etta said and nestled tighter beside Angus.

"My parents were very impressed with you," she said. "Have you thought about… us?"

His mind in turmoil, Angus sipped his aperitif.

"I think about you all the time," he said.

"I've been thinking, too," she said. "Would you like to have children?"

Caught off guard, Angus smiled wanly as the thought of Rose and Aidan flashed through his mind. *Children*?

"That's one thing I *haven't* thought much about," he said.

"We'll have plenty of time to decide on that," she said.

The reality of Etta's expectations gripped Angus as he put his glass down and sat back.

"Can we go shopping next weekend?" she said. "There's a new jewelry store in the mall."

Angus refilled their glasses and said, "You need jewelry?'

Etta put her finger on Angus' chin and smiled. "Like… a ring?"

"A ring?"

Etta put her hand on Angus' thigh and whispered into his ear.

"Don't you know diamonds *are* a girl's best friend?"

Angus eased back as the meaning of Etta's words jarred him.

"I… don't think I'm quite ready…"

"Ange… I've been under the distinct impression that our relationship is serious."

"I just meant… I'm not ready right now to think about getting married."

Etta softened, lowered her voice. "I didn't say I want to get married tomorrow."

Jolted by Etta's bold overture, Angus groped for words he hoped would get past the moment. He turned to Etta and said the only thing he could think of: "We haven't really talked about getting married… like… where would we live?"

"Right here!" Etta said. "You can move in anytime."

"But… what would your parents think? They seem pretty… conservative."

"What are you so tentative about? I love you! Don't you love me?"

"Of *course*… I *do*," Angus said. "I just want everything to… work out right."

"You sound like you're lost in a fog. What's your problem?"

Angus put his glass down and stood up.

"Getting married is… huge! I just want to *think* about it."

"Then go think about it," Etta said.

"I will… I promise."

4. TRUST IN ME

Dabney Merritt took the elevator up to Logan County Citizens Bank's executive offices on the third floor. Carter Duffy stood at the door of his opulent office suite, hacked into his brown silk and cashmere sport coat sleeve and beckoned Dabney to enter.

"What's on your mind this ugly morning?" Duffy barked.

"With all due respect… I was going to discuss Mr. Sewell and the Inn…"

"I know all about Charlie and the Inn," Duffy wheezed.

Dabney leaned forward. "We should call the Inn's note," he said flatly.

"I'll handle it. I'm the one who has gone along with Charlie and the Inn since the beginning."

Nodding, Dabney said, "With all that bad publicity… the cancellations the Inn is getting… the latest appraisal…"

Duffy shot him a frosty look.

"Where are you going with this?"

"Won't the Inn have to file bankruptcy?" Dabney asked.

"So what? The Inn's collateral on the note. We'll repossess it."

"Take it over?" Dabney said.

"I got some people I can talk into making an investment… get the bank off the hook," Duffy said and coughed into his fist.

"Should I say anything to Claire?" Dabney said.

"When the dust settles and the family calms down, I'll talk with her," Duffy said. "If we decide to take over the Inn, I want our ducks in a row."

"What about Bernie Walker?" Dabney asked. "She's very tight with Claire."

"Walker's just a numbers mechanic," Duffy said, "So don't tip our hand."

Duffy coughed into his fist again and lit up a *Havana* from his private stock.

"Don't drop the goddamned ball, Dab."

~~~~~

In accordance with the family's decision to put her in charge as the Inn's General Manager, Rose had transferred her office to Charlie's old office. It had taken several days for her to adapt to the eerie sensation that she was intruding on the sanctity of Charlie's former domain.
~~~~~

As soon as Rose entered her new office with Aidan, she called her mother.

"I hate to ask you on such short notice," Rose said. "Could you and Dad take Aidan for a few days until I line up another nanny?"

"Dad will pick him up at ten," her mother said.

Rose sipped her coffee and thought about what she had asked Angus to consider. But she had to be realistic. He had an important job at an exclusive country club and an attractive girlfriend he was serious about. Admittedly, Rose knew nothing about Etta since they had only met briefly at Charlie's funeral. And while there was no particular reason for her to dislike Etta, it seemed as if Etta didn't fit with what Rose knew about Angus.

Mulling as she sipped her coffee, Rose admitted that she had once believed that marriage was a matter of choosing cleverly. How wrong she had been. Cleverness had nothing to do with it. How had she been so blind to Angus? Had she hurt him so deeply that he hated her? She longed to be with him. When she had kissed him in her living room that night after work, why hadn't she thrown her arms around him and told him that she loved him? He was outgoing and affable and thoughtful; Etta seemed stuffy and possessive and remote. She felt sad about how coldly she'd returned the *Claddagh* to him as if it were a trivial trinket.

And there were times when she'd been aloof and mean to him. But whatever she asked him to do, he always tried to please her; the prom, the botched thunderbolt. Angus had taken an interest in Aidan and coached him to play the xylophone. She'd gotten angry when Angus tried to help her after Aidan had bitten Marcy. Had she been so self-serving that she had lost Angus for good – to another woman? She thought of Angus being with Etta and shuddered. She would make one more appeal to him. She would never give up.

As she read over the agenda for her staff meeting, her father entered her office.

"Looks like you're pretty comfortable in your office," he said. "Charlie Sewell left you some nice digs to work in."

"I'm so… Aidan can't wait to see you," Rose said. "He's so-o-o ready to do some *girling"* – Aidan's version of "grilling."

Rose's father arched his eyebrows. "Your mother told me that you're still looking for a new nanny."

"Do you know of anyone?" Rose said.

"Not offhand, but I've been thinking about your situation," he said.

"I've learned that when you have that look in your eye, you usually have some surprise," Rose said.

"Not really," he said. "Over the weekend, I was talking with Sean Sweeney up at the Waterbury Resort on the lake. He's looking for a management partner for his resort. You and Aidan could live with your mother and me…"

"I appreciate your concern, but I can't think about such a drastic change right now."

"It was just a thought."

~~~~~

As her staff filed in, helped themselves to pecan rolls and the coffee Bucky had delivered, Rose greeted them. When Bernie arrived, she brushed past Rose and plopped down in a chair at the conference table. She wore a tightly tapered wide-sleeve, black mini-dress, a double strand of black pearls adorned her plunging neckline. Her open-toed black snakeskin pumps showcased her brilliant red lacquered toenails, matching her fingernails. Suppressing her dismay over Bernie's gaudy get-up, Rose took her seat at the conference table and addressed her staff.

"I realize we're all terribly saddened by Mr. Sewell's passing, so I won't keep you long," she said.

Heads nodded as Rose glanced at her agenda.
~~~~~

"The Sewell family has asked me to act as the Inn's general manager… until they decide what they want to do."

As the others offered their support and promise to help, Bernie glowered at Rose and began filing her nails.

Angered by Bernie's insolence, Rose turned to her. "Bern… I'd like to get with you and review the payroll." Bernie stared out the window as Rose continued. "And I'd appreciate it if you would give me a set of updated financials for this year's outlook so I can go over them with Claire and talk about our line of credit at the bank."

Bernie dropped her nail file on the table, drew a sharp breath and said, "Nothing's changed since I gave them to Mr. Sewell."

"Any word on that mouse thing?" Cliff said.

"Our attorney is meeting with the Thomsons later this week. Hopefully we'll hear something right after," Rose said, glanced around the table to the others, then turned to Theresa Loar. "What do our bookings look like for the next few weeks?"

"This weekend, President's Day, we have a total of thirty," Theresa said as she passed a sheet of paper entitled, *March Bookings,* across the table to Rose.

Studying the bookings, Rose arched her eyebrows.

"Other than St. Patrick's Day weekend with thirty-five reservations…" she glanced at the paper again, "… we have fewer than twenty-five reservations for the whole month of March?" She shook her head. "Do you remember what we did last year in spring?"

"Not much," Theresa said. "We were in the middle of all that remodeling."

"Mr. Charlie laid off most of my help," Gracious put in.

Bernie scowled at Gracious. "You better get ready to service the rooms yourself, the way things are going," Bernie said.

"If there's nothing else…" Rose paused, "Let's go to work."

~~~~~

Bernie stalked into her office, slammed the door shut behind her and locked it. How dare the Sewell's put sweet *Little Miss Perfect* in charge of the Inn when Bernie clearly knew far more about its finances and business affairs. Rose had never even bothered to acknowledge that Bernie and Chef Byron had forged a solid working relationship that had benefitted the Inn with dependable purchasing arrangements Bernie had set up through JoJo. But now, with the Inn's business downturn, the risk of losing her consulting commissions had changed everything. Boiling with vengeance, Bernie vowed to get even. "Someday, Rose, " she muttered, "You'll need me and I'll tell you to kiss my ass." Searching frantically to find her stash of coke, Bernie rummaged through her desk drawers. Nothing! Shit! She dialed JoJo's number.

"Can you come over… right now?" Bernie pleaded.

"I'm busy," JoJo said. "Can't it wait?"

"Don't put me *off*," Bernie rasped. "I need…"

"I'll see you later this afternoon," JoJo said and hung up.

Distraught by JoJo's denying her what she so desperately needed until it was convenient for him, Bernie swore under her breath, "Fuck you, JoJo… you can keep your pants zipped up for a while!"

~~~~~

Mid-afternoon as promised, JoJo knocked lightly, pushed the door open and entered Bernie's office. When she stood and rushed to his side, perspiration glistened on her forehead… her hands felt cold and clammy.

"You look ruffled, Little Flower," he said.

Bernie sat upright, leaned toward him and blinked.

"Did you bring me something?"

JoJo reached into his coat and tossed a baggie of coke on her desk.

"No more freebies, remember?" JoJo said. "But consider this a bonus for getting me the credit cards."

Her heart hammering, Bernie opened the baggie. Strung out and agitated, she poured out more coke than her usual fix, pushed it into two fat lines, snorted them quickly, sat back and pinched her nose. Seeing blood on her thumb, she wiped it away with a tissue, waited for the coke to transport her and lay back for a moment until she felt its wondrously soothing effects.

JoJo chuckled.

"If I liked that shit as much as you do, I'd be dead."

Bernie blinked her eyes and turned to him.

"This morning... we were all told that the Sewell family put that bitch Rosemary in charge of the Inn now that Charlie's gone."

"Get me the credit card numbers by Saturday night and you can forget about Rose," he said. "We'll go to Lima and celebrate."

~~~~~

Home alone that night and between snorting six lines of coke, Bernie thought about Rose and the Sewell family putting Rose in charge of the Inn; the Rose she once liked had become a flaming, ass kissing, self-serving bitch.

Bernie spread more coke on her coffee table, pushed it into two lines, snorted them and closed her eyes. Since JoJo's commission plan was now in the dumper, she needed to make up for the loss. She wondered how much she could make on JoJo's credit card idea.

At midnight, she ate a bowl of dry cereal and drank the last of the second bottle of *Chardonnay* she'd opened two hours earlier. Lurching into her bedroom, she undressed, tossed her clothes in a heap on the floor. She glanced at her figure in a full-length mirror. She'd lost weight, her skin not as tight as it had been, her breasts flaccid. Before going to bed, she went to the bathroom. Standing in front of the medicine cabinet mirror, she peered into it and saw white exudate gathered in the corners of her bloodshot eyes.
~~~~~

She dampened a face cloth with cold water, pressed it to them. When she drew the cloth away, her eyes looked clearer. After scrubbing her face with the freshly dampened cloth, the cloth was dotted with blood. She turned on the magnifying cosmetic mirror next to the medicine cabinet. Tilting her head back to examine her nose, Bernice could see the lining of her nasal passage was peppered with tiny red blisters. Though her nose was tender and sensitive to her touch, she squeezed it, then tried to stanch the blood flowing out with the cool face cloth. Minutes later – her nose still bleeding – she opened the medicine cabinet and extracted a styptic pencil she had used for razor nicks on her legs. She ran water over it, twirled it around inside each nostril, pressing it against the ruptured blisters. The smarting sting of the caustic hemostat made her eyes water. As a further precaution, she reached for a jar of petroleum jelly and squished a finger full into each of her blistered nostrils.

~~~~~

Lumbering into her office early, Bernie tried to concentrate on the task as hand.

Her door locked, she stood at the Inn's financial records cabinet and started to open the drawer. She stepped away, nervous about what she knew she had to do, then sat at her desk and polished off most of the remaining coke. Her courage restored, she opened the filing cabinet and culled through the credit card charges of Inn guests for the previous two years. Passing over the guests who lived anywhere in the vicinity of Fountain Point, she pulled more than two hundred records, threw out the repeat visits and noted that of the remaining hundred, many guests had visited the Inn from as far as Tucumcari, New Mexico. She loaded the single-page records into the copying machine and as she watched it kick out the copies, she resolved to forget about Rose's impertinence and take comfort in the fact that her bank account would soon be flush, her worries about her debts and Rose – a thing of the past.

When the machine was done, she bundled the copies, stashed them in a file folder, clamped the originals together with a green alligator clip
~~~~~

and put them safely away in the back of the bottom drawer of the filing cabinet.

Bernice snorted the last of her coke after donning her winter coat and shearling boots. Flipping the office light off, she thought about what she'd just done. Ignoring a pang of guilt, she tucked the file folder under her arm to give to JoJo.

5. PERDIDO

Monday morning – relieved that Aidan was at her parents' home – Rose still felt awkward sitting at Charlie's desk as she browsed through his computer business files: a few outdated, many current and relevant to the Inn's operations, several notes addressed to Bernie about staff cuts, overhead cuts and other financial questions… a separate note about meeting with LCCB was clipped to a copy of the Inn's loan agreement with the bank. Leafing through a thin sheaf of papers, she spotted the spreadsheet Charlie had copied and left on his desk for her the day the TruTech meeting was delayed. Comparing it with her copy and Charlie's computer screen, she saw they were identical. Charlie's notes reminded Rose that she would need to check with Bernie that the Inn's staff and advertising cuts had been put in place.

Rose strode over to Bernie's office to compare Bernie's financial records with hers. She knocked on Bernie's door. When Bernie didn't answer, Rose decided to check Bernie's files for herself, but was surprised to find her office door locked. Where was Bernie? It was nine o'clock already. Using her master key to open the door, she entered, surveyed Bernie's cluttered office, spotted a bulging file on Bernie's credenza marked, *Private, Bernie Walker.* Knowing that Charlie would expect her to be thorough and not waste time, she picked up the file and returned to her office, leafed through the worksheets, doodles, scrawled notes and innumerable figures; notations about payroll periods, withholding taxes, staff headcount and confidential salary information. There were pay period calculations for hourly workers and another spread sheet showing the names of the hourly employees and their wage rates. Three names appeared on the worksheet that puzzled Rose – the first two, Lucy Fuller and Noreen Baker – were two maids Charlie had furloughed the previous year. The third name, Jack Connor, had been an hourly kitchen helper. Why were they still on the payroll roster? Scribbled in what appeared to be Bernie's handwriting next to their names were two words: *Escrow Account.* The three names were bracketed with a date and number entered next to them – $30,940.08 – and a second number labeled *Annual Inn Payroll Recovery to date:* $36,096.76. Of all the vague scribbles and notations, *Payroll Recovery,* was the most puzzling.

She turned to the notes Charlie had made about cutting the advertising budget at WOFP Radio by $10,000. Studying Bernie's hand written worksheet marked '*WOFP*', Rose noted several references to the Inn's advertising spending to see doodled figures with different percentages calculated on different sums of money.

Two hours of sorting through the pile of papers, Rose felt that, finally, despite no help from Bernie, she had enough of a grasp on the Inn's financials to go over them with Claire and decided to go see Cliff Williams in the kitchen.

Rose passed the vendor file to Cliff.

"Do these invoices look familiar?"

Cliff leafed through the file and nodded.

"Recognize the names, but don't know a whole lot about 'em."

"The largest ones are from State Wholesale and Lima Linens," Rose said.

"That'd be Bernie," Cliff said. "Byron and her handled all that."

~~~~~

Back in her office, Theresa Loar was waiting... nervously fingering a sheet of paper. Handing it to Rose, she said, "As of an hour ago, our President's Day reservations are down by nine from the thirty I told you about this morning."
~~~~~

Rose slumped into Charlie's former executive chair and shook her head.

"We'll just have to work through this mess until this weather and all the bad publicity get behind us," she said. "Have you had any luck finding a nanny for Aidan with the temp help agencies?"

"Not yet," Theresa said.

Before leaving to go home that evening, Rose called Bernie at home. When Bernie answered, her voice sounded as if she were desperately ill.

"Are you all right?" Rose asked.

"The doctor said I have severe bronchitis," Bernie muttered. "I need a few days off."

"Take whatever time you need," Rose said. "Do you need anything else?"

Bernie coughed into the receiver as she said, "I'll be fine."

"I'm worried about you," Rose said. "Are you taking any medication?"

"Don't worry, Rosemary, I'll get the payroll done," Bernie said.

"I'm not…" Rose started to say, but before she could finish, the line went dead.

6. CHEATIN' IS RISKY BUSINESS

The law office of Lewis Watkins & Associates, LLP, welcomed Harrison Thompson and his law partner, Myron F. Clark. With a professional but cool demeanor, Speed gestured for the group to be seated. Noticeably absent were the traditional accouterments of morning conferences…coffee, juice, pastries, bottled water.

"Gentlemen, shall we begin?" Speed said.

The conference table accommodated just the six attendees: Speed; Rob McCrory; Zach Barton and his forensic chemistry partner, James "Stonewall" Reese. Harrison Thompson and his law partner, Myron F. Clark, who sat next to each other on the opposite side of the conference table.

Speed made the introductions and the two guest attorneys nodded to everyone around the table. "Gentlemen… my name is Myron Foster Clark. I represent Harrison Thompson and his wife, Blanche. It's our hope that we can come to an amicable resolution to this nasty food poisoning Mrs. Thompson has suffered."

"Hopefully so," Speed answered. "I'll be very surprised if we don't make a lot of progress on what we're here to discuss."

Harrison Thompson – nodding to Clark – placed his elbows on the conference table, took a deep breath and pursed his lips.

"Let's set the record straight," he said. "The facts speak for themselves. This is a serious case of out-and-out negligence. We – that is, my wife and I – seek only our just due."

"We'll address the matter of negligence and justice in a few minutes," Speed responded. "But first, we thought that you might be interested in what we've discovered."

"By all means," Clark said. "But you'll have to admit there's very little wiggle room here. What could be more certain than Mrs. Thompson's discovery of that mouse in her chili? Dreadful crime."

"Granted Mr. Clark, indeed, there was a mouse in her chili," Rob McCrory said. "The question is… how did it get there?"

"It's a matter of record," Clark said.

"Of course, that's the issue," Speed said. "If you don't mind, I'd like to re-introduce you to Mr. James Reese, our expert."

"We're comforted that you have sought expert opinion in this matter," Clark said as Reese opened a thick file folder and spread the contents on the conference table.

"Allow me to present my findings and analysis of what happened at the Inn on Friday, February thirteenth at noon," he said. "There's a lot of data so bear with me."

"Our time is yours, Mr. Reese," Clark said.

"First, here is a list of the tests we conducted," Reese said and passed a one-page document to them, entitled: *Analytics*. "We confirmed the rodent's taxonomy. We looked at body characteristics, condition of the skeletal structure, stomach contents, hair, vital organs."

"Get to the point," Thompson said.

"The mouse had been trapped. Its skeletal X-ray showed that it's back had been broken... by a conventional 'snap trap'... before it was found in the chili."

"That's speculation," Clark said.

"Second... it's stomach contained only ordinary bread crumbs – no chili."

"What's that got to do with anything?" Thompson growled.

"Third... when a rodent is cooked, the hair loosens," Reese continued. "So if a rodent was cooked in the chili, hair would have loosened and detached and been present throughout the chili sample."

"More speculation," Clark said.

"Fourth. We conducted an enzyme test. Enzymes are deactivated when exposed to heat. If we determine that a particular enzyme is active, then we know the rodent had not been exposed to a high degree of heat. Since we found our mouse friend to have positive enzyme activity, he couldn't have been simmered in a pot of chili, or for that matter, in anything else like something fried, boiled or baked."

"You're wasting our time," Clark said.

"Fifth. There was no food substance worked down into its hair... there were trace amounts barely on the surface. The mouse couldn't have been in the chili for more than a few minutes... at most."

"My client and I have been very patient," Clark said. "We see no reason for continuing this charade."

"Mr. Reese has one final point," Speed said and nodded for Reese to continue.

"The last and most telling finding is this," Reese said. "There was no evidence whatsoever that the mouse's lungs had any chili in them. The mouse definitely did not drown in the chili, it was put in the chili seconds before Mrs. Thompson discovered it."

"You can't put that libelous fairytale over on us!" Thompson roared. "How much did they pay you to tell that pack of lies?"

Speed bristled, pointed his index finger directly at Thompson's rage-filled face.

"I'll overlook that outburst, Mr. Thompson."

"You damn well better overlook it," Thompson sputtered. "I thought we'd come here today to make a friendly agreement. Now, I see we'll have to take you to a court of law! This is nothing but harassment. I can sue for that, too!"

"Here's something you should think about," Speed said sharply. "You're on a collision course with counter charges against you for felony fraud."

"We'll see about that!" Thompson snorted.

"That we will," replied Speed. "If you don't back off, here's our draft of the complaint we'll file against you for fraud by deception."

Speed handed a document to attorney, Myron Foster Clark.

"It's all there, counselor," Speed said, as Clark examined the document. "If you want to check legal precedent, I suggest you review the brief I've attached on an identical case. The plaintiffs enjoyed a nice stint in Joliet Prison for fraud… and a hefty fine. Read it and let me know if you want to proceed with your client's phony claim."

As Clark turned each page, perspiration beaded on his forehead. He massaged his glistening forehead and turned to Thompson.

“Harrison, I think we should review this closely before we go any further,” Clark counseled his petulant client.

“More lies,” Thompson hissed.

Speed stood and waved Thompson off.

“Don’t think for a minute that The Inn at Mary’s Gate would hesitate to prosecute you to the fullest extent of the law,” Speed warned.

“This isn’t over yet!” Thompson bellowed.

“Gentlemen, let us study on this,” Clark said. “Good day.”

As the pair huffed out, Speed slammed the office door behind them – and against his own no smoking rules – lit his *Meerschaum* pipe, glanced at the ivory engraving of a weathered sea captain on the front of it, exhaled a pungent cloud of smoke and turned to his colleagues.

“Rosemary needs some good news,” he said and dialed her number. Hearing the voice recording, he left her a cheery message.

~~~~~

Rose brought Aidan, his xylophone in hand, with her to the Inn after her parents dropped him off on Friday night. Her old office vacant, she plopped Aidan down in front of the VCR she used for training new employees, inserted his favorite movie, *Snow White & the Seven Dwarfs,* and punched play.

After starting the movie for Aidan, Rose stepped into Charlie’s office. The drudgery of realigning the staff due to the Inn’s dismal bookings and dissecting the Inn’s financials had drained her. Things didn’t add up. Additionally, there were the current bills. And the Inn’s note payment… she would count on Claire to help with that. Picking up the file of unpaid invoices she had shown Cliff, she noticed her phone message light blinking, picked up the receiver and listened to the voice of Speed Watkins:
~~~~~

'Speed calling... Thompson's lawsuit is down the drain. Feel sorry for that dodo... you can relax now. Any questions, call me.'

Smiling smugly, Rose opened the vendor file. With Bernie still out sick, Rose stepped into Bernie's office and pulled Bernie's records for vendor billings.

Back in her office, she checked the Inn's advertising expenditures. It struck her odd that she'd never heard of High Point Advertising. Before delving into the details, she heard Aidan yelping and rushed to see him. Without the slightest acknowledgement of his mother hovering over him, Aidan tapped the mallet on the xylophone as Rose listened to him sing: "Hi-ho! Hi-ho!"

Shocked that her son was playing the "Heigh-Ho" song from *Snow White,* Rose knelt down and hugged him.

"Ango! Me Ango!" he said and pushed her away.

~~~~~

Rose sat by her fireplace after finally getting Aidan to bed for the night and stared into the crackling flames. Tense, anxious, she dialed Angus' phone number. When he answered, his voice sounded irritable.

"This is Angus... what's up?"

"You sound like you're in a bad mood," Rose said.

"Rose? No... I..."

"I just wanted to tell you... I think Aidan would rather live with you than me."

"I don't blame him," Angus said.

"You *are* in a bad mood."

"My main prep cook called in sick at the last minute this afternoon and I got zapped," Angus said. "How *is* the music man?"

"Behaving... more or less... but doesn't bother to tell me goodnight anymore. The last word out of his mouth is *Ango.* Speed called... the mouse law suit is history."
~~~~~

"I'll call Robby and congratulate him." Angus said.

Rose sighed and fell silent. His instincts up about Rose's call, Angus waited. Finally, Rose broke the silence.

"Have you thought anymore about what we discussed?" she asked.

"A little," Angus said.

"Ange… you're the only one who can help me get through this mess at the Inn."

Struck by Rose's plaintive tone and her disquieting plea for help, Angus struggled to be direct. And though a fleeting thought of Etta crossed mind, he wished he were sitting next to Rose talking with her in person.

"I'd love to work with you…someday… but I'm committed here at the Country Club," Angus said.

Rose's audible sigh of dejection echoed in Angus' ears.

"That sounds like a 'no' to me," she said.

"I don't see it working out right now," Angus said.

"Thanks… for thinking about it, Ange," Rose said softly.

"I hope I haven't misled you," Angus said.

"You haven't… really… I guess my hopes got too high."

The silence on the dead line rang in Angus' ears.

7. MY ONE AND ONLY LOVE

Hanging up the phone, his mind on Etta and his promise to "think about it" after they'd talked about getting married, he trekked down to the Shock Room. In the darkened safety-lit bar, he filled a glass with two fingers of Black Bush.

Vexed, he fixed his gaze on the funky lava lamp sitting on the corner of the bar. He watched the lamp's ambient glow of ruby red amoeba-like blobs of wax rise aimlessly and fall randomly through the clear viscous liquid, disappearing to be reborn again… anonymous… pointless… as though hinting at what Hell might be like. He sipped on the Black Bush and thought about Etta. They were *sympatico* in many ways. Artistic… a shared love of music… and food… cooking… wine… and travel. But Etta had jumped ahead. Hadn't she? They had never discussed marriage; never even mentioned it. Now it was: "*Haven't you heard that diamonds are a girl's best friend?*"

Staring at nothing, he wondered where the word *love* fit into his life. He adored Etta's personality, her openness, her sensuality. It was hard to imagine being without her. But did he *love* her? He'd promised her that he'd think about getting engaged. He owed her *that.*

Angus shifted his gaze to the doorway leading into the kitchen. He thought of the times that he and the kitchen staff at the Club had labored together… as a team. Charlie Sewell had imbued that same *esprit de corps* among his employees at the Inn. Yes, he was indebted to Charlie and the Inn. Despite having told Rose that he was happy with his job at the Country Club and in a relationship with Etta, images of Rose dogged him; images of having worked with her – grown up with her… gone steady with her… shared confidences with her. Deep down, he couldn't escape his feelings for Rose. They were more than a tug of nostalgia. Whenever they were together he felt something stronger, more acute, a special connection. She was intelligent, assertive. She was confounding and truly grating about always having to be right about everything. But the truth was, she usually *was* right. Now Rose needed him to help here through an uncertain, chancy situation. But Rose had left him to get married. She had dismissed him from her life when she'd so coldly given him back the one thing he had held onto as a sign of his feelings for her; the *Claddagh.* It had taken months to put that behind him but now she was divorced and struggling to raise a difficult son and reaching out to him for help…

Angus finished his Black Bush, refilled it, knocked it back and trudged up the stairs to bed.

8. HOW CAN I TELL HER

All the following week since he'd spoken with Rose, Angus' gut churned.

At his prep station cleaning up after the Club's Thursday night monthly Board meeting dinner, his thoughts roiling, Ruby's voice jolted him.

"Take a break, hombre, and let's talk in my office," she said.

"I'll clean up first," Angus said.

As if the prep tables were infested with deadly pathogens, Angus spritzed them three times with sanitizer, rubbed and scrubbed them until they gleamed. Stepping back, he stared at the gleaming stainless steel work surface.

"Are you coming in?" Ruby yelled from her office doorway.

Seated in their usual across-the-desk chairs, Angus leaned back.

"You've been in a funk all day," Ruby said. "One of your honey's dump you?"

"Just bustin' my ass to cover for Jewell being out sick all week."

Ruby propped her cowboy boots on the desk.

"Don't blow smoke up my ass," she said.

Knowing Ruby's irascible temperament, Angus groped for the right words.

"I'm trying to make a decision," he said. "Maybe you can help me."

"What's got your dauber down, Sunshine?"

"I'm thinking about going back home… to Fountain Point."

Ruby dropped her feet to the floor with a thud.

"Have you been chewin' peyote?" she said. "You got the bull by the horns right here."

"I've just been thinking…"

"Last time someone told me he was 'thinkin' I kicked him in the nuts for being stupid."

"I'm serious," Angus said.

"So am I!" Ruby said. "Do your moping somewhere else!"

Angus stood, moved toward the door, then turned back to Ruby.

"I'm moving back home," he said. "I'll come back to help you out on the weekends for couple of weeks…"

Her face and neck purple, Ruby stood, kicked the side of the desk.

"Take your greenhorn ass and saddle up tonight," she bellowed.

Angus stood and extended his hand. "I appreciate all you've done..."

Ruby swiped his hand aside. "If you get home and decide to break camp, don't even think about hauling your lame ass back here crying to me!"

~~~~~

Angus rambled up the steps to his room, showered, changed and surveyed his belongings. As he assembled his sparse wardrobe, swept his few personal items off the dresser into a plastic bag and packed his suitcase, he recalled Milt's quip about his audition for Berklee: "*You're in the water now, let's hope to hell you know how to swim.*"

Drained by the kitchen's busy workday and Ruby's anger over his decision to leave the Club, Angus plopped down on his bed. Had it not been for Dominic – and Vincenzo at the Roma – he would never have had the opportunity to bounce back from his injury and pursue his new career as a chef. He wouldn't have met Etta. Etta deserved his honesty, but his decision to return home and work at the Inn was his… alone.

He latched his suitcase and, for the last time, trudged down the stairs to the Columbus Country Club's foyer, glanced at the portrait of the CCC Founder, Orlando A. Miller, tipped his straw hat to him and drove to Etta's apartment.

~~~~~

Etta met him at her door in a plain white t-shirt and boxer shorts; her face covered with cold cream.

"You surprised me. Let me get rid of this mess," she said. "I'll see if I can find something to drink."

"I didn't come by for a drink," Angus said. "I just want to talk… "

"You don't have to be in a hurry," she said. At her bedroom door, she turned back to Angus and said, "Pick out a CD and I'll be right back."

As Etta disappeared, Angus leaned against the back of her sofa. Uneasy about what he would say to her, his neck muscles cramped.

When Etta returned from her bedroom, her complexion sparkled with fresh make up; her lips glowed warm pink. She wore blue satin pajamas, partially unbuttoned, her black tresses pulled back in a ponytail. Angus nodded but made no move to sit down until Etta nudged him.

"Before you say anything, I want to apologize for talking about our relationship the way I did last week," she said.

He'd not expected this. He felt a pang of indecision where before, there was only certainty. But he had no choice, no other answer. He'd promised Etta that he would think about her wishes and he had done that. As he took a step back, Etta said, "You seem like you're in a hurry. Can't we sit down?"

"I'd rather stand," Angus said.

"What's going on?"

Angus put his hand on Etta's arm. "I just… wanted to tell you that I quit my job at the Club."

"What? You loved working there."

"I've decided to make a change," Angus said.

Etta stepped back, furrowed her brow.

"You're making me nervous," she said.

"I've decided to accept the job at the Inn back home," Angus said.

Etta put her hands on her hips.

"I don't want to live in some little burg in East Jesus."

"I'm not asking you to move there," Angus said.

Her eyes blazing, Etta slammed a fist on Angus' chest.

"This is about that bitch Rosemary! The Sewell *family* wants you to come back? Bullshit! *Rose* asked you! Begged you! At least be honest about *that.* I heard her *pleading* with you when we were sitting with her at the family reception after thc funeral!"

Angus brushed Etta's hand aside.

"She wasn't... pleading. I'm *not* a goddamned bleeding heart!"

"And I wasn't born yesterday!"

Etta pounded her fist on his chest again.

"She's got you so wrapped around her finger... I could throw up!"

Angus slapped Etta's hand aside as he said, "This isn't about..."

"Stop insulting me with more bullshit!"

"Then here it is in plain fucking English," Angus shouted. "I'm moving back to Fountain Point to take the chef job at the Inn!"

Etta slapped his face. Hard. His flesh stung. His eyes watered.

"Vaffanculo! Bastardo!" Etta bellowed.

Recoiling at Etta's fury, Angus edged toward the door.

Etta bounded to her CD rack and pulled out Angus' recording of "The Christmas Song" he'd given her.

"And take your fucking chestnut crap with you!" she yelled as she hurled the CD at Angus and thrust her middle finger at him as he stepped quickly out the door.

9. SMOKE GETS IN YOUR EYES

From where he sat at the head of the table, Speed surveyed the family members gathered around the executive conference table in Charlie's former office. According to Charlie's instruction to see that his wishes were followed about Rosemary being in charge of the Inn, Speed had invited her to attend the family meeting and, as a courtesy to Claire, had also invited Robby.

Passing a thick folder to them, he said, "These documents don't paint a glorious picture about the Inn's financial situation. It's going to take some maneuvering to get things worked out."

"I've been aware of Dad's financial issues," Claire said. "I think the bank will be willing to work with us."

"Don't count on that," Speed said. "Merritt told me the bank was considering foreclosure."

"Why didn't you call me?' Claire said. "I'm a senior officer at LCCB. I'm the one you should've called."

"You're a relative… you have a conflict of interest."

"That's not the point!"

"Merritt told me plain and clear," Speed said, "You can't have a role in satisfying your dad's financial obligations with LCCB. The bank examiners would sniff that out in a minute."

"Dabney Merritt would sell out his own mother if he had to," Claire blurted.

"The bank isn't saying that foreclosing on the Inn is a done deal," Speed said. "I'm hoping we'll have a chance to work through that."

As the two of them wrangled, Rosemary sat quietly and studied the Inn's financial records she'd reviewed in Charlie's office.

Speed drew in a deep breath, exhaled slowly. "Actually, there is some good news," he said. "Charlie has a current will. Additionally, he has the Inn covered with an all-peril insurance policy for $2 million. He has two life insurance policies, but I have to tell you, he borrowed so heavily against the cash values, a big chunk of his death benefits will get eaten up… I'll say more about that, later."

Speed opened a bottle of water and continued.

"Last year, in January, with the Inn's good financials and Charlie being a Board member, the bank gave him a million-dollar line of credit to refurbish the Inn. At the time, the Inn was appraised at two-point-three million. So Charlie didn't hesitate to pledge the Inn as collateral."

Studying everyone's solemn face, Speed continued.

"Merritt pulled a new appraisal on the Inn this past January; it's now at one-point-nine million…"

"He never said anything to me," Marianne said. "He always seemed very confident about things."

"Since the remodeling, Charlie paid back three-hundred seventy-five thousand on the line…plus the interest," Speed said. "Unfortunately, things went south after the Thompson incident."

"I've seen some of his notes to Bernie," Rose said.

"Dad completely trusted Bernie," Claire said. "He knew when he hired her that she'd had some rough times, but he thought the world of her."

"There were some things Charlie kept to himself," Speed said. "You weren't always completely in the loop, Claire, so Charlie asked me to handle all the banking details. It wasn't that he didn't want you to know, he just didn't want the bank to think anything negative about you being his daughter." Speed paused, tapped his pencil on the table. "That's why I talked to Dabney Merritt… and whether you like Dabney or not, he's been an important buffer between you, the Inn and the bank."

"I'm just… fed up with his arrogance," Claire said.

"Here's the bottom line," Speed said. "Number one… the Inn's latest appraisal. Number two… the Inn still owes the bank six hundred-twenty five thousand. With the Inn's lower appraisal and bookings way off, the bank is champing at the bit."

Speed stood, paced the short distance from the conference table to the window overlooking the Inn's garden, stopped and turned back to the family.

"On top of everything, Charlie has missed paying the Inn's taxes as well as his own personal taxes. I got payment extensions for the time being, but there's still a big problem. All of this is not to mention..." Speed glanced at Marianne, "... your home mortgage, and his trust is under-funded."

As everyone sat mute, Speed paced the area again, stepped back to the conference table. Pressing his hands palm-down on it, he groped for the right words to say next.

"Here's the jolt," he said. "For all practical purposes... if we don't find a way to handle the Inn's debt... then, technically speaking... Logan County Citizens Bank owns the Inn at Mary's Gate."

The silky sound of Frank Sinatra's "My Way" became annoyingly audible over the Inn's music system. Sipping on his bottled water, Speed waited for the toxic facts about Charlie's estate to sink in. "All together, he owes taxes and penalties of about two-hundred-thousand."

In the balm of silence... each person around the table absently leafed through Speed's voluminous documents. Then, Rosemary lifted her eyes.

"I may have an idea," she said.

"I love your spunk," Speed said, "... but... I want you all to think about one last thing... and it's a big one."

Dour and hesitant, Speed continued. "The smartest thing... to protect everyone..." Speed turned to Marianne, "... especially you Marianne... Charlie and the Inn should file for bankruptcy protection. That will forestall the bank's foreclosure and give us time to work out a plan with all the creditors."

"You can't be serious!" Claire gasped.

"It's the best way for us to get out of this mess," Speed said. "Reorganize and live to see a better day."

Claire said, "Mr. Duffy… he wouldn't just… take over the Inn… would he?"

"Don't kid yourself," Speed said.

"I'm going to see what I can do at the bank," Claire said. "I'll talk with his eminence, Mr. Dabney Merritt. Meanwhile Rosemary, let's plan to go over all of the Inn's financials after I talk with Merritt."

"I have everything from Bernie but there are some definite questions I could use your help with. Do you really think the bank would take over the Inn?" Rose asked.

"Knowing Duffy… he'll have Dabney do his dirty work," Claire said.

Staying back to review Speed's file and think about her idea of how she might be able to help, Rose leafed through her pages of notes and didn't hear the sound of soft rapping on her office door. Only after hearing a voice say, "Anyone home?" did she look up to see Angus.

Rose dropped her notes, rushed to greet him.

"You have an uncanny sense of timing," she said.

"I got your message," Angus said as he removed his Amish straw hat.

"I didn't leave you any message…"

"I thought you wanted me to give Aidan music lessons," Angus said.

Shaking her head in mystery, Rose circled back to Charlie's desk, sat down and gestured for Angus to be seated.

"Yes… I… he'd love it," she stammered. "You came all the way from Columbus to give Aidan a music lesson?"

Angus tossed his hat on Rose's desk.

"Won't have far to drive after I move back home," he said.

Rose stood, folded her arms across her chest.

"Angus... I can't play these games," she said. "You told me that you weren't interested in coming back. What's going on?"

Smiling at Rose's bewilderment, Angus said, "Is the job you mentioned still open?"

Rose plopped down in her chair.

"Please... quit kidding around."

Angus reached for his hat, tossed it at Rose.

"I was wearing this when I got fired from my job at the Country Club," he said. "I told you it was my good luck charm."

"You got fired?" Rose said.

"I quit," Angus said.

"Are you... what are you telling me?"

"I'm here to take the job... if it's still open," Angus said.

Her eyes welling, Rose grinned. "Sorry... it's been filled. You're too expensive... and too late."

As Angus made a mock move to leave, he said, "In that case, I'll go see if Vincenzo has an opening for me at the Roma."

Rose reached into her desk drawer and extracted a printed sheet of paper.

"Well, why don't you fill out this job application... just in case?" she said. "Our Human Resource staff will review it when they have time."

"Do you think they'd pay me for something I'd love to do?" Angus said.

"Maybe after a probation period..."

Angus got up, stepped around the desk to Rose and put his hand on her shoulder.

"Would I be allowed to fraternize with the help?"

Fighting back her emotions, Rose took Angus' hand and held it to her cheek.

"It's against the rules," she said. "But maybe on weekends… after Aidan's music lessons."

Rose wheeled around in her chair.

"His grandfather is picking him up at noon tomorrow to stay for a few days with them at the lake. So... if you're not too busy, I think I can manage grilled cheese sandwiches for dinner," she said.

10. A LOVELY WAY TO SPEND AN EVENING

Seated with Rose in her breakfast nook, Angus relished the grilled cheese sandwich she served with a green salad and old-fashioned bread and butter pickles.

"Fill me in on Aidan," Angus said.

"His behavior is getting worse so I'm going to take him to the doctor," Rose said. "Will you go with us?"

"Anything to help out a fellow musician," Angus said.

"What about dessert?" Rose said.

Angus eyed Rose's figure and said, "I'm enjoying it right now."

"You're worse than you were in high school," she said, grinning.

"You didn't give me the time-of-day in high school," he said. "You were all gaga over that twerp, Thurman."

"Thurmy was very… thoughtful," Rose said.

"He kept calling me *Agnes.*"

"You know I liked you."

"Until Patrick."

"I'm going to have some coffee," Rose said as she got up from the table.

"Cream and sugar," Angus said.

"I only have skimmed milk," Rose said as she reached for two cups from the cupboard, placed them on the counter and filled them from her Krups Grind and Brew coffee maker.

"Fancy machine," Angus said as Rose placed the cups on the table.

"Aidan loves to hear it gurgle... he thinks it's music."

"Maybe he'll be a barista when he grows up," Angus said.

"Maybe a musician-barista."

"You have a couple more kids and they can drink coffee and play jazz together."

As Angus spooned sugar into his coffee and sat back, Rose dropped her eyes. After a moment, she forced a weak smile and spoke quietly.

"After Aidan was born, I had to stay in the hospital because of a problem."

Puzzled over the turn in their conversation, Angus sat forward.

"Ange... Christmas Eve at the Inn... I was so thrilled to see you, I didn't want to ruin things by telling you about my messy divorce."

Angus fidgeted in his chair.

"In the hospital after Aidan was born, they couldn't stop the bleeding. The nurses tried to contact Patrick to tell him what was happening but couldn't find him. Panicked, I asked them to call my parents. The next morning, they flew to New Jersey and arrived just in time."

Rose lifted her cup to her lips, sipped quietly and replaced the cup on the table.

"That afternoon, the doctors performed a hysterectomy. The next day, my father found Patrick and two of his drinking buddies passed out in our apartment in a drunken stupor... supposedly celebrating the birth of our son. They'd been doing drugs, too. After I got home and Patrick found out I couldn't have any more children, he stalked out of our apartment and disappeared for three days."

The lump rising in Angus' throat grew bitter with anger. As Rose's shoulders slumped, he reached for her hand as she continued.

"When Patrick finally sobered up and came home, he was so abusive I couldn't take it," Rose said. "After I found him snorting cocaine in our kitchen… my father helped me get the divorce."

Angus stood, paced, and turned to Rose.

"When I saw you in your office this afternoon, I had no idea that quitting my job and coming home would be…"

Rose stood up and said, "I think I said that you have an uncanny sense of timing."

Rose took his hands in hers and whispered into his ear.

"I don't want to… but we'd better stop while we can," she said.

~~~~~

Driving from Fountain Point to Indian Lake on Sunday afternoon, Rose turned onto the bridge road leading to Orchard Island and entered her parent's driveway. Three short beeps was her traditional signal that she had arrived. She hoped to see Aidan come running as she walked around the east side of the house to the lanai entrance.

"I thought I heard you beeping," her mother said. "Come in and let me get you something to drink."

"A glass of wine sounds good… where's Aidan?"

"Your dad took him. They're on their way home with some fresh fish. Aidan always wants to help… you know he loves to watch Poppy *girling* on his new grill."

Inside the house, Rose savored the aroma of her mother's apple pie as she made her way to her bedroom, the room still decorated with her high school memorabilia. On the dresser, sat her senior prom pictures. The Goddess of Olympus… *My, how Aphrodite has changed,* she
~~~~~

mused. The picture of Zeus made her laugh… the thunderbolt fiasco with Angus... him giving her the *Claddagh* at Percy's… Victory Dances at the Inn. Where had it all gone?

Rose examined another photograph of her posing with her mother and father and Dave Thomas, the founder of Wendy's. Since the early 1980s, her parents had been on the front edge of Wendy's long-sustained growth curve. As with most other franchisees, they had enjoyed the 15-year fruits of the company's most prosperous times. After they sold their Wendy's franchise back to the company. After she had grown up and moved away, they had lived comfortably in this very house where Rose had grown up. Returning the picture to the dresser, Rose brushed her hair. While looking closely in the mirror to search for any hint of premature graying strands peeking through her raven tresses, she thought about Angus...

"Rose?" her father called. "Have you fallen asleep in there?"

"I'm on the way," she answered, as Aidan ran into her bedroom.

"There you are, Aid… I've missed you."

"Poppy… *girling*," Aidan yelped.

~~~~~

Pushing the food around on her plate during the family banter, Rose fretted over how she would broach the idea that had been inspiring her since Friday afternoon at the family meeting. After her mother cleared the dishes and coaxed Aidan to go with her to read his new wordbook, her father tapped on the table.

"Rose… I've watched you pick your way through your meal. What gives?"

"Let Rose relax," her mother said. "She's going to be here overnight so we don't have to rush."

"I wasn't planning on staying overnight… I should get back home with Aidan," Rose said.
~~~~~

"Please don't go," her mother said. "You hardly ever have time to talk with us… we'll bring Aidan home tomorrow evening."

"I'll have to leave early," Rose said.

"You and Dad take your time… I'll let you know when Aidan is ready for bed."

~~~~~

As the sun disappeared and a blustery wind picked up, Rose's father studied the Inn's financial documents she had given him. Rose watched as he quietly lit his pipe, exhaled a thin curl of smoke.

"I know that mouse lawsuit hurt like hell," he said. "A good business gets damaged, conscientious hard workers get over extended and trouble takes over."

"But Dad… bankruptcy? I'm shocked."

"It *is* shocking… no one wants to face it."

Rose moseyed over to the lanai windows. Having turned choppy, the lake's surface reflected shimmering broken nightlights from the mainland highway. Cars zipped past the water and disappeared as if they were sucked into a giant whirlpool; Friday's meeting with Speed and the Sewell family – its own consuming vortex. Her idea not sounding nearly as good in her mind as it did when it first came to her in Charlie's office, she hesitated, turned to her father and said, "Dad… I want to ask you something."

"Nothing's ever stopped you from asking me anything," her father said.

"It's hard for me to say this…"

"I doubt if it's something I can't handle."

"Dad… I need some money."

"That doesn't surprise me," he said. "With the Inn having problems, I'm sure you're worried about what's going to happen to you and Aidan."

"No dad… I need some real money… like six hundred twenty-five
~~~~~

thousand dollars. And I'm going to need it in the next week or so."

Amazingly calm, as if Rose had told her father that she needed a glass of water, he stepped to her side.

"Rosemary… sometimes I don't know when you're kidding and when you're serious. I assume from your tone that you *are* serious?"

As the two of them stood by the lanai door, Rose's mother appeared with a pot of coffee and two empty cups and sat them on the table. "What in the world are you two talking about so long? I've put off poking my nose in to tell you that Aidan's fast asleep on the sofa."

"Dad… I should…"

"Let him sleep … come in, Helen, and let me fill you in on our conversation.

A half-hour of sipping through the entire pot of coffee while the three talked, Rose's mother turned to her.

"Your dad and I have done very well," she said. "If he thinks we can help you, I would be thrilled. You two finish talking, I'm going to check on Aidan and watch television."

Watching his wife retreat into the kitchen, Rose's father said, "You've been everything a father and mother could want. We've been hoping for an opportunity to help you get out on your own."

"I realize I'm asking you for a lot of money… but I think with the Sewell family's help… and Angus returning… we can make things work."

"About Angus… I know Charlie Sewell thought highly of him, but... do you have absolute confidence in his abilities?"

"Mr. Sewell isn't the only one who thought highly of Angus," Rose said. "He's had a big job as a sous chef."

"One of the things I remember learning from Dave Thomas is to give people you respect the opportunity to prove themselves worthy," her father said. "I respect Angus, so I'm happy for you he's back with you at the Inn."

He motioned for Rose to join him on the lanai settee.

"Fortunately, other than that numbskull you married, I've never had to guess about whether or not you'd be successful," her father said. "Charlie Sewell told me that the Inn – present problems excepted – wouldn't have gotten where it is without you."

"Thanks."

"But with all the turmoil, it might be the time to make a move," her father said. "Sean Sweeney would love to have you manage his Waterbury Resort. It would please your mother and I no end to have you here at the lake. You and Aidan could live right here..."

"But I love working at the Inn," Rose said.

"You have two choices, Rosemary. You can choose to stay at the Inn with an uncertain situation or join up with Sean Sweeney and have more control over your future," he said. "You could end up owning the Waterbury... just *think* about that."

Rose sat quietly.

"Ever since I sold my Wendy's franchise back to the company, I've put that money to work... first, for your mother's security," he said. "If anything ever happens to me, she'll be a very wealthy widow... that's just between us."

Ambling to the lanai bar, her father opened a soft drink and said, "Split a Coke?"

"Sure."

Returning to the settee, he sat next to Rose, "About the money... your mother and I have set up a trust fund for you and Aidan."

Rose swallowed hard.

"We were going to surprise you for Aidan's birthday next month."

Thirty minutes later, Rose's father had explained the details of her trust fund, finished his second pipe, rubbed his chin and said, "You have to make a decision. From the financials you showed me, I would be very leery about investing in the Inn...you could lose the entire six hundred thousand... almost half of your trust fund. Why would you risk it?"

"Because I believe in the Inn... and the Sewells... and Angus."

Putting his arm around his daughter, he patted her on her shoulder. "I won't say *don't do it*, but pride and emotional decisions have taken down a lot of people. If I were you, I'd be very careful not to let my heart overrule my head."

At midnight, Rose's father kissed her goodnight and left her sitting alone in the lanai.

~~~~~

Rose sat at her desk. The gusty winter wind swirling around her parents' home the night before and her rambling imagination had made for a sleepless night. Even the short drive from her parents' home back to Fountain Point had been a blur.

Thinking back to her romantic evening with Angus, she was reminded – after virtually pushing Angus out the door – that she'd told him she would get with him to talk about the Inn's kitchen operation. She dialed his extension.

"Yes, boss."

His voice lifted her spirits as she replied, "Can we get together this afternoon about four... to go over the kitchen operations?"

"I'll be ready to educate you," he said.

"The word is *enlighten,* not *educate...* OK?

"Yes, boss. See you at four," Angus said.

"You know, Ange... as creative as you are, you should try to come up with something more original than *'Yes, boss'*... OK?"
~~~~~

"Only if you try to come up with something better than *'OK'* when you want me to roll over and agree with whatever you say."

11. DON'T TELL ME YOUR TROUBLES

At 10:00 o'clock Monday morning, Claire marched into Dabney Merritt's office. Indicative of Dabney's vision of himself as the most important person on the planet, pictures of him shaking hands with politicians, well-known bankers, minor celebrities and local dignitaries plastered the wall behind his desk. A bust of Adam Smith sat on a desk-side-pedestal. Engraved on its silver legend medallion was one of Adam Smith's most prosaic quotes:

No complaint, however, is more common

than that of a scarcity of money. A.S.

~~~~~

"You're telling me that the Inn is finally admitting that it can't meet its obligations to our bank?" Dabney fumed.

"I think we should work with them," Claire said.

"If we rolled over for everyone with financial problems, the bank would be broke. How do you mean, *work with them?*"

Flushing at Dabney's insolence, Claire frowned and said, "Well to start with, we could take a *deed in lieu...* at least that would..."

"Out of the question. We're not in the hospitality business!"

"Then let's give them a six-month moratorium on the debt principle and let them pay just the interest."

"Another bad idea," Dabney barked. "With all that negative publicity about the mouse killing the Inn's business... we might as well get it over with and foreclose."

"But it would give them some time," she protested. "They might be able to find another investor. Let's give them a chance."
~~~~~

"That's silly talk, Claire. That's how the Inn got in trouble in the first place. Your father sweet-talked Carter Duffy into borrowing a lot of money to sink into that Inn." Dabney pursed his lips in mocking irony. "It was a bad decision and they won't recover from that mouse scandal until who knows when."

Claire shook her head in despair. "Then what do you suggest?"

"We'll call the note, auction off the property and get whole. Meantime, we'll look at your father's personal assets."

"I'd appreciate it if you'd show a little sensitivity, for God's sake."

"There's no place for sentimentality in the banking business," Dabney said. "You should know that you can't fix one bad decision with another bad one. What about his other assets?"

"He's used them to keep the Inn operating."

"Haven't we gotten a recent financial statement from him? Do you mean to tell me that we wouldn't have noticed a change in his net worth? Who's looking at this guy?"

"My father has been a loyal, private banking client of Mr. Duffy. Maybe you should speak with him."

"I already have... he agrees with me… we'll take over the Inn. It's that simple."

12. HOW LONG HAS THIS BEEN GOING ON

"I brought all of the kitchen orders to go over," Angus said as he sat down at Rose's worktable. "I sorted them by month."

"I checked Bernie's files. Look at these," she said, pointing at the payables folder. "Tell me what you think about these invoices."

Angus studied the invoices. "I can't tell without checking, but the unit prices from State Wholesale Foods, seem high."

"How can we check it?" Rose said.

“I’ll call a wholesale distributor friend of mine who called on me when I bought for the Club.”

“Use my phone,” Rose said.

As Angus made a quick call, Rose leafed through the other papers. He hung up and pushed the State Wholesale Foods invoice across the table to Rose.

“Based on the prices my friend quoted – and his company isn’t always the lowest – the Inn is paying anywhere from a ten-to-fifteen-percent premium for the privilege of doing business with State Wholesale Foods,” Angus said.

“Why would we do that?”

“Only one reason,” Angus said.

“And that would be?”

Angus twirled his pencil around on the worktable, then said, “Let’s say… I agree to pay you a higher price for something because you give money back to me under the table.”

Rose cocked her head. “But why wouldn’t I just keep what I’m overpaying in the first place instead of giving it to you?”

“One of the things I love about you Rose is your wide-eyed innocence.”

“For God’s sake, Angus, give me some credit. What are you talking about?”

Angus raised his hands in surrender. “What I’m saying is that someone is pocketing a lot of money from all the extra charges.”

“That can’t be,” Rose said.

“I hate to say this,” Angus said, “But being completely objective, if I had to guess who was pocketing money, it would be Bernie.”

“Bernice?” Rose shrieked. “You can’t be serious. She’s been a trusted employee… Charlie… Mr. Sewell hired her before he hired me.”

Swigging his water, Angus said, "Byron specified what to order and gave it directly to Bernie. There was no one else in the loop."

"Maybe that's the way it was when she started working at the Inn and she hasn't changed it for some reason we don't know about," Rose said.

"Even giving Bernie the benefit of the doubt," Angus said, "She would have had plenty of opportunity to correct overbillings."

"There're always mistakes," Rose said. "Some vendors aren't the most meticulous bookkeepers."

"I'm not talking about a misplaced decimal point or errors in addition," Angus said. "There's a consistent pattern of overbilling on every item."

Rose shifted in her chair.

"But… that's calling Bernie… a crook!"

"I don't know what else to call it," Angus said. "Some vendors set up incentives to get buyers obligated to them. Whether it's free goods, merchandise, entertainment or money under the table, there are a lot of ways to work kickbacks."

Angus paused for a sip of water.

"When you and I and Cliff went over the Inn's food inventory, no one in his right mind would carry that much excess… half of it outdated."

Angus let Rose absorb the thought, then said, "So not only is Bernie paying too much, the more she buys the bigger the kickback she gets."

Rose put her hand to her forehead, pinched her brows.

"But why... why would she risk *doing* that?"

"What do you know about that Gardini guy Bernie works with?"

"JoJo?" Rose said.

"That day – the day you got pissed about Bernie hugging me in her office – she told me that she was working with Gardini. I met him at Mr. Sewell's funeral. I'd check on his involvement with Lima Linen and State Wholesale," Angus said.

"I don't have to check… Bernie and I discussed him when Charlie asked her to see if our suppliers would extend our payment terms while we waded through the financial mess we're in."

"You get the picture?" Angus said.

Rose slipped the Lima Linens invoice across the table to Angus and said, "What about these?"

Angus studied the invoice. "My guess is that the linen deal wouldn't be the same arrangement as the food," he said. "Sometimes, the linen guys charge an outright fee just for keeping them on emergency call. If they're crooked, it's easy to overcharge on the fee and kick back some money."

Rose rocked back. "How could Bernie *do* this? How could she do this to the Inn… and... Charlie?"

Angus stretched and took a deep breath.

"Here's something else, Rose. I didn't think much about it when you mentioned that kitchen helper, Jack Connor, being laid off … until you said he was still on the payroll. And you told me that Charlie had released two maids. If I were you, I'd check on the payroll details to see if she's been siphoning off funds and hiding them somewhere."

"That's odd... I *did* come across something in Bernie's files called 'Escrow Account' and the names of three employees who had been laid off, along with an entry about payroll recovery of over thirty thousand dollars."

"I'd check on that escrow account. It sounds suspicious to me."

Rose squeezed her eyes shut, opened them, blinked. "*Why?* Why in the world..."

"Bernie's been in financial trouble before," Angus said.

"How do you know that?"

"I helped bail her out."

"You gave her money?"

"Not that much… only three thousand," Angus said.

"You gave her three thousand dollars?"

"*Loaned.* She paid me back… after she got divorced."

Rose frowned. "Divorced? She told me she'd never been married."

"Bernie tends to forget things," Angus said. "If you look at her lifestyle, you'd have to wonder how she affords everything." Angus paused. "She has an expensive car… she dresses like the Queen of Sheba and she told me she owns the duplex where she lives. I don't know what she makes, but I'll bet every credit card she has is maxed-out."

"I don't know… what to say," Rose said. "But while we're at it, have you ever heard of High Point Advertising?"

"Wouldn't know a thing about them. Why?"

"Because I'm looking at an invoice from them for our fourth-quarter advertising… it's twenty-five thousand. Does that sound like a lot to you?"

"It's been a while, but when I bought radio advertising for my band, I found out that advertising agencies get discounts from the stations where they buy time. Their clients don't pay any more… the stations just give the agencies a discount. That's how agencies make their money… they get a cut. That's what I remember."

"So… if an agency billed us here at the Inn for our radio advertising, they'd get a commission?"

"That's the way it works. What are you thinking?"

"Just wondering who High Point Advertising is," Rose said. "I guess they must be our advertising agency. It's funny… I've never heard of them. And I don't remember Charlie ever saying anything about them."

Donning her winter coat, Rose hurried home to Aidan. Every inch of the drive… she thought about Bernie cheating and dreaded the thought of taking Aidan to see the doctor.

13. SOMETHING'S GOTTA GIVE

Seated around the conference table in Rose's office, Speed, Marianne and Rose listened to Claire's brief but stressful recap of her meeting with Dabney Merritt.

"What's the bottom line?" Speed asked.

"No dice. The bank isn't going to bend. It can take over the Inn and sell it or auction it off to cover the debt."

"You mean we'll lose the Inn?" Marianne asked.

"Not as fast as they think," Speed said. "We could sell the Inn, too, but before that, we can buy some time with a bankruptcy filing. That's the best route."

"What if we can find someone to invest in the Inn?" Rosemary asked.

"Who would step in with that kind of money to bail us out?" Claire said.

"That's a wild card," Speed said. "Meanwhile, the bank has creditor priority so our best gambit is to get the other creditors to go along with our reorganization plan. And if a buyer turns up, we'll work through that… but it'll be on our timetable."

"What about Bernie?" Claire asked. "You may want to tell her… she's our Business Manager."

"I have reservations about Bernie," Rose said. "I'd like talk with you about her."

"If we file for the bankruptcy late this Friday, we can stay ahead of the bank," Speed said.

"I think we owe it to our employees to give them heads-up," Rose said.

"What will happen to them?" Marianne asked.

"I think we can explain it in a way that they'll understand," Rose said.

"I'm so glad you talked Angus into coming back to help," Claire said.

"I'll draft a bankruptcy notice letter to the Inn's creditors and a news release for the *Examiner*… the radio station, too," Speed said. "The weekend will give us some breathing room."

"But what if we find an investor?" Rose asked.

"If we get that lucky, they'll want to do their due diligence," Speed said. "The bankruptcy procedure spells everything out… be just as easy to work under the bankruptcy rules."

~~~~~

In Claire's office, Rose unbundled the Inn's financial records, spread them out on Claire's conference table and sorted through the notes she'd made from the papers she'd culled from Bernie's files. After spending a disheartening two hours confirming Bernie's duplicity – the bogus escrow account, her *High Point Advertising* account, its check deposits signed by JoJo Gardini – Rose scrubbed he eyes with her palms and muttered, "That conniving little bitch! Tell me if I'm wrong, Claire, but I want to fire Bernie. What do you think?"

"If you don't have solid proof of wrongdoing, you could be heading for a lawsuit from Bernie. For some reason, she hasn't withdrawn any money from the escrow account. It's a very clever scheme and my hunch is that she's playing a waiting game by *forgetting* to tell you that she's escrowed that money from the laid-off employees and is waiting for the right time to run with it. But if she ever withdraws cash from that account, you could make a good case for fraud. The advertising account is problematic. She could claim Dad approved it. It would be her word against yours that he didn't."
~~~~~

"I'm sure she'll cover her ass," Rose said. "But I can't sit around and do nothing. I just...can't do that."

"Here's my suggestion," Claire said. "Confront her and see what she says. Even if she's playing us all for fools, if she has an ounce of conscience, she might fess up."

Rose stood, gathered up the financial papers and stuffed them into her briefcase.

"I hope you're right but something tells me Bernie will lie her way out of things," Rose said as she closed her briefcase.

14. THIS LITTLE LIGHT OF MINE

Rose and Angus arrived at the pediatrician's office with Aidan pushing, pulling and screaming every step from the car. A nurse opened the inner clinic door into the waiting room. "Aidan... Miss Gracewood?" As Rose, Angus and Aidan stepped through the nurse led them down a narrow hallway and into a brightly lit examination room.

"I'll take those papers you filled out," the nurse said. "Dr. Meyer will be with you in a few minutes."

Snugged against the far wall of the examination room was an elevated, rectangular black leather bench sheeted with white paper. Angus remembered his visits to Dr. Vincent's office for his hand injury. The room had an antiseptic aroma and electronic monitors affixed to the wall.

Aidan sat quietly until being startled by the sudden opening of the examination room's door and a man entering.

"I'm Dr. Meyer," the man said. Under his clinic coat, he wore a red and gray striped tie over a darker gray dress shirt. He was of medium height, slightly built and had an authoritative bearing. His wide-set eyes peered out from behind a thin wire frame glasses that emphasized his large brown eyes with scant eyebrows; his thin hair graying at the temples, Angus guessed he was in his mid-forties.

Before Dr. Meyer could say anything, Aidan burst out crying. Rose tried to calm him as the doctor reviewed the information record Rose had completed. He peered at Aidan for a moment then reached over and touched Aidan's head. Aidan pulled back, buried his face in Rose's shoulder, sobbed louder. Dr. Meyer turned to Rose, gestured to Aidan and said, "Fine looking young boy you have here…" he glanced at the clipboard chart, "I assume you're his mother, Miss Gracewood?"

"Yes," Rose said. And this is my friend, Angus McCrory."

Dr. Meyer nodded to Angus, glanced at the clipboard then looked up. "Your son looks like a very healthy two-year-old to me."

Angus stood behind Rose as she explained why she brought Aidan to see the doctor.

"I'm concerned that he seems… different from other children his age," Rose said.

"How so?" Dr. Meyer said.

Rose cuddled Aidan and said, "Well… as you can see… he doesn't like for anyone but me… and Angus… to touch him. He's very moody… misbehaves a lot."

"Not unusual for a two-year-old," Dr. Meyer said. "You should see my kids. Does Aidan seem moody every day?"

Rose glanced at Angus. "I would say so… wouldn't you agree, Angus?"

"Except when we're doing music," Angus said.

Dr. Meyer arched his eyebrows. "He likes music?"

"He's *obsessed* with his little toy xylophone," Rose said. "Angus has taught him to play little melodies…"

"He learns them after only one or two tries," Angus said

Dr. Meyer nodded. "What does he say when he's playing with the xylophone?"

Rose shook her head.

"Other than shouting 'no,' 'Ango' or 'me'… he hardly says anything… not even calling me Mommy."

"Limited vocabulary isn't unusual for a two-year-old," Dr. Meyer said. "How does he play with other children?"

"He doesn't," Rose said. "His nanny had a little boy next door come to visit, but Aidan wouldn't get near him."

"Does he respond to his name when you call it?"

Rose nodded to Angus as she answered. "He does to Angus… but not me."

Dr. Meyer made several notes on the clipboard chart, then walked a few paces, turned his back to Aidan, whistled loudly and clapped the clipboard against the surgical dressing cabinet. Startled – Aidan burst into tears. Meyer shrugged and said, "I was just checking to see if Aidan might be hearing impaired."

He paused, made a note on the clipboard. "Do you read to him?"

"Every night. He has twenty different picture books," Rose said.

"What does he do when he sees the pictures? Does he point to them or react in any way?"

Rose paused. "No… not really."

Dr. Meyer turned to Angus. "When you're playing the xylophone with him, does he look at you… make eye contact?"

Angus put his hand to his chin and said, "To tell you the truth, I've never noticed."

As Dr. Meyer made more notes, Angus whispered to Rose, "I think you should tell Dr. Meyer about Aidan biting Marcy."

Dr. Meyer had looked up from the clipboard and squinted at Rose. "Is there anything else I should know about Aidan's behavior?"

Her voice quavering, Rose said, "Aidan… bit his nanny on the arm… then bit himself. It was awful."

Dr. Meyer studied Rose's worried look, rubbed his chin and leaned back against the examination table.

"That isn't unheard of, but..." he paused, and as he made another notation on the clipboard, Angus and Rose exchanged puzzled glances. Dr. Meyer put the clipboard on the cabinet, turned to Rose and took her hands in his.

"I know it's difficult for you, but right now," he said, "I'd try not to get overly worried. My preliminary thought is that Aidan shows signs of *Autism Spectrum Disorder.* There's no specific test, but..."

"Is that a disease?" Angus interrupted.

"Not in the classic sense of the word," Dr. Meyer said. "There are different theories about the cause of autism. It's complicated, but the interesting thing is that many therapies involve music."

"What should we do?" Rose asked.

"For now, it sounds like you're doing the right things."

Dr. Meyer turned to Angus. "It would be good for Aidan if you keep working with him on the music."

Driving home, Angus turned to Rose.

"Dinner at my house Saturday night?"

"If I can farm Aidan out to Mom and Dad for the night."

15. HERE COMES THE SUN

When thc doorbell rang, Angus shivered in expectation. Stepping quickly to the door, he opened it to see Rose. She wore a scoop neck, floral print dress and flat-heeled shoes with subtle green eye shadow and ruby red lip gloss to match her fingernails. Her raven hair was neatly pinned in a French braid. Kissing him on the cheek, she handed Angus a four-bottle wine bag.

"I hope you like these," Rose said. "The red is Villa Antinori Chianti... and my favorite white... Marlborough Sauvignon Blanc"

"What's your preference... red or white?"

"I've never tried the red… Nikko said it's very smooth."

"Be right back," Angus said and turned to the kitchen.

"It smells glorious, let me help."

"Restricted area, off limits," Angus said.

Returning, he placed a serving tray on the coffee table in front of the sofa… two crystal wine glasses, the bottle of Antinori, an oval china plate of the fresh tuna ceviche, six Boursin cheese-laden crackers on a smaller plate, cocktail forks, napkins and snack plates.

"Cheers," he said as he handed Rose a glass of the Antinori.

Clinking their glasses together, Rose said, "I've been looking forward to this. The only thing missing is your straw hat."

"I'm using it for a pasta strainer," Angus said.

"You're using your good luck charm to drain spaghetti?"

"You'll love the taste," Angus said.

"Ugh!" Rose said and sat down on the sofa and sampled a cracker with Boursin.

"Maybe you'll play something for me later?"

"Only if you bribe me," he said.

"I didn't bring any money," she said, sip-tasting her Antinori.

"I prefer the barter system," he said. "We'll be alone in the basement."

"I was down there once," Rose said. "Your Valentine's Day party."

"Do you still have the poem?"

Rose pursed her lips, tapped on them with her index finger.

"Let me see… do you mean, '*If I were lightning I would shock you… if I were a band I would rock you'*… that poem?"

"No, *'If you were a breeze I would feel you… If you were a grape I would peel you.'*"

"Doesn't sound familiar," Rose said.

Angus hoisted his glass in a mini-salute and let the Antinori's luxurious bouquet of subtle Tuscan blackberry notes mixed with oak, tease his palate.

"How's Aidan?" he said.

"Same little monster."

"Maybe he just needs another music lesson," Angus said.

"I had to take his xylophone away from him this afternoon," Rose said. "He was on another rampage."

Rose munched on the *Boursin* and took a sip of her wine.

"He finally snapped out of it when I took him to Mom and Dad's at the lake this afternoon."

"I'll put the pasta on," Angus said, stepped to the bookcase behind the sofa and extracted a thick, black loose-leaf family photo album and put it on the coffee table in front of Rose. "This should keep you entertained for a few minutes."

His sumptuous spread orchestrated as if it were an elegant symphonic composition, Angus carried his freshly baked pretzel rolls, slab of creamy country butter, salver of *Parmgiano Reggiano,* pepper mill and two arugula salads to the dining room table. Shuffling back into the kitchen, he opened the Marlborough Sauvignon Blanc and circled back to the dining room through the living room.

"Would you care to join me for dinner?" he said.

Rose squinted at Angus. "No… you go ahead, I'm not hungry," she said.

"You'd better *get* hungry or you'll have to go straight to bed… no dessert, either."

"In that case, I'm starving."

Seating Rose to his left at the side of the dinner table, Angus sat at the head and passed the pretzel rolls and butter.

"They're warm," Rose said as took one from the wicker breadbasket.

"I just took them out of the oven," he said.

Rose smiled as she buttered a corner of the roll. "You're a regular Mr. *Poppin' Fresh.*"

"Let me fill your glass," Angus said, reaching for the chilled Sauvignon Blanc.

"I'll wait for dinner," Rose said. "I want to be alert enough to steal your recipe for… what are we having for dinner?"

"It's a surprise," Angus said. "So what's the deal with Bernie?"

"I hate to ruin the evening," Rose said.

"It's that bad?"

"I checked on the payroll records," Rose said. "Bernie has deposited money into an account as if three laid off employees were still on the payroll… the account has more than thirty-seven thousand dollars in it that no one knows anything about."

"Hold that thought," Angus said.

In the kitchen, Angus put the linguine into a pot of water and with thoughts of Bernie in the back of his mind, stirred the noodles until they were perfectly cooked… *al dente.* He dumped the pasta into a colander and let it drain. While stirring the clam sauce and inhaling its garlicky aroma, he unwrapped a stick of butter and dropped it into the sauce. He heaped the linguine onto two plates and ladled the rich sauce over each portion… adding four whole smiling clams around the edges of each plate.

He draped a white towel over his arm, balanced the plates carefully to keep the oil from spilling on the floor and sauntered into the dining room. "Clams a la Angus," he announced as he placed Rose's plate in front of her, sidled around the corner of the table and sat down.

"O my God," Rose muttered. "I had no idea..."

"Not too bad for a piano player, huh?"

Angus sprinkled a liberal spoonful of the freshly grated cheese over the tantalizing clam sauce and passed the salver to Rose.

"Have some Parmesan," he said.

"I... don't know what to say," Rose stammered

"Say '*buon appetito*' and dig in," Angus said.

Shaking her head, Rose said, "No... I should have told you..."

Angus stopped twirling his fork through the linguine. "What?"

Rose furrowed her brow. "I'm allergic... to shellfish."

Angus dropped his fork.

"You're allergic... to clams?"

Rose tried to smile as she said, "Especially clams... they make me deathly ill."

Angus arched his eyebrows.

"And just when I think I'm getting to know you..."

"That's the price you pay for hanging around with a wide-eyed innocent," Rose quipped, grinning.

Rocking back in his chair, Angus burst out laughing.

"Why didn't you say something? I would have made something else."

"You never gave me a chance... you kept doing your cloak-and-dagger thing."

"I wanted to surprise you."

"You did... I never suspected you would try to poison me."

"There are a lot of things I would like to do to you, but poisoning is not one of them," Angus said. "Can you eat some plain pasta with a little butter and cheese?"

"I don't want you to go to any trouble for me, OK?"

"Yes boss," Angus said as he got up and strolled toward the kitchen. "Try the salad… if you're allergic to that, we'll go to Wendy's."

~~~~~

Rose sipped the last of her favorite Sauvignon Blanc and said, "Would you be with me when I have the showdown with Bernie?"

"I'm here to help," Angus said.

"I still don't understand why she would lie to me about being married," Rose said.

"Easy enough to check it out," Angus said. "I'll talk with Robby."

"Piano time?" Rose said.

With Rose at his side on Aummie's piano bench, Angus played the song he knew was Rose's favorite, "The Impossible Dream." As he played the fourth phrase, *To run where the brave dare not go,* Rose sang the lyrics. Her voice – a sweet lilting alto – surprised Angus. "You have a nice voice," he said, "Keep singing."

"I don't know the rest of the words," she said.

"Here's my favorite song, "All The Things You Are,"" Angus said. As he played, Rose rested her head on his shoulder. When he finished, he pulled Rose to him. Enfolding Angus in her arms, Rose lifted her head and kissed him gently on the lips. Their kiss lingering, Angus caressed her breast. Rose moaned softly and put her hand on his leg. "Are all piano playing chefs as…" Her words trailed off as the jangling phone interrupted their moment.

"I'm not answering the damned phone," Angus said as he held Rose close.

"It might be Mom," Rose said and pulled back.

Reluctantly, Angus picked up the receiver, said "Hello" and quickly handed the phone to Rose. "I didn't know you were clairvoyant."
~~~~~

As Angus sat quietly, Rose's face clouded. She finished talking with her mother and handed the phone back to Angus. "I have to leave. Aidan burned his hand. Mom was taking a pie out of the oven and Aidan touched the hot rack when she turned away. They just got back from the hospital."

~~~~~

His face somber, Rose's father met them at the door.

"The doctor said Aidan's burn isn't too bad," he said. "He gave your mother some baby Tylenol for him… she's with him in our bedroom watching cartoons."

"Do you mind visiting with Angus for a few minutes while I go see Aidan?" Rose said

As Rose rushed to the bedroom, her father turned to Angus. "Let's sit in the living room," he said and gestured to the expansive, richly furnished room Angus remembered so well. As they sat down, Rose's father crossed his legs and focused on Angus.

"Rose has too much on her plate right now," he said, "She has her hands full with Aidan let alone working at the Inn. I wish she would just quit and move back home here to be with him."

"I… Rose is the most… determined person I've ever met," Angus said.

"She's the most *bullheaded* person *I've* ever met," Mr. Gracewood said and smiled. "How do you manage to get along with her?"

"We're very complementary," Angus said.

"If I know Rose," her father said, "She dishes out the orders and everyone scrambles to keep her happy."

"Rose and I have a difference of opinion now and then, but I love working with her," Angus said.
~~~~~

They sat quietly until Rose's father leaned forward and said, "Rose told me about your leaving a good job as a chef in Columbus to come back to the Inn."

Angus sat forward, touched his scarred thumb. "Mr. Sewell… helped me out after I injured my hand. The Sewell family has been very supportive…"

"I'd like for you to think about something," Rose's father said. "If you can persuade Rose to partner with my friend, Sean Sweeney, up here at the Waterbury Resort… I can set *both* of you up with a very good situation."

Angus turned away briefly then leveled his eyes at Rose's father.

"I couldn't do that, Mr. Gracewood. I wouldn't feel right doing that."

Rose's father reached over and tapped Angus on his knee.

"I like that," he said. "Honesty and loyalty go a long way with me."

Before they could talk further, Rose appeared with Aidan in her arms. "Looks like the big boy is fine," she said. "Just a nasty boo-boo." As Rose bundled Aidan up to leave, his eyes lit up when he saw Angus. "Ango! Boo-boo!" he chirped and brandished his bandaged hand for Aidan to see. Angus stood and patted Aidan on the back.

"Know just how you feel, Aid," Angus said. "Been there myself."

~~~~~

Riding back to Fountain Point, Aidan slept soundly in his baby seat secured in the back seat of Rose's car. As they turned onto SR-33 toward Fountain Point, Rose leaned toward Angus and whispered, "What did you and Dad talk about?"

"He said you were the most loving, selfless daughter a father could have."
~~~~~

16. REVELATION BLUES

Before Claire could hang her coat up in her office closet on Monday morning, her phone rang, the caller ID: *Carter Duffy.*

"Yes, Mr. Duffy?"

"I'm here with Dabney Merritt. Come up to my office immediately."

As Anna Belle welcomed Claire and escorted her into Duffy's inner sanctum, the two men sat mutely at Duffy's mahogany inlaid conference table. Approaching them, Claire was startled when Duffy slammed a copy of the previous Saturday morning's *Examiner* on the conference table. Tapping on the front-page article about the Inn's filing for bankruptcy, Duffy barked, "Take a seat, Claire."

"I spoke with Mr. Duffy about our conversation regarding the Inn's obligation to the bank," Dabney said.

"I'll handle this, Dabney," Duffy snapped, coughed into his fist and slathered a dollop of Purell on his hands. He turned to Claire. "Tell me about the Inn's filing for bankruptcy. Did you know about it before I read it in the paper?"

"I knew about the possibility…" Claire said.

"I'm not talking *possibilities*," Duffy fumed. "Did you know it was going to happen?"

"Not when I spoke with Mr. Merritt," Claire said. "I suggested several ideas about working with the Inn but he rejected them out of hand."

"All bad, I might add," Dabney put in.

"Here are my notes about out conversation," Claire said and handed the file folder to Duffy. "Mr. Duffy… not to be disrespectful, but Mr. Merritt said that you handled all the financials on Dad's loan. In fact, he told me that I had a conflict of interest."

Fingering the file folder, Duffy said, "I'll look at this later. Tell me why you didn't talk to me personally about this… I'm in goddamned charge at this bank."

"Mr. Merritt said that he had already talked with you and you agreed that the bank should take possession of the Inn."

"When did he tell you that?"

Dabney squirmed in his chair as Claire continued.

"When we met last Monday," Claire said.

Duffy glowered at Dabney. Boring in on him, Duffy growled: "When did you look at the Inn's last financial statement… Charlie's too?"

"Claire is in charge of all the loan financials… I only see them when there's a problem," Dabney said.

Duffy's cough rocked the conference table.

"So you didn't think all the problems with the Inn, the bad publicity, missing a line-of-credit payment the first of this month… filing for bankruptcy…you didn't think *any of that* was a goddamned problem?"

"I didn't see it. I…"

Reaching for the Purell, Duffy slathered his hands again and scowled at Dabney.

"Mr. Merritt! You mean to tell me you want to be president of my bank and you screwed up on something as basic as not looking at a borrower's goddamned financial statement?"

Dabney's face flushed as he scowled at Claire.

"I'll thank *you* for this, Ms. Sewell… or McCrory, whatever," Dabney sputtered. "You had every opportunity to bring this matter to the attention of Mr. Duffy before the Inn filed for bankruptcy. It was up to you to… "

"Don't blame your bonehead blunder on Claire," Duffy said. "Your screw-up is going to cost me and my bank a lot of money!"

17. THOSE ENDEARING YOUNG CHARMS

As Rose, Angus and Robby finished Claire's traditional St. Paddy's Day dinner, Robby rambled into the kitchen, returned with a file folder and took his seat.

"Got the dope on Miss Bernie Walker," he said.

"Do we have to talk about her?" Rose said.

"I asked Robby to check on her marriage," Angus said. "I thought it was weird that she told you she'd never been married."

Robby took a long draught of Guinness and tapped on the file folder.

"Hold onto your gonads, little bro'," Robby said.

"Don't be crude," Claire said.

"The old man always said, 'a mule doesn't change his spots,'" Robby said. "Looks like he might be right. Did you ever hear of a woman named Joan Christian?"

Angus shook his head.

"AKA Misty Coleman?" Robby asked.

"Bernie's friend?" Angus said.

"Great friend," Robby said. "She's wanted for theft by deceit, solicitation, extortion and conspiracy to defraud. On top of that, she's been busted for coke… three times."

"Holy shit," Angus said.

"I talked with a detective on the Orlando Vice Squad. He told me she's been involved with ID theft from credit cards. Says she scammed them while working for a strip joint in Orlando. She also had an extortion charge filed against her by a man named Richey Ames. He owns Ames Payroll Service, but for some reason, he dropped the charges."

"Bernie told me she worked for Ames Payroll Services," Angus said.

"On a hunch, I checked that out," Robby said. "Ames said that Bernie quit to get married. He refused to discuss his extortion charge against Misty."

"What do you think that's all about?" Rose said.

After another draught of Guinness, Robby said, "With Misty's profile, my guess is that she was shacking up with Ames and threatened to blow his cover by telling his wife if Ames pressed charges."

Angus pinched his eyebrows and sat back.

"Anything on Bernie's marriage?"

Robby flipped through his notes. "Bernie and her husband, Lloyd Marshall, got married in Orlando. Orange County records show their marriage date of March twenty-six last year. Misty... a fine felon... stood up for Bernie."

"That was the weekend after I saw her on St. Paddy's Day," Angus said.

"You were with Bernie the week before she got married?" Rose said.

"I had no idea she was getting *married*," Angus said.

"She got that Lexus she drives and has an account at the Huntington Bank where she tucked away her divorce settlement of fifty thousand dollars," Robby said.

"I might be able to find out a little more," Claire said. "I have a friend at the Huntington I interned with a few summers ago."

"Don't bother, Claire… I don't want to know," Rose said.

18. TOGETHER AGAIN

After welcoming Rose and Susie into her office to discuss the final May Day Parade plans, Mayor Bunny scrunched into her swivel chair and squinted at the list of parade floats Susie handed her.

"Looks like you done your homework," Mayor Bunny said. "See you got the Lions Club and the Masons. First time that Cadillac dealer ponied up, too."

"I talked to Mrs. McCrory at the Logan County Citizens Bank. She's the bank's community relations person," Susie said. "The bank will contribute twenty-five hundred dollars to the fireworks."

"What about Fountain Point Savings?"

"Mr. Inskeep was very nice when I asked him if it was OK for LCCB to participate," Susie said. "As long as Fountain Point Savings can have the only banners along the parade route and at the fireworks, he didn't have a problem."

"We need to get you on the City Council," Mayor Bunny said. "Those old buzzards couldn't talk a starving coyote into a steak dinner."

"The only thing…" Susie paused, "…is the grand marshal."

"Who ya' got lined up?"

Susie shuffled her feet.

"I haven't asked anyone, yet."

Mayor Bunny leaned her fat arms on her desk. "Damn girl… gettin' pretty late, ain't it?" she said. "How come?"

"I've been thinking… it's always been a man… but maybe it could be a woman this year."

Mayor Bunny rocked back in her chair. "If you're thinkin' about me, forget it. I was the grand marshal a few years back. All I heard was a lot of damned catcalls about fixing potholes."

Susie stifled a laugh. "I was thinking about a woman who works at the Inn… and sings over at Bountiful AME Church."

"I know Pastor Lionel over there," the Mayor said. "He's got a whole passel of ladies singing every Sunday. Who are you talking about?"

"Gracious Maxy," Susie said.

Mayor Bunny rocked back in her chair.

"Hell… I remember her," she said. "She sang at the high school graduation the year I was the guest speaker. Bunny turned to Rose. "Memory serves me right, you were the valedictorian."

Rose nodded. "Gracious has a beautiful voice… she sings all the time at work."

Mayor Bunny tapped a chewed-up ballpoint pen on her desk and turned back to Susie. "Will you have her sing during the parade?" Bunny asked.

"Angus said he has a portable sound system… he can set it up on the back of her convertible. Is it OK to ask Mrs. Maxy?" Susie said.

"What kind of music is she going sing?"

"Gospel… spirituals… she can start the fireworks with the National Anthem."

"Some of the jokers in this town could use a good dose of Gospel music… go ahead, sign her up," Mayor Bunny said. "What else ya' got on your mind?"

"Rose… I mean Miss Gracewood and I thought that maybe… you might help out judging the floats," Susie said.

"Like to help you out girl, but can't do it," Mayor Bunny said. "Some knucklehead will accuse me of playing politics with the awards."

"Well… Okey-dokey… "

"Try that art teacher up at the high school," Bunny interrupted. "Her name's Gillepsi… something like that."

"I remember her," Rose said. "Evelyn… Evelyn *Gillespie.* Her husband owns the Cadillac dealership."

"He's letting us use one of his convertibles for the grand marshal," Susie said.

Plagued by arthritic joints, Mayor Bunny struggled to her feet. "Gotta get ready for Council meeting tonight," she said. "I'll ramrod your budget through so fast those bozos won't know what hit 'em. We'll make it the best fireworks show this town has ever seen."

19. THE PARTY'S OVER

Rose's father arrived Saturday morning to pick up Aidan. Sleepless the entire night after rehearsing what she would say to Bernie, Rose – clutching her robe, her eyes bleary – met him at the door as Aidan played on the floor. When her father lifted Aidan into his arms, Aidan yelped, "Poppy… *Girling…* Mimi… Boo-boo!"

Rose kissed Aidan and pecked her father on the cheek.

"You look like you need some time off," he said.

"I'll relax after my meeting this morning," Rose said.

"Your mother has to come to my office Monday afternoon… we'll bring Aidan home by dinner time but we'd like to have him stay for a few extra days sometime."

"Aidan will love that… so will I…"

"Let us know when you can come home for a few days."

~~~~~

A hundred thoughts clashed in Rose's mind as she unlocked her office, stepped through the door and stashed her handbag under her desk. Not daring to signal Bernie that there was anything less than casual about their meeting, Rose dressed in her normal work attire. Granted, she had no solid proof of Bernie's intentional wrongdoing… it was just the agonizing issue of firing a once-trusted employee, a former friend... devious and deceitful.

She rang Angus' extension.
~~~~~

"Hey-hey… it's going to be an ugly day. Are you up for this?" Angus said

"I'm so nervous, I could throw-up. Can you bring in some coffee?"

"Should I put a shot of Bailey's Irish Cream in it?"

"Maybe at home tonight… after this God-awful meeting!"

~~~~~

Angus and Rose had been talking for nearly a half-hour in Rose's office when Bernie arrived. Though Angus had helped Rose brace herself for the troubling scene about to unfold, her hands dripped with perspiration. No handshaking… get right down to business.

"Greetings," Bernie said. She put out her hand. Rose ignored it. "Have a seat," Rose said.

Disheveled, her eyes watery, her face pale, Bernie wore no make up, her skin patchy with red marks clearly visible on the corners of her nose and her upper lip. Jittery, she slouched to the conference table and plopped down across from Angus and Rose.

"Bernie… there're several things I'm concerned about," Rose began. "Actually more than just concerned… I'm livid!"

"Livid? What's this about?" Bernie said, sitting erect.

"Bernie," Rose paused, "You may think I'm naïve or even stupid, but I know you're doing a lot of dishonest things as our business manager."

Bernie reared back.

"I resent that! I'll be damned if I have any idea about what you're talking about. Tell me one thing I've ever done that's dishonest."

Rose shook her head nervously.

"For one, you've set up your own advertising agency to bill the Inn for our advertising and keeping the fifteen percent commission for yourself."
~~~~~

"That's legitimate," Bernie huffed. "The Inn doesn't pay one penny more just because I bill it through my advertising agency!"

"So, you admit that you're making commissions on our advertising billing?"

"I'm entitled to it! I..."

"You are *not* entitled to it," Rose snapped. "You work for the Inn at Mary's Gate. If you want to run an advertising agency, be my guest... but not here."

"That's petty bullshit!" Bernie blustered. "You called me in here today to tell me I shouldn't have set up an advertising agency? I can turn that off in a heartbeat."

"There're a few other things I'd like you to explain."

Bernie glared at Rose. "I can explain everything I do!"

Rose glanced at Angus, his dejection clear at Bernie's imminent self-destruction.

"You've made arrangements for so-called emergency linen services and some kind of a deal with State Wholesale Foods to overcharge us," Rose said. "Explain that!"

"First of all, we've used the linen service. I don't remember where or when or how many times, but for sure, that laggard, Gracious Maxy, can't keep up with laundering things. That's why I use the linen service."

Angus hunched his shoulders, sat forward. "Quit bullshitting, Bern. I know for a fact that JoJo Gardini is mixed up with Lima Linen and State Wholesale. You're paying at least a fifteen percent premium over the published prices from other reputable vendors. JoJo's whole act is a scam."

Bernie sniffed hard, pinched her nose. Feeling a trickle of blood on her upper lip, she quickly reached for a tissue from her purse and covered it.

"I've done everything possible to keep our yearly prices protected from increases," she said, dabbing at her nose.

"Let me finish," Angus said. "State Wholesale is notorious for giving kickbacks. How much are you making from those bandits?"

"I don't have to sit here and take that crap from some two-bit kitchen jockey," Bernie hissed. "Where the hell do you get off accusing me of taking kickbacks? I make legitimate commissions! I play the game…"

"Stop it," Rose demanded. "You're in over your head, so I'd suggest you listen up."

Bernie shot Rose a withering stare.

"I have a hair appointment," she rasped. "When you have something you think you can prove, you know where to find me."

"I'm not finished!" Rose shouted. "You've been scheming with our payroll records, too. And don't deny it. You want proof, I have it."

Panic clouding her face, Bernie perched on the edge of her chair.

"It's all here, Bernie," Rose said, as she passed a copy of the bank documents across the table to her.

Bernie scowled at the documents. "What's all *this crap?*"

"Just a couple of *small* items," Rose said, cynically. "You're secreting payroll amounts in the bank for people who don't work here any longer. You opened an account at the bank called *Escrow IPR*… it's bogus. You might think I'm not smart enough to figure this out, but you set yourself up to steal the money you squirreled away from three laid-off employees. Should I name them?"

Slumping back, her face ashen, hands trembling, Bernie burst into tears.

"Honest, Rose, I… I planned to surprise Mr. Sewell with a year-end refund on all the money. I thought he would be happy to find out that I'd saved the money from those three employees."

"Come on, Bernie," Rose said. "And you know what else? Mr. Sewell's death gave you a perfect smoke screen."

"That's not true!"

"You knew you could use all of the chaos to conveniently forget about telling anyone about that escrow account. It would be easily overlooked and you'd wait until it was completely forgotten and take the money."

"I *never* took any money..."

"And you know the truth? You were almost right. Except for one little problem... I figured it out!" Rose barked.

"You've always been a goddamned smart-ass, Rosemary."

"Stop it, Bernie," Angus said.

"Don't give me any of your shit, Angus. You've had a hard on for Rosemary since grade school."

"You're way out of bounds, Bernie," Rose said. "Don't even bother to apologize."

Bernie looked at Angus... then back to Rose.

"At least I fucked your boyfriend!"

"Get out, Bernie... you're fired!" Rose screamed.

"Piss off! Admit it... you're firing me because I screwed Angus.... something I doubt you have!"

Her heart racing, Rose's face flushed crimson.

"You're lucky I'm not going to press charges for fraud," Rose said. "And don't think for a minute you're getting any severance pay. Keep the stupid commissions on the schemes you've wangled... and you can thank JoJo for his thieving generosity."

"He's not..."

"Give me your keys!"

Bernie slammed the keys on Rose's desk and stalked out.

Rose sighed and turned to Angus who took her hand and pulled it to him as she murmured, "I'll never, *never* understand *why* she did this."

~~~~~

At home, Rose took a long soothing bath, then dried off and dressed in a pleated, slim-waist aqua linen blouse with pearl buttons, tucked it into her slinkiest blue satin slacks, inserted a pair of aquamarine ear studs and – completing her ensemble – fastened the matching pendant necklace and slipped into a comfortable pair of black flats. Checking her image in the dresser mirror, she applied a thin coat of eye shadow matching her Lilac Champagne lipstick, adjusted the tortoise clip in her French braid. In the kitchen after icing a bottle of white L'Alycastre '91 Nikko had recommended, she cracked the seal on bottle of Black Bush. Searching her cupboards, she found the fish poacher, opened the refrigerator and unwrapped the fresh, wild king salmon filets Cliff had ordered for her. She glanced at the recipe, but Bernie's crude remark, *At least I fucked your boyfriend,* had so rattled her, she had difficulty concentrating. Did Angus really… go to bed with Bernie? Or was that something Bernie said just to hurt her? Angus had admitted that he'd been with Bernie the week before she'd gotten married. Was *she,* Rose, herself... the '*wide-eyed innocent'* Angus had accused her of being? Did it matter? Even if it were true… Rose had left Angus and Fountain Point to marry a man who'd proved to be no more honorable than Bernie. Now… she and Angus had grown close. Though never having actually said it to him, she had tried to show him her love.

~~~~~

Preparing for dinner with Rose, Angus dressed in a new pair of tan wool pants and a dark blue crew neck sweater over a white collared long sleeve shirt. He dug into his closet and pulled out his lace-up cordovan Dockers, brush-polished them and slipped them on. Donning his straw hat and winter coat, he drove to Rose's home.

The scent of lavender greeted him as he stepped into the foyer. Strolling into Rose's living room, he spotted a lighted candle on the coffee table, a salver of candied cranberries and cherries, a silver plate with a wedge of blue cheese. A silver cocktail fork lay atop a copper compote of mixed olives… a plate of water crackers next to it. Doffing his coat and straw hat, he stepped to the kitchen door and said, "Knock, knock."

"I thought I heard you come in," Rose said

"How'd you know I wasn't the local axe murderer?"

Rose moved next to Angus. "I don't remember inviting him," she said as she left a light imprint of her lipstick on Angus' cheek.

"Anything I can do to help?" he said.

Reaching for the wine, she said, "Open this," and handed Angus a corkscrew and two crystal wine glasses.

"Not very much for me, I don't want to miss dinner," Rose said.

"I'll think of some way to keep you awake," Angus said as he handed her the glass of white wine.

She tugged Angus toward the living room. "I'll put on some music," she said. "Do you like Tony Bennett?"

"I like being here with you even if you liked Def Leppard," Angus said.

Music playing softly, Rose sat next to Angus on the sofa. "Do you really like teaching Aidan music?"

"He has more musical intuition at two than I had at ten."

As Angus reached for a cracker, Rose touched his right hand and felt the scar of his knife wound.

"I'm so sorry about your accident... and not going to music school."

Angus felt a tug of regret. "I can still play good enough to have a lot of fun."

Angus topped a cracker with a chunk of blue cheese. "I've been thinking about Aidan's autism. He's a different little person when he's with me playing music."

"No question... there's something magic about it."

Angus popped a cranberry into his mouth.

"Pretty fancy spread for a cheerleader turned business mogul," he said.

"I've been thinking about the Inn," Rose said.

"Not me," Angus said. "Not after that scene with Bernie today."

Rose's eyes looked brighter, less fatigued than they'd been over the past few weeks, Angus thought. But he knew Rose had a way of asking questions with her eyes without saying a word. He sat back into the sofa cushions, touched Rose's arm and said, "If you want to know about what happened between Bernie and me… "

Rose shifted slightly on the sofa. Her voice barely audible, she said, "No… I don't need to know, it just… it hurt me."

Angus put his hand over Rose's hand.

"It hurt me, too, to find out I was so gullible about her," he said. "I regret it."

"We don't need to talk about her," Rose said.

Angus lifted Rose's chin and looked into her eyes. "She was right when she said how I've felt about you since St. Pat's."

Smiling, Rose put her hand on Angus' chin. "No way," she said. "I had no clue."

"Sure. I never gave you the slightest inkling I thought you were anything but a dud… that *Claddagh* I gave you was a bad joke."

Rose broke into a wide grin. "That was…"

"I still have it at home in my dresser drawer along with that funky plate you gave me with the *Irish Blessing."*

"Before you get too maudlin, there's something else I'd like to discuss."

Angus freshened his wine and nodded to Rose's glass. "More?"

"Just a splash," Rose said.

Lifting her wine glass to her lips, Rose collected her thoughts.

"If we don't find a buyer or a business partner for the Inn to get out from under the debt... I'm worried that it will end up closing or the bank will auction it off," she said.

Mulling her remark, Angus sniffed the flinty bouquet of the L'Alycastre.

"You think that could really happen? The Sewell family would lose the Inn?"

"The Inn owes the bank six-hundred-twenty-five thousand dollars," Rose said. "Talking with Speed and Claire over the last three weeks...there's no doubt the bank will make some grandstand play to get off the hook."

"I wish I could help, but... six-hundred twenty-five thousand dollars?"

"You *can* help..."

"Should I stop by a cash machine?"

"I talked with my father. What would you say if I told you that I have the money?"

Though Angus knew that Rose and her family were wealthy, her comment was a total surprise. Angus cocked his head and said, "What... did he say?"

"He's very conservative, but I know he'll help me decide if I would be doing the right thing by investing in the Inn. I'd like for you to help me decide, too."

Angus stood, paced Rose's living room floor. "I have no idea what to say. I was never very good at business except for running my little band… and running a kitchen… and…"

"But you *could* help me… I'm asking if you'll work with me… on everything… not just running the food and beverage operations."

He put his hand on Rose's shoulder. "I think I'll run home and get that *Claddagh,*" he said.

"Is that a 'yes'?"

"If I say 'no'… I'm afraid you might poison me with your dinner."

Angus sat down on the sofa and turned to Rose. "Where do we go from here?"

"I'm going to the kitchen and fix dinner while you put on another CD," she said.

"Can I watch you fix dinner?" Angus said.

"If you're bored, you can open another bottle of wine."

~~~~~

As Ray Charles sang, "I Can't Stop Loving You," Angus and Rose sat down at her dining room table. Angus surveyed the array of dishes: fresh salmon poached in a *court-bouillon* topped with dill weed and capers, thin spears of asparagus scented with fresh lemon, curly endive with warm goat-cheese and pistachios. Rose passed the salmon platter to Angus and said, "Dad caught this salmon off our dock at the lake. It's the only salmon ever caught in Indian Lake."

Angus nodded as he helped himself to the salmon. "Bet the grizzly bears are pissed."

Rose passed a blue wicker breadbasket to Angus.

"Roll? Shirleen made them."

"You swiped rolls from the Inn?"

"You've got me mixed up with our friend Bernie," Rose said.
~~~~~

“Let it rest, Rose. You’re serious about investing in the Inn?”

“I owe a lot to the Sewells. I loved Charlie. He gave me a chance to prove myself when I came home and tried to get over my divorce.”

~~~~~

As Rose cleared the table, Angus selected a different Ray Charles CD and punched ‘play’… “Someday.” Glancing toward the kitchen to see Rose making coffee, he turned up the volume on the CD, strolled into the kitchen, stood behind Rose and touched her shoulder.

“OH! You scared me,” she said, as she turned toward him.

“How’s the coffee coming?”

“It’ll be just a minute,” she said, as she turned back to the coffee maker.

Encircling Rose with his arms, he gently pulled her back into his body.

“I made a special dessert...”

Turning Rose around to face him, he felt her tremble as he kissed her.

Nuzzling Angus’ neck, she whispered in his ear. “Ange… I don’t want you to be disappointed,” she murmured, but her words disappeared as Angus’ lips smothered her mouth.

Sitting on the edge of her bed, Angus watched Rose at her dresser as she removed her necklace. She sat on the bed and kicked off her shoes. As Ray Charles sang, “What Would I Do Without You,” Rose turned her back to him.

“You can undo me if you like,” she said.

Willing his tentative fingers to function, he released Rose’s bra and marveled at her creamy bare back, tracing his fingers in circles around it.

“Mmm…” Rose murmured, “Don’t stop.”
~~~~~

Angus rushed to undress. Bending over to untie his shoes, he lost his balance and slipped off the bed. As he lay on the floor, he grappled with his uncooperative shoelaces then wrenched his shoes off and pitched them aside.

"Do you have as much trouble getting dressed as you do *undressed*?" Rose said.

Angus stood, pulled his crew neck sweater up over his head. As it bunched up under his chin, Rose said, "If you don't hurry up, I'll be out of the mood." Pitching his sweater aside, Angus said, "If you're not too bored, you can unbuckle my belt."

They lay back on her bed and embraced. Rose shivered as Angus put his lips to her ear and kissed her. She felt his firmness press against her, but from somewhere… the thought of finally satisfying her suppressed desire for intimacy with Angus filled her with fear. It had been a long, long time since she'd shared intimacy with Patrick, a lothario she had come to detest. Now, her feelings deeper than she could imagine, Angus was in her arms. As Angus pulled her close, she twisted her body away.

"Wait. My arm…"

"What?"

"You were laying on my arm," she said, as she freed her arm.

"You all right now?"

"Are you comfortable?" Rose whispered.

"Yes… I'm… " he replied, as Rose kissed him. The sweetness of her tongue left him breathless. "I love you," Angus said.

"I've wanted to hear you say that for a long time," Rose purred. "I love you, too."

"Do you want to… now?" he whispered.

"You don't have to ask," she said as she pulled Angus onto her.

20. COKE TIME

On his way back to Fountain Point after meeting with Johnny Mocha late Sunday, JoJo checked his cell phone… three calls from Bernie. Oddly, she didn't answer his return call until the fourth ring, her voice barely audible.

"JoJo?"

"Bernie… you sound hung over."

"Where are you?"

"Coming home from Lima."

"I've been trying to call you."

"How much have you had to drink?"

"I… got fired… Rosemary…"

"Fired?"

"I'll tell you about it… when I see you."

"Where?" JoJo said.

Bernie slurred her words. "I left some of my things at the Inn… I still have a key to the back door."

"What about security?"

"That old man watches TV at night. Besides, he knows me."

"What about any guests?"

"They always check out early on Sunday. I'll meet you in the parking lot."

~~~~~

Sitting in her Lexus waiting for JoJo, Bernie finished the second bottle of vodka she'd started swigging after finishing the first one earlier that afternoon. As JoJo pulled onto the Inn's parking lot near the back entrance, Bernie cleared her eyes and watched as he got out of his Mercedes, spotted Bernie's car and sauntered over.
~~~~~

"Bernie… what the hell happened?"

"Let's go inside," she said.

Wobbling as she stepped out of her Lexus and led JoJo to the back door, she unlocked it and entered the Inn ahead of him.

"I have a master key to the rooms. We'll use the bridal suite," she said.

Bernie tottered up the stairway to the second floor and entered a spacious, richly appointed bridal suite. Unsteady, Bernie worked her way to the end table next to a settee, turned on a dragonfly *Tiffany* lamp, tucked her handbag under the corner of the coffee table and flopped down on small couch.

JoJo moseyed around, took in the array of period antiques. *Belle Epoch* prints and vintage posters accented the room's unique décor. A framed panel of leaded art glass featuring the Muses of Comedy and Tragedy, hung over the William Morris settee where Bernie sat.

"Nice pad," JoJo said. "Tell me what happened."

Bernie sat on the edge of the settee and told JoJo about the scene in Rose's office.

"Quit worrying… those credit cards are gold. We start doing business next week in Chicago," JoJo said. "Couple of months and you'll be rollin' in cash."

"Did you bring anything?" Bernie said.

"Say hello to Aunt Nora," JoJo said, as he put Johnny Mocha's package of pure coke on the coffee table. "One line of this blow and you'll quit worrying about everything."

JoJo snorted a line, rocked back... pinched his nose.

Bernie snorted the other line, sat back, blinked her eyes. Within minutes, her worries dissolved into a state of bliss.

With Bernie in his arms, her body supple under the coke's spell, JoJo fondled her. The king-sized bed of the Inn's bridal suite beckoning, she disrobed in the sitting area, held up her hand signaling a pause. "Don't want to fly on one wing… just one more little snort?" JoJo pushed the envelope in front of Bernie. "Go easy!" he said. After Bernie inhaled her second line, she tossed her head back and murmured, "Jesus...oh… God…"

His high piqued by the sight of Bernie's voluptuous body, JoJo led her into the bedroom. Her naked body lying beside him, Bernie suddenly wrenched back and clutched her chest. "JoJo," she croaked. "I… can't breathe!"

"Relax… you'll be fine in a minute," JoJo said.

"I… I…" Bernie gasped and slid off the bed onto the floor. Rolling to the edge of the bed to see her pallid face contort in agonizing desperation, JoJo bounded out of bed, knelt over Bernie's convulsing body.

"Goddammit, you dizzy bitch... I told you to *go easy*!"

He glanced at the phone, deliberated. He couldn't be linked to an OD. He picked up the room phone and dialed 911.

"This is 911," the voice said. "Is this an emergency?"

"Yes… my friend… she… collapsed… " JoJo sputtered.

"Talk to me! Is she breathing?"

"She's… she's not moving. We're at the Inn at Mary's Gate… bridal suite."

"Stay with her until the squad arrives. They'll need your help about what happened. Try to stay calm," the voice ordered.

JoJo scrambled to dress, picked up the packet of left over coke, ran down the stairs and headed for the back exit. Nearly running into a gnarled old man shuffling toward him, JoJo shielded his face, pushed past the old man and bolted out the door, leaving it ajar.

Minutes later, the emergency squad arrived and burst though the back door to be greeted by Snuff Guffy.

"You the one who called?" the squad leader said.

"No... I was getting ready to leave after checking things out for the night," Snuff said. "I heard the emergency call on my hand set."

"Where's the bridal suite?"

"Follow me," Snuff said.

~~~~~

As the medic administered CPR to Bernie's motionless form, he yelled, "She's breathing but we'll have to get her to the ER!"

With Bernie laying comatose on a portable gurney, the emergency squad rushed out the back door to the ambulance. As Snuff followed, a Fountain Point police cruiser pulled onto the Inn parking lot. Patrolman, Clint Mitchell, jumped out of the cruiser and approached Snuff.

"Checking out the 911 call," he said. "Everything under control?"

Snuff handed a scrap of paper to the patrolman. On it was the Mercedes' license plate number Snuff had scribbled.

"Saw some guy busting out the back door," Snuff said. "Seemed like he was in a god-awful hurry."

"Who are you?" Mitchell said.

"Security," Snuff said.

~~~~~

Snuff Guffy and Clint Mitchell stood quietly while Rob McCrory inspected the bridal suite. As Rob picked up a stylish handbag tucked under the settee in the sitting area, a premonition gripped him. Rummaging through the purse, he extracted a lizard skin billfold, opened it and flipped to a driver's license. His heart skipped a beat as he stared at the photo of Bernie Walker sealed under plastic. Returning Bernie's ID to her purse, he closed the handbag, passed it to Clint Mitchell.

"Hold onto this, run a check on that license number Guffy gave you and get back to me pronto."

Rob turned to Snuff.

"After I call Rosemary Gracewood, lock this room and don't let anyone in!"

Anxiously, Robby dialed Rose. "Sorry to call you so late on a Sunday. It's Bernie," Robby said. "She and some man were at the Inn tonight. He called the Emergency Squad but didn't identify himself. Looks like a drug overdose."

"What?"

"Bernie is critically ill in Mary Rutan," Rob said. "I'm heading there right now. Give Angus a shout and meet me as soon as you can."

~~~~~

An Asian man dressed in green hospital scrubs approached Rob, Rose and Angus as they sat in the Emergency waiting room. His eyes serious, he spoke in a confident, assertive tone.

"I'm Dr. Yee... you are...?"

"Detective McCrory," Rob said and turned to Angus and Rose. "This is my brother Angus and Rosemary Gracewood from the Inn at Mary's Gate, where the emergency squad found the victim."

Dr. Yee nodded. "A very sick young lady," he said. "She's had three seizures... profuse bleeding from her nasal passages. Her heart stopped but we got it started again. We'll have to wait for the lab report to confirm the substance but I think it's cocaine."

"Is she awake?" Rose asked.

"She's in the ICU, but you'll have to wait until tomorrow morning to see her."

As Dr. Yee departed, Patrolman Clint Mitchell burst through the ER door, spotted Robby and rushed to his side.

"Got the info on that car," he said. "Mercedes 500SL convertible. Owner listed as Patrice Gardini. Last known residence... Dakota Drive."
~~~~~

"Pick him up and bring him down to headquarters. I'd like to talk with him… tonight!"

~~~~~

11:00 a.m. in Bernie's dimly lit room, the sound of her heart monitor beeped ominously. An antiseptic odor filled the air… tubes taped to her... an I.V. drip perfused her veins. When Rose touched Bernie's arm, Bernie turned her bleary eyes to her unexpected visitors and whispered, "I'm so sorry…"

"Take it easy, Bernie," Angus said.

"We're here to help you," Rose said.

"But…"

"You need help," Angus said. "We'll get you into rehab somewhere."

"I don't have any money…"

"If you'll get help, I'll work something out," Rose said.

"I owe you… " Bernie cried.

"Will you go along? Let us get you some help?" Angus said.

"I can't believe you'd be willing…"

"Bernie. Will you *cooperate*?" Rose said.

"Yes," Bernie muttered... "JoJo…"

"JoJo's in jail… where he belongs," Angus said.

Bernie rolled her head to the side and sobbed.

"JoJo," Bernie cried. "I gave JoJo copies of some of the Inn's guest credit card numbers."

"For crissakes," Angus said.

"They're clipped together in the back of the filing cabinet in my office," Bernie murmured.

~~~~~

Angus and Rose rushed into Bernie's cluttered office. Rose stepped to the metal filing cabinet along the wall next to Bernie's desk, opened the top drawer labeled, *Guest Records* and rifled through it. Nothing. She opened the second drawer… nothing. At the back of the bottom drawer, she saw a thin file folder with sheets of paper held together by a green alligator clip. She picked the file folder out of the drawer, sat it on Bernie's desk, unclipped the papers, spread them out on the desktop and ran her finger down the list of names and credit card numbers. With Angus looking over her shoulder, Rose studied the five pages of entries.

~~~~~

Rose, Angus and Robby sat in Rose's office as Robby leafed through the sheaf of papers with the credit card information, shook his head and turned to Rose.

"If the Feds find out about this, they'll be all over it," Robby said. "You have to contact these card holders and the credit card companies immediately. If we can short circuit this mess in time, Bernie might get lucky."

"How lucky is *lucky?"* Angus said.

"If Bernie signs a statement as to her complicity with JoJo, I can buy a day or two by saying the investigation is still under way," Robby said. "Meanwhile, the *Examiner* knows about the emergency squad run last night. I'll have to give them the story."

"Do you have to give them Bernie's name?" Rose said.

"I can only protect her up to a point," Robby said. "I don't know what JoJo told his lawyer, but he'll shit when he finds out about the credit card theft. You can bet he'll pull Bernie into it."

"Bernie will cooperate," Rose said.

"If Bernie will testify against JoJo and the cards get cancelled before any serious damage, the credit card companies might be open to a plea bargain… if the Feds agree."

"And if they don't?" Angus said.
~~~~~

"Someone gets burned," Robby said as he got up to leave.

~~~~~

Seated with Angus at her conference table, Rose rested her head on her hands.

"What a way to start the week," she said.

"I'm still thinking about our dinner Saturday night," Angus said as he slid a small package wrapped in green tissue paper across the table to her.

Rose took the package, rotated it slowly between her fingers and said, "If this is what I think it is, you'll never get it back."

"I'll never want it back."

"You have an uncanny sense of timing," Rose said.

"Musicians," Angus said.

As the delicate green tissue paper parted to reveal Angus' gift, Rose's eyes misted.

"You're so..." her words trailed off.

Slipping the *Claddagh* onto her fourth finger, Rose held her right hand under the light to inspect it more closely. She slipped the *Claddagh* off, turned it around so that the crown pointed to her fingertip, its heart to her heart. She grinned at Angus.

"I think you should move your piano into my house," she said. "It'll be a lot more convenient for giving Aidan music lessons."

"How's he doing?" Angus said.

"Since you're working dinner at the Inn tomorrow night, I'll take Aidan to the fireworks at the Lake tonight and the May Day regatta tomorrow."

"Will you be back for the fireworks at the high school tomorrow night?"

"I'll meet you at the south gate about nine," Rose said. "I asked
~~~~~

Nikko to open the Pub after the parade so we can stop by after the fireworks for a drink."

As Rose moved to leave with Aidan, she turned to Angus.

"Susie Merriman called... she was trying to track you down about getting the microphone and speaker set up in Gracious' parade car."

"I have it covered," Angus said.

~~~~~

After closing the Inn following its May Day dinner service Sunday night, Angus showered and relaxed with a glass of Black Bush on ice. Sitting at Aummie's piano, he played "Now Is The Hour." He refilled his glass with two fingers of Black Bush and played his favorite blues tunes. Refilling his glass the third time, he sat again at the piano and played Rose's favorite song, "The Impossible Dream." He mused over Rose's plans to invest in the Inn and thought about how lucky he was to have her in his life... and Aidan. Rousing from his reverie, Angus tossed off one last Black Bush and realized he had to meet Susie early to set up the speaker system for Gracious. Shuffling into Rose's bedroom, he pulled back the comforter, switched off the nightstand lamp.

~~~~~

Startled by the jangling from his nightstand and foggy from the evening before, Angus fumbled to find the phone.

"Mr. McCrory," Susie Merriman said, "We're all waiting for you to set up the speaker system on Gracious' float. The parade's about ready to start!"

~~~~~

Searching for the grand marshal's lead vehicle at the parade's starting point, a sudden strong gust of wind buffeted Angus as he caught his breath. Spotting Susie, he pushed through the judges evaluating each float's decorations for the awards ceremony. Without warning, the superstructure of Simpson Realty Company's float wavered in the wind, collapsed and toppled over into the street. As his son tried to salvage it,
~~~~~

Nelson Simpson gestured to the pile of debris and bellowed, "Mike! Forget about it… too damned windy to worry about it now!"

Disheveled and hung over, Angus set up the speaker system on the back of the grand marshal's Cadillac convertible loaner from Gillespie Motors, and tested it: *"One-two-three… this is a test… one-two-three."* Annoyed by the interference of gusting wind crackling over the speaker, Angus snatched the foam wind-protector from the box, snugged it over the microphone and retested the sound, *"One… two… three."* He handed the microphone to Gracious. "Try it out," he said.

Grabbing the mike from Angus – and in her sweet alto voice – Gracious sang, *"Lift me up above the shadows, yes plant my feet on higher ground."* Gracious nodded to Angus and yelled, "God bless!"

Strolling the parade route against a brisk wind, Angus felt a tap on his back. He turned to see Cliff with two young girls. "Glad you could make it, chief," Cliff said. "Windy as hell but a mighty fine day."

"Thought you'd be on the Inn's float," Angus said.

"Got my kids with me," Cliff said. "Shirleen's got it covered."

Just ahead of the color guard and the grand marshal's convertible, Susie handed out the list of more than fifty parade floats and pointed to the third vehicle in line where Mayor Bunny's car had paused to avoid getting too close to the color guard. Beaming her warmest, most ingratiating political smile, Mayor Bunny waved to Susie and the crowd as if she were the *Queen Mum.* Angus caught up with Susie. "Other than the wind, it's a gorgeous day."

Following the parade as it inched lazily forward, Angus took in the beauty and perfume of the spring flowers decorating the streets, sidewalks, lawns and porches of homes along the parade route. Block after block, lampposts festooned with hanging flowerpots swayed in the wind… long strands of spiraling Azalea blooms cascaded half way to the ground.

Along East Columbus Avenue as the parade passed by The Inn at Mary's Gate, Angus' admired Snuff's long curving flower beds with sweeps of blooming red emperor tulips, bobbing yellow daffodils and delicate lavender phlox tucked in and around corners of the stone-lined sidewalks.

Standing at each corner of Inn's façade were two, twenty-foot-tall tri-color beech trees, their deep red, pink and green almond-shaped leaves just beginning to unfurl; the very tops of the trees rustled in the wind, teasing at the Inn's overhanging ancient wood-shake roof.

As the parade advanced, Angus waved at Claire who waved back from the Logan County Citizens Bank float. Following just behind was the Fountain Point Savings float. To the screeching sound of a siren, Angus turned to see a shiny black-and-white police cruiser, Robby tucked behind the wheel. A blast of wind kicked up as Robby tooted the cruiser's horn and yelled at Angus. Robby's words swallowed by the wind, Angus doffed his straw hat and bowed in acknowledgment.

Following behind Robby in the Fountain Point Fire Department's 1929 vintage Seagrave Fire Engine, Fire Chief, Forrest Toomey, waved, tossed packets of chewing gum to the pleading children scrambling to retrieve them.

With the parade lurching forward, Angus stayed in front of the Inn and surveyed the myriad of passing floats: high school bands, decorated bicycles, vintage Corvette convertibles; Boy Scout Troop 55; Brownie and Girl Scout Troops and Fountain Points High School's soon-to-be graduates. Following the graduate's float was Fountain Point's popular, Satan's Angels Drum & Bugle Corp. After it paused to play "This Is My Country," Angus turned to see the Inn's float entitled, *It Takes A Village*. Seated on the Inn's front porch watching the parade were Theresa Loar, Snuff Guffy and Shirleen from the kitchen. Spotting Angus, they waved to him. As Angus waved back, a blast of swirling wind sent Shirleen's bonnet sailing into the street. Angus retrieved it, ran to return it to her.

Breathless from his quick sprint and still woozy from his bout with Black Bush the previous night, Angus watched the last two floats teeter in the wind and move on. He strode to the Inn's side door and shuffled back to the kitchen to be sure the kitchen was ready for Tuesday's food audit.

Slouching at his desk in the kitchen office, Angus held his head, nursed a fizzing double dose of *Alka-Seltzer*. He rested his arms on the desk and desperately in need of a nap, dropped his head onto them and dozed off.

Startled by someone knocking on his office door, Angus bolted upright to see Nikko standing in the doorway.

"Came back to get some olives out of pantry," Nikko said. "The way this wind is kicking up, they still having the fireworks?"

Angus shook the cobwebs from his head and rushed out of the Inn to meet Rose.

21. BLUES IN THE NIGHT

Seated with Rose in the high school grandstand, Gracious Maxy's rendition of the "The Star-Spangled Banner" boomed over the speakers. To a thunderous explosion of an M-80 silver salute signaling the start of the May Day fireworks, Angus glanced at the sky to see the smoke and sparks drifting away on the gusting wind.

Gasping at the assortment of aerial displays – bursting Roman candles, flaring color stars, Horse Tails, Diadems, Peony and Spider patterns crackling, popping and multicolored strobing flashes with floral-patterned parachutes – even the most critical pyrotechnic aficionados watched transfixed.

After thirty minutes of the spectacular display and the echo of the ear-splitting finale ringing, Angus and Rose made their way through the smoke still swirling above the football field toward the exit gate. Walking side-by-side down Park Street toward the Inn for a drink, they stopped on the corner of Brown Street.

"That smoke from those fireworks still stinks," Rose said.

Angus lifted his eyes to the starry sky shimmering as if illuminated by a million candles. Ghostlike billows of smoke danced in the flickering overhead glow as the piercing sound of sirens punctuated the thick night air.

"That isn't fireworks," Angus said. "Someone's house must be on fire."

Running to the corner of East Columbus Avenue, Rose and Angus stopped short and stared down the street in the direction of the Inn. Jammed together, clogging the street in front of the Inn, fire trucks and police cruisers blocked the area; adding to the spectacle, their red lights whirled through the smoky haze. They ran toward the Inn until they were stymied by a Fire Department blockade. Rose held her hand up to defend against the raging inferno's searing heat. Acrid smoke fouled the air. A voice blared orders from a bullhorn: "Picker! Into position! … Ladders! West portico!"

Angus yelled at Rose, "I hope to God everyone got out of the Inn."

"Nikko! I saw him at the Pub!"

Fire hoses attached to every fireplug in sight crisscrossed the street like spaghetti. Four firefighters hoisted ladders from two trucks and ran with them toward the Inn. A fifty-foot cherry picker with two firefighters wrestling with spurting hoses tried to maneuver closer to the Inn, but the driver struggled to navigate between the power lines. Suddenly, the neighborhood house lights blinked and went black as one power line broke apart sending a sparking, serpent-like tendril whipping to the ground. A voice boomed over a bullhorn: "Get back! Move!"

Flames licked the trees in front of the Inn. The trees flailed, shedding charred leaves that danced in the wind and skittered to ground.

Angus and Rose jockeyed through the chaos to get closer until a firefighter stopped them. "Too dangerous to get any closer, " he said. "The crowd's already bollixed everything up."

Recognizing the firefighter as Red Marmon, Rose pleaded, "Red… I work here!"

"I know, but…"

"Did everyone get out?" Angus said.

"Everyone's safe."

Red pointed to a house across the street. "Go stand on that guy's lawn…you'll be safe there… you can see all you need."

Angus and Rose edged through the milling crowd, crossed the street and stood on a small rise near the side of the house. To their left, a second pump truck – siren screaming, red light whirling – blasted its way up the alley beside the house and screeched to a halt next to the other pump truck in front of the Inn. Riveted to the chaotic scene unfolding before them, Angus put his arm around Rose's shoulder and pulled her close. He could feel her trembling as she buried her head in his chest. As he hugged Rose, there came a horrific explosion so violent that Angus felt the blast strike his back as he turned away and shielded Rose. Looking back over his shoulder to see billows of black smoke belch up in ugly testament to the funereal scene, he knew the Inn's propane tank had exploded. Gouts of flame burst out of the ground at the side of the Inn. Bullhorns exhorted the awestruck crowd: "Clear the area! Clear the area!" As the third pump truck arrived, flames shot from the roof gutting the old structure.

From their safe distance, Angus and Rose watched the fire consume the Inn as strong winds wafted the smoke and embers up in swirling patterns… times past vanishing into the eerie light of the night sky.

"I can't look at this any longer," Rose cried.

As Angus led Rose around the safety barrier, the Inn collapsed with a resounding crash.

"Move back people!" Chief Toomey shouted through a bullhorn, "Get back!"

Rose and Angus shifted back with the heaving crowd to see a water cannon whip around overhead to target the flames still shooting out of the raging inferno.

"Let's get the hell out of here," Angus said and tugged on Rose's arm. They edged away and heard a voice yell, "Rose… over here."

Seeing Claire, Rose and Angus pushed their way through the crowd. As Rose embraced Claire, she saw Mayor Bunny standing with Marianne Sewell and stepped over to them. "I'm so sorry," Rose whispered.

"Charlie's whole life… gone," Marianne sobbed.

Rose huddled with Claire and Marianne as Mayor Bunny approached Angus.

"In all my years," she said, "Never had a disaster like this!"

"Do you know how it started?" Angus said.

"Fire chief said the damned fireworks. Wind caught 'em... sparked those old wood shingles on the Inn's roof."

~~~~~

Standing under their umbrellas in the Tuesday morning mist, Rose and Angus surveyed the still smoldering ruins of the Inn. The bitter odor of wet ashes and charred wood reeked from the pit of black debris.

"Thank God for Nikko getting everyone safely out of the Pub," Rose said as a car pulled up to the curb, an *Examiner* emblem on its door. Scoop Wilson emerged, slogged through the mucky grass toward them. Sizing up the disaster, he turned to Rose. "Everyone in the whole county knows about the fire, but I have to do a story. Do you think the Sewell family would give me some quotes… and some of your thoughts about the Inn's history and heritage?"

Rose gazed past Scoop at the Inn's remains across the street.

"We'll meet at my house tomorrow at noon," she said.

22. WHO COULD ASK FOR ANYTHING MORE

Seated comfortably around Rose's coffee table – Marianne and Claire in upholstered arm chairs, Scoop Wilson on the piano bench –
~~~~~

Robby perched on the shoulder of the sofa where Rose and Angus sat. Rose wore a blue tweed business suit… an emerald broach pinned to the lapel. Angus crossed his feet, bounced them anxiously, ruminated over the discussion that he, Rose and her father had had earlier that morning.

Rose handed a file folder to Scoop and Claire.

"I assembled all of the historical information I had on the Inn," she said.

Scoop paged through the file folder's contents.

"Plenty to go on here," he said. "A few thoughts from everyone… a quote or two… I'll be all set to run the story tomorrow morning."

"Mom and I hope you won't mention the bankruptcy," Claire said. "Or anything about Dad… I mean the Inn… and the money we owe the bank."

"That's old news," Scoop said. "I plan to pay tribute to your father's contributions to Fountain Point… his good work… his generosity…"

"Would it be news if the Inn's debt got paid off?" Rose asked.

The group's collective gaze fixed on her.

"I hate to rehash the Inn's financial problems," Claire said.

"I visited Fountain Point Savings this morning," Rose said.

"Where are you going with this?" Claire asked.

Reaching for an envelope tucked under the corner of a rotund ceramic figurine of Shakespeare's Falstaff, Rose handed the envelope to Claire.

Cautiously, Claire opened the envelope, unfolded the single enclosed sheet, studied it and dropped her jaw. "What… what *is* this?" she blurted.

"It's a certified check for six-hundred-twenty-five-thousand-dollars…payable to the Logan County Citizens Bank," Rose said.

Everyone sat in stunned silence as Claire handed the check to her mother.

"You... you're paying off the Inn's debt?" Marianne murmured.

"Angus and I... and my dad... reviewed Speed's work up on the Inn's finances," Rose said. "With your permission...Ange and I want to rebuild the Inn."

"You... and Ange?" Claire sputtered.

"The check I gave you will pay off the Logan County Citizens Bank... and with the fire insurance, Fountain Point Savings will arrange financing on the new Inn," Rose said.

"You're... are you *serious?*" Claire gasped. "Rebuild it... you can't be serious... really?"

"I couldn't just stand by and let the Inn disappear," Rose said. "It's been an icon in Fountain Point... forever. It's been the most important thing in my life..." Pausing to put her hand on Angus' arm, "... except for Ange," she said.

"Now that's a story!" Scoop said.

~~~~~

After dressing for their trip to Indian Lake to pick up Aidan, Rose and Angus digested the *Examiner's* feature story about the Inn and re-read the last paragraph:

"Having resolved the Inn's financial obligations with its creditors, plans for rebuilding the Inn at Mary's Gate will get underway immediately," Rosemary Gracewood said.

23. WHAT NOW MY LOVE

A blazing orange sun burned through the oppressive August morning haze shrouding the construction site of the new Inn at Mary's Gate. Sonny Askren – construction engineer for the Fountain Point Development Company – stood sweltering over a makeshift wooden
~~~~~

worktable. Mopping his brow incessantly, he studied the renderings of Fountain Point's leading architect, Tom Lewis. As Sonny scratched his head, he felt a tap on his shoulder and looked up.

"Seems like things are moving awfully slow," Angus said.

Sonny pushed his glasses onto his forehead and peered at Angus.

"Busted water main been holding us up," he said and pointed to pools of muddy water dotting the site. "Foundation's got a foot of water needs pumping."

Angus scanned the site. "I don't see anyone working on it," he said.

"Pump broke down yesterday," Sonny said. "Got my best man, Billy Mac, workin' on it back at the shop."

Rose dropped her tote bag next to the worktable.

"Labor Day is next weekend," she said. "It'll be winter before long."

Sonny mopped his brow, shot a hopeful glance at a cloud drifting lazily overhead.

"We need rain," he said, "But we should have everything under roof by Thanksgiving."

"Can't you hire more people?" Rose said.

"Already got dang near everybody in the county knows anything about construction work," Sonny said.

Angus pointed to a truckload of fieldstone mired in the mud near the foundation.

"When will they finish the stone work?"

"Got Stump Merkel comin' today with the crane to set the corner stone," Sonny said.

Surprised by Sonny's news, Rose glanced at her wristwatch: 9:45.

"What time?" Rose asked.

"Pending the weather… should have it set by dinner time."

"I mean what time will he be here?" Rose said.

Sonny peered through the piercing sun at Rose.

"About noon," he said.

Rose hefted her tote bag onto the worktable, extracted a cube shaped, clear acrylic box and handed it to Sonny. "I didn't know the corner stone was today or I would have given this to you sooner."

Puzzled, Sonny frowned as he examined the curious box.

"What's this little doo-dad for?"

"I want a time capsule in the corner stone," Rose said.

Further in the dark, Sonny flipped the box around to examine it closer.

"Don't know anything about no time capsule," Sonny said. "Where's it go?"

"Inside the corner stone," Rose said.

Sonny rolled his eyes. "That thing's solid sandstone."

Rose shifted her stance. "Don't you have a stone mason?"

Sonny pointed to three men on a scaffold. "Got three of the best," he said.

Rose pointed to the box. "Can't they drill out a simple little space?" she said. "That box isn't any larger than my hand, OK?"

Sonny paused, curled his lips into a tight frown.

"Hate to slow things down but… I expect we could rig something up."

"I'm no expert," Angus said. "But couldn't your stone masons figure it out in a couple of hours?"

Sonny glanced at the scaffolding and pointed to a balding man, the tallest of the three stonemasons. "I'll get Wilbur Talbott on it," he said.

"He'll get 'er done." Sonny tapped on the acrylic box and squinted at Rose. "You want just… this plain old box in that cornerstone?"

Reaching into her tote bag, Rose extracted a sheet of white paper. "This goes inside the box before you seal it inside the cornerstone," she said. "Twenty-five years from the date of our grand opening… " Rose paused and focused on Sonny. "… Can you give us any idea when the Inn will be completed?"

"Shootin' for next summer," Sonny said. "Barrin' some disaster."

"Take a minute and read it," Rose said. "It's about the Inn… you and everyone who's a part of the Sewell family's legacy."

Sonny pulled his glasses down and squinted at the document:

> *Generations of your ancestors have contributed to the loving legacy you are experiencing this day at the new Inn at Mary's Gate. More than a physical structure, the Inn is an icon of our community; an anchor of stability and tradition; a beacon of friendship and a symbol of values rooted in quality, service, caring and giving back to a community which depends on it in part for jobs, recreation, commerce and philanthropy. The Inn's current structure – finished in 1995 – is symbolic of not only a new beginning after a disastrous fire which destroyed the revered old landmark, but also a preservation of the core values of its founder, Billy Sewell, his progeny, Willis Jr. and Margaret Lahey Sewell and their son and his wife, Charles and Marianne Sewell. Some have said that Fountain Point is just a small rural community with limited resources and modest amenities. While that may be true, it's important to recognize that, together, Fountain Point and the Inn at*

Mary's Gate are a silver lining in the clouds of doing without some things in the interest of living a simpler life. Think of the Inn and its heritage as you work to foster, promote and protect this valuable legacy.

Sonny shoved his glasses back up on his forehead.

"Who's going to read this if it's locked up in that cornerstone?

"You'll have to make a seam in the cornerstone so when the time comes, someone can open it and share it... OK?"

~~~~~

Rose and Angus sat at the picnic table on Helen and Chris Gracewood's cottage beach and watched Aidan splash around in the water. Waiting for the right moment, Angus touched his pants pocket to be sure the paper he had concealed from Rose was still there. Seeing Aidan content, Angus eased the paper out of his pocket and turned to Rose.

"I have a surprise for you," he said. "Something I think will be familiar to you."

Squinting through the evening sun at Angus, "How can it be a surprise if I'm familiar with it?" Rose said.

"Don't be so picky," Angus said. "It isn't that big of a deal."

Unfolding the paper, Angus read:

"'IF I WERE'... by Joanna Fuchs," he began.

"If I were a key, I would lock you;

If lightning, then I would shock you;

If I were a pier I would dock you;

If I had a band I would rock you.

If I were a spoon, I would feed you;
~~~~~

If I were a house, I would deed you."

"Now for the best part," Angus said:

"If I were a horse I would carry you
If I were a boat I would ferry you
But since I am neither
And don't think you are either...
The best thing I can do is marry you.
with my straw hat no less,
I hope you'll say yes!"

Tears trickling down her cheeks – Rose bounded onto Angus' lap.

"Yes! Forever! Tomorrow, we'll call Mom and Dad... and you can tell Aidan the news, OK?" Rose said.

"There's one condition," Angus said.

Rose frowned.

"Stop saying '*OK*' every time you want me to agree with you."

THE END

ABOUT THE AUTHOR

Born in Lansing, Michigan and raised in Bellefontaine, Ohio, Charles W. Rath graduated from the University of Notre Dame and launched a successful career in sales, marketing and advertising, which he culminated as Executive Vice President and Chief Marketing Officer of Wendy's International Inc.

Rath initiated the popular ad campaign featuring Wendy's founder Dave Thomas that led to 15 consecutive years of record sales and earnings for the company.

As an author, Charlie Rath has written a youth musical, a collection of short stories and a science fiction spoof about our culture of excess consumption. This is his first novel.

Charlie and his wife, Susie, reside in Bexley, Ohio. They have three children and nine grandchildren.

Made in the USA
Charleston, SC
09 March 2015